Praise for *The House of Erzulie*

"Blurs the edges between dream and reality, madness and magic, beauty and brutality, darkness and desire."

— Gayle Brandeis, author of *The Art of Misdiagnosis*

"Intriguing and compelling at every turn."

—Maisha Wester, author of *African American Gothic: Screams from Shadowed Places*

"Skillfully blends an atmosphere of hallucinatory tension with well-researched explorations into 19th-century beliefs."
—*Library Journal*

"A propulsive read, full of commentary on ethnic identity, mental illness, and power."
— *Booklist*

"A spellbinding tale ... that brims with masterful, uncanny language ... while also delving into more complex topics like generational trauma and the horrors of slavery."
— *Foreword Reviews*

"A fascinating and surreal look into troubled minds.... Kasai's settings are lush, and her sometimes-brutal tale is compulsive stuff." — *Historical Novels Review*

"Sits on the shelf with *Wuthering Heights, Frankenstein,* the work of Edgar Allan Poe, and Daphne du Maurier's *Rebecca.*"
—*Adroit Journal*

"From sensuality/passion to the stark cruelties of slavery, Kasai weaves her word magic from the first page to the final page." — Alma Luz Villanueva, author of *Song of the Golden Scorpion*

The House of Erzulie

Also by Kirsten Imani Kasai

Ice Song

Tattoo

The House of Erzulie

Kirsten Imani Kasai

Shade Mountain Press
Albany, New York

Shade Mountain Press
P.O. Box 11393
Albany, NY 12211
www.shademountainpress.com

Kasai, Kirsten Imani
The House of Erzulie / Kirsten Imani Kasai
  ISBN 978-0-9984634-1-4 (paper)
1. Plantation life—Fiction. 2. Spiritualism—Fiction. 3. Vodou—Fiction.
  4. Creoles—Fiction. 5. Mental Illness—Fiction.

Printed in the United States of America by Spencer Printing

10 9 8 7 6 5 4 3 2

Book design by Robin Parks

Shade Mountain Press publishes literature by women authors, especially women from marginalized groups (women of color, LGBTQ women, women from working-class backgrounds, women with disabilities). We aim to make the literary landscape more diverse and more truly representative of the nation's artistic voices.

Shade Mountain Press is a sponsored project of Fractured Atlas, a nonprofit arts service organization.

Of all ghosts, the ghosts of our old loves are the worst.
—Arthur Conan Doyle

Contents

Lydia Mueller
Philadelphia
Present Day

"LYDIA! FOR CHRIST'S SAKE! Come down. You've let the roast burn." My husband's voice shreds my reverie. A bloodletting blade quivers in my fingers, eager to sever scar-quilted skin. I pause, the blade's edge dull against my flesh. The memories persist. Even after all this time, I know how hard I'll have to press to make the first cut.

Smoke wafts up the attic stairwell, filling my office with the sharp stink of blackened blood and meat. Irritation boils. He'd rather let the roast go to leather than take it out himself. Had he done that, there'd be nothing to blame me for, and what would my husband do for sport if not make my life miserable?

But no. He senses my impending self-destruction, or so I imagine. I put the antique blade to bed beside its brothers and sisters; tuck them into rotting, blue velvet covers and close the lid of their arcane box. Isidore's pain is not mine to appropriate.

"Take it out, Lance!" My voice cracks with the effort. Laryngitis has kept me mute for almost three weeks. No amount of ice cream, lozenges, warm scarves, quiet, or Throat Coat tea had made a difference. It was only when Lance departed for a conference in New York that I began to recover. Just yesterday, I greeted the mailman and spent an hour on the phone with my good friend Marcella. My voice was all milk and honey then, but as soon as Lance parked his custom-painted BMW in the drive, my throat swelled up as if I'd swallowed a beehive. Choking on wax and fibers, bits of broken cellophane wings and the sticky ends of lost stingers, I imagined coughing up stiff little black and yellow hairs, vomiting honey and pollen globs, but still I couldn't clear the obstacle and once more receded into silence and pain.

"Lydia!" Lance shouts again. "Twenty-four dollars, wasted!" Of course he knows to the penny how much that meat cost. No doubt he's rounded up for effect. He mutters, "Fuck." Appliances clatter in the kitchen. I must do my wifely duty, and so descend the stairs.

The smoking roast sits in the oven, its open door accusing me of neglect. Lance has retreated to his study, savoring the excuse to have bourbon for dinner. My husband has lost his patience for me. Says that I'm tetchy and paranoid. Argumentative. That since I've been back, I've become difficult in a way he doesn't recognize. That it's like sharing his bed with a stranger. I was only gone for a short while, but in my absence, his kindness soured like a lemon. I no longer recognize him as the man I married and I watch, hopelessly, as the affection between us erodes.

Hackett's disappeared for the weekend, and I'm glad. My colleagues frown on the slackness of my parental tether, but my son's earned his freedom. At seventeen, he's old enough to look after himself and he certainly doesn't want interference from two people who haven't proven themselves any more capable of managing their own lives than his peers.

I have always been exceedingly careful to hide the damage done by my own hand. The stigma of the "crazy" label was a strong enough deterrent to keep my activities a secret. Maybe if my grandparents had paid better attention to me or been less dismissive of the "mixed-up mixed girl" they'd brought home, maybe if I'd been a less convincing liar, they would have seen the marks. But people often fail to see what's right in front of them, more so when they are elderly and willfully blind to the Devil's handiwork upon their own.

I managed to finish high school with a high enough GPA to earn a scholarship to Tufts University. I was seventeen when I started college, nineteen when I met Lance, and twenty-two when we married, the year after graduation. I liked college. I thrived in the rigorous program and stopped seeing black bugs skittering around the corners of rooms and the shadows of dogs slinking beneath the furniture. Stopped feeling the floor shift and buckle beneath my feet. And then I was a young bride marrying the most handsome professor at Tufts, a Rhodes Scholar and a generous man—all the girls said so. All the girls…Hadn't I been warned?

Dearest Sarah, the only one I ever allowed to meet the gruesome spirits of my dark heart, Sarah the fairest—too coolly blond and aggressive for Lance—wanted to rescue me from folly, but young girls in love are stubborn as mules and deaf as posts to warnings from those more clear-headed than they. For hadn't I been nubile as a nymph, bright-eyed and gleaming, when we met? One of many glittering baubles from which

Lance might choose, I was dazzled by his attention, having had only one boyfriend before him—the requisite summer romance terminating in heartbreak.

I knew it forbidden. Our late-night dinners at fancy hotels in Cambridge crossed a line. Believing myself unique, I ignored the whispers. His first marriage, to another graduate student when he was earning his PhD, was brief. Two years at most before he fell out of love with her and ended it. But I'd held onto him, hadn't I?

At my wedding, Sarah had pressed an envelope stuffed with hundred-dollar bills into my hand and whispered, "A leopard can't change its spots." She hugged me and slipped out the door, a bottle of my champagne in her hand. That was the end of our friendship, the best I'd ever had. But I had Lance, didn't I? He was supposed to be enough.

Our move to Philadelphia when Hackett was two came as a profound relief. I started work on my own PhD, possessed of a naïve expectation that a geographic cure would squash all the little crawlers of doubt that skittered around in my mind at night. For the most part, it had. But lately they'd been back, persistent as roaches, as glib as serpents' tongues.

They say "love is not a cup of sugar that gets used up," but it is. Spoonful by spoonful, grain by grain, the greedy, the needy, and the hungry consume it and demand more until the bowl is empty. Then they run away, jonesing for a fix from another source. Each betrayal, every insult or injury depletes the loving cup and leaves the holder bitter. It's a bitterness I can taste, and it sits on my tongue like the foulest medicine.

I wake to an empty bed. Silence but for the faint hum of the appliances. Lance has already gone to the university to teach morning classes, and hopefully, my son has gone to school. The doorbell rings through the empty house like storm wind, startling me out of my skin. Shaking, I descend the narrow staircase to the front door. A Fed Ex man waits on the stoop. I briefly imagine inviting him upstairs to occupy my empty bed and unloved, ignored hole, but when I open the door and see him, shiny and almost infantile in his youth, my stomach clenches. His dazzling smile and friendly eyes offer a genuine greeting. This must be his first job—he hasn't become jaded by repeated contact with humanity.

I sign to accept a box from New Orleans and take it back to my office for examination. Adelaide Randolph's assistant at the Foundation, Owen, has included a brief note:

Lydia,

These were found beneath a floorboard on the property during a recent retrofitting. Ms. Randolph wanted to dispose of them but I thought they might be worth a look.

Best,

O. Winslow

Thank god for idealistic interns! The box is sealed with old-fashioned string tape; it's been sitting untouched for years. Aside from the plastic shipping label window, there are no markings on it. Faint odors of heliotrope and jasmine waft from its opened flaps and fade, an olfactory mirage. Cautiously, I excavate this gallimaufry of memorabilia. First is a packet of tiny letters tied up with faded ribbons and addressed to the same recipient—Geneviève Stockton. Then several mildewed account ledgers, their pages flannel-soft with age and rot; a musty, leather-bound journal smelling of decay; and a water-stained, silk pocket square bearing the embroidered initials *ISA*.

Isidore Saint-Ange was the only son of a French naval officer and a free Jamaican woman. I know from the Foundation's notes that Isidore spent his childhood on a small estate outside Boulogne and was educated in England from the age of ten through college at Cambridge. A distant cousin of Monsieur Bilodeau, he'd been imported from abroad to marry Emilie Bilodeau, her parents' only surviving daughter and second in line to inherit the vast wealth of Belle Rive.

Lastly, there are three paper-wrapped daguerreotypes and several wood-framed ambrotypes detailing Belle Rive's esteemed "big house," its outbuildings, slave cabins, and fields.

One photo shows an early Greek Revival structure overshadowed by heavy tree branches. Draped in lacy balconies and hugged by the prototypical Southern veranda, a wide, double-storied wooden rectangle sits atop a low slope. The image is empty of people, but the head and forelegs of a bridled horse lurk at the edge of the frame, and a white, oblong blotch floats above the lawn like a specter risen from the grave. Fields stretch into the distance on either side of the house, and a gray thread of smoke lines the far sky. For all its grandeur, it's a stark and lonely place.

Another shows a stern but earnest couple in formal garb—Emilie and Isidore Saint-Ange. Petite and ordinary-looking, the woman appears to be drowning in the sea of her gown's ruffles and flounces. Her large eyes hold a somber hopefulness as she stands beside a seated gentleman, a nosegay in her carefully posed hand. The man is handsome, with sensuous lips, high cheekbones, and unfashionably long wavy hair oiled to a high shine. His dark eyes appear to gleam. His suit betrays a European dapperness and he holds an open book in hand, as if disturbed from his studies. Their youth clouded over by a sepia patina, they have the stiffness of corpses in rigor.

The last daguerreotype is a memento mori. A toddler wearing a lace christening gown is propped in his tiny coffin as if sleeping in a close cradle. His neatly combed hair and folded hands do not divert from the sunken eye sockets and obvious signs of a wasting illness that have hollowed the plump cheeks of their son, Théodore Saint-Ange.

There aren't often such juicy, personal artifacts in my workload. My primary focus is nineteenth-century antebellum and Georgian architecture. I concern myself with columns and cornices, gables and foundations, porticos and verandas. It's not my place to poke around in private histories unless they directly pertain to the building. Of course, the records I don't see, the ones overflowing with family secrets—illegitimate children, illness, poverty, crime, theft, suicide, madness, and tragic deaths—are reserved for family archivists' quiet perusal, the most salacious details gleaned for display and promotion in museums of the grotesque, or suppressed and tidied over.

Carefully wrapped in acid-free paper is an official document stamped with a fleur-de-lis seal that's obviously served as a snack for many a booklouse. Its brittle page sends a jolt through me as I read.

State of Louisiana, Orleans Parish

Warrant: The people of the state of Louisiana
to Joseph A. Call

You are hereby commanded forthwith to arrest
Isidore Saint-Ange of Belle Rive Plantation, who has been
declared to be insane and to convey him to the Louisiana
State Insane Asylum (and you are hereby authorized to
take you aid and assistance if deemed necessary) and of this
Warrant, make due return to this office after its execution.

Witness my hand and the seal of Alfonse Du Lac, Clerk
Recorder, Orleans Parish Court of Louisiana,
this 13th day of May A.D. 1854

Received this 13th day of May A.D. 1854, the patient named in the within Warrant by Victor N. Kloat, Superintendent, Louisiana State Insane Asylum.

Why does my heart sink so for a long-dead stranger? The very idea of arrest and containment is appalling enough in my day. Treatment for the mentally ill in the mid-nineteenth century consisted of confinement in straitjackets or chains, beatings, cold-water baths, starvation diets, and regular doses of opiates, emetics, or laxatives supplemented with bloodletting. Inmates were kenneled like animals and left naked in dark rooms to stew in their own madness. Were he fortunate enough to be caught up in the wave of reform, when doctors began asserting that mental illness was a physical disease rather than a spiritual one, Isidore may have received rudimentary talk therapy, rest cures, adequate nutrition, and a sanitary environment. But my mind fills with images of shaven heads dotted with staring, haunted eyes and patients who lurch howling and groaning through icy corridors heaped with piles of human filth.

I cut the tape and begin to flatten the box when a crumbling fabric pouch plops out, grayish-brown with patches of shine as it has been oft-rubbed by nervous fingers. Tiny objects crinkle and shift inside, something like eggshells or mouse bones, twiggy snips of herbs and tiny metal beads.

It's a gris-gris bag, a vodou charm meant to imbue the carrier with protection, blessings, or special powers. Perhaps Isidore had turned to vodou to find relief from whatever disease he'd attempted to cure through bloodletting.

Lance cautioned me about taking this job. Told me I wasn't yet ready to resume the trappings of my old life, but I was inexplicably compelled to take the assignment and so I'd said yes against his wishes. Hadn't I dreamed myself opening these boxes and reading these old papers? Seen myself wandering a lightless Gothic house with many rooms to explore and heard voices calling my name? Belle Rive's pull upon me was as inevitable as the tides. Now I must prove myself solid, capable. Sane. Ace the test whose completion will deem me well again.

The morning passes easily. Hunkered down at my desk, I get the most boring stuff out of the way first. The project entails compiling a history of Belle Rive, currently undergoing structural renovations. There are plans to turn it into an event center for weddings and such, though the idea of beginning a marriage attended by the ghosts of slaves revolts me. While the Foundation prides itself on its deep roots in the Louisiana Creole community, it seems eager to divest itself of its sordid history by rolling it back in time to the antebellum era, when the wealthy Bilodeau family had the dubious honor of being the only slaveholding plantation in New Orleans owned by *gens de couleur*—free people of color. The keepers of Belle Rive wish to pave over the bones buried all around the grounds to make this picture as pretty as possible. In ways it little recognizes, the Foundation perpetuates the very legacy it seeks to deny. Much like the white grandparents who raised me (and wouldn't let me keep the figurines from my Black mother's vodou altar when they took me from our house), ancient Adelaide, the Foundation's director, is a throwback to a harsher, crueler era.

She's requested that I highlight only the most historically salient events and limit my discussion of less savory topics to anecdotal footnotes or asides. In our most recent phone conversation, she stressed—in a carefully worded way akin to a caress from a velvet-gloved iron hand—that it would behoove both myself and "our beloved Foundation" to "bring to light only that which best supports modern lifestyles and preferences." Adelaide's polite way of requesting that I present the plantation as a stately old home filled with honeyed light and perfumed air that exemplifies the very best of Southern living. I am to dress the set and create a beautiful façade to disguise the festering rot and horror of slavery's legacy. Then, honeymooners will pay five hundred dollars a night to make love in remodeled sugar shacks and breathe in the dewy scent of magnolia blossoms while the bones of the dead molder six feet below the ground upon which they recline, heart to heart.

Receipts and ledgers make for dry reading, but as dreary as they can be, one can paint quite a detailed picture from them. For example, in 1842, owner Marcel Bilodeau purchased thirty-five acres of land to add to Belle Rive's five hundred. He planted the new acreage with sugarcane to compare its cost and yield to the fields of cotton. His letters detail dates of planting, harvest, and weather events. Not much else is discussed, except for a minor slave revolt in North Carolina and that Marcel feared the insurrection would spread to Louisiana. Brief notation of a cholera outbreak, the deaths of seven slaves and the first-born Bilodeau child, Honoré, age one.

I've often wondered how parents manage to survive the loss of so many little ones. My projects are always tainted by the shadow of death. For our forebears, life was cheap. Mothers expired in childbirth or shortly after. Babies routinely died. Toddlers vacated life with a whisper. Children succumbed to astonishing accidents and illnesses—fevers, plagues, infections, and defects of heart, lungs, and brain. Inheritance was a numbers game. Outlive your siblings and win. A family might produce ten children but only two or three would survive to adulthood. Reading further into the Bilodeau history, I began to understand why Isidore's arrival and integration into the family was so vital. Many of their bloodline suffered weak hearts. Emilie's mother, Floriane Bilodeau, had lost five of her children to stillbirth and miscarriages. Emilie's sole living sibling, Prosper Bilodeau, died childless. Emilie was the only one left to carry on the family name and prevent the estate from being divided into shares for far-flung relatives.

Hackett was my only pregnancy, and he lived a safe and comfortable life. Genetically, ours had been a risky strategy. Lance and I put all our eggs in one basket, literally, and hoped for lucky snake eyes with a single roll of the dice. But I have no worries about leaving behind a legacy, financial or otherwise. Lance will see to his. He's tenured and takes special pride in his academic accolades. I want none of that, preferring my behind-scenes work to the pressure of professional notoriety. Mine is a quiet little enclave of secrets, sex, blood, and dreams. It is where I am happiest, and where I best belong.

The afternoon lengthens into evening. Shadows creep across my study walls and steal into me, filling me with darkness. Dusk is the best time of day, for it's when magic stirs and the fey come out to play. But it is also a dangerous time, when one can be seduced away from an ordinary life by the charms of the Spirit world. My house is empty; my soul as lightless as the house in my dreams. I am lonely and require a companion. So I tuck myself into a knot of blankets on my little plum-colored chaise with the packet of tiny letters. Each one is artfully penned on the palest pink paper, the neat handwriting feminine and delicate. The romance between Emilie and Isidore promises to be a sweet one, much more so than my own tepid marriage. I shouldn't be too envious, though. Lance and I were once just as giddy. I anticipate a boring recitation of domestic obligations and concerns, but the letters draw me in. That is how I begin to fall in love with the engaging, thoughtful young woman in the photograph, dead more than a hundred and fifty years—Emilie Bilodeau.

The Collected Letters of
Emilie Bilodeau Saint-Ange
Belle Rive Plantation, Louisiana

to

Geneviève Stockton
New York
1851–1854

April 19, 1851

Dearest friend,

Monsieur Saint-Ange has been detained in New Orleans, and this delay throws Belle Rive into a phrenzy of anticipation. We have exchanged many cordial letters over the past year, and although he strikes me as the soul of gentility, I know nothing of his true nature. Is he kind and good-humored? Ill-tempered and brusque? Will my heart quicken at first sight of him or will dread chill my frame, knowing that I am to be forever harnessed to one whose form repulses me? I have received but one daguerreotype, of which he is very proud (having sat for this portrait at the Great Exhibition in London with the famed Crystal Palace glimmering behind him) and so I know him to be fine-looking, of deeper complection than myself, with black pomaded hair longer than is fashionable. There is a certain poignancy to his expression, a longing perhaps, expressed in the intensity of his gaze and the sensuous, mustachioed mouth that belies the sorrows of our ancient race. It is a face I shall have to look upon each day for the remainder of our natural lives, and I nightly pray that his countenance shall gaze upon my own with tenderness.

Maman, however, will let nothing slow the impressive march of her command. Mme. Durand came today to finalize the fitting of my wedding gown. Cream silk faille with princess seams, a pointed waistline, and ruffled lace sleeves. Against Maman's urgings, I chose a fairy ring headpiece, which will leave the top of my head bare, rather than a full veil. I should not wish to greet my new husband entirely draped in white and resembling nothing so much as a haint! The irises are in bloom and we shall use our own flowers to make everything lovely.

Clothilde is charged with making the wedding cake, much to the consternation of Cook. Maman trusts Clothilde's careful hand in any matter which requires one, whether it be the education of her only daughter or the application of icing scrolls. We are to have three layers— black, fruit, and white. I've already put in a petition for Clothilde to stock the fruit layer with plenty of currants, almonds, and brandy, as this is my very favorite.

Yours in faith,
Emilie

✤◈✤

April 24, 1851

Darling Geneviève,

My fiancé has arrived! Hearts are aflutter. Maman ordered all the slaves and workers to line up to greet him as he stepped from his carriage, and one and all gawped at him, for he cut a very fine figure in his starched ascot and frock coat, bowing and nodding as he progressed through this phalanx of admirers, treating slave and master with equal concern and asking each one his or her name. Naturally, Maman scorned this behavior. She remains fixated in her beliefs that polite social gestures are wasted on our Negroes, but I was heartened to see that my intended shows no such pretensions to those whom our society deems lesser.

Maman put on her usual show of airs. How I wish she would hang up her masks and retire from the stage! As soon as she senses her performance has an audience, she becomes an actress prancing before the limelight. Papa was off fishing that day or she never would have put on such a display. Isidore (I thrill to such intimacies, but as this is my private letter to you, my friend, I can dispense with archaic formalities if I like) was very kind about it, yet I felt I must excuse her. She is a product of her time and unmoved by modern talk of freedom and the evils of enslavement. I am always careful to keep my readings on the topic under lock and key for fear that she will burn them and ship me off to Jamaica to become the wife of a planter and thus see how the world treats "silly girls with too-lofty ideals." So much reading, she insists, will weaken my skull and force my swollen brain to protrude over my eyes. Curious that this disease never seems to affect any male scholars, teachers, lecturers, or writers; it is apparently an affliction unique to women who read novels and seek to over-educate themselves.

I had to seek out my betrothed to make amends for Maman. He appeared entirely unconcerned. I suppose in France they are quite used to attitudes of all sorts, including those which seem ridiculously antiquated as well as those of the most forthright thinkers of our age.

You shall be ever so pleased to learn that he is the soul of gentility, very refined and soft-spoken, with a tender inclination toward me and an expressive and open face. He charms Maman with his suavity of manners and appraising ways, while Papa subjects him to much scrutiny and presses him with endless questions about the ancestral estate in Boulogne, the health of Isidore's mother (Papa's second cousin, you recall) and his opinions about various agricultural matters and politics. Very dreary! I could go on endlessly, but Maman calls to me. Isidore and Papa have returned from their tour of the plantation and dinner shall soon be served. While Papa was very kind to Isidore, it is yet to be revealed if there is to be a true affection between them. A day spent in one another's company shall soon reveal the future of their friendship. I hope that it blossoms, for if I were made to choose loyalties between them, I should not know which way to turn.

Yours in faith,
Emilie

❧❦❧

May 5, 1851

Darling Geneviève,

He is to be my husband, this gentle man from across the sea, handsome of face and carriage, well-mannered and sweetly spoken. If I am correct, he has already quite taken a shine to me. He smiles upon seeing me and examines my face with serious thought, as though he means to commit every line to memory. It makes me quite giddy!

We have but three weeks until we are united. Mother spent the evening writing cards to all her friends, family, and acquaintances, and come tomorrow, another set to be distributed to Papa's people. It will be a whirlwind of activity for the coming days. I float through it like a cottonwood seed, a little piece of fluff amidst storms, awaiting my landing.

He kissed my hand upon bidding me goodnight. I know it is most improper of me to entertain ideas of our wedding night, but I simply have no conception of what we are meant to do. Twenty-two years of age and Biblical knowledge continues to elude me. Mother refuses to speak of such things. You and I shared our giggling speculations when we were girls (does a husband mount his wife as does a dog or horse?), but now you are a woman and a mother, and too far away to inform my notions. Even if I asked, your reply may not arrive soon enough to serve me. How I long for all those lost years, dear friend, while Mr. Stockton toured the Orient with you and our correspondence withered to a trickle scarce enough to wet my parched lips, thirsting for news of you. Now that you have returned, you should anticipate the deluge of letters that will arrive at your door, for words pour like rainwater from my pen! Perhaps I'll ask Clothilde. She must be in her seventies and has borne several children, so at least she can educate me about that. If not for Clothilde, I'd be as ignorant as a fence post, and just as rough.

Yours in faith,
Emilie

⚜

May 8, 1851

Beloved friend!

How could I have been so stupid? Each time I consider my ignorance, a fresh surge of horror overtakes me. I feel myself revealed to be but a child, not a speck of the woman I have pretended to be. I'll be a woman soon enough, I fear, and the thought makes my stomach leap like a trout in a net.

Clothilde educated me on the particulars of the wedding night. Maman was away visiting, and I cornered Clothilde at laundry, washing the family dainties. It seemed an apt moment for our conversation, her standing there with my pantalettes in hand, a mountain of soiled sheets waiting their turn at the scrub board.

I begged her, quick, while Maman was out of sight and hearing, tell me the truth!

"Mademoiselle Emilie," Clothilde said, "you know Maman don't want you wise to what men do. The truth apt to frighten a girl right out of bed! Madame Floriane skin me if she hear I give up the secrets of marriage."

Bed! The first I'd heard of it. Of course, I realized that we were to share sleeping quarters, but the thought of a man seeing me without my nightclothes left me quite unnerved. She said of Isidore, "Strong back but a pretty face for a man. Handsome men know what they like. You may come to enjoy what he do to you, p'tite! Keep him happy at home. Just you be careful you don't catch the clap."

The clap! Honestly, I cannot abide the thought. Not that I presume a Frenchman possesses no carnal experience with those of my sex, but Clothilde rattles my nerves with her loose talk. In my charitable work at Poydras Orphan Asylum, I have witnessed those poor infants born to diseased mothers who soon develop foul crusts about the eyes and almost certainly go blind. God forbid the same happen to our child. The discussion terminated with the return of Maman, intruding upon the washing as though she knew of what we spoke, commanding Clothilde to add more borax to the water. Clothilde is a master of deception where Maman is concerned. She smiles, nods (somewhat dim-wittedly, to my eye), and says, "Oui, Madame Floriane!" As soon as my mother's attention is drawn away by some other trifle, Clothilde continues as if Maman had never spoken.

My curiosity about the specifics of the act remained unsatisfied and I again attempted to pry from Clothilde the secrets of Eve. An opportunity presented itself the following evening and I pressed her for answers, "Quick-like!" Oh, that I had not asked and let it remain a surprise! Such coarseness! I nearly quiver at the thought of kind Isidore wielding his animal vigor and impaling me!

"Gwo zozo, ti zozo," she said. Though Clothilde can easily understand our French, her Haitian Creole is often too obtuse for my ears. She repeated, "Big cock, little cock…which one you like? He gon' guete ou! Get his pecker hard and stick it in your dolly. You know? Like the sow and boar. Never you mind, p'tite, it only hurts once. If he's a good lover, he grease the pot with plenty o' kissin'!"

I can scarce look at him now for the roses popping in my cheeks. It is almost certain that he senses my trepidation and compensates with extra tenderness, as if I were a trembling, wild mare spooked by the carriage wheels. Clothilde laughs in that sly manner of hers and continues to grin with one side of her mouth whenever Isidore is present.

The flesh of my thighs rises in goose pimples whenever my thoughts linger too long upon the event to come. I am marked a scarlet woman before I have ever been touched.

Blushing,
Emilie

May 28, 1851

Darling Geneviève,

Belle Rive is aswarm with activity—our rooms boil over with noise, merriment, and bustle. I scarce had a moment to slip away and write you, such are the demands on my person. Dress fittings, Cook sweating away in the kitchen to clean the suckling pig that Maman wanted butchered, the boiling of nuts and shelling of peas. I admit I find it thrilling. When else shall I ever be so fêted? So prized? Two days until Isidore and I are united under Our Lord's watchful eye. I am ever hopeful and give Him thanks that my fiancé is a gentle, thoughtful man and not one of our own, a strutting peacock with social aspirations and a head full of clay. His European ways refresh and delight me, and I am eager to name him as my own. Did I tell you, darling, that Cook will attempt to make marsh-mallows? It's a new sweet I tasted at the Rose Society's annual gala last spring. A spongy cloud of vanilla sugar which dissolves in the mouth. Pure delight—and all for me! (And Isidore, too, naturally.)

Cousins from as far as Atlanta have traveled to Belle Rive to stay the week, but not Papa's scandalous brother, who received no word of our event. Maman has little family, as you remember, but she has extended welcome to the ladies of her circle, many of whom have known me since infancy. We had a tea yesterday in the English fashion with Maman's flock in attendance. Each married woman has taken a minute to proffer her own sage advice, some of which is quite stunning and often makes me laugh (later and privately). For example Mme. C—— insists "a good wife refrains from marital congress a full fortnight after ceasing her feminine courses and a fortnight prior to their commencement," which, if I correctly calculate, would leave me completely untouched (but perfectly illustrates the reason for her lack of heirs). Mme. D—— inscrutably cautioned me against the slightest show of repulsion at exposure to the male form. Any expression of mine that confirms the feminine notion that husbands are foul servants to desire would only inflame his temper. Best to praise the "Greek glory of his temple's firm pillar." I had to bite my cheek to keep from giggling aloud!

The sagacious and sharp-tongued Mme. L—— took my elbow and whispered that I should best ignore the gossip of "ancient cows who have never enjoyed the invigorating thrill of passion singing inside their skins." I have always liked her greatly. Among Maman's friends, she is my favorite. In fact, it has always struck me odd that a bond as enduring as theirs was ever forged, for more disparate of morals and temperament they could not be.

She explained that a husband and wife should always begin and end the day with affection, even if tempers are frayed. "A kiss upon the mouth 'good day' and one 'goodnight' shall pave the way to happiness." That is the only advice I intend to keep.

Must dash, for there are garlands of Spanish moss and ivy to weave and white crepe to hang. Be certain that I shall write to you of the details of our ceremony and the all-important Honey Moon.

Yours in faith,
Emilie

⁂

June 12, 1851

Dearest darling Geneviève,
I raise my hand to pen this letter to you and admire it with new tenderness, for mine is a hand which has been kissed, which has felt the soft skin of a husband, which is free to stroke the hair of a man and press his head to my breast. Mine are hands grown wiser in the ways of love. Mine are hands which have received tender kisses upon their palms. Mine is no longer the body of a girl, pure and ignorant, chère Geneviève, for I now inhabit the form of a woman.

Naturally, our wedding was a splendid if exhausting affair—very gay and vibrant. So much so that Maman's physician, M. Fournier, warned us against acquiring that particular delirium of excitation which results from strenuous dancing and physical exertion. I would lead you through our minuet minute by minute, but I have not the time! The sun has just risen and the kitchen maids scurry to and fro, bringing trays of brioche, boiled eggs, fruit, and cold ham to the breakfast table in the hotel's dining room, where I have tucked myself into a corner to afford myself a pinch of privacy.

I expected Isidore, as a man of the Continent, to have some knowledge of lovemaking, but I must confess that when the time arrived, and we were at last alone, my heart beat so loudly it seemed that all the world would hear it and must block their ears to the sound! We had only exchanged a few chaste embraces prior to our wedding, and though I steadfastly refused to entertain those grim and loathsome stories that Maman's ladies had poured into my head, they were resolute in their insistence. How I trembled! Isidore asked if I should prefer to wait to consummate our marriage, but as you know, I am not one to shirk my duties or dash from a challenge. "No," I said. "You are my husband, and I am your wife, and we shall do the things that husbands and wives do."

And so, we did! Though there was pain, there was joy too, and we lay curled up together afterward, fondly conversing until dawn. I cannot express how absolute my relief! I thank Our Lord that He has seen fit to provide me with such a genteel example of masculinity. Now the maids cast sly glances at me. I'm certain they imagine me a refugee of the bedchamber, and in my unbound hair and wrapper, I look the part! Imagine how scandalized Maman would be to learn that her *petite fille* was seen wandering about the best hotel in Baton Rouge in her nightclothes! Now I must pass this to the concierge for post before I return to our suite, and my sweet husband.

A thousand thanks for the French *négligée*. I've never owned anything so fine as that and shall treasure it always, for the sentiment it carries from you and the new memories Isidore and I have imparted upon it.

Yours *en déshabillé*,
Emilie Bilodeau Saint-Ange

July 9, 1851

Dearest one,

Trust that I have thought of you affectionately and with longing nearly every hour of the day, for I have spoken to you so often within my mind, conversing about the meager trivialities of wedded life, such as the way that shopkeepers and hoteliers address me with startling deference now that I am a married lady with a ring upon her finger and a handsome husband to boot. How quickly the addition of a hat and somber trousseau affects opinion! I am no longer viewed as a silly schoolgirl or an old maid, but as an adult woman with her own firm opinions. Mind you, rather than being asked, "What does your father wish for you, Mademoiselle?" now they simply confirm that I have my husband's approval for my purchases, not understanding that Bilodeau money—not Saint-Ange—buys every thread of fabric we wear or morsel of food we consume.

I have been preoccupied with the other duties and callings of a wife, and confess to you that I take pleasure in granting pleasure to Isidore and thrill to his masculine touch. My slumbering form has blossomed into womanhood, and those Honey Moon weeks spent with my husband served to forge a deeply affectionate bond between us. He is very pleasant to my eye, and mild-tempered with an easy smile that reassures me of our sincere compatibility.

Papa's acquaintance, Mr. Badcocke, invited us to join him for a celebration at his modest but comfortable bachelor's home for an Independence Day ceremony. As Isidore has never experienced our treasured American holiday, we were delighted to attend.

Such an overexuberance of food, I cannot tell you! The table groaned and sagged beneath the pilings on of platters and dishes overladen with cold boiled ham, oysters *étouffée*, lobster salad, floating jellies, pickles, corn pudding, cordials, biscuits, cakes, blancmange, punch, and phosphate in bottles. Grand, patriotic speeches were made while we languished on the esplanade taking refuge from the pressing heat under my parasol. Just after sunset, fireworks enlivened the velvety sky and magnificent, thrilling bursts of noise and color inflamed my senses while Mr. Badcocke's housekeeper sang a stirring rendition of "America," then our host took up the fiddle and played "Old Roisin the Bow" and "Afton Water." After those sentimental tunes, we danced sprightly to "Camptown Races" and "Oh! Susanna" until we panted and grew red-faced from twirling and laughing. Lastly, Badcocke sang "Coal Black Rose" to the crowd, but his gaze never strayed from one female guest, a beautiful Mulatress dressed in fine white lawn and lace. You know that I have never enjoyed minstrelsy, and his performance had the peculiar effect of souring my pleasure in his company. Though he bade everyone to attend Mlle. Laveau's salon for a card reading, one sensed that his jest had scurrilous motivations, for he made great show of offering the Mulatress money for a private reading in his rooms, at which many of the men rudely guffawed and tittered. Isidore was quite put out by the showyness of Mr. Badcocke's expenditures and thus departed the festivities in a grim-faced mood.

Now we have returned to Belle Rive, and Isidore assumes his new role as plantation manager alongside Papa. Prosper yearns to be master of Belle Rive, but he has little patience for tedium and leaves everything he starts incomplete.

Do write and tell me more about your children. By now, darling Sylvie must be saying "Maman" and eating from a spoon.

Yours in faith,
Emilie

※※※※※

September 4, 1851

Geneviève, gift of my heart,
You cannot know the joy that fills me upon learning that I carry a child. Yet here I must laugh at myself, for you are a mother many times over and so comprehend the singular happiness that has blossomed in my soul! I daily give thanks and praise to He who is most generous and loving.

Nothing passes by Clothilde unremarked, I tell you! Even my own Maman noticed no change in me (but you are well familiar with her inclinations, eagle-eyed only where spending and social breaches are concerned), yet dear old Clothilde, who professes to know me as well as she knows her own reflection, saw tell of it the first moment that the new life took root. She hurried me into bed and brought me a posset with sherry and bits of bread as soon as she saw my face turn green at the breakfast table.

"You done good, Miss Emilie! Gonna be a little one runnin' these halls by spring. Been so long since we had a babe here. Not since your poor brother Honoré"—and here she wiped her tears on her apron, for though he is many years gone, that boy was the apple of Clothilde's eye, and I think she shall never recover from the heartbreak of losing him.

I wanted to tell Isidore first, but Maman was so suspicious of my return to bed that she had to see for herself what troubles I'd sprung. I simply had to confess to her or risk being harangued to death by my own

mother, thus depriving her of the grandchild she so desperately antici-
pates. Maman was in a tizzy, her flounces and ribbons all aflutter as she
cooed and cackled about the bedchamber—truly she quite reminded me
of Papa's ridiculously overwrought lavender frizzle bantam when he was
enthralled by the breeding of fancy chickens two summers ago. It gave
me such a headache! But Clothilde diverted her with talk of creating the
baby's layette and left me in peace to sip my posset and await the passing
of sickness.

Isidore, as you imagine, is delighted in his solemn way. I suspect
he is startled to have found success in me so soon after the wedding, but
he is obviously relieved. He thinks me too delicate to comprehend the
precariousness of his position in this household and the purpose of his
presence here, but I too am grateful that his seed is strong.

Meantimes, we settle well into the daily routines of married folk.
Each morning, Lavinia brings us coffee, trifles, and savories, and Isidore
and I breakfast together in our room, then Isidore is conscripted to plantation duties with Papa while I tend to my small affairs at Belle Rive.
Namely, putting all the necessary items in the nursery, supervising the
papering (I chose a cream and pale blue stripe), clearing cobwebs from
the old bassinet in the attic, and sewing a muslin christening gown
trimmed in Bucks Point lace, which I have recently learned from a pattern in *Southern Ladies Monthly*. There is a tiny bonnet, shoes, and a
blanket to make as well, so I expect to be kept busy for the next few
months. Maman wants to hire a seamstress for the layette, but I take
especial pride in being able to make it myself. I am Maker of my child,
am I not? Therefore, I should also make whatever my child needs. I have
not yet told anyone of my assertion that I shall not rely on a wet nurse
but feed my babe with my own milk. Maman will fall into fits when she
learns of my plan. Perhaps that is a healthy portion of my desire to do so!
Truly wicked!

Please do tell of your troubles with Fanchon. You say she is too
headstrong to abide your wishes, but I persuade you to think upon your
own set-aside desires. Do you remember how very badly you wished to
visit Paris before your marriage to see the great masterpieces with your
own eyes and to sip champagne with the Romantics? Recall, please, how
fourteen-year-old Geneviève schemed to stow away on a sailing ship and
make her own way on the Continent. I was but ten, and found you to be
the most daring, invigorating person I had ever met! I'll admit now that

it crushed my spirit to watch you take vows at seventeen. You have been a married lady for over a decade now and still have not seen those gay lights of the Champs Elyseé or trekked the ruins of Athena's temple at the Parthenon. Pray, dear friend, that you look upon the girl's future with the same hope and bohemian spirit that her *chère maman* once possessed.

Should we abandon our hopes so lightly and with such ease? Would you ask your child, the light of your life, to do the same? Though you and I may find ourselves entrenched in ancient ruts worn by generations of women before us, I suggest that it is also within us to begin the climb up constraining walls and to lead our daughters into the light of a new day. Dear Geneviève, inasmuch as our parents would have us hold fast to tradition, my sense that revolutionary change soon approaches grows each day. Now that I am a respectable Madame, might you consider sending Fanchon to stay with me for the summer? I promise to only take her on adventures appropriate to her age and understanding.

Yours in faith,
Emilie

❧❀❧

September 29, 1851

Dearest Geneviève,

Monsieur et Madame Saint Ange (isn't it thrilling?) have entertained several visitors over the preceding weeks and been the glad recipient of many congratulations. Maman's excessive planning irritates me less. Most occasions, I enjoy her company as we work on the layette or browse the mail order catalogs for iron cribs and prams (she has decided her grandchild is too precious a treasure to sleep in a hand-hewn wooden cradle like all the other babes here) until she becomes strident and insists that I know nothing of what a babe needs for I am just a countrified, American ignoramus—never mind that Maman hasn't been back to Lyon since she left it as a girl.

Isidore has taken a private study on the top floor and is most happily installed there among his books and drawings. He retreats there for a time in the evenings to write in the naturalist journal he has begun here, for he has shown deep interest in our local flora and seeks to catalog each species he finds merely for his own edification. Papa has taken quite a shine to Isidore, and they have twice ventured to Papa's club in New

Orleans to play cards. One almost feels Papa's interest in his son-in-law is more keen than in his own boy, for Prosper has crass habits when he's in his cups and is dismissive of the old guard, calling Papa's companions a bickering passel of rusty-guts.

This missive bears sad tidings, I fear. Do you recall Fair Japheth, the cane cutter? He is the one who whittled all those darling animals for us when we were young (of which I still have the sow and her little family of painted piglets in my keepsake box). Last night he passed over after a grisly accident whence his arm was mangled in the grinder and grew gangrenous in this oppressive heat. Often have I pleaded with Papa to apply leniency with the aged slaves, to allow them to take jobs that are less dangerous or taxing to their fatigued eyes and limbs, but Fair Japheth was always the fastest, despite the tremors that have assaulted his body this past year, and Papa would not consent to relocate him. Now he has died in a ruinous and painful manner, denied any portion of the dignity that a man of such character should be allotted. Once more, I strain against the bonds of this place and yearn for a life free of such insults against humanity, but how should we leave it? What should we do? Isidore's occupation was that of amanuensis to an elderly professor, but he resists the pursuit of a similar vocation here, for he feels himself inadequate to find another such position. He mentions, sometimes, having sold illustrations to the newspapers, but likewise refuses the re-initiation of that trade. For the present time, we yearn for the freedom of the soaring breeze uplifting our wings but remain trapped, two birds in a gilded cage, both too afraid to fly.

Yours in chains,
Emilie

❧❦❧

November 5, 1851

Sweet friend,
The cold grows contrary to, but in pace with, the warm glow in my belly. Now that my sickness has eased, I enjoy robust health. Isidore says there are roses in my cheeks, but not just any rose, Heaven forbid. Mine are the precious Souvenir d'un Ami. My flesh the buff-colored petals with a salmon center, pink and bright, fragrant and much admired. He stroked

my cheek when he said this and cracked open one of his library volumes to show me the exact flower he means. It's a small thing, but quite pleasing. One of the benefits of having a naturalist for a mate, I suppose.

The entire family passed All Saints' Day in a state of merriment in New Orleans. We attended Mass at St. Augustine's, afterwards taking supper at L'Hôtel Dauphine. Most delicious! We concluded our meal with frosty iced creams and crisp macarons, which I enjoyed immensely. My taste for sweets has increased tenfold and I can get no fill of petit fours, éclairs, groundnut candy, fudge, and suchlike. Isidore delighted me by securing a box from the kitchen that was filled with delicious trifles. Darling man! (Even as I lie abed writing this, my keen nose gladdens to the scents of fresh butter and chocolate, which emanate from that box on the dresser.)

The following day, we decamped the Dauphine and went to the cemetery to picnic at the family tombs and pay respects to the old crumble-bones, as you and I once deemed them. We had the great fortune to witness a funeral with music! The trumpets and choir sounded from a long way off, a steady, mournful buzz that increased in volume and clarity as the procession drew near. I recognized the tune "Nearer My God to Thee," but sung with such beauty, sorrow, and longing that it transformed into its own magical element, so imbued with the Spirit that I wept. Those voices were hands, pulling the tears from me much as the knitter unspools yarn from her ball of wool. As they entered the cemetery, I spied at the head of the procession that beautiful woman in white who had been the subject of rude commentary at Mr. Badcocke's, walking and singing with such grace that I found myself enthralled by her presence. How I clung to Isidore's arm, filled with emotion! He, too, was quite overcome and could not take his eyes from the spectacle, so powerful was his response to the processional's sights and sounds. We departed shortly thereafter, so I was only able to hear a few faintly distant notes as they sang their way home.

Now, I must tell you that we have acquired two more slaves, altho' I wish it were not so. Papa took Isidore to a slave auction to locate a replacement for poor, dead Japheth and came home with a young man, very robust and black-skinned, with a permanent scowl carved upon his face, and a girl about ten years of age, very agreeable, but who is so thin that her little brown arms and legs resemble kindling sticks rather than human limbs. Maman calls her "Poupette," for she is very much like a marionette, and fawns over her like a pet.

Isidore calls to me, and so I must close this letter.

Your friend,
Emilie

⋇⧂⧃⧂⧂⋇

November 10, 1851

Dear Geneviève,

How I love the delicious Rose Drops you sent! The Anise Drops are likewise excellent for soothing my quarrelsome belly. Thanksgiving at the Tontine Hotel in New Haven—how lucky you are! Lucky too that Mr. Stockton tolerates your disaffinity for the kitchen and spared you and your cooks that task. I pored over the menu that you sent. Perhaps someday I'll dine on such delicacies as chartreuse of vegetables and broadbill ducks in wine sauce. We had the usual holiday repast of glazed ham, turnip greens, gumbo, biscuits with creamed onions, and custard pies.

Now, on to more serious matters. Tell me, do you truly wish to attend a séance? I confess your fascination with this new Spiritualist craze leaves me anxious for your immortal soul. Do not be taken in by charlatans! How is it possible that ordinary women and men can communicate with the spirits of the dead? Does that not defy God's natural laws? How is it possible to cast aside the teachings of our Church in favor of these untried ideas? You plead with me to read the material that you send, but I fear that an abundance of fanciful aggravation could dangerously affect the child within me. Truly, I find myself precipitously vulnerable to suggestion of late as the nights stretch longer and colder and I sleep more poorly with the discomforts of confinement. Sometimes I have sharp belly pains, and streams of cold and heat rush through my body, one after the other, which leave me gasping. Maman pleads with me to abandon my novels, for she is convinced their ideas infect my imagination and leave me susceptible to moral weakness.

Indeed, last night I had the most horrid dream! In it, I slept in the dim and insecure room of a monstrous Gothic mansion whose timbers shifted and groaned about me as I lay abed twisted in tattered sheets. I sensed a malevolent presence elsewhere in the house, and though I struggled mightily, could not free myself from the tangled bedding to

27

flee. My heart knocked about frightfully in my chest, and every beat of it signaled the advancing tread of one so loathsome and inhuman that I could scarce draw a breath to scream. A spirit entered, a tall, thin woman arrayed in a flowing white shroud, but her ethereal face was no thing of beauty. It was the very image of rage and aching misery. Crimson tears of blood flowed from her black eyes, and her long jet curls appeared to float in the air as if tossed by a violent wind. She drifted close to me, closer still, until it seemed that she pressed the very breath from my helpless form. The malevolence of her wicked presence occluded the room like marsh vapors. She overpowered me and I struggled wildly, knowing that she would wrench the babe from my womb should I let her touch me. With exhausting effort, I forced myself to rouse and woke to the sound of my own screams.

Oddly, Isidore did not evidence his usual compassion when I described the horror of it, but instead hunched beside me and chuckled, a low juddering sound which appalled me so much that I wept. Upon seeing my tears and distress, he appeared to regain some semblance of himself and held me until I slept again. It would be easy to let wifely worry get the better of me. If not for our tender and ardent lovemaking (yes, I can claim it freely now!), I would question his happiness here. Whatever passions or agonies stir his mind, they are not yet troublesome.

Yours in faith,
Emilie

❧❦❧

November 30, 1851

Dearest friend,

I was very saddened to hear that Mr. Stockton would not allow Fanchon to journey to New Orleans next year for a summer with your oldest and most faithful friend, but I console myself with knowledge that the cruelties of plantation life might prove scarring to such a young soul not accustomed to our ways. Perhaps it is best that she be spared the indignities and ugliness with which we are daily assaulted.

Sincerest gratitude for the package of five novels! You indulge me wonderfully! I have already raced through Féval's *Les Belles-de-Nuit* and begun Hawthorne's *House of the Seven Gables*. I begin to believe M. Fournier's conviction that my condition leaves me more susceptible to dark fears and fancies, for I feel myself growing nervous in the night and starting whenever the big linden tree shakes its creaking branches as if alive and stretching, rattling its ominous leaves against the window panes. That dreadful dream lingers, still.

I shall endeavor to read the pamphlets on this new craze for Spiritualism that you include, but I cannot promise you that I shall in any way be persuaded to divagate from my Christian faith.

On a happier note, I have been teaching Poupette how to read, using those old issues of *Robert Merry's Museum* that you passed to me when we were young. It still galls that Maman and Papa would never purchase a subscription for me, but this feels a suitable revenge, does it not? I have ordered a slate and chalk to present to my eager student on Christmas morning. How I delight in anticipating her pleasure! Meanwhile, Maman and I have been occupied with taking measurements of every slave at Belle Rive to give each one a new suit of clothes from Father Christmas. Thus far, it promises to be a very jolly holiday for all.

For you, I enclose a needlepoint pillowcase I have decorated with the image of the old swing under the arbors where we spent so many pleasant hours.

> Buried in books,
> Emilie

December 8, 1851

Geneviève,

I write to you colored black and scarlet with heartbreak. I know these things happen, I know it! But knowledge does little to ease the terrible sting of my loss. Yes, dear friend, the child within me is no more. About one week ago, I began to dream that I would visit the chamber pot and see streaks of fresh red blood upon the cloth. You can imagine my anxiety, but I ignored those dreams. Have I not always been told that dreams are but the waste product of an active brain? That night's purpose is to cleanse the foolish fancies we have accumulated throughout the day? I clung to that absurd notion when in my heart I felt it wrong. I was certain that my dreams, repeating themselves over several successive nights, were harbingers of some terrible omen, and I could not rid my mouth of the taste of dread. So certain that I was being foolish by believing in trifling superstition, I did not even tell Isidore of my fears. Consequently, when I did visit the chamber pot and discover swaths of bright blood, the sickness that rose in me was frightful and all-consuming. Shortly after, the pains started. I took myself to bed, but the cramps increased and the blood steadily flowed. I had no choice but to summon Clothilde, who in turn called for Maman. Dear friend, this was the one time in memory when Maman put aside her own concerns and devoted herself to another.

I will spare you the unpleasant details of the ordeal that followed. It was a long night of sorrow and unhappiness such as which has certainly left its scar upon my soul.

Clothilde took the pot out back and buried the contents beneath the tallest oak tree. She said every soul needs a home, even one as tiny as that. I do believe that innocent spirit safe in our Father's heavenly embrace, and yet, Maman insists on berating me with these abominable tales of a limbo crammed to the breaking point with unconsecrated souls. I refute her preposterous claims, and yet they linger most drearily in my imagination, where they too easily take root in its fertile soil.

Did I tell you that I had picked out a name for her? (I am certain she was a girl.) Fern Aurore Bilodeau Saint-Ange. And that I had begun to embroider that lovely moniker upon one of the small blankets I made? Foolish! Foolish of me! Those ancient wives' tales have terrible merit. I should not have breathed word of it to anyone. My lips uttered the curse that killed my child, Geneviève! Please don't expend any breath attempting to persuade me that it is otherwise. There are powers in this world far beyond my understanding and yours. We are blind, groveling animals to think ourselves omnipotent masters of a world that cares so little for our aspirations.

I think of your tremendous luck that you and Mr. Stockton have escaped such tragedies. Isidore has been the epitome of kindness, though I know he does not share my pain. When Maman had another mishap after darling Honoré passed, Papa grew quite impatient with her grieving and carried on as if the whole affair had never transpired. My husband is a kind man, and makes a show of attending to my needs as much as he is capable. He pats my hand and tells me that we shall try again when I am returned to health, but despite his ardent professions, I cannot quell the disturbing notion that he is rather relieved to have been spared fatherhood and begin to get the sense that he prefers our lives to remain easy and unencumbered. Thus I am alone in my suffering and keep a brave face to please the others, all the while I feel myself as barren as a cut-down cotton field after the harvest—without life, and as bleak as winter.

Emilie

December 29, 1851

My dear friend,

You among all women will understand that the mind is a flexible thing, how Imagination preys upon it much as a rodent does when burrowing through winter grain stores. I am still abed. Maman insists me well enough to rise and take visitors (her friends, not mine), but I refuse every invitation. I complain of the cold and flaunt my pale hands, drained of blood. Would you make me suffer so? I ask her, for the indignities she would force upon me are legion, spitting up my story like so much cud to be chewed over again and again.

Only Clothilde (as always!) is any comfort. She tells me stories of her native religion and the vodou *loa*—stories you probably know as well as I, having grown up just down the road, cutting your teeth on the tales of your old nanny Delphine. (I do remember those little tea cakes she made for us, how I would love to have one again!) Clothilde says that the first child born to a family after the passing of one of its members is that same cherished soul returned for another life. Honestly, I can't say I easily believe such foolishness, but it does afford me a certain measure of comfort. It also leaves me eager to conceive again, once my body is fit to do so, so that no other may stake claim on my darling child's soul!

You will be heartened to know that I take comfort as well in the pamphlets that you sent me, most especially Hammond's *Elements of Spiritual Philosophy* and *The Practical Christian*. Cherished friend, I confess that a profound change has altered me. It is as if my faith was an obstacle lodged within me—hard and unyielding—just as the stone nestles within the peach's honeyed flesh, but my loss served to sever it from its moorings and cast it out on a tide of blood and twigged limbs, for my prayers for a healthy child fell on deaf ears. God chose to end my babe's life rather than spare it, and my fury swells unabated. No longer do I take comfort in the Bible, for my pleas for release from this spiritual agony languish unanswered, and during Mass, the face of Jesus looks

upon me with unfeeling eyes. I have devoted myself to reading Spiritualist accounts of the afterlife, for it heartens me greatly to consider that I,
too, might communicate with my Fern through the agency of a medium.

All about me, the great portals between life and death swing open
and closed, offering tantalizing glimpses of the Great Beyond and an
Earthly existence tempered by the succoring assistance of dear, departed
ones. Veritably, I am haunted with questions. Where is precious Fern?
Why did she leave us? That I may obtain answers to these queries fills me
with a mania to pursue them.

Your soul-weary friend,
Emilie

✦✦✦

January 21, 1852

Dear Geneviève,

How intrigued I was by your account of the Fox sisters' séance and mys-
terious table rappings! Did you truly hear this communiqué from the
departed with your own ears? I become ever more convinced that we
exist alongside a phantasmic realm invisible to us.

Today, I chanced upon Clothilde treating Papa's rheumatism with
a poultice. Clothilde has been with us so long and her healing talents
are so accepted in this household that it never occurred to me to inquire
about the source of her skill. I questioned her about her history and discovered that she is the first child born after twins, which gives her a great
sense of power and the ability to heal the sick and troubled upon instruction from the voices of her ancestors. Papa listened with a grimace upon
his face and told Clothilde to shush her mouth, quoting Leviticus in retribution: "A man also or woman that hath a familiar spirit, or that is a
wizard, shall surely be put to death: they shall stone them with stones:
their blood *shall be upon them.*" He accepts her favors but rebukes her
natural talents, ever mindful to keep her in her place.

I have sent Isidore into town to procure several books for me. I am
very eager to delve into Elliot's *Mysteries* and deepen my understanding
of the nature of spirits and their mystical properties. (Isidore is dismissive of anything not scientifically verified and tells me I'm foolish and
gullible, yet he indulges me still. And sending him to town provides him
a welcomed reprieve from his duties at Belle Rive, so I feel I do him a

favor.) Please do tell me more of your investigations into Spiritualism. I am most captivated by the tales of the medium Mrs. Hayden and her travels in England.

Your eager student,
Emilie

❦

February 5, 1852

Treasured friend,
Belle Rive is thrown into chaos! Albert, the slave most recently procured by Papa, has vanished. Simply vanished, as if he had never existed. Oh, the uproar and madness as one and all have searched from house to field to riverbanks and beyond. The men wade through the water and comb the trees, anxious for any sign of the escapee, while Maman frets uselessly. I begged Papa to let it go so that Albert might have a fair chance of escape, but he is set on his course. I have always wondered why more did not attempt it, for life at Belle Rive, while certainly being no worse than that of slaves on the neighboring plantations, is little better, and though I know there exists in the breast of each one an intense yearning for freedom, the law is so strictly prohibitive that only the most desperate or foolhardy attempt to flee on pain of death. Papa has summoned the slave catcher and Isidore expresses his astonishment at the proceedings, for indeed, to his foreign understanding our habits seem strange. This event merely sharpens my own convictions that our future does not reside at Belle Rive but in the free North among such conscientious brethren as yourself and the Abolitionists of whom I hear so much (mostly, when Papa and his acquaintances rail against the vagaries of politics and Maman complains about the ineptitude of her lady's maids).

My health bounds back like a faithful hound. I feel myself ready to resume relations with my husband and try again for a child. Do be pleased for me! We journey to visit Maman's cousins soon and meet their new infant, for which I scarce feel ready, but believe it will do me well.

Yours,
Emilie

❦

Dearest friend,

You inquired after the runaway, Albert. Woeful news! It grieves me to report that he was apprehended near Hammond and returned to us, whereupon the slave driver Mr. Plunkett (I have often spoken to Isidore about my dislike of that vile and odious man) had him whipped and brined. Much to my relief, I was away when it transpired and thus did not witness this cruel punishment, but more regretfully, I was not present to force an attempt to stop or ameliorate it, but oh! how profoundly it has marked Isidore, serving only to impress upon him the barbarism of our natures.

My husband is distracted of late, a mental quality evidenced by his utter revulsion with Albert's handling, about which he speaks in a grim and cold tone. He journeys to the City sometimes to visit the botanical gardens and make sketches of the orchids there, but I suspect this new fascination merely provides a reason to evade Belle Rive's cruelties.

I devoured the tracts you sent to me. They further convince me of the wrongness of our ways and speak to my desire to emancipate not only the slaves but ourselves from this peculiar institution. Maman and Papa would fly into rages if they found my papers, for they complain bitterly about the Quakers and their teachings against slavery. Yet, the more tightly they clamp down, the more I struggle for release. Their ignorance tires me, Geneviève. Something has changed within me. My loss has broken me open—the scales have fallen from my eyes and I chafe, I chafe! beneath the constraints of the life afforded me.

Poupette is a dear girl, shy and eager to please but even more eager to learn. Her sunny disposition is a delight to us all, and she simply drinks in whatever I can teach her. What differentiates her from us? An unlucky birth? Should she be forever marked and doomed to servitude? I am ever more aware of the hypocrisy of this family. Papa waves the French flag and trumpets the claim of his European bloodline, but his grandmother was Haitian, as is her sister Clothilde. He and Maman are fixated on color and heritage. Once, when I still carried, I heard them speculating on the complection of my child, for though Isidore is Mulatto and myself Octoroon (how deeply etched is this slur upon me, overheard in childhood and never forgotten), they feared it would be dark.

You recall that I have my own trust—enough to pay for our passage to New York and perhaps secure a small house for us. I hold this vision close to my heart. It gives me much comfort to imagine leaving Louisiana for a free, new life in the North. There is too much ugliness here. It's a wonder I did not see it before, but I was as coddled as a kitten, an innocent girl with childish interests and hopes. Naïve about the world's harsh realities and unconvinced that cruelty could dwell within the breasts of those I knew and loved. Albert's back is a mass of scarred skin, so raw and evil looking I cannot face it. To know that my own father caused such pain (though his hand didn't wield the whip, his authority permitted it) is injurious to my God-fearing soul.

Yours in clarity,
Emilie

❧✣❧

April 2, 1852

Dearest one,

Thank you for your letter of the 25th. I was so pleased to receive news of Mr. Stockton's kind offer to employ my husband. I hold your suggestion under advisement. Isidore is very proud; if he sensed that his position in Mr. Stockton's firm was in any way the result of charity or our pitiable machinations it would surely sour his enthusiasm. Naturally, I shall employ my feminine wiles to elaborate the North's many fine qualities and liberties, but in light of recent events, he may need less persuasion than we believe.

Despite my efforts, my womb still proves inhospitable. I'm certain that Isidore has been avoiding our lovemaking, and I suspect he's afraid of causing me injury or another loss if I conceive again. You'll think me naïve, but I've asked for Clothilde's help. She's given me a sachet to add to my bathwater and made a tincture for me that smells of blackstrap and has an iron filling rolling around the base of the bottle. Together we laid flowers and cakes on the altar in her small room and lit a candle while Clothilde invoked Maman Erzulie (our Christian Mother Mary, to whom I whispered prayers) to bring me a child.

Not yet ready to join its processional, I walk alongside the Spiritualist path. I have so many questions and want to experience its wonders myself. Indeed, these readings and my brush with Death have parted the curtains between worlds, leaving me newly attuned to the Spiritual vibrations and energies surrounding me. I resonate with them as does the toll of a bell when the clapper strikes.

Yours,
Emilie

⚜

April 30, 1852

Dearest Geneviève,

I read with great interest the articles you enclosed about the new trade in Chinese sugar workers from Hawaii. You ask how I think this will affect Southern plantations and Belle Rive, but I cannot imagine that a society so deeply invested in its practices could be convinced to abandon its slaves to hire indigent workers. Nor can I imagine that the Chinese would fare any better here than the Negroes, for suspicion runs rampant among the whites and many Creoles who fear the Oriental as a despotic swindler. (Yet, the fashionable often dine at Ping's Imperial Palace in the French Quarter, where it is reputed that wealthy patrons may speak a secret password and be admitted to a back room to gamble, play mahjong with Chinese ladies, and indulge in the smoking of opium—therefore, I ask, where is the true source of corruption? In the purveyor of immorality or in the customer who cannot control his immoral appetites?)

It is with a glad heart that I report Isidore has befriended a Welsh gentleman, Mr. Crunn, who shares my husband's affinity for the natural world and discussions of a philosophical nature. It pleases me greatly to see his excitement at having found a kindred soul with whom to express his enthusiasms. (I do try to indulge his interests, but my attention easily wanders once the discussion turns to horticulture. I can scarcely manage to arrange an attractive bouquet of blooms, so it is a great relief to me to be able to advise my sweet husband that he should save his stories for a more appreciative audience—though I do so gently, and his eyes sparkle when he proclaims my suggestions of a letter to Mr. Crunn "splendid" and dashes off to write one.)

This upright man about whom Isidore had spoken so highly came to Belle Rive to collect Isidore, and I must confess to you that we women were quite taken with this dapper and exceedingly charming visitor. Maman primped in excess, and I could see her rouge from across the room, so vigorously had she applied it, but the imperturbable Mr. Crunn flattered one and all with his flirtatious wit.

Isidore's buoyant mood convinces me that now is the perfect time to kindle a new life within me. Though I am hale and hearty, I pleaded with Clothilde to assist me with a bit of her native magic. She just nodded in her sage way and patted my hand, saying, "Leave it me, child. The *loa* know how to fill that belly!"

I await a second "treatment" and do my best to make myself alluring to Isidore by bathing with milk and rose petals before bed, donning my sheerest linen gown, and leaving my hair unbraided at bedtime to entice his hands to run through it.

> Your harlot-at-heart,
> Emilie

May 16, 1852

Darling Geneviève,
I begin to think the African gods (or *loa*) more powerful than our Catholic saints, for while my Savior has not answered my prayers for a child, Clothilde's offerings to the spirits had immediate effect. She has given me an amulet blessed by her gods and "humming," she says, "with good woman power." Dare I confess to you that I donned this strange item and felt myself becoming radiant with foreign vibrations and the emanations of its command? Truly did I sense myself taken over by a profound and mystical force, such that I approached my husband and appealed to his masculine senses, which he rewarded with ardent reply! Marriage has allowed me to reveal and express a side of myself hitherto unknown, and I find that I like it very much, this new sense of feminine confidence. Even should others find my actions shameful or deceitful, my own daring inspires me.

At last, I begin to confide to Isidore my wish to leave Belle Rive. Yes, I hear how callous my words are, that I would be willing to abandon my own family, my home, and everything familiar to me. But Geneviève, you have done so and survived. You have built for yourself a magnificent free life in the North, liberated from the petty superstitions and prejudices that so demean and dehumanize our Creole and Negro brethren. I have no wish to earn my bread on the forced labor of others or to uphold my parents' traditions. My Spiritualist readings have awakened a great hunger in me and kindled a fire which starves for fuel. My present ambition is to secure an appointment for magnetism treatment from Joseph Barthet in the City. Not only will it strengthen my womb, it will help to prepare my mind to receive communications from the deceased and, it is my fervent hope, from my darling Fern Aurore. I have not received any message from her, but remain convinced that her spirit hovers above me, awaiting entrance into this world through a new birth.

Isidore, I believe, is amenable to the change, for he too is vastly discomfited by slavery and fumes about the absurdity of his life here. But something restrains him from full-hearted commitment to a future in the North, and I cannot comprehend its source. I grow desperate to remove him from this environment lest he take root here and become too difficult to pull up.

Your friend in inspiration,
Emilie

May 29, 1852

Geneviève,

How thrilling to hear your travel plans for next year, and how very fortunate you are to experience the world as you do! By nature, I consider myself a person who refuses to entertain jealousies when they arise, but I admit to many sharp pangs of envy when I read your itinerary. I have always longed to travel overseas and find the notion of an ocean voyage on a well-appointed steamship exceptionally romantic.

Do you recall the La Forets? They have been displaced after a dreadful fire that burned down much of their plantation and acreage. You know the terror that fire inspires. Any stray spark or hot ash can take the wind and catch the next place alight and up it goes, too. We have Mme. La Foret's eighteen-year-old niece Loucille staying with us for the time being. The circumstances are grim but I do enjoy her company.

Papa practically keeps Isidore in his pocket. They're forever riding the grounds, poring over the account books or disappearing into New Orleans to visit Papa's clubs. Prosper is quite put out to be replaced as favored son, especially by a "foreign interloper," which is how he describes my husband, and often grumbles about this favoritism. Maman is always on hand to coddle her precious boy and ply him with gifts, but he is too selfish to do anything to increase his esteem in Papa's eyes. He would rather pout like a child or drown himself in drink than break a sweat with hard labor.

There's a fancy-dress party at the club in a few weeks, and Isidore's accompanying Papa. It's funny, but he seems nervous about it, my husband. He thinks I don't know what those fellows get up to at their clubs, but I've heard plenty of stories from other wives about dancers in scanty costumes and too much drink. Would I trust any other man to go and behave himself? Maman makes Papa buy her off with a new broach or a shopping trip to Miss Tilly's for some ridiculous *chapeau* after one of his parties, and the whole time he's gone she capers about telling one and all about the important work he's doing. I won't entertain such delusions!

Maman is having her ladies to the house today for a tea so that Miss Loucille won't feel too excluded from society's doings while she is displaced. Mainard went yesterday to purchase a pound of Ceylon tea, a half pound of Souchong, and cocoanuts for Clothilde to make her famous cookies to accompany the custard, sherry cake, and butter sandwiches. My appetite for sweets stayed with me after the miscarriage, and I take much more enjoyment from these things than ever before. I enclose the receipt for Clothilde's cocoanut cookies. The measurements are not precise, but if you have a good cook, I'm certain she will be able to replicate the original with success.

> Yours in faith,
> Emilie

June 15, 1852

Beloved confidante,

Happy news! I am with child once again. I have waited to announce it, not wanting to tempt the fates as I did before. Dear friend, I accept your advice and warnings with a good heart and sound conscience, for I know that you worry about me and fear a second loss, but I am certain that I shall be successful in bringing to bear this time. Yet I withhold the news from all but my intimates—Clothilde and Maman—for fear of speaking too soon and disappointing my husband once again.

In Mr. Crunn, Isidore has found a patron to support his dream of building an orchidarium at Belle Rive that will lure naturalists from far afield and serve as a showcase for some of the rarest floral species. Frankly, I fear it a wasted effort. Our climate won't be kind to the European delicates Isidore hopes to raise here, but it gives him pleasure and purpose, and I can't deny him or speak against such high hopes. I suggested that Albert be his assistant, and so they work together on the project. It's a reprieve for Albert, and I think Isidore appreciates the camaraderie. He tends to hold himself apart from the family in small ways, and Papa's best efforts to make a son of him fail. Isidore tolerates Prosper, certainly there is no love lost between them, and he has yet to make anything more than an acquaintance of the fellows at Papa's club. He says he is not lonely for he has me, and so I've come to accept his dreamy, rather solitary nature. Though he and Albert work in near silence, it's a companionable one, and they both enjoy a respite of lemonade and biscuits when the air cools.

Today is baking day, and Cook has just rung the bell signaling that new bread and butter have been laid at table. I dally no longer!

Fondly,
Emilie

✦✦✦✦✦

July 7, 1852

Dear friend,

Your reports of the stirring discussions enjoyed at the Daughters of Temperance meetings move me deeply. It is a great thing you do, dearest, to speak of reforms against the evils of liquor you describe. As you know, my own brother is woefully enslaved by his love of liquor, and it has been years since I have enjoyed his company free from the reek of fumes on his breath or emanating from his skin. Maman coddles him foolishly, and Papa's evident disgust with Prosper's lassitudinal habits serves him no better. Your letter convinces me that demon drink is another evil we must fight against, as daughters, women, and mothers, to preserve the sanctity of our happy homes.

I am delighted that you liked the hair flower that I enclosed in my last letter to you. My experiments with the art form have quite satisfied me! The work is even easier for me now that my abundant hair so quickly fills the brush. Clothilde says it will make a pretty wreath for you in no time at all. Have I mentioned that Clothilde grows superstitious in her dotage? You know she has always spoken to the *loa* spirits and treated all at Belle Rive for their pains and heartaches using her herbs and native religion, but it appears to have taken a malicious turn. She insists on filling my head with wicked thoughts about Isidore. She tells me that I must not be a fool in marriage, lest my husband discover he can deceive me without effort and begin to do so.

Can you imagine? This morning she insisted on emptying the chamber pots herself, a chore normally done by Lavinia, saying that if I will not fend for myself, she shall do it for me! The gall of that woman! I know she is family and have always felt a closer bond to Clothilde than my own Maman, but her accusations and insinuations about my marriage tax me to no end and only serve to incite an icy fury in me.

Papa gave Maman permission to purchase a new set of Willow ware for their anniversary, and she was quite over the moon when it was delivered today. Geneviève, please slap me if ever I become the kind of woman who goes into raptures at the prospect of new dishes! Maman will pass our current setting to the La Forets, who are rebuilding the portions of their home that burned and in need of many items. Isidore has accepted the task of delivering the crates to La Foret plantation on his route to New Orleans.

The New Orleans Garden Society has invited him to give a lecture about the cultivation of orchids and rare botanicals, at the home of Madame Laveau this summer. When the letter arrived, he could scarce control his anticipation and trembled with such an influx of emotion that he nearly suffered a fit of apoplexy. I am so pleased for him and know that his theories will hold his audience in thrall. It's my hope that an involvement with an audience of educated gentlemen will counter the mood of distraction that consumes him.

A wind has lashed at the trees all afternoon, and fat drops sprinkle from a burdened sky whose deep gray clouds glimmer with a spectral greenish light. Poupette asks if we have a storm cellar, for she's been caught in "a beastly gale" and tossed "arse over tit from bow to stern." Darling girl, she makes me laugh sometimes with her seafaring witticisms, speaking as though she's some seasoned old, peg-legged pirate. I asked her the source of these colorful expressions, but she merely clamped her lips together, and I could get nothing out of her but silence.

Presently, I sit on the veranda to watch Isidore and Mainard pack the carriage, and Maman flustered and bustling about fruitlessly trying to orchestrate the whole affair. Now they have finished and Isidore steps up into the carriage, briskly and with an arresting, gentlemanly ease (I do wish you could see him—he cuts such a fine figure) and leans out the door to wave farewell to me, his dark eyes sparkling, the long hair he refuses to style to American fashions blowing in the wild wind. How did I manage to become so fortunate?

But now my gaze slides to the right and here stands Clothilde, wiping her hands on her apron and frowning from the doorway as she watches them depart. Despite the wild wind, Clothilde's muttering, and the sound of the cane grinder chewing up stalks in the sugar house, I can hear the scratch of my quill against the paper and the thumping of my own heart inside my chest. I watch the goose pimples spring upon my skin as the clouds surrender and drop their burdens. The sky darkens and I cannot shake this sudden sense of foreboding that chills me.

You'll think me foolish for giving credence to such subtle warnings, but as I write this, I cannot help but feel that the mystical world crowds around me too closely, and strange, malevolent energies impress their ill designs upon the pattern of my future. Why does my happiness shift so soon to foreboding? Tell me I'm afflicted with the Hysteria of the ancient Greeks, that my condition weakens my brain and leaves me susceptible to fantasy. Tell me, dear friend, that I have naught to fear.

All atremble,
Emilie

✦❦✦

July 13, 1852

Adored Geneviève,

I write to you now because there is no one else who would believe me, unquestioningly, when I admit that my discomfiting premonition of the 7th has proved itself true. In one respect, I could rejoice in this new awareness that bares my protected, tender insides to the world as if I were a perch fileted by a fishmonger, but my raw flesh and naked spirit are unshielded and thus easily wounded.

Isidore did not return the following evening after his journey to La Foret and the City.

What had promised to become a deluge of significant force ceased after a few moments, and the sky cleared, revealing a crisply golden and lushly hued twilight. Dearest, I did not become alarmed until the stewed pears and cream had been cleared from the dinner table and Papa had tottered off for his evening brandy. Another of Maman's headaches sent her to bed, and Prosper had gone to play Faro with the overseer, Ramón, and some of the other fellows, leaving me on my own. I made myself busy as best I could while I waited for my husband's return and finally, Clothilde brought me a glass of milk punch to help me sleep, for the night had grown intolerably still and muggy.

The moisture was so thick in the air that it clung to the linden tree and dripped listlessly from its branches in imitation of the promised tempest. I passed a strange and restless night and woke alone, thinking Isidore must be in his study, but he was not. Papa dismissed my worries, saying Isidore was a grown man who knew the roads and dressed like a gentleman. None around here would harass him, for Papa has made sure all the landowners know that his son-in-law is Mulatto and free, and not to be trifled with. Still, anxiety nibbled away at me as the day lengthened to bring yet another twilight and solitary night of waiting. On the 9th I begged Papa to send Ramón out to scour the roads for sign of my husband, but once again he deemed me silly and said Isidore had likely remained in the City an extra night or perhaps returned to assist the La Forets, who are in dire need of hands. Surely he would send word if he were delayed! Isidore can be forgetful, but he is always conscientious of his duties to me, and his absence worried me to no end. I waited on the veranda while Maman busied herself with Cook, planning the menu for the week. Were they all mad, I wondered? Did no one but me care that my husband might be lying broken in a ditch, the victim of some gruesome attack?

Then Poupette cried out, high and gleeful, dashing from the house to the road where Mainard was driving the carriage with Isidore inside, wide-eyed and startled by his reception, with me and Maman flying out to greet him.

"What sourced those tears, dear wife?" he said blithely, climbing from the Rockaway as if he'd been gone but hours and not days. I gaped at him, uncomprehending. Who was this callous stranger that returned to me?

The day passed as if in a distorted dream, my husband steadfastly refuting all claims that he had been gone two nights. Maman told me to leave it alone, and Papa chided me for meddling and contradicting my husband's word. I felt as though I should go mad. Isidore barricaded himself in his study and avoided me until bedtime, when he finally staggered into our room long after midnight, having fallen asleep on the study room divan. Once more I entreated him to tell me what had transpired during his absence, but he dismissed my worries as the product of an overexerted brain.

"Will you be this man when you are a father, Isidore?" I asked. "Are you really so quick to dismiss me, when I do nothing but care for you?"

The lamps were doused, so there was little light save a pale moon glow from the window that shielded his expression from me. He said, "Ahhh," with a great exhalation of breath like the crush of a bellows and nothing else.

Then I added, "I presume you are anxious about the result, as am I, but there is every chance that we shall hold our own dear little one soon enough. I know that we will be successful this time." I hoped my words would reassure him, but he did not speak again until the following day, when he approached to assure me that he does not wish to nurture false hopes but is very pleased at the news. Yet his words belie the quality of his voice, weighted with a reluctance or sadness whose origin I cannot identify. Geneviève, you are well versed in the heightened senses afforded our sex, which grant us a surety of Truth as we move through this dishonest world. Mine tingle with the certainty that Isidore keeps some secret from me, likely for fear of hurting what he perceives as my "delicate" sensibilities at this most important time. Subtle changes take him over in minuscule ways that prick the fabric of my awareness and cause it to snag. I am deeply tempted to write to Mrs. Greaves at the Société de Magnétisme et Hypnotisme to plumb the mysteries of Isidore's perturbation. It may be possible that he is troubled by convoluted spiritual energies which require the guidance of a professional to sort.

Yours in faith,
Emilie

Dearest one,

A hundred thanks for your kind letter brimming with gentle reassurances. Your words soothe my restless heart, which seethes with unvoiced queries and aches for a Truth not forthcoming. I bear them like an amulet against the anxieties that dart 'round my brain like swallows in a barn. You say I labor too long at the loom, endlessly knitting my questions into new shapes, but you are not here to experience what I do or to capture the furtive, creeping stance that my husband adopts in private moments when he believes himself alone. Tell me, then, what you make of a scene such as this:

A week after his return, Isidore accosted me in the parlor after tea. Immediately I noted the sharp gleam in his eye and what appeared to me, most oddly, as what can only be described as that wicked curl of lips more commonly pursed in serious thought. A subtle chill shivered its frightful way through me, and it appeared that the warm sunlight glowing through the tall windows dimmed and turned cold, casting bleak shadows into all the corners of the room.

His words, when uttered, struck me with the force of a blow, for had we not been arguing just earlier that day about that lost night, and hadn't he graciously conceded to an error of timekeeping and memory? Yet, here he was again, firm in his assertion that I was wrong, that Papa, Maman, and all the other people in house and fields sat in error. Insistent, he railed, "I was only gone but a single night. One, do you hear me?"

Dear friend, that statement shall forever live in my imagination, for it upset the balance of our carefully weighted world. He had been away two full nights. Why did he not understand that? We stood across the parlor from one another, and in the few seconds it took for his words to reach my ears, I took in everything about him, fully and with great immediacy. The slight, almost imperceptible crookedness of his face—as if his head tilted slightly to one side. That the left jaw listed while the right was sharper and squared with more finality, and how the set of his mild brown eyes was just beginning a very slow slide off a canted fence rail. Even his fine, long nose appeared pinched by an aggressive hand, as if the modeler had grown impatient with his medium and allowed that pique to tighten his grip upon the living clay.

I saw these things and wiped my eyes, grown suddenly untrustworthy. His familiar face had warped into one I no longer recognized, and it was then I understood that he is lost to me.

You think me childish to be so consumed by these speculations, but I am ever more convinced that we must renounce Belle Rive and whatever undue influence affects my husband before our child is born. I search for answers among the many Spiritualist books that now mount up on the nightstand, certain that I shall find a remedy for the disharmony I sense all around me.

Fervently yours,
Emilie

❦

August 7, 1852

My darling Geneviève,

You are terribly brave to assail New York's "seedy rum-holes" in defense of Temperance! I live through you and your expeditions into suffrage, Spiritualism, and those social reform movements which promise the betterment of our sisters' lives. Truly, you are a virtuous paragon of inspiration to your countrified friend, and I shall do whatever I can to honor your efforts by replicating them to the best of my abilities. Admittedly, I have much less opportunity than you to do so, and little occasion to exercise my freedoms. Now that I carry the "Belle Rive heir," as Papa says endlessly, my circle of influence tightens measurably. I am barred from riding a horse. Even the jostle of a carriage is too frightfully rough for me, Maman insists. I'm all but prevented from leaving home unless it is with Isidore, whom I must beg to be allowed to journey with him into New Orleans. He promises to take me soon, and at last, I have good cause to insist upon it!

Mrs. Greaves, of the Société de Magnétisme, has sent me several letters, and she has worked to secure a place for myself and Isidore at a séance hosted by the esteemed and somewhat notorious Madame Marie Laveau, the vodou priestess. Everyone knows of Mama Marie— the Laveaus are famed for their vodou rituals at St. John's Bayou—and the slaves speak of her conjuring skills with hushed reverence. Firstly, I shall ask if you recall the striking Mulatress to whom Mr. Badcocke so rudely sang "Coal Black Rose" at his Independence Day fête? We spoke briefly at that party when we were introduced, and she inquired if I read novels, for she needed a good recommendation. Little did I realize then that she is the daughter of Marie Laveau! She's called Petite Marie, and I had the incredible good fortune to speak with her again at the Romans' celebration at Oak Alley. She attended as a guest of the esteemed novelist Alexandre Dumas (you'll be thrilled to know that he is very charming), else I'm sure the Romans would never have consented to the presence of a vodou priestess there. Her manner and words are most soothing, and Mrs. Greaves assures me that Madame Marie will be able to communicate with the spirits responsible for Isidore's distraction and strange moods.

Maman and I spend afternoons working a crazy quilt and refining our potichomanie skills. (A peddler with a cartload of Yankee notions was by a fortnight ago and sold us painting brushes and several pots of colored enamel.) Prosper slammed the sash too hard and cracked a window pane, so we are using the broken pieces to assemble a mosaic of sorts in the Persian tradition.

I have also commanded a steady supply of groundnut candy from Clothilde, since we have molasses in abundance right now. She is quite happy to have an excuse to clear Cook from the kitchen and commandeer the baking. I enclose a tin of candy for your four lovely little ones, I pray you won't mind. Do tell them it comes from me, won't you?

> Bursting at the seams,
> Your Emilie

September 10, 1852

Charming friend,

We have all been delighted by your gift of the game "Mansions of Happiness" and spend many an evening together in the parlor after supper playing round after round. Maman, especially, seems to delight in playing with Poupette, as she considers the game an education in virtue that she is thrilled to enforce. It's quite amazing to think of families across our beloved country playing on replicas of the very same board, and we have speculated at length about the treasures you describe on display at Mrs. May's Toy Shop in Manhattan.

Now I shall answer your many questions about the séance at Madame Marie's! She received us very warmly, seating us at her daughter's side during the ceremony. I was quite tickled to be taken for an intimate of the family and favored over the other guests. The event went much as I'd imagined—it was exceedingly refined and mystical. The séance began with a vodou incantation, which I recall here to the best of my ability: *Papa Legba ouvri baye-a pou mwen, pou mwen pase. Le ma tounen, ma salyie lwa yo.* I understood enough to recognize a summons to the gatekeeper of the Spirit world, Papa Legba (similar to our Catholic Saint Peter), to open the gates and let us in. Madame Marie easily connected with her Spirit guides to soothe the grief of those in attendance, and thus, with Mrs. Greaves' assurances in mind, I asked for a message of my own.

I closed my eyes, concentrated on opening myself to the Universal Mysteries, and waited. But it was not Fern who answered my call. The atmosphere changed, Geneviève. At once I felt stifled and breathless, pinned beneath the penetrating stare of some powerful presence. I opened my eyes to meet the sordid, burning gaze of a bizarre, feminine apparition—the very same figure I saw in those dreadful dreams that plagued me before I lost the first child, don't you recall? It materialized atop the table within the circle of our joined hands as if formed from the breath of our young hostess. Isidore gasped, but the warning flew too late from my lips. The apparition dissolved into my husband as if he had inhaled a puff of smoke. Then all was chaos!

Madame Laveau quickly broke the circle and lit a lamp. She wore a strained look upon her face as she attended to her daughter, slumped in her chair. She shook and slapped Petite Marie and called a servant to fetch smelling salts. Her lips tinged with blue, she came to at last, and allowed herself to be led away. Everyone swallowed tumblers of brandy and departed in silence, unsure of the gravity of her illness.

We were briefly shaken, but I remain charged with excitement days later, for here is the proof of the Spirit world that Isidore had so long refuted. Truly, it was more than I had hoped for, and I am positively glowing with my newfound awareness. The Fox sisters can't top Madame Marie, I assure you! I reflect on the experience often, savoring every supernatural aspect of that night, but am most transfixed by the odd qualities of the ghost, who appeared as vividly to me as the painting on my walls, for she wore trousers like a man and strange, plain clothing unlike any woman I know. I cannot begin to decipher her identity, and

Isidore claims he suffered no ill effects, and so it remains a fascinating mystery to enliven my dull days.

Yours in faith,
Emilie

Geneviève,

Horrors abound at Belle Rive! Albert has been thrown in jail for murdering Mr. Plunkett, the slave driver. The tale is a vicious and gruesome one whose particulars make even the staunchest heart quail. Suffice it to say that Plunkett abused Poupette horribly and Albert retaliated with passionate violence. Since they arrived together at Belle Rive, he has been her protector, and they have looked after one another with unusual tenderness. Superadded to these tumultuous burdens is the revelation that Poupette is several years older that we supposed, as much as fourteen years. Maman says that the girl hasn't yet had her monthlies, but Fournier warns us that she may yet conceive. Papa is like to wake snakes, ranting about that "no account cracker" he hired and stomps about in a vicious mood, terrorizing everyone with his cane.

Maman is destroyed that her "pet" is less a girl than she supposed and now casts a gimlet-eye her way, muttering about the destructive nature of the African libido, as if Poupette herself, that sweet child, were the seductress and to blame for the attack upon her innocence. Does Maman know nothing of what those men get up to? The gross liberties visited upon female slaves? I have read much about this in the Abolitionist tracts put out by the Quakers and find it appalling. This incident simply encourages me to pursue my political education so that I may, in some small way, be of service to causes far greater than my own.

You know, I had the oddest sensation at Petite Marie's salon. Perhaps it was the leaping flame reflected in an eye, or the syrupy cadence of a hushed voice somewhere in the flickering lowlight. I have thought upon it greatly and still cannot pinpoint what unsettled me. I would dismiss it as nervous fancy but for the certainty of my intuition, which confirms that humans are receptive to the unseen energies and forces that surround us. But let us say no more on the subject, for my poor Isidore is particularly troubled by this tragedy coming so hard on the heels of that séance, which (he has at last admitted) disturbed him. He shares

Kant's philosophy that "knowledge begins with the senses, proceeds to understanding, and ends with reason." When I challenged this assertion, Isidore grew agitated, insisting, "Kant said there is nothing higher than reason and I concur! I won't be swayed by chicanery and parlor tricks, my dear, and I suggest you do the same."

I begin to feel that I never quite know who shall greet me when I waken each morning, the soft-spoken man of pleasant mien whom I married, or this new, hardened stranger who sometimes takes his place.

Yours in perplexity,
Emilie

～⊱⊱⊰⊰～

October 7, 1852

Darling friend,

We have a son! Our little angel came into the world a week ago, a wee spindly thing wearing a little brown cap of curls. Clothilde calls him "early bird," as he arrived a month in advance of his expected date. He's beautiful and adorable. Such a bonny baby! I recovered quickly from the birth with Clothilde's help. She has delivered nearly every baby born at Belle Rive for the past forty years and knows many a remedy to ease pain, stop and start flows, and return mothers to full vigor.

How I delight in caring for him! Isidore is quite enthralled and very attentive to his first boy—fatherhood has transformed him from a brooding philosopher to a tender and affectionate parent. Naturally, Maman and Papa have made much ado over "Little Bit" as we call him, although his formal name is Théodore Marcel. Poupette is my shadow and follows me everywhere, ever ready to take him from my arms.

Despite this ray of glorious sunshine in our lives, some subtle torment is at play within my husband's mind. His nights are restless and he struggles in his sleep as if fending off invisible enemies and desperate to awaken. But most days are gay and pleasant, and he sits with me when I bathe or feed Théodore, marveling at his tiny toes or his long, grasping fingers. Isidore calls our boy "perfection in miniature" and declares himself the happiest he's ever been. We are to host some visitors in the next few weeks—Loucille La Foret is coming to stay for three days, and I'm very much looking forward to her companionship. Aside from Poupette and Maman (when she can tear herself away from her own concerns), I am starved for female company. My world has gotten very small indeed. I scarce have time to write to you, much less enjoy my books and the leisure time which was so abundant just a few weeks ago.

Isidore ventures to the City next week to meet with Fr. Lázaro to arrange Théodore's baptism. My husband insists on making the journey unaccompanied, but I spoke to Papa in private and he has agreed to insist that Mainard drive Isidore in the Rockaway carriage. Since the incident of the missing night, we are all in silent agreement that Isidore must be Watched. It's easiest to deem him simply forgetful and treat him as one for whom time, perhaps, keeps a different pace. Aside from these trivial incidences of moodiness, I consider myself quite blessed to at last have a family to claim as my own. Once we free ourselves from the stranglehold of this place, I feel that Isidore will recover the inquisitive nature and optimistic spirit he first brought to me.

Maman Emilie

⁂

December 11, 1852

Dear Geneviève,

What a delight to receive your gifts! Théodore already widens his eyes and smiles at the charming music of the silver rattle you sent him. I wish I could do more for your babes, but you are so ardent in stressing that they need for nothing, I cannot go against your wishes and send the penny sweets and trinkets you refuse. It's my hope that I will someday be able to return the generosity you shower upon me.

Our darling boy was baptized at St. Augustine's on All Saints' Day. While I adore the Gospel choir and the beauty of our Catholic rituals, a part of me stood distant on that day, observing the spectacle as if I were a visitor from a strange land. Can our insignificant routines of prayer and holy water truly consecrate and save an already innocent soul? Will a priestly blessing serve to guard him against demoniacal forces when my skin prickles with the nightmarish sense that we are no longer safe?

I have refused to entertain this notion, but I cannot divest myself of it. I confess—since that séance at Mme. Laveau's, I have been haunted by a lingering premonition of calamity and tremble with foreboding. Strange rattlings disturb the night, as if a body walks the floors and searches our cupboards and drawers. The sepulchral atmosphere grows heavy with moisture and a sour breeze pushes in from the river, whipping through the cane like a lamentation. Clothilde will not cease her alarming talk of some vengeful *loa* she calls Erzulie Ge-Rouge, for she claims to see her "ride" various female slaves and send them thrashing and flailing across the fields. I cannot shake the distinct sense that a malevolent spirit prowls these grounds hungering for something I cannot identify. (Maybe it's only the fice dog we've spied wandering the roads outside Belle Rive, a large, filthy stray with a nervous manner.) It would be easy to dismiss Clothilde's gossip but for the fact that Isidore *does* look different. His altered appearance matches his disconsolate mood. Sometimes I glimpse a simmering agitation behind his eyes, as if some sinister spirit temporarily possesses him, but then his countenance reconfigures itself into a comely man of gentle temper and I am left flustered, questioning my own sanity.

Your Emilie

❧❀❧

February 5, 1853

Darling companion,

What a welcome relief to receive a letter from you after your weeks of absence. (I shall save these beautiful foreign stamps in my scrapbook!) I relish your reports of life abroad and the many wondrous sights you've seen, the glories of the Hagia Sophia and the bazaars of Constantinople. Your eloquent descriptions fill my head with rich, heady images so that I too can smell the cinnamon and peppercorns at the spice trader's table and envision the beautiful women with their exotic jewelry and clothing.

Don't you miss your precious little ones? I don't know that I could bear to be away from my sweet Théodore for more than a night without suffering terribly for worry and want of him. Maybe it changes when you have a fine healthy foursome, and know that brothers and sisters will look after one another and keep each other in good care. Still, you are very bold to travel so with Mr. Stockton, but then how could you deny yourself this grand opportunity to see the whole wide world?

I long to get away, to pack myself, Poupette, and poor Isidore into a coach, hitch up Shaggy Maggie and ride her until she drops. No, I wouldn't be so cruel. But when I see the packet ships and steamers gliding up the river, I long to wade out and climb aboard. To hoist my dripping skirts, shimmy up their rope ladders, and sail away to some other place where there are no *loa* or spirits to haunt the grounds around my house and bedevil my loved one to insanity.

Isidore accuses me of sending Mainard to spy upon him when he goes to town. Mind you, I have given no such instruction, but now wonder if I ought to! His tone grows vicious whenever he thinks upon my supposed betrayals and says I do not trust him a whit, sending my minder to tail him like a child. I defend myself as best I can, but how this change sickens me! The sweetness of having my own small family sours and melts away and I cannot hold onto it or reassemble it.

Isidore's nights are tormented by strange, intense dreams, and when he wakes, feverish and violently agitated, he tells me again and again of visiting a hideous house beset by ghostly shadows and slinking vermin where he runs endlessly through its dim, shifting corridors, pursued by a spirit intent on draining away his masculine vitality.

Admittedly, the content of these fancies shocked me upon first hearing, but I have grown used to them. Isidore speaks of nonsensical things, too, that he feels watched when no one is near, that he is privy to the private thoughts of those around him and knows they are convinced he is deranged. I no longer take comfort in my Spiritualist readings or my Bible. What is left to me? Forgive me the dreariness of this missive, but I long for a true friend to support me in this troubled time. If only I could hear your voice, speak with you as easily as I once could by skipping up the road to your house. You suggest I confide in Loucille La Foret, but she is nineteen now and engaged to marry a military man. She is consumed with preparations for her wedding and married life, just as I was such a short time ago, and I have no wish to burden her with my woes.

Yours across the miles,
Emilie

March 9, 1853

Treasured friend,
A dreadful tragedy has taken my brother's life. Some weeks ago, he was bitten by that malignant cur we'd seen. I told Ramón to chase it away for fear of it coming into the yard and savaging the children, but Prosper (in his cups, as usual) took the lead against it, grabbing a shotgun

and dashing off on his own when he next spied it. We heard a few shots and he came back an hour later, red-faced and furious, shouting that the damned mongrel had bitten him. Clothilde would have cauterized the wound but he was so enraged, he verily attacked her. I was glad for the bite (it shames me greatly to admit that now) and I told Isidore that it served Prosper right for trying to play the hero when he's but the fool.

Prosper died in a gruesome fury from that bite, so frantic that Maman and I were barred from seeing him in such a tortured state. His passing casts a deeper shadow upon us at a time when all of us are already burdened by the weight of sorrow. Aghast, I don my mourning black and usher Death in the door.

Yours in distress,
Emilie

❧❧❧

April 19, 1853

Dearest Geneviève,

Our own Poupette has surprised us by delivering a little boy. Maman promptly snatched the babe from the girl's arms and proclaimed him "Petit Prosper." Maman insists on hovering over the girl in every aspect of the infant's care, but Poupette takes it in good-natured stride (not that she has a choice to do otherwise). I intervene where I can to allow Poupette time to nurse her child and lavish him with her abundant love. It is my intention to bring the both of them with us when we move North, whenever that may be. My ambitions are delayed, not stymied, and I continue to hold fast to my hope that Isidore and I should one day soon escape Belle Rive. The malignancies that have lain dormant now stir, like poisonous serpents waking from hibernation to creep through our dreams, feeding on the last shreds of our happiness.

I mentioned Isidore's consumption with his orchidarium and his deep devotion to its construction. It seemed to be the single source of joy in his life, outside of our sweet Théodore. Yet some unwholesome obsession has infected him. To my horror, Isidore suffered a violent fit terminating in a vengeful explosion of rage upon the precious glass house, which he had labored so long and hard to build. Frantic, he smashed the expensive panes and bent the frames until nothing remained but a glittering pile of rubble, which he then tried to set alight. Profoundly agitated, he came into the house, dripping blood and excoriating us with his fierce gaze. Geneviève, I did not recognize him! He was a stranger and stranger still he grows, muttering to himself and casting suspicious looks at myself and Maman and Papa. Yet, still we share a bed and raise our child. He works with Papa and reads his books or takes his journal along on his walks and sketches the flowers. I care for him deeply, and sometimes still feel that he cares for me with identical intensity.

One night last week, Clothilde, who never seems to sleep, came from her room in her wrapper to warn me that Isidore was roaming around in the front yard and I'd better come and get him before Maman or Papa found him for he was fully nude, not even a pair of shoes to protect his feet! We brought him back inside, shivering and mud-streaked, wiped the grime from his skin and bade him lie down. He did not speak throughout the whole ordeal, nor did he blink his eyes until I closed them for him.

Clothilde frightens me with her ominous talk of witchcraft and spirits. She insists that Isidore is a cursed victim of evil medicine, a power so much greater than hers that she can little counter it. She cautioned me not to wake him or his soul would be left out wandering. It was deeply distressing to find him thus, and Clothilde insists, "Your man possessed by the witch's prowling spirit. Soul climb out the body when it sleep. When his left, someone else come. You got to find that witch and sprinkle red pepper on her skin while she sleep. That will keep her tied to her own wicked body where it belong."

"How do you know this?" I asked, to which she replied, "There's more than one conjurer at work in this house. I seen Ge-Rouge, too. Crying her bloody tears and hunting for the man who done her wrong. She eat his heart if her teeth could cut!"

A terrible thrill ran through me, as if I had fallen into a swift, icy current. How I moaned and sobbed at the persistency of that awful unwanted visitor from the Spirit realm. All the Spiritualist readings assert that the dead reside in a place of comfort and pleasure, that they wish no living person ill, but *something*, be it a human spirit, *loa* goddess, or manifestation of an unknown evil, plagues this house and I cannot divest my family of its presence. You think me foolish, no doubt, to fall prey to such lurid imaginings, but what else could it be? What else would slither beneath the fabric of our lives to disrupt and disconcert us so?

Clothilde puts all her trust in vodou gods, and I'm very nearly convinced to follow her faith. I don't believe in witchcraft, but I grow desperate for any solution, any explanation that will lend me some peace, so once again, I consented to allow Clothilde to work her magic on him. She procured a hen with frizzy feathers to scratch up the yard and find any vodou charms planted there, but none were discovered, thus amusing Papa and infuriating Maman, who laments the destruction of her garden.

Now, to end on a more pleasant note, I'll tell you that I very much enjoyed your description of riding in an elevator! I can hardly imagine the marvels you've witnessed in your travels. Imagine being transported vertically through space in such a short period of time. It sounds absolutely marvelous! Mr. Stockton is so kind to you, Geneviève! How many women have been lucky enough to be gifted a new Steinway piano on their anniversary? Very few, I'm sure. You're in exalted company. When I get to New York, I will lay myself down beneath that instrument, and your beautiful music will shower upon me like a warm spring rain to soothe all my troubles.

Admiringly yours,
Emilie

May 3, 1853

Dear Geneviève,

My brother's death and Isidore's macabre obsessions have tipped us into calamitous seas and here we flail, seeking purchase for our thrashing feet. Belle Rive's stately beauty now appears to me as very garish and overwrought, and our lives here both cruel and trivial. I am desperate to abandon this place and join you in New York, but my family will not hear of it. Papa insists that I am never to leave Belle Rive as now that Prosper is gone, I am the only inheritor of his legacy. It's as if the calm, clear pond in which I swam stagnated into a rank and foetid bog. My ankles tangle in its eelgrass and pondweed snares my hands so that I cannot free myself, no matter how intently I struggle.

Isidore's strange dreams plague him night after night, and often, I hear him cry out, as if in ecstasy or horror. He will rise from our bed in a trance and stand by the window gazing into the night, or claim a privy visit and vanish for what feels like hours. To do what? Last night, the suspense was too great to bear and my husband so agitated when his wandering began that I feared for his safety so I followed him, my slippered feet silent behind him as he moved through the house in a strange, stilted manner, whispering words I could not understand. He unlocked the kitchen door and passed over the moonlit yard, down the path to the waterside, arms outstretched as if grasping at unseen reins. The night was thick with a damp that dragged at my gown and soaked my slippers, and yet I pursued him through the clangorous reeds where ghostly blue flickers of will-o'-the-wisps danced amidst the bogs. He reached the riverbank and disappeared into the black interior of a ramshackle fishing hut, from whence emanated such tortured cries that I must cover my ears, for I would have wept to hear his pain.

Why did I not disturb him, you wonder? Why should I cower in terror from the sounds of my darling husband in distress? I tried, dearest friend, I tried to assuage his pain and enter that coven of shadows to rescue him from his nightmare, but upon marshalling my resolve to brave the beastly darkness of that Stygian hut, a strange influence overtook me and fastened my feet to the ground. I could not move forward, only back, as if repelled by some supernatural force. Isidore's cries increased in strength, but I could venture no closer. I peered into the blackness and called his name, and Geneviève, had my mind not been open to the awareness of our Spiritual brethren, I would have dismissed what nearly dismantled my resolve. Isidore stumbled to the door of the hut, entirely unaware of me as I stood before him. His horrific eyes were staring and empty as if drained of all life when he lurched out, hair mussed and clothes asunder. I stretched forth my hand to rouse him from that dreadful state and glimpsed, almost as if at the edge of my consciousness, the ephemeral glimmer of some wicked phantasm, so faint as to be imagined. Yet I did not imagine what I saw! I recognized the face of that feminine spirit who had stood upon the table at the séance, the one who dissolved into a buzzing cloud and flew into my husband's throat. She turned her wretched visage to me and for one brief moment, our souls touched—hers frigid and mine life-warmed and passionate—and I immediately experienced that distinct sense of icy pain one has when plunging cold skin into very hot water.

Then, dear friend, the vision, faint as it was, was no more. I rushed to Isidore and guided him back to our bed, where he collapsed into a deep sleep to awaken at sunrise, pale and drawn but completely unaware of his fugue. He remembers nothing and I struggle with my own memory, doubting if what I saw was real or just some figment of an overworked brain. I have little time to dwell on it. Fussy Théodore has the grippe again and Maman spends much of her day abed, weeping over her foolish, dead son, so I am left to manage Cook and the house on my own before I fall into bed, myself exhausted. I cannot imagine how you cope with your brood, when one child taxes me so greatly.

Très fatiguée,
Emilie

❦

May 21, 1853

Chère Geneviève,

If this is vodou magic at work, so be it. Clothilde spells to protect Isidore from the evil spirits that assail him, and while I do not invest my faith in her remedies, she is the only one attempting to cure his strange malady. During the days, if it is warm and bright, Isidore appears as a semblance of his old self, working alongside Papa (albeit still begrudgingly), bouncing Théodore on his knee, singing French ditties to him. It is almost as if we have returned to the early days of our marriage, and it fills me with fleeting hope. But when dusk settles over Belle Rive and the sunlight dims, so too does my husband's bright light.

Despite my insistence that he is unwell, Isidore is in staunch denial about his illness, though wracked by a lingering melancholia and no appetite for the savories of which he is usually so fond. He takes little but broth or bread, and his formerly virile body appears fragile and thin. Isidore's caprices keep him in his study until very late at night. Sometimes he comes to bed and climbs in beside me and kisses me with tender lips, but more often, he is already exhausted when he finally lies down. He traipses about the house without a candle and startles me from sleep when he materializes, spirit-like, from the midnight gloom. His dreams are desperate. I hear him murmuring and gasping in his sleep. Geneviève, only because we are bosom friends of such long acquaintance do I dare tell you that my husband dreams so intently that he cries out in his sleep, as if reaching the apex of passion.

I've been consumed with a morbid fear that he will soon die or somehow be taken from me, and I convince myself that another child will increase his zest for living. Our son entices his papa back from the realm of his ghoulish fancies, silences Isidore's grumbling, and brings smiles to his face. Wouldn't another bonny babe double his joy?

I confess, I have taken advantage of his arousal, for I have hungered for a touch not forthcoming and I long for the easy, amorous nights of our Honey Moon. I guide his limp hands to my breasts, turn his mouth toward mine and press my thighs around his. I mount and ride him in the night as he sleeps, unaware and uninhibited. My loose hair hangs down and tickles his chest as I sweep it over his burning skin. He cries out, "Oh beloved! Intoxicant flower!" and writhes as do Lavinia and Mainard when the *loa* possess them during their secret ceremonies in the fields. Of what does he dream, or who? For he never cries out any name, and if he opens his eyes, he does not see me.

Yours in secret sin,
Emilie

May 30, 1853

Darling Geneviève,
Your charming and delightful recounting of your travels were such a pleasure to read and greatly elevated my low spirits. It is better that you are far from Louisiana in any regard. There have been a growing number of reports of a bilious fever in the City and much anxious discussion in the newspapers as to whether it is cholera or something worse. Presently, the illness seems confined to the impoverished, immigrants, and sailors, and so the wealthy panic and urge the mayor to quarantine those unfortunate souls to prevent the contagion of the upper classes.

Rest assured, we feel ourselves quite safe here at Belle Rive. Last week, I overheard Papa, Isidore, and Ramón speaking about the need to keep everyone from town until the plague has ended. They agreed that our stores and supplies are sufficient to carry us through the next two to three months, so long as there are no emergencies requiring outside aid, such as journeying to town to replace a broken wagon wheel. Maman is quite annoyed that she cannot have the trifles she wants, being barred from any shopping trips for the foreseeable future, and I feel the constraining garrote of my duties here encircle me more tightly.

Isidore's fascinations and distracted qualities worsen toward evening when he grows costive and sullen, anticipating another unpleasant night without rest, and those wrathful torments of the figure he sees pursuing him through his dreams. At last, I consented to allow M. Fournier to attend Isidore. The doctor came yesterday and stayed for dinner and (several) glasses of Papa's fine port afterward, all for the purpose of observing my husband, who evidenced few of his manias. I admit to having warned him of the doctor's assessment, cautioning him to be well-behaved, for I do not want to allot my family the satisfaction of labeling my husband demented or defective in any other manner. To you, I speak of him as a source of confusion, for indeed, he is ofttimes an enigma to me, yet I hold him in highest esteem for he strives to be kind and considerate, to express his adoration to me and embrace me tenderly. When I am nestled in his arms, I feel myself to be a small bird in a nest, warm and safe despite the blowing winds and threatening storms that shake our branches. How should I evaluate my husband, then? Do I place faith in the dying embers of his passion for me, or do I succumb to the quarrelsome doubts that assail me when I watch him dismantle his food, picking a single cut of fish into a hundred tiny flakes and know that he is searching for the iron shavings he confides are hidden there? Do I call attention to the unusual vibration of his eyes, the distressing sense that when he looks, he does not see? Or the skittishness exhibited at the movement of small shadows, how he jumps as does our Shaggy Maggie, when a rat scampers through the stable? The nervous picking of his fine, long fingers against any minuscule wound or irritation of the skin, how a faint scratch that might normally heal in a day or two, lingers and festers because he cannot let it alone?

Complaining of indigestion, Maman took herself off to bed early with a bottle of Browne's Mixture, and Isidore removed himself to his study, so I settled myself outside the parlor door to overhear M. Fournier tell Papa that he believes Isidore suffers paranoid delusions and phobias, for which he prescribed paregoric to remedy Isidore's malingering.

Later that evening, Papa and M. Fournier entered our chamber to advise me of their decision and tell me the dosage (two teaspoons at mealtimes) to aid digestion and another at bedtime to aid sleep. The first night he refused it, but he slept very poorly, if at all, and thrice woke me with his outcries and flailing limbs. Today, I succumbed to the promise offered by that little green flask of liquid and persuaded Isidore to take it. I pray that he shall recover his good health again soon.

Keeping a weather-eye open,
Emilie

◈

June 13, 1853

Dearest friend,

I am much gladdened to hear that you and the children are keeping fit during this season of pestilence. The plague worsens day by day, and grievous news arrives with every post. The mail carrier will not even venture onto any property, but drops our letters in a bundle beside the fencepost delineating our land. Word of my friend Loucille La Foret's passing was delayed by several days, as we could not decipher why we'd received no letters until Mainard spotted a great pile of our newspapers and correspondence when he went to haul some fallen branches.

You recall that Loucille La Foret married a military man and the past year, she has kept a townhome in the French Quarter while her husband is away. She succumbed very quickly to the black vomit. Terribly sad, indeed! The only comfort to her poor family is that she took sick and died three days later (she has always had a weak constitution and suffered coughs and digestive upsets), so she did not linger, suffering a grotesque and drawn-out decline like some do, inching toward wellness then collapsing again into wretchedness.

We are kept occupied with the disinfecting of Belle Rive, and wash every surface and useful item with a solution of chloride antiseptic. We labor through these stultifying days, with our babies rashy and crying from the smothering heat, with Isidore sluggish and vaguely dopey from the paregoric's effects, our ears filled with Papa's ceaseless grousing about "God damned Democrats," "medical board hucksters," and those "blathering bamboozlers on the City Council."

Papa's complaints aggravate Isidore's nervous condition and so he removes himself from our company for great lengths of time, most recently from before sun-up past moonrise, so that we did not see hide nor hair of him for an entire day. We have barricaded ourselves at Belle Rive like those quarantined immigrants you described from your charitable visits to Ellis Island on behalf of the Association of Vigilant Women.

We cling fast to the notion that this scourge shall pass us by if we remain cloistered on our plantation, while the Angel of Death toils so busily in the City.

Do send something gay and bright to cheer me and lift the oppression of illness that hovers so threateningly nearby!

Yours in good health,
Emilie

～⚜～

July 4, 1853

Dearest Geneviève,

How I wish we had flown north to your side all those months ago! Yellow fever rampages across New Orleans and hundreds are stricken, from the lowest dockyard tavern to our own Great House. Lavinia and Cook have taken ill, along with several field hands. Contagion spreads and every one of us walks as if asleep, suspended in a God-awful limbo of fear. We labor through the long, stifling days of intense heat and unrelenting sun. Maman and Papa are very somber with the loss of so many of their society friends to yellow fever. The slaves endure heat exhaustion to the point of dropping in the fields, but I cannot convince Papa to suspend their labor. He is terribly surly and anxious about our fortunes, and this makes for an exceedingly depressed atmosphere at Belle Rive. Théodore appears unusually thin—he will not take milk and complains whether he is held in my arms or laid in his crib.

I read in the *Daily Picayune* the fever is spreading beyond Louisiana's borders, carried by travelers on the steamships and railroads. Does Yellow Jack's insidious influence reach as far North as New York? Will you take the children and abandon your home if it arrives?

It is all we can do at present to manage the daily maintenance of our fields and people, to run the kitchen in Cook's absence (Clothilde is managing nicely, so blessed we are to have her!), and to keep the house in some semblance of order. Of course, today should be a day of festivity and fireworks displays, such as those magnificent ones we witnessed two years ago at Mr. Badcocke's, but the atmosphere here is one of torpor and quiet labor. Even the slaves in the fields do not sing, nor do the birds, and the river languishes without a current, casting brown froth against its shores. One and all weary of the growing list of deceased the *Daily Picayune* publishes every week, and we have initiated a macabre routine of reading it on Sundays, searching the list for names we know so that we may add them to our prayers.

I feel myself growing quite dull and uninspired. I have no time to read, and I enjoy no companionship but yours. Metaphysical quandaries of the Spirit world, the origins of faith, and our Savior's loving embrace little quench my thirst for comfort in these dreadful hours, when so many languish in the Reaper's cold shadow.

Your Emilie

⚜

August 18, 1853

Cherished confidante,

My precious Théodore sickened with the fever that claimed so many and expired in my arms on July 11. He is buried under the oak tree beside Fern, where I can see the grave from the veranda and my bedroom window. Papa has commissioned a granite headstone from Tennessee topped by a carving of two angels as a gift to me, but likely it will not arrive for months.

Nothing is as it was. A dreadful pall has sunk itself over Belle Rive, insinuated itself into every happy moment and stolen its luster, leaving behind nothing but dull suspicion and ruin. If I were unable to write to you I think I should go mad! Your letters are my only consolation through this harrowing time.

Each day presents itself as an agonizing test of endurance through which to labor. Each one of us struggles with sorrow over the loss of our darling boy and other members of the household. Somehow, I manage to cope with the arduous expectations that the days bring, if only because I am entirely numb to any sensation but obligation and duty. Just when I believe that I have exhausted my supply of tears and cannot possibly cry any more, they spring up fresh and hot at the slightest provocation. Sometimes I wish I had never married, never borne a child, for the intensity of my heartbreak erases whatever joy I took in those events. There are moments, too, when I become irrational and consumed with an anger whose heat cannot be doused.

I have rediscovered my old cello in the attic, where I can play without disturbance. I had not touched my instrument since you left us, but its music leapt to fiery life with a single stroke of the bow. Only the vibration of the strings beneath my fingers and the elegant notes of the Stabat Mater or sonatas by Brahms and Boccherini alleviate my agonies. There is nothing in the attic to remind me of any life but my own. Every other room in Belle Rive is a container of memories, accosting me with images and souvenirs of my life as a happy wife and mother when I have no wish to be reminded of what I have lost.

Théodore's death has loosed Isidore's mind from its flimsy moorings. My husband suffers from some expression of Dementia whose sinister hold on him daily increases. His actions turn erratic. By turns strangely jolly or morose, he begins to lose his footing in the daily world. He misplaces things, cannot recall what has been said to him but an hour prior, and speaks of mystical energies that harass and bedevil him throughout both waking and sleeping hours. When I asked him to describe these energies to me, he pronounced them the "disenchanted spirit of an in-dwelling orisha manifested through light beams" and "she who haunts me, drinker of tears and swallower of seed," or "Queen cock-a-hen." Never has he spoken this way, and worse, will not be dissuaded from his conviction that he speaks truth and all others are blind, unknowing fools.

Papa, Maman, and myself had a very somber conversation about what is to be done. Mainard has complained to Papa that he fears Isidore will strike him or otherwise lash out during one of his fits and cause him injury. Maman, as you would expect, speaks only of the aggravations his delicate stomach cause the kitchen girls, as nothing seems to suit his palate and he returns every dish to the kitchen, insisting that it is over-salted or tastes of bicarbonate. After the last outburst, both girls and myself tasted the porridge and did not find it spoiled. He insisted on straining the yolk of a poached breakfast egg because it had a meat spot that would have corrupted his bowels. If his food is found wanting, he becomes quite agitated and accuses Clothilde of bothering him even if she is nowhere near.

Most reluctantly, I concurred with my parents that Isidore requires additional treatment. He sleeps poorly and neither paregoric, chloral hydrate, nor our home remedies have brought relief to him or us. M. Fournier has promised to come tomorrow evening to bleed him if Mrs. Browder delivers her child in the morning.

But all is not lost! This afternoon, I pressed Isidore to take a glass of fortified sherry and some biscuits. (Forgive my deceit, won't you? For

I told him I had baked the biscuits myself and churned the butter, too, so that he would accept it.) He grew drowsy as I sat beside him reading Trollope's *La Vendée* and his eyes fluttered with the welcome approach of sleep. I made to creep from the room, but he stirred and reached for me. Clasping my hand in his own cool one, he gazed at me steadily, with a tender warmth I had all but forgotten, and said, "How greatly I care for you, darling Emilie! Even in the throes of this mania, I do adore your bright spirit."

These are the wonderful moments of full lucidity that assure me we shall recover Isidore from the clouds that obscure his normally clear mind. I shall do everything within my power to see that it is done.

Yours in hope,
Emilie

November 17, 1853

Chère Geneviève,

Trust that your words are a great comfort to me and your compassion for my situation deeply valued. You cannot imagine the burdens that I labor under. With Prosper gone and Maman and Papa absorbed in their own woes, I shoulder much of the work to keep us all afloat on the stormy seas of our misfortune. I am utterly alone in my care of Isidore, and my growing suspicions that his sanity and health shall not return. He is profoundly unwell, I see that now, and it is more than a father's grief at the death of a child or a man's disappointment in the loss of his avocation. Our nights are fractured by his nightmares, screams, and thrashings. Sometimes I wake to discover him moving about the darkened bedchamber in perfect silence, his open eyes shining among the shadows like two wet, black stones just plucked up from the riverbank. Last night, I woke to an empty bed and room. He does not answer when called, for in this wandering state he is as firmly asleep as if he were lying in bed and will not respond to my voice. (Or perhaps because another speaks to him, a voice that fills his head and summons him from our bed to prowl the house and fields on these strange errands!) Searching the house, I found no sign of him. Restless tree limbs flung themselves against the house, a sound of battering hands thumping upon the clapboards, and a wild disturbance of lashing winds soughed through the cane.

For one fleeting moment, I considered staying abed. What duty have I to track my wandering mate and restore him to his rightful place, to make life quiet and easy for Maman, who cares for nothing but her own comfort and pleasure, to assure my cantankerous father that his fortunes are secure and he need not compromise his station among the other gentlemen and landholders?

I cannot allow Isidore to suffer alone, languishing among these unfamiliar torments when I care for him and see how far from the path he has strayed. At last, I took a candle and passed through the house, but not locating him, went to the fields and down to the river and that rotting shack where I'd found him before. It was nothing more than an uninhabited pocket of gloom festering in the moonlight. He was not to be found and so I returned to my room, whereupon I heard sounds akin to the whimpering of a small animal, and opening the wardrobe, discovered my husband cowering there, naked and bleeding from an old wound he'd opened. I bandaged him and returned him to bed. My warm arms and bare skin did not comfort him, nor settle his trembling, for what felt like hours.

M. Fournier comes every other day to bleed Isidore, but today's incident was completely appalling. Isidore would not allow Fournier to touch him. He fought and complained, wrested the lancet from the doctor's hand and gouged his own arm, saying that the doctor cut in the wrong places and very lucidly explaining to me, "He makes holes for bad things to come in rather than making holes for the bad things to get out," all the while gashing his flesh and watching his life force spill onto the carpet with a ghastly grin on his face.

Fournier very quickly produced a metal syringe (I had never seen one before and found its appearance quite unnerving) and gave Isidore an injection of morphine to calm him while we bandaged his wound, advising me that "the mania has reached its pitch and now we must prepare ourselves to meet whatever demons lurk within his tormented, fevered mind."

The grim atmosphere and lingering specter of disease promise a very dour Thanksgiving celebration and holiday season for all of us. I am very nearly tempted to write a letter to Father Christmas and request that he bring me my husband as he was when he first landed on our shores.

Your adoring Emilie

Cherished friend,

You are my sole comfort and refuge in this time of great distress, for although I judge myself terribly and agonize over my every thought and deed, I know you would not penalize me for the exceedingly difficult choices I've had to make.

Isidore is undone by grief over the death of our son. The spirit inside him has broken beyond repair. No cure or treatment, no medicine or number of embraces can remake the shattered eggshell of his mind. His morbid delusions are a great source of anxiety to him, and no amount of reason, prayer, compassion, or medical treatment restores his sanity. Papa threatens to commit him to the State Asylum in Jackson as we can no longer safely manage him, and Maman is frightened by his nighttime ravings. He is still plagued by those gruesome dreams of a succubus preying on him during sleep and stealing his vital masculine fluids (how I used to blush when thinking of such things, but necessity and compassion have inoculated me against such girlish embarrassments) and he causes many a perverse commotion. It is heartbreaking to witness his agonies, but even I am not beyond his reproach. Now he accuses me of conspiring with Clothilde to poison him, so he refuses all foods but the bottles of claret he hides in his study—for they were sealed when taken from the cellar and thus cannot have been tampered with. Papa has raged about cutting him off, but as wine is Isidore's sole source of nourishment, I forbade it against the threat of never speaking to him again.

Only when the morphine takes effect is there peace in this house. I am committed (and I use that word fully aware of its irony here) to healing Isidore, and if not restoring him to jovial good health, then to alleviating his suffering. I am much encouraged by the reform efforts of Miss Dorothea Dix, who has petitioned state legislatures for humanitarian care of the insane, and Dr. R. John Galt, of Virginia, who advocates a radical therapy consisting of simple conversation between doctor and patient. That quack M. Fournier would bleed Isidore within an inch of his life despite obvious indications that bloodletting is more harmful than helpful. Isidore is pale as a peeled banana these days, a wretched mess of bloody scabs, oozing sores and scars, and worse off, I believe, for Fournier's medicaments.

You ask how I am. Read the above and parse for yourself my state of mind. I am Tired, dear friend, so Tired of Belle Rive's brutalities and false notions. My own life unravels in my fingers and I cannot repair it. My Savior sits silent on his high cloud of judgment and extends no hand to help me. I beg the spirits of my departed children to come back in new bodies, to visit me in a dream or otherwise communicate with me as the Spiritualists assure me is possible, but they, too, are silent. Clothilde's vodou spells offer false refuge, for no matter what we do, Isidore worsens. I begin to hear a very quiet voice within speaking almost in a whisper, that voice of Intuition, of Wisdom. I suspect my husband suffers a physical ailment that no prayer or magic can treat or cure. Haven't we tried everything? We prayed for Théodore and Prosper, Cook and Lavinia, and they died anyway. I am convinced that the spirits cannot affect lives *in* this world because they are no longer *of* this world.

Therefore, I am convinced that his is an illness of the mind— which as an agent of the body is susceptible to those same diseases which weaken its organs—like the pox, tuberculosis, or cancer. Should we not treat it thusly, as we would any sickness? I propose a course of purgatives and emetics similar to the Brattleboro cure to rid Isidore's body of Fournier's poisonous narcotics and remedy the cachexia that has left him so frail and weak.

More and more often, I feel myself to be a stranger in my own home. My parents appear to me as useless reliquaries of superstition. I am a solitary traveler on the road toward Truth and Reason, thus I am irresistibly drawn toward a second and far greater life. Lacking husband and children, I am a free agent once again, as I was before I married. Is it my obligation to marry again, bear more children and possibly endure the loss of them, too? How many times can a heart be broken before it is beyond repair, its shards irredeemably damaged and too brittle to withstand mending? I have no faith in this life, or the spirits and saints we believe guide us, for have they not failed to answer my prayers to grant me any measure of peace? I go happily into old maidhood! At least I shall not suffer further love's battering storms or know my heart absconded with. Work and education will be the remedy that restores me. Perchance some good shall come from our sorrows after all.

I write to several sanitariums in the hope that they will find a place for my husband. I believe wholeheartedly that his sense would return to him if he were removed from these toxick environs and allowed to sleep undisturbed by nightmares. If you have any solutions to our troubles, your kind assistance would be most valuable.

Yours in hope,
Emilie

◆◆◆

January 12, 1854

Beloved confidante,

M. Fournier is a complete and utter imbecile who has abused Isidore with his ridiculous notions. The man is the very epitome of quackery, for he is completely dismissive of my pleadings to cease this infernal routine of bleeding and dosing which leaves Isidore pallid and catatonic, or else gibbering and wild. At the very least, Fournier subscribes to an outdated school of thought where treatment of the mind is concerned. Rather than believe that Isidore's mania has origins in some undetected disease of the physical body, he insists those delusions spring from a spiritual weakness that leaves him susceptible to the damaging influence of his dreams and hallucinations. I say Fournier's treatment only exacerbates Isidore's delusions, for he grows progressively worse and we see no improvement in body or mind despite Fournier's insistence that we increase his chloral and bleed him even more aggressively. Twice this week alone, I have taken Isidore's medicine tray and emptied the contents of all those bottles into the chamber pot, but a new bottle of paregoric or chloral hydrate soon materializes in its place, as if by magic.

The Furies are in me, Geneviève! Papa and I practically came to blows over Fournier after I blocked his entrance into Isidore's study. One can smell blood from the passage, so great is the stench of corrupt bandages and festering wounds—for Isidore worries his injuries with anxious fingers, complaining that the exposure of "nerve wires" under the skin will lure some specter who comes in at night to spool them out if he doesn't hide them from her. With Poupette's help (Clothilde is barred from the third story due to Isidore's absurd terror of her), we bathe and spoon-feed him, and I brush his hair (very slowly, for he claims to hear the rustling of each individual strand as loudly as a cane field thrashed by a hurricane, but so can he hear worms tunneling the soil of the graves beneath the oak tree and voices of the *loa* berating and ridiculing him from under the floorboards and echoing out from walls and ceiling).

69

Fournier forcibly removed Isidore's books and other volumes from his study to grant his over-taxed brain a period of quiet restoration away from such arousing influences, but what else is he to do with himself? Make lace with Poupette and me? In place of reading, we encourage him to exercise by strolling around the grounds with myself or Albert's replacement, Coffee. (Mainard is too nervous to be alone with Isidore. The last time Mainard took Isidore for a walk, they passed the shattered remains of the orchidarium and Isidore collapsed in a fit of what Fournier deemed "religious excitement.") But while the walks provide temporary relief, Isidore always succumbs to his fixations.

At last, my many letters brought my hopes to fruition. I have secured placement for Isidore at Castile Sanitarium in Wyoming County, New York. Dr. Greene (a former Quaker and proponent of the new style of mental illness care), will give Isidore the water cure for two full months. He will not be bled, I made certain of that, and Dr. Greene promises to wean Isidore off the paregoric and chloral, which he believes contribute greatly to Isidore's mania, insomnia, and delusions. They depart tomorrow, loathe as I am to further delay Isidore's treatment. Mainard will travel with Isidore as his valet, and with Isidore being so lethargic and compliant, I doubt Mainard will suffer any of the old fits and furies that made caring for my husband so difficult. I yearn to travel with them, but Belle Rive is in a catastrophic state after last summer's fever outbreak. We lost twelve slaves and did not get a large enough portion of the fields tended according to schedule, and so our yield this year is much less. The ground is unusually dry. We have lacked adequate rain and Papa fears ruin. His solution is to work the remaining slaves twice as hard, but as Prosper is gone and Maman is detached from all participation in the accounting or planning, the decisions are often left to me, and I insisted that we will no longer invest in the sale, purchase, or barter of human lives. I miss Isidore's advice in these matters. However reluctantly he participated, he did so successfully.

Théodore's grave has sprung up with unseasonal buttercups, and I revere this cheerful reminder of his cherished, genial soul. There is still one glimmer of love left on this godforsaken plantation.

Yours for always,
Emilie

Dearest one,

I am very sorry to hear that you are unwell, but take comfort in your assurances that your cough is just a seasonal catarrh. I do recall how violently you used to sneeze when all the spring flowers were in bloom. Clothilde has always treated bronchial catarrh with this simple remedy: chop one large white or yellow onion and place the pieces in a clean jar. Pour raw honey over the onion, until completely covered. Seal the jar and let sit overnight on a warm cookstove. Then you may take the honey by spoonfuls to ease your cough.

It has been eight months since Yellow Jack stole away my poor, lovely boy. The pain of his death is no less; I have merely grown used to the presence of enduring grief within me.

Papa has come down with shingles, and this illness combined with rheumatism makes it much too painful for him to walk the grounds, mount a horse, or ride comfortably in a jostling carriage. He can hardly even hold a quill, his fingers have grown so decrepit and gnarled. Ramón is my helpmeet most days, good-natured and devoted but not excessively bright or forward-thinking, more often he simply proposes keeping a steady course and following Papa's planting ledgers from prior years.

I am so pleased to hear that both your boys recovered from their bout with scarlatina. You must have been terribly anxious about them, but do not entertain Mr. Stockton's notion that their illness is in any way connected to your protests against Temperance. Since he is a teetotaler, I'd presume him to be very much in league with your organization's goals, or has he finally broken his Christian vow of sobriety to enjoy a glass of after-dinner sherry with you?

I am taking advantage of Isidore's absence to rid Belle Rive of every bottle of claret, brandy, sherry, and port. I packed all the bottles into a crate and sent them to Mme. C——. (She is very fond of entertaining.) This shall be a dry house when my husband returns from Castile.

Your abstemious Emilie

April 16, 1854

Dearest Geneviève,

Once upon a time we were sweet as figs and the whole of life was a sumptuous banquet spread before us from which we could pick and choose the most savory morsels, the prettiest of glistening fruits. Now I tell you that I have supped at the king's table and found myself deceived, for what appeared delicious has spoiled upon my lips and fermented in my belly.

My husband is no more. By which I mean that derangements of the head have so entirely consumed him, I no longer recognize the man who first came to Belle Rive, full of gentle hope and happy anticipation. We exist now as patient and nurse, rather than man and wife, or ward and guardian, now that Papa has grown so weak from rheumatism and Maman is gone to stay with Mme. C——. Did I ever imagine myself in such a role? Never! But I wear that hat (and pants!) at Belle Rive now, and discover myself master and mistress of a plantation.

Margaret Fuller's book *Woman in the Nineteenth Century* has been a great source of comfort and inspiration to me. I side with the advocates of moral treatment for the lunatic and morally insane, and though I shed the blinding mantle of my old faith, I do believe it's my ethical duty to protect those incapable of defending themselves against insult and violence. For just as the bondage of marriage parallels the bondage of slavery, the insane are bound by laws they cannot comprehend, laws which seek to deprive independent adults of the right to choose the manner of their own care or the quality of their living conditions. If nothing else comes of my experiences, at least I now move through the world with a fresh awareness of wrongdoing and maltreatment against those who cannot otherwise defend themselves, and a keen hunger to better serve humankind. My life has been very insignificant and my concerns fixated on trifling matters, but I have risen from the murky deeps of female despair with a steely sense of purpose. How shall I apply it? To whom shall I deliver my gifts?

I return to prayer, of a fashion. I play the cello with reverence, and that, I believe, is a form of worship. I tend to Fern and Théodore's graves, care for my parents, and do whatever I am able to ease strife or strain for those at Belle Rive, both my relatives and our charges. Reverend Logue has passed by again and led a small service on the veranda, so that Papa could listen from his usual spot on the divan in his office. When he departed, I walked with Reverend Logue as far as the crossroads, so that we could continue our conversation about faith and the living vitality of prayer. I had confessed to him that my connection to the Holy Spirit had been severed and that my Catholic faith has wavered under the duress of my sufferings. Reverend Logue assured me that the Lord does not judge my lapse. "He is ever present, watching, listening. You pray through your actions. You show your faith by your works and deeds." He quoted Philippians 4:6, "but in everything by prayer and supplication with thanksgiving let your requests be made known unto God," confirming my belief that my reverence is demonstrated through my music, and the care that I lavish upon my unhappy husband. He has no advocate but for me, and were I to slacken my vigilance, Papa would surely toss him in the "loony bin" without a second thought.

Were you here, I would play for you a tune of my own creation and ask that you accompany me on your Steinway, so that we may find that easy camaraderie of our youthful years and think upon nothing more taxing than where to place our fingers to induce the most beauty.

Yours *à deux*,
Emilie

✦❁✦

May 2, 1854

Dearest friend,
Each day when Mainard brings in the post, my heart leaps with anticipation that I may at last have a missive from you, and every day I am disappointed. Why do you not respond to my letters? I have told myself that perhaps you are traveling or ill, but even then, you have always managed to keep me current on your movements. Yet each day that passes without word, I grow more fearful that I shall never hear from you again. Do put my mind to rest! A quick word to assure me that you are well would ease my suffering mightily.

Like you, devotion and hope have newly abandoned me. I nursed them within myself as I nursed my dying child as he suckled at my breast, growing ever weaker. At that time, I set my mind against the possibility that he might be taken from me, his little warrior's body not be strong enough to withstand the onslaughts of that disease, wicked Yellow Jack, dressed in the Reaper's gray gowns, and my faith was proven false. Do you see how morbid I have become? This life has drained all joy from me and left me a husk. Does it wrench your heart to hear your jolly friend speak thusly? For it does mine to hear the words in my mind, much less put them on paper. All the prayers and pleas to the various Gods and Spirits that Belle Rive has entertained over recent months languish unanswered.

I sought comfort in my Catholic faith. Lit candles and prayed to St. Dymphna to slay Isidore's demons. I danced around the revival bonfire and sang hymns, cast my troubles into the flames, prayed with Reverend Logue, and gave offerings to Erzulie for the return of love. At my lowest, I even wrote to the vodou queen's daughter, Petite Marie, to come to Belle Rive, adorn Isidore in amulets and cast her spells of healing. (She did not reply.) The Loa, the Saints, the Holy Son and Father and all the Helper Spirits in Summerland cannot return him to his former health. All sweetness is wrung from him! He is a spent lemon, a hollowed rind. I hold fond to my heart memories of his smile, his kiss, his hands gentle upon my ripe and yearning skin, for I am convinced I shall feel those no more.

Only his time at the Castile Sanitarium seemed to impart any measure of stability to his emotional disorder, but once home, how quickly he slipped into mania! As if it were a pool of jungle quicksand sucking at his ankles, drawing him ever deeper down. It is agonizing to watch him fade away hour by hour as those dark visions and fancies return to vex and bedevil him, grinding him down as surely as the millstone crushes grains into dust. Daily I send letters to Dr. Greene begging his aid to secure a permanent place for Isidore, but my requests go unanswered. Papa threatens to summon the sheriff to lock him up if he causes another disturbance, while one and all about the place creep through halls and fields like timid mice dreading the cat's appearance.

Keeping company with the death of my hopes for my husband's recovery is the demise of my devotion, for how can I persist in believing what has so far proven to be entirely faulty? I confess I can sense my belief languishing just as a wick burns down and sputters to death in the bobeche, and I am helpless to rekindle it. It is a terrible feeling to find myself without a light in this wilderness. Whence shall I seek comfort and strength? I have relinquished all faith in Christ and the Spiritualist mediums. Who shall hold my hand as I stumble through life's brambles or catch me if I fall? The answer is No One. I am utterly alone but for you, dear friend, and you are gone from me. Oh, but I weep! Weep for the losses and my heart, arms, bed—all empty.

Yours in sorrow,
Emilie

Absent Geneviève,

Your silence perplexes me. Please do write to me, dearest! I long for news of you, and my wounded soul craves the balm of your healing words, for you alone know how my poor heart aches for my many losses. You cannot imagine the depth of our suffering here. As I have mentioned, Isidore's nights have been sundered by excessive wakefulness, and we have all lost hours of sleep for the constant tread of feet pacing the creaking floorboards above our heads, and the mournful wails and hostile mutterings of his restless wandering soul. I was afraid to give him the high doses of chloral required to quiet him, but his hallucinations grew more threatening when he was not fully alert to fend them off. I should have done it, despite my hesitations. Had I been stronger, less swayed by the compassion and empathy which are my feminine flaw, I would have seen him dosed and securely strapped down, and none of this would have transpired.

Oh, cherished friend, my poorest Isidore has done unthinkable violence to himself! He once told me about a classmate's illness and the subsequent, curative measures he witnessed at a surgeon's college in England, but I did not imagine the depths of fascination it has since held for him. The details are too horrible to repeat here. Indeed, I can scarce recall it without conjuring a sense of sickening, physical revulsion that leaves me legless and sobbing.

We were all woken by the screams of the little carpenter's boy who opened the tool shed that morning. Panic whipped through the household like a wildfire, scorching one and all who witnessed it.

I could not save him from the sheriff and his bailiff. They came three weeks ago to escort Isidore to the asylum in a padded wagon. I discovered that Papa had already initiated legal proceedings, and as soon as the crisis occurred, he sent Mainard riding to collect the order of confinement. Tears coursed down my cheeks when they restrained him and bore him away—a rain of crushing sorrow and guilty relief, for I had reached the limits of my abilities to care for him and could no longer quiet the subtle resentment and frustration brewing within me.

Because I cannot concede to his abandonment in an institution, because I refuse to accept that there is nothing more to be done for my husband but let his delusions fester within that suppurating seat of moral and spiritual infection, I shall labor on towards resolution. Despite his continued delusions and fancies, there are occasional moments wherein

I feel the strong presence of his sanity, and I remain convinced he will return to me, in full possession (how I do hesitate to use that word!) of his charming faculties.

Pain has burned away all traces of those innocent, hopeful fooleries which shaped my younger self, leaving behind a figure of staunch purpose and dedication. Isidore's illness has given my yearnings shape and weight, and clarified the murky waters of my future. To you alone I confide that I have applied for admission to Boston Female Medical College to begin training as a Physician. Like the mythical Phoenix, I rise from my ashes to take wing and launch an ascension into boundless skies. Pray for me, dear friend. Though prayers are but paper kites set alight, flaming into the oblivion of a hostile atmosphere, the knowledge of their brief flight is a beautiful comfort to me.

Faithfully yours,
Emilie

❧

July 10, 1854

Madame Saint-Ange,

It is with the deepest regret that I write to inform you of the passing of our mutual friend, Mrs. Geneviève Stockton. As you know, Geneviève had taken ill in recent months and was never able to fully regain her strength. After suffering yet another relapse in March, she died of protracted pneumonia on May Day of this year. Mr. Stockton has departed for Montreal, Canada, for six months, at least, to handle business affairs and has left the care of his children to various relatives and associates. Fanchon remains with her Aunt and Uncle in Baltimore, while the two boys are in the care of Geneviève's cousins, Mme. and M. Picot, of Brooklyn. I have charge of the baby, Sylvie, until such time as Mr. Stockton returns or possibly longer, depending on his fortunes.

I know this news must come as an appalling shock to you, as I believe that no one has yet written to you about your beloved friend's death. Mr. Stockton, as you know, did not involve himself too deeply in his wife's personal affairs, and he was often traveling for business. There was only a very small funeral service, attended by Mr. Stockton and my husband, M. Lafitte, solicitor for Mr. Stockton's estate. I have taken it upon myself to contact Geneviève's friends and relatives as Mr. Stockton was deeply distraught and incapable of managing such formalities himself.

Geneviève and I grew quite close over the years of our husbands' acquaintance, and I was honored to call her Friend. I see from your frequent correspondence that you are also an admired intimate of that delightful and most considerate and charming of ladies. Thus, I enclose your letters to her so that you may keep alive the memory of her cherished affection for you and let her luminous spirit brighten your gentle Heart.

Sincerely,
Mme. Agathe Whitehead Lafitte

New Orleans, September 22, 1854

Dearest Geneviève—my truest friend,

How I have missed your wise words and gentle guidance, your humor and sharing this journey of life with you, sister of my soul! Though you have departed this Earthly realm, and my own ideas about what may await us on the other side are so uncertain after my recent heartbreaks, I do still believe that you are held safe in God's embrace, that you dance among the stars and that the streaks of cosmic dust crossing the night sky are but the lacy trails of your skirt hems as you waltz through heaven.

And though you are gone, I continue to speak to you as though you were but down the road, dwelling with your maman and papa as when we were girls. We are tied together with ephemeral yet unbreakable threads and will eternally inhabit our invisible web. Is it possible for our alliance to transcend time and this earthly bondage to persist beyond our meager understanding of this world and what lies beyond? I pray it is so, and place my trust in such things.

You would scarce believe all that has transpired for me in recent months. Isidore still languishes in the throes of his illness. I labor to transfer him to a Reformation asylum in New York State, where he will receive treatment from the very finest of doctors. The doctors at Jackson diagnosed Softening of the Brain with Illusions of Persecution, Suicidal and Periodical Mania. They soak him in cold water baths and bind him entirely in wet sheets in an attempt to cool his fevered brain. The meager food is cheaply prepared. The meat, when they have it, is all fat and gristle, and there is no fresh milk. Too often, he is left alone to wander the corridors at the mercy of violent lunatics with criminal minds. The poverty of these attempted remedies leaves me frantic because I feel in my bones that they do not help him, but serve only to make him and the other asylum residents easier to manipulate.

Whenever possible, I visit him at least weekly to ensure that he is adequately fed and clothed, but no matter what I do, too often I feel my efforts to be in vain. Noting the chill of the rooms, I knitted Isidore a large shawl with a backing of combed under-fleece and a cotton lining that could be used as a wrap or blanket. My foolish pride swelled to observe the pleasure he took in my gift, for he was somewhat himself that day (though trembling and weak, with a loose and limpid gaze that slid about the room like a marble on a tray). He said to me, "No man could be more fortunate than I to have you, dear wife." It was almost as though the years of grief and turmoil had melted away and returned us to the bright blooming days of our early marriage, and stupidly, I left that day certain that my husband was returning from that dark netherworld that had kept him away for so long. Yet, upon my next visit, I spied my beautiful shawl cut in twain and unraveling upon the shoulders of strange lunatics, and learned from the Nurse that Isidore rejected my shawl during one of his fits, claiming that its Paisley eyes followed him unceasingly. Because his fits have taken a violent turn and the magistrate claims that Isidore constantly requests tools for his surgery, they lock him into a Utica Crib, where he must lie prone and caged for hours until his mania subsides. Though touted as humane treatment, I can scare tolerate the sight of him sequestered there on a rough bed of straw, his long hair hanging betwixt the crib's wooden spindles and the constant fretting of his thin fingers fraying the edges of his pajamas. Just as I was helpless to keep my child from the Reaper's grasp, so am I powerless to pull my husband up from the otherworldly depths of madness. Thus does my oft-broken heart gain new fissures.

I am much inspired by Miss Dix's strident, eloquent pleas to our Congress to alleviate the sufferings of the insane in prisons and asylums. Most assuredly, she is one of Us! I have insisted throughout this dreadful ordeal that my husband is not possessed by spirits, but instead has been struck down by a bodily illness which Science has not the faculties to comprehend. All treatments attempted so far have resulted in little to no healing and restoration of his true Self. Yet when I sit with him, caress his hands, speak to him softly, I begin to see that he is still within, and perhaps the gentle guidance of a beloved voice may yet serve to guide him from his frightful labyrinth. I very much hope to meet and speak with

Miss Dix when I am up North, after ensuring Isidore has settled into a new hospital with ease.

You will be pleased to know that your darling daughter Fanchon has taken up our cause. She has your fiery spirit, dear friend, and I shall make it my duty—in your stead—to ensure Life not damp it down or snuff it out! Mr. Stockton has consented to allow Fanchon to travel with me and Poupette to Philadelphia, Boston, and New York. There are several very fine universities for women in New England, and we intend to tour them all. He has not yet granted her permission to do so, but it is my hope, and Fanchon's, that he will acknowledge the great promise her young mind holds and approve her admission. Fanchon is beyond delighted at the prospect of our journey together and even more so at the notion of a college education. Your young lady has quite an extraordinary talent for numbers, mathematics, and the physical sciences. Her capabilities dazzle me! Having no girl-child of my own, I shall take utmost pleasure and satisfaction in guiding your darling daughter steadfastly toward her dream. Never you fear, Geneviève, I shall lavish upon her devotion unbound, my own and your portion alike! I retain your letters to me for Fanchon, so that she will know intimately the wit, grace, and compassion of which you were the soul, for your words will surely be a comfort to her and to petite Sylvie as they age and move through life missing their beloved Maman.

Having no sons or grandchildren to inherit her, Belle Rive will pass into my hands after Papa's death. I have told Maman that when he is gone, I will sell the plantation and use the profit to buy freedom for all its slaves. Whatever is left will secure a small home for myself and any who need it, near whichever college accepts me. I expect that Maman will resent giving up her lifestyle for my more frugal one, but she'll have to get used to it, for she has been spoiled too long. Her way of life languishes. I am very much encouraged by these Abolitionists who speak out against slavery and wish to add my efforts to theirs, in whatever way I can. All the troubles of recent years have irredeemably transformed me, and I cannot sink back into ignorance. The world beckons me forward, and I go, gladly answering its call.

All my love,
Emilie

Lydia Mueller
Philadelphia
Present Day

SWALLOWING THE LUMP in my throat, I fold the last letter and return it to its envelope. My eyes blur with emotion. I want to reach through time and press Emilie to my breast as if she were a rag doll and commend her incandescent spirit, struggling to keep joy alive amid such mental torment and emotional squalor.

Retying the ribbon around the letters, I set them down with a sigh. Such heartbreaks! The loss of Geneviève strikes me as especially sad. Her absence from this one-sided correspondence mirrors my own. I know what it feels like to have but one true friend in the world and to lose her. Memories of Sarah linger in the back of my mind. We haven't spoken for years after falling out of touch the way friends do when their paths widely diverge, and all the unsaid words between them have piled up into ramparts.

Emilie's abortive romance has left me aching for a loving touch, but there are no hands here except my own. So frequently am I alone I forget that anyone else lives with me. The hollow house ticks around me, empty as a grandfather clock without its pendulum. The ghosts of Belle Rive are trapped in the storage boxes lining the floor beside my desk. Boxes of smoke and sorrow. Bloodstained papers that emit fragrant coils of memory, their great exhalations like the press of a bellows. I hear them breathing all around me, a faint and spectral choir. Rhythmic breathing to match the aching pant of lovers in coitus, sighing, gasping in deathly ecstasy. *Pleasure, you gorgeous beast.* No hands except my own, and my skin ripe and wanting.

I IMMERSE MYSELF in the Belle Rive project. There's nothing else to occupy my mind. Hackett so rarely makes an appearance that my mothering duties are reduced to occasional texts and simple observation. Have the leftovers been eaten? Has his bed been slept in?

Lance chides me for my concern. "Leave the boy alone," he says. "He's seventeen! He doesn't need his mommy intruding in his life." But seventeen is far from grown, and there are many dangers for boys of his age. Boys with some money of their own, a car, and permissive parents. Boys whose college admission is guaranteed because their father's a professor and they needn't even pass the SAT to get in. He's a smart kid, but takes too much after the worst in myself and Lance. It's as if during his conception, all the irresponsible genes in our DNA sought out one another with the express intent of creating a being with zero compulsion to hard work, efficiency, or foresight. It troubles me to think such things about my own child, but aren't we to blame for his failings? Or failing to curb the worst traits when they were still fledgling and underdeveloped? Lance says I worry too much. Hackett will come around in his own time and we must wait out the discomfort.

HACKETT GOT SUSPENDED from school. A teacher caught him and Tommy Galicki smoking a joint in an empty chem lab during lunch. Naturally it's Tommy Galicki, the only one of Hackett's oddball group of friends whom I actually like. Hackett's bust simply wearies me, but Tommy's is surprising. Hackett typically pairs up with the worst-behaved kid in any crowd. I thought Tommy would be a good influence, so I encouraged them to spend time together. My bullshit meter's batteries must be drained.

I'm summoned to collect my son from detention while Lance convenes with the principal via Skype—two busy men too important to meet face to face. Lance had coerced me into sending Hackett to a private Catholic high school, even though we aren't affiliated with any religion. (Lance is certain that the strict disciplinary codes and narrowly focused curriculum will groom his son for a career in academia—like father, like son.) Hackett, our amiable, restless boy, resisted at first but soon capitulated when we toured the co-ed campus and discovered that the freshman peer liaison was a pretty girl he'd met at the mall during vacation. Fourteen and still affable, he confided his connection to the girl during the ride home. He wouldn't shut me out completely until the summer after freshman year.

Lance handled Hackett's enrollment and has chauffeured him back and forth nearly every day of term ever since; I haven't returned to St. Agatha's since that first tour. Now, warm afternoon sunlight bathes the building's vaguely familiar, red sandstone façade. Autumn leaves blush and tall sycamores spill vivid shadows across the still-green lawns. Unlike most schools' ambient noise of ringing bells and children shouting from distant playing fields, St. Agatha's is eerily quiet. A crinkled gray nun in a blue cardigan, shapeless polyester skirt, and sensible shoes waits to unlock the creaking doors and admit me.

"Mrs. Mueller? This way, please." She shuffles down the corridor two steps ahead of me and guides me down a flight of stairs. Detention is held in the dingy basement, a small grim room occupied by six ancient wooden desks, a teacher's desk and chair, a loudly ticking wall clock, and my son. I can smell him from the door—subtle cloying reek of marijuana and sweaty teenager. A stern, bald man in a clerical collar sits in front, watching Hackett write on a sheet of paper. Folded awkwardly in his seat, long legs jammed beneath the tiny writing desk. I see no trace of my little boy. Hackett turns his brown eyes to me. They're empty of emotion. He doesn't fear my anger. He isn't relieved or pleased to see me; no fleeting spark of childish joy that I've come for him enlivens them. It sends a chill through me, to know another love lost. My bright boy is buried within that stiff sarcophagus, his face unsmiling and cold. Neither Lance nor Hackett ever turns to me with joy in their gazes or smiles lighting their faces. They have both been infected by the same terminal disease, a viral decline of emotion that feeds upon the scant and fleeting grievances of my small soul. Or so I imagine.

How have we become so lost from one another? I cannot think upon it without my heart splitting. The father has become a cliché of ambitious detachment. The son models his tender young life upon a man's grown-up, callous sentiment, growing bitter before he's fully bloomed.

The balding priest stares up at me. I've stood rooted here for far too long, as if announcing my idiocy.

"Hackett," I murmur, my voice gone weak again. I clear my throat and extend my hand. "Come home."

He unfolds himself like some reticulated, stiff-jointed animal, picks up his skateboard, and slings his messenger bag over his shoulder. "Lydia."

God, I hate his formality. What's wrong with "Mom"? I nod to the priest and thank him. He finally opens his white-lipped mouth, revealing jagged rows of yellow teeth. Soft and slimy, his voice burbles over a dam of phlegm in his throat. "Of woman came the beginning of sin, and through her we all die."

Shocked and suddenly livid, I recoil from his rancor. Is this what my son learns at school?

"Let's go," I snarl, turning Hackett toward the door, angered that my voice remains limp.

The priest stands, corncob teeth clacking. "But I suffer not a woman to teach, nor to usurp authority over the man, but to be in silence. For Adam was first formed, then Eve. And Adam was not deceived, but the woman being deceived was in the transgression." He grins luridly, his stare never wavering. "The apple doesn't fall far from the tree, Eve."

I shudder, pushing Hackett along the hall toward the stairs. "What an asshole! This is exactly why I didn't want you going to St. Agatha's." My protests are weak. I'd put up very little opposition. This is my own fault.

Hackett shrugs. "Just ignore it, Lydia. I do."

We retrace my steps through empty, echoing corridors. Outside, gray clouds have swallowed up the golden sun. Wind-tossed candy wrappers and empty paper cups flutter along the street. I open the car door for my son, but Hackett just shakes his head and mounts his 'board. "See you later." He kicks off and is gone. I stand stupidly on the street, the gaping car door beeping a nagging warning. My face grows hot, and I swipe at futile tears. My sadness is unremarkable. It has no power to move its witnesses to compassion. I don't really see myself as a terrible mother. Isn't it possible that children might turn out a certain way—badly—despite one's best efforts? I close the car door. Am I meant to chase him down the street? I never know what to do with him anymore. It had been so easy when he was little. Feed, change, rock, soothe. But now my almost-man wants none of my solace or care. I have become useless.

At home, I drink a tumbler of scotch and wait for Lance's return. He texts me an hour later to tell me that he's extended his office hours till 8:00 and will see me later. No inquiry about Hackett or me. No recounting of the meeting with St. Agatha's headmaster. Out of boredom and curiosity, I perform a rudimentary search of Hackett's room. He's taken his tablet and phone, and there's nothing unusual to be found until a tiny plastic envelope falls into my hand—four little pink pills stamped with smiley faces. He'd taped it to the underside of his desk. Childish. I pocket the E and leave. At what point do I worry? What sign will he give that teenage rebellion has morphed into something bigger and more dangerous? Who will catch him if he falls?

I SPEND THE night alone. Lance chooses to sleep in his study. Throughout the following day, I wander from room to room, unable to concentrate on anything or complete any task. One would think that Lance would be eager to engage in a head-shaking session with the mother of his delinquent child, but he's not. I no longer bother texting or calling him. He seldom responds. Eventually, I return to my routine of the night before, sipping a large glass of scotch and staring out the living room window until the room grows dark and a chill sets in.

I sleep. I dream. Dark shapes drift through drunken nightmares. The sinister figure of a man forms within the twisted, malformed rooms of my subconscious mind. Impossibly tall and hovering, lips cracking open into a gruesome, toothy grin. Hands under my clothes, hot flesh against mine, scratchy with stubble and reeking of sweat, sex, and drink.

"Wake up, little sunflower." Loving words spoken with the mouth of a monster. Why does this devil torment me so? Clawing my way out of the clinging, vile dream, I open my eyes.

Lance stands over me, his handsome face creased into appealing laugh lines. "When we first married, your gaze would follow me everywhere. You were a bright sunflower, tracking your sun." He kisses my cheek. "You must have been dreaming of me. You were moaning."

I frown and raise a hand, shielding my eyes against the harsh morning light. "Sunflowers are ugly! I've always hated that nickname. You know that." My head's throbbing. I can't remember what, or when, I last had anything to eat or drink besides whiskey. "Get me some water, will you?"

"Been on a bender?" Lance asks, heading into the kitchen. "I couldn't wake you last night." He returns with a glass of ice water. The tumbler has a heavy base with a fat dollop of crimson inside, a floating globule of blood.

"Is Hackett here?"

My husband shakes his head. "Haven't seen him."

"He's been out all night. Aren't you worried?"

"I checked his bank records. He bought a pizza last night, probably for delivery judging from the exorbitant price, and this morning, he treated himself to a rather nice breakfast at a café in Rittenhouse, so aside from his impaired financial judgment, he's obviously doing just fine."

"Rittenhouse? What's he doing over there?"

"Probably spent the night at Tommy's. I think his mother lives there with her new husband."

"Are you fucking kidding me?" Anger rises in me, a cobra flaring its hood. "Go get him!"

Lance sighs heavily. "Lydia, I am not going to retrieve him like some parole officer after a truant. He'll have to learn from his mistakes the hard way."

"No! You're his father! *You* should be the one punishing him, not *life*."

"Don't fret, darling. I put a hold on his debit card. He's had his fun and now he'll have to come home and face what's waiting. Anyway, I spoke to the headmaster. St. Agatha's will amend his suspension. He can return on Monday."

"I don't want him going back there. Find another school."

"He's getting a good education. I won't pull him out just because of a stupid, teenage mistake."

I can still feel the old priest's grimy words clinging to my skin. "They told me *I* was the problem."

Softening, Lance sits beside me. "What do you mean?"

I parrot the verse back to him. "'Of woman came the beginning of sin, and through her we all die.' What kind of talk is that?"

Lance offers a benign stare. "Catholic talk. I'm sure whoever said it didn't mean anything by it." He averts his gaze, and rises to leave the room. Without looking at me, he adds, "Wash up. You stink of liquor."

HACKETT COMES HOME on Sunday. Lance and I are reading the newspaper at the dining table, sharing coffee and bakery brioche when our son pokes his head around the door and sheepishly offers a greeting.

"Well, well, well," smirks Lance. "Look who's decided to join us. Run out of money already?"

Hackett gives a nod that's more of a shrug.

"Come and sit down."

Hackett moves to the table, his gaze flickering between myself and his father, looking for a safe place to land.

I push the plate of pastry toward him—a motherly gesture. "Start talking."

"I'm sorry." He hesitates, wavering between an adult admission of culpability and a childish impulse of blame and rebellion. "Really sorry." Genuine contrition. I'm relieved.

"You shouldn't worry your mother like that," Lance says. Those few words are laden with meaning, and we stare at each other, daring someone to break the spell, say what Lance will not. That I'm fragile. Shattered and repaired, like a china cup, its shards glued back together. Not like a broken bone, stronger for its healed fractures.

Hackett dips his head. "I know," he whispers. "Sorry, Mom."

And my heart is full, seething and liquid with love for this child of mine. I blink away tears and Lance squeezes my knee beneath the table. He changes the topic, and we abandon this knot of turmoil as if it had never happened.

LANCE IS HOME from work at an early hour and in an unusually good mood. "Just us tonight?"

"Yes. Hackett's gone to see a movie with some friends."

"At least he has friends. You should see the sullen kids that I put up with. I don't know what they think they're going to do in this world—spoiled little brats, the lot of 'em."

"The boys maybe. Not the girls, Professor. Never the girls." I'm teasing but we skate along the treacherous edge in my voice.

"My poor darling," Lance purrs, sliding a hand over my hip and cupping my bum. "You know I love you best."

I turn to face him, hungry for affirmation. "Do you really?"

A glimmer of surprise lights his face, then he frowns. "I always have and I always will." His voice thickens. "And I've done a poor job of showing it since...since you've been back. I'm sorry."

Finally, we make love. Sweetly. Tenderly. He treats me with great care because I am Damaged. Defective. After such a long time, I had thought I'd forgotten the scents of his body, the taste of his sweat-damp skin, but they're still firmly embedded in my head and I relish them. He makes me gasp and howl and cry, and when it's done, I feel whole—for the moment.

TONIGHT, LANCE HAS a faculty dinner with a visiting professor. Rather than play the part of adoring spouse, basking in the light of my husband's brilliance, I claim a migraine and lie facedown on the couch, waving him away. I suggest he take Marcella in my stead. She is a better companion anyway, and they get along very well. She's much more impressive, professionally, and conversation of the erudite, tinkling sort comes naturally to her, whereas I have to force it and leave a gathering feeling as though my face has been twisted out of place and stretched wide by too many deliberate, false smiles.

When I first met Marcella, her name delighted me. Marcella was the little girl in the Raggedy Ann stories, which I had loved when I was small. As our friendship deepened, I'd come to think of us (privately, of course) as them, for like in the books, Marcella was adored and privileged while I was the doll—dull-witted but kind-hearted. Except I suspect that my heart is no Valentine candy, sugar-sweet and pure. Mine's more like a cholla cactus covered in barbed spines. My brain a tentacled Cthulhu, whose seething and malevolent thoughts lurch among its muddy pits.

It's as if I've been captured in a portrait entitled *Dark Mood Descends*. The Dark Mood is an infestation inside me. It started small. In the beginning, its shoots and seedlings were easy to pluck, and I managed to keep further encroachment at bay. But life is wearying; time must be invested in other pursuits besides the maintenance of one's inner landscape, and again I find myself nearly buried by the weeds that my neglect has nurtured. There's a plant called creeping spurge, a toxic invasive that spreads itself along the ground like a fallen woman hoping to avoid stoning. From a single taproot, it unfurls long stems, radiating out in a growing circle like a spider's web. It's deceptively cute. Easy to pull, fortunately. But it's also easy to become dismayed when viewing a spurge-infested yard, for the weeds appear completely dominant and the nature of their takeover totalitarian. Likewise does my despotic and omnipotent Dark Mood grow.

It's easy enough to detach and drift off. When I wake some time later, a glass of water and two painkillers rest on the coffee table, courtesy of my dutiful husband. He'll be gone for hours.

LATER, I HEAR him tiptoe up the stairs, hoping not to wake me but failing. I think I sleep as dolphins do—with one half of my brain at a time, or the albatross, who sleeps mid-flight. My sleep is a flickering pattern of vivid hallucinations overlaid on the gauzy screen of my actual surroundings. I talk in my sleep. Laugh and giggle, weep and cry aloud, carry on two-way conversations. I hold my dreams as close to the vest as a prime hand of cards. They seep through my waking hours and leach into my consciousness, trick me into looking for things I've purchased or misplaced, leave me believing that certain conversations or events have taken place, when in reality, they only happened in the Land of Nod.

Lance has always tolerated it well. He sleeps the sleep of the dead, and when I confuse real-world and dream-life events, he merely gives me an exasperated, tolerant smile. This happened so often in the early days of our marriage, he employed a double-wink to signal me that I'd ventured too far from reality. How quickly I came to rely on those winks during conversations with his peers, Hackett's doctors, teachers, and the parents of his friends. They rarely occur now. Either I've got a firmer grip on reality or my husband has hauled up the anchor and set me adrift on the sea of my imaginings, exhausted by the flexible reality I inhabit.

He steps quietly into the bedroom, takes pajamas from his dresser, and exits the room. Pipes groan and the water gurgles and splashes in the hall bathroom. He's showering in the middle of the night. His defining personality quirk is his insistence on a proper bath. The only time I've ever seen him take a shower was during a long-ago summer vacation to Myrtle Beach. His bathing habits have been the subject of much irritation—he can never be rushed to get ready. My heartbeat quickens, a steady, up-tempo cadence. Something is Wrong.

Shower quickly concluded, he comes to bed, smelling of toothpaste and soap. I reach for him, placing my hand on his penis, lying warm and soft in the nest of his damp pubic hair. His body contracts away from my touch, then quickly—forcibly—relaxes. He presses my hand to his cheek, kisses the back of it, and tucks it beside me. He rolls over, presents me with his back, and sleeps the sleep of the dead.

I YouTube the Kinks' "Destroyer" and click the repeat button. Paranoid, is what I am. But isn't that always my way? Never been the snooping sort of spouse. Had I fears or worries, I simply talked myself out of them. Then again, I want no part of any knowledge that would destroy me, or Us.

I meet Marcella for lunch. I need to talk, and she's a competent, empathetic listener. She'll dispense a few nods and mm-hmms before dismissing my fears and turning the topic to something else.

The café is too bright and crowded—a sensory onslaught like someone hurling tiny, sharp blocks at me. The gleaming lights, sharp clatter of dishes, and raucous cackling of voices grate on my nerves.

Marcella wears shiny taupe pumps and a sleeveless camel-colored dress that complements her perfectly blown-out hair. Her square face is 1960s movie star beautiful and her amber eyes crease into a smile when she spots me.

"Outside maybe?" Marcella takes my elbow and propels me toward a patio table in the shade. I can breathe again. She knows me well, this woman. Again, I feel a rogue flash of gratitude for her friendship, her humored tolerance of my quirks and unflagging interest in the subjects that unite us.

"Thank you." Humidity makes my long curls rebel; they flop in my face like flaccid snakes. We order a forty-dollar bottle of Viognier and make small talk until our salads arrive. Marcella refills our already-empty glasses. I can't do the whole preliminary-thing—wait for a suitable moment in the conversation or until she asks how it's going at home. My voice is tight again. Familiar sensations of bees and choking (mental flash of séance spirits flying into Isidore's throat—my throat). There is a transitory moment between silent thought and speech. Speaking aloud gives birth to malignant wraiths, summons the undead from some limbo netherworld where fantasy and grim imaginings coalesce in hostile gloom. Speaking aloud gives flesh to fancy, clothes my suspicions in blood, skin, and fat. They become ambulatory, grow sharp, poking fingers—golems brought to life with the intention of wreaking havoc.

All I seek is consolation, the brushing away of fears and suspicions. A friend's assurance that I am a paranoid self-destroyer. She is a good friend. She'll play her part.

I start to speak but must clear my throat, again and again. I choke on strangling words. Marcella frowns and looks away; I fear she has no empathy for me, that my oddball neediness has already drained her well. "Lance...," I choke out.

Marcella's eyelids flicker faintly, a nervous twitch I've not seen before.

"It sounds so clichéd," I say, twisting the napkin in my lap. "But I think Lance is seeing someone. After all these years, everything we've been through. Why would he do it now? Tell me, Marcella," I plead. "Tell me I'm being stupid."

Color plummets from her face. She is white as chalk. It's such a dramatic statement, white as chalk, white as a sheet. I always thought it was a ridiculous idiom, but seeing it happen before me now, a prickling chill jets up from my belly into my heart. She becomes a corpse before my very eyes, her mouth locked in a strangely jagged gape.

"You knew about this?" Suddenly, I recognize her expression. *Guilt.* But more shameful than guarding my husband's secret, she is hiding one of her own. Tears pool, magnifying her sad, lovely gaze.

"I'm so sorry," she whispers. "It just *happened*. We never planned it, obviously."

"I don't understand. What just *happened*?" Mimicking her emphasis, even though it's suddenly all brilliantly, cut-glass clear. I'm consumed by a razor-sharp desire to wound and torture her, to extract a confession and smash her pretty porcelain face to pieces.

"It was so difficult for him when you were...ill. We met to talk—about you. Your absence was a loss for both of us." She is stricken, yet coldness underlies her fragility. Her mouth tightens; her chin lifts with the subtlest defiance. "He just wanted a friend and it—it became something else."

One time. A hundred times. How many doesn't matter.

Treacherous bitch. Fury is my name. Blinding anger swirls within me, a dark maelstrom. The betrayal is devastating.

"And yet you sit here with me, having a ladies' lunch and building up your façade of friendship. You look me in the eye and ask how I am when all along you know you're slipping me poison!"

"Poison?" She looks confused. A hand flutters out as if to cover her drink, but is quickly retracted. Our eyes meet. She looks frightened.

Hot tears fill my eyes, but I'm shamed by them. I have so few friendships. I don't know why it's always been like this for me. Maybe because no one wants to play with a broken toy.

Vaguely aware of the distant grumble of thunder in the sky's unsettled belly and a sudden patter of raindrops, I realize I'm standing. Marcella looks at me with pity and it's all *too much*. The edges of my life blacken and crackle, a photograph tipped into the flames.

And then I am walking up the steps to my own front door with no memory of having returned to my car and driven home.

Muted pops of gunfire sound in the living room. I pass the open French doors and see my son engaged in a video game. I patrol the house, looking for Lance. My husband is absent. Has she called him yet? Did she reach for her phone the minute I staggered from the table and call to console him, or to warn him? *Your crazy wife is on the loose. She knows about us and she's pissed. She said something about poisoning me, can you believe it?*

Wet wind slices in through the open window in our bedroom. Raindrops damp the carpet. Rummaging through the medicine cabinet, I search for something, anything, to take away the pain. I want to drink a bottle of glue and have it pour through my cracked insides and fix all my shattered pieces. I want to cut out my heart and replace it with a clockwork, feelingless fixture. Numb my brain, settle the turmoil, scrub away my insanity.

Would bloodletting make me feel better? Drain the wastewater accumulating in my head and heart, tears that run clouded with my pollution?

Lance keeps a pack of blades in his dopp bag, refills for his heavy, vintage razor.

But another image leaps into view—the antique, dovetailed mahogany box that had arrived in the first collection of artifacts I'd received from Belle Rive. The one that Fournier had employed to drain his patient's mania—Isidore's bloodletting kit.

The house is still, as if holding its breath. My feet are silent against the thick carpet, but my own breath is loud and labored as I retrieve Isidore's box from my desk, enter the bathroom, and grab a towel.

I pop the lid. Nestled among the fleshy, velvet folds sits an engraved silver scarificator, its twelve steel blades stiff and reluctant to launch, its spring-loaded device either damaged or rusted. Warm waves of pleasure pulse through my organs, raising goose bumps on my skin. Pewter bloodletting bowls. Suction pump and connector. Glass cups for wet or dry cupping and a silver heat lamp, each piece inscribed with the maker's mark, Charrière.

Running my fingers along the bottom of the pewter bowls, I think about how much blood they've held. That they will soon hold my own. It's gruesome yet fascinating to imagine a troubled gentleman seeking relief for his illness—just as likely to be depression as syphilis—by slitting a vein and letting ill humors flow. Whatever my own disease—I prefer the quaint term "domestic illness"—there are no convenient remedies to alleviate its stresses. I, too, might seek relief from any source that promised it. But I'm not so bad, yet.

A scuttling silverfish drops onto my lap. I jump up, shivering from the startle and shaking out my clothes. The silverfish lands inside a blood bowl and crunches beneath my thumb when I crush out its life. Once more, the pewter has tasted blood—of sorts. I imagine that an insect's hemolymph isn't the rich pudding these bowls have enjoyed before.

A feather-light blade slides into my hand.

Maybe I've cut too deeply, for the flow pulses, a syrupy gush. Red Niagara Falls. Lethargic and taken over by a luscious sense of peace, I rest my arm on the bloodletting bowl, which is in danger of overflowing onto our white wool carpet. I close my eyes and slip immediately into a dream.

Whereupon I find myself slinking through a draping jungle of powdery Spanish moss and high, brutal sprays of razor grass to clamber upon the pedimented portico of a degenerate Greek Revival townhouse with odd Gothic gables, a Frankensteinian example of architecture. Towering three stories high, its slender, Ionic columns support a sagging double gallery and twisted iron railings. Blisters bubble its grayish-purple paint, and tattered lace curtains flap in a preternatural breeze thick with buzzing clouds of mosquitoes and bumbling bluebottle flies. A splintered green door with a black iron knob stands askew in its frame, several feet above the ground. I reach overhead and twist the knob, sunshine-hot in my hand. My knees crack as I crawl over the high sill into cool, dank air. Dark wood paneling patterns the walls. A dense, abstract swirl of stained glass rebuffs the light and puddles blue and crimson on the floor. The house smells of dust and camphor.

Now I'm in the servant's stairwell, creeping upward into clinging blackness. Dust motes as big as paper snowflakes sashay through narrow beams of light. I cannot see my feet, lost in a sea of deep pile and rotten sagging wood. As always in dreams, I move with purpose, relentlessly exploring the endless house. It's bottomless, unknowable. There are sub-levels, new rooms, and forgotten passages. Secret rooms and corridors with cracked, sweating walls. Doors open upon doors. Stairways curl into infinite Mobius strips and strange players people the building, circulating with unknown intent.

The staircase sways beneath my tread, its boards spongy, the deep indigo of its oriental carpet soaked and squishy. To ascend the steps is to take my life in my hands. There's a parlor on the second story, which has retained the flavor of its original occupants. Chalky walls the color of the Dover cliffs. Sloping Gothic arches and slender black beams collide at their apex in a froth of Art Nouveau–styled flowers and curls. Porthole windows framed in brass stud the walls. Peacocks fan green tails among Tiffany irises. Soot blacks the round fire grate, grays the walls, and smuts the cracked, emerald-green ceramic tiles. A large telescope weights a sheaf of curling papers on the desk beside inkwells and mischievous porcelain fairies with twisted sausages of woolen hair.

Nine men and women in dusty black period dress gather at a circular table, the softly tinted light reflected in their spectacles and the sepia patina of their dense, dewy skins. A forlorn, petite white girl with a snub nose acknowledges my presence with a nod before lowering her eyelids. Next to her sits a beautiful, keen-eyed woman in cream lace who holds very tightly to the hand of a slender man whose unfashionably long hair falls in waves over his padded velvet shoulders. He is roguish and troubled, an open-mouthed vessel waiting to be filled. I want to fly into his throat and curl into his empty shell as the genie does the bottle.

The people link hands as an older, Creole woman wearing a yellow tignon and layers of fringed fabric begins to speak in patois. Whether prayer, chant, or incantation, the words make my stomach twist and flood me with absurd terror. The people raise their voices like bludgeoning cudgels and batter me into submission. Candle flames gutter and smoke. I want to leave the room, but the door through which I entered has vanished.

"Show yourself, Spirit!" the woman cries, rolling her head upon her neck, sweat beading on her brow and quivering lips. The table shakes and thuds and her apostles moan and cry out in tormented bliss. "I sense your presence! I smell your perfume and feel the agonies of your soul in the air around us!"

Her words snag me like fishhooks and reel me in. I'm crouching on the table, the beast in their midst, howling and ravenous. *Feed me.*

The petite woman's eyes pop open and widen in horror as she stares into the abyss of my tormented soul. "Spirit! Speak your name!" she whispers. "Tell me, what of my child?"

Blood veils my vision and fills my mouth, tasting of rusting metal and dirt.

I wake dizzy and bloodied, lying on the bathroom floor in a tumble of red. My carpet is ruined. Flickers of the dream ascend and evaporate. I bandage the cut and clean up the congealed mess on the rug as best I can, watching in horror as it spreads. Shaving cream, hydrogen peroxide, laundry detergent—they diminish the mark by degrees, but an hour later, there's still a bloom like a squashed rose. My ruined clothes go into the garbage.

Though relieved, I'm ashamed and confused. I haven't cut myself for many years—I thought those impulses long-dead and far behind me, but now I see that they've only lain dormant, awaiting an opportunity to reawaken.

I TIDY UP and make myself presentable before going downstairs to fix croque-monsieur for Hackett. We eat in companionable silence, flipping through magazines at the breakfast bar before I say goodnight, kiss his cheek, and return to my room. I haven't the heart—or the stomach—to check my phone for messages. I silenced its ringer and stuck it in the nightstand drawer, hoping to fall asleep before Lance gets home, thus delaying the sight of his deceiving face for a few more hours, but my insides tighten into impossible knots. Sleep does not come. I lie half awake, captive to a shifting stream of furtive images, reliving the warm gush of my blood and the dream house's sickly scents.

The rain that's sporadically pattered down all evening gathers speed. Sheets of water lash the windows. Wind rattles the old panes in their frames. I lie curled up on the mattress corner, and my marital bed seems enormous around me. Unwanted imaginings flicker, persistent as moths—Marcella twisting herself up against my husband like some vile, needy cat. Lance fucking her on Marcella's living room couch and kitchen counters, or in his office. Both of them grappling, sweaty and naked, in my very own bed, laughing like fiends. Marcella wrapping her legs around my husband's head and grinding her probably perfectly groomed cunt against his face, smearing her juices all over the mouth he would come home and kiss me with. Lance coming into the bedroom, lightning flashes illuminating his grin and glinting off the long scalpel and rib spreaders he will use to slice me open and pry out my barely beating heart. Obviously, he no longer has a use for it.

But those things aren't real. Because I'm still alone, floating in a puddle of horror, too frozen to even cry.

The cut on my arm throbs. I peel back the bandage and pinch it, forcing it open like a pair of lips, and push my tongue into the sticky slit—salty and slightly spoiled. It stings, and the buds of my tongue feel like a cat's raspy lick against the raw flesh. There are other things that I don't want to think about, memories better buried, easy to punch down into the soft dough of my past. *It's your fault*, a bad voice says. *Of course he would tire of taking care of a horrible girl like you. Lucky you kept him this long. Head full of worms, tunnels full of shit. Shit for brains.*

Finally, I unthaw and cry. Deep, choking sobs pour like vomit from my throat.

What can we say to one another that will numb the sting of his duplicity? Should I apologize for my faulty brain, the crazy in me that drove him away, the sheepdog chasing down the wolf while the sheep run in frenzied pointless circuits and butt their heads into fence posts? For I am the sheep, docile, stupid—tasty mutton for tough teeth—and my crazy is the snarling, frothing beast—the fice dog—that keeps it all penned in. Or is it the other way around?

"Lydia, you're not making sense." Lance sounds weary, emotionally exhausted. "I don't understand what you're saying." My eyes focus and I recognize him, sitting on the bed beside me. Have I spoken out loud? A hazy light illuminates the room, just enough to showcase the heavy circles beneath his eyes. Has he been crying, I wonder?

"I didn't say anything."

"Yes," he sighs. "Yes, you did." He drags his palms over his face, and sighs. "It's not your fault."

I weep silently, but my tears are a hot, salt river flowing around an icy, granite boulder. My heart's a stone. It will take eons to erode beneath these tides.

His lips part, a wet, tiny noise that makes me want to scream. I know what's coming and shriek to ward it off.

"Don't tell me! I don't want to know! I don't want to hear any of it—your explanations, your excuses. Spare me that, at least."

"It was just once!" he says. "A stupid, terrible mistake. I need you to know that."

My voice returns in all its maniacal glory. Rising like a hurricane, gathering speed and force till its fury is unleashed and rips from my throat in a torrent of demonic sound. I howl and cry and scratch till blood dyes the sheets. Lance grapples with my flailing limbs, pins them down. I writhe and wail, nipping his flesh with my teeth, chomping and gnashing.

This is the way it goes. His weight suffocates me. The mattress sucks me into its cushioned belly. His bones are iron bars imprisoning me. We thrash and fight and buck. Clothes tear. Nails dig. No kisses, no tenderness. We are animals, thrusting and clawing. Brutal sex—we match and master one another, he is my war prisoner, and I am his. I cannot get close enough to him, even as repulsive images of him fucking Marcella fill my head and shatter my eyes. I would open up his skin and pull it closed around me, drown myself in the red, raw meat of him. Eat him from the inside out.

I ask the same stupid question uttered by millennia of women before me. Its plaintive neediness makes me want to slap myself, staple my mouth closed simply to escape its whine. "Do you love her?"

"My feelings for her are nothing compared to those I have for you."

I think of the cut I made on my arm and wish I had severed an artery.

My life has played out like a Greek tragedy, and finally I've been rescued by the god in the machine. Adelaide Randolph tells me that the Foundation has requested my presence in New Orleans right away. They're retrofitting the main house to bring it up to code and have hit a few snags. They need me to verify that the fixtures they're being told to remove are integral to the house's historical legacy so that they can remain. Adelaide tells me to catch the Tuesday morning flight and spend a few days on premises to oversee inspections. The email includes a copy of my potential itinerary and flight info. All I need to do is confirm and show up at the airport day after tomorrow with my bags. This opportunity for escape couldn't have come at a better time. Without hesitation, I reply "yes" and hit "send."

I spend the rest of the afternoon checking the weather in NOLA and packing. There's plenty of food in the freezer for Hackett, and Lance can supervise whatever else needs doing. Freedom is one of the blessings of children growing older. The sting of them needing (and wanting) their parents less is ameliorated by the rediscovery of the buried self, that independent identity that gets shelved when babies are born, demanding every ounce of energy and love that we once kept for ourselves.

I try not to think about how Lance will spend the time alone. Already, it is too much to see his face, to encounter him in the house when we happen to occupy the same room at the same time. He's retreated to his study and its comfortable couch. Through my gnarled shroud of anger and grief, I sense his conflict, a self-righteous protection of his egregious infidelity and a truly repentant desire to ease my pain. It's better—easier by far—simply to avoid or ignore him.

My own feelings about what he's done are muted. I should feel enraged and devastated, but I'm simply numb. It feels like the memory of a dream or a story I read long ago. Already, his infidelity is anecdotal. However, Marcella's role in the affair is an endless source of kindling to fuel my rage, for in some incomprehensible, socially sanctioned way, she's become the instigator in this scenario. A wily seductress of my hapless husband, when in fact I know that the largest portion of blame is his. But I have to live with him. I am dependent on him, our history, and his love to be the roost into which I settle myself after flight. He is my family. She is not. Therefore, it is easier, and safer, to dress her in the enemy's clothes. We haven't spoken since our lunch. I float within the hurricane's eye, lost inside the maelstrom. I cannot even mourn the death of our friendship when it is the victim of Marcella's deliberate homicide.

ADELAIDE RANDOLPH DOES not meet me at the airport. Instead, she sends the intern, Owen, to fetch me. A scrappy little man-boy who looks as if his mother has just finished scrubbing him up for church waits outside the curb at baggage claim, holding up a sign that reads "Mueller: Belle Rive Plantation."

He offers his hand and I pretend not to see it. Handshakes are the Devil's germ-delivery system.

"Hey, I'm Owen. Flight okay?"

I nod as he grabs the handle of my wheelie bag and steers us out to the parking lot, his mouth going the whole time.

"I've really been looking forward to meeting you! I don't know if Ms. Randolph mentioned the glass house and gardens on the property, but I was hoping you could find some time to tour the grounds with me. I'm in my final semester at GSU earning my Master's in Heritage Preservation with a focus in historic landscape architecture, and I would love to be able to sit down with you at some point to discuss my project." He pauses for a great inhalation of breath before continuing at warp speed. "But first you should assess the workshop original to the house. Ms. Randolph wants the whole structure removed and sold. She wants to put in a gazebo and dance floor, which if you ask me totally destroys the integrity of the property."

He doesn't seem to need any reply to push him along to further revelations, so I tune out, and recline against the car seat, enjoying the scenery. I can't imagine what it must have been like for Isidore, leaving France to come to America knowing that he might never return home. Was he eager for the adventure? Full of trepidation? What must it have been like to step off a wooden ship after weeks at sea and enter an alien culture? I don't know if I could do it, leave my life behind for so much unknown. Maybe I would go mad, too.

Oddly, I feel connected to them, Isidore and Emilie. All their anxieties about race relations and skin tone, their disgust over their profits from slavery, their guilt, or lack thereof. I sometimes feel little better off than them. Both Black and white, I'm ambiguous enough to pass for a multitude of ethnicities. If not for the quirk of being born in the twenty-first century, I'd be subject to the same scrutiny. And with all the violence I see on the news, the racial tension and political back-pedaling, it's easy to feel that we're still stuck in the caste system of the nineteenth century.

Owen has finally ceased talking. I see little of the city on the drive to Belle Rive. Following the curve of the Mississippi River, we wind along a freeway through flat fields empty of slaves, carts, horses, and sugarcane. Instead, there's an occasional gas station, a fly-harried nag nibbling grass while staring into space, and eventually a few driveways that lead to other restored plantations.

We arrive at Belle Rive at dusk, driving slowly up the two-hundred-year-old oak alley. Enormous tree branches lock fingers over the paved road, drowning it in shadow. Belle Rive sprawls atop the low hill, looking a bit like a wedding cake that's collapsing in the sun. It vaguely resembles the house in the daguerreotype. There've been many changes over the years, but the bones of the original structure are still visible.

Yellow Caterpillars—backhoes, excavators, graders, and a forklift—crowd the front lawn, tracking up the thick, clumpy soil. Dumpsters line the railing beside two stinking blue porta-potties. There is no magic here. It is a work site being razed and paved, repainted, retiled, and dressed up in strangers' antiques purchased from estate sales and eBay.

My skin prickles. Here walked the ghostly footsteps of Isidore and Emilie Saint-Ange. Here, Albert succumbed to ownership and the proprietary label "field slave" after he'd been bought at auction. Here, Madame Floriane chastised Poupette, berated her daughter, her husband, son, and legions of human chattel for failing to please her. The history of this place hovers like some simmering contagion awaiting the right conditions to breed and spread, and I fear its infection.

I suppose that I imagined the Foundation was run by descendants of the original owners, the Bilodeaus, but I recall reading that it was sold in 1859 to a white family who joined the Confederate side and turned Belle Rive into a field hospital during the Civil War. In fact, on my list of duties (after authenticating the multiple layers of wallpaper uncovered during restoration) is verifying that the wooden floor planks in the parlor were stained by blood soaking through the carpets when the room was used as a surgical suite for amputations.

I follow Owen up the steps onto the veranda. No scents of jasmine or heliotrope fill the clinging, humid air, only the faintly mucky odor of brown river water flowing half a mile distant and the smell of my own perspiration. I am glad for the distraction. I have wanted to cut again and resisted. Logically, I understand that it will be nothing more than a temporary high, a short-lived analgesic to dull a deep, abiding pain. But still, I have yearned for the caress of the blade against my skin, opening a little sliver of flesh like a doorway to usher out the negativity inside me.

Instead, I run a furtive fingernail through the crease of my earlier wound, ripping apart the ardent romance of knitting vessels and cells. The sides of the cut are Romeo and Juliet, lovers who must not meet lest they become one. Without my fingernail inside that wound, gliding like a luge along its sticky, scabbed track, I might be a robot. That red line keeps me grounded. Without it, I doubt my presence on earth. Little red anchors, holding me down.

Adelaide Randolph appears before me. Compact and round, with a cap of steely gray curls, she's stout, primly proper, and shrewdly staring at me. I've lost a bit of time, I suspect. Slid over into dreamtime for a quick coffee break, because I suddenly find myself mid-conversation.

"Mrs. Mueller? What do you think?" Adelaide's voice a syrupy concoction pouring all over me and clogging up my ears.

"Yes, that's fine," I say. I have no idea what I'm agreeing to, but I've learned to smile and nod and make the best of my lapses.

Adelaide's plum-colored mouth curves faintly. "I'm so glad you feel that way. The main house is uninhabitable. Plaster dust everywhere, you see, and the workmen—" She lowers her voice. "They might not give you the respect you deserve. What man could resist watching such a pretty young woman through a wall of plastic sheeting? May as well be washing up out in the yard. We'll do a full tour in the morning. I presume you're tired after your travels. Everything you need is in the guest house. They've all been remodeled with a full bath. Owen will show you the way."

She dips her head, austere and tight-lipped. "I wouldn't advise you to go traipsing about tonight. There are holes on the property where the plumbers and electricians are working. You might stumble into one in the dark and break an ankle. Owen will fetch you come sunup, all right?"

I nod agreeably. Suddenly I *am* very tired. The heat and humidity are taking a toll. Owen chatters all the way to the "guest house," one of eight wooden structures mounted on bricks about eight hundred yards from the big house. The weathered wooden slats are silver with age. A rocking chair sits on the porch next to a big milk can stuffed with drooping irises. Gingham curtains flank the small window.

My skin crawls. I imagine blood spray on the slats, a stench of sweat, a sharp ache of futility. It's like someone putting makeup on a skeleton and making it do a two-step. Adelaide has stabled me like a horse, and I'm going to spend the night in a fucking slave cabin.

"Come on in." Owen smiles, holding the door wide for me. The walls have been plastered and papered with a cheery floral print. An iron-framed bed with a chenille counterpane and a profusion of decorative pillows fills half the space. There's a wooden dresser with a washbasin and pitcher, a porcelain chamber pot (stuffed with fake flowers), an electric teakettle, two mugs, and a few teabags and sugar packets in a basket.

Owen shifts nervously, loitering in the doorway like some damned bellhop awaiting a tip. I raise my eyebrows at him.

"I read your dissertation online, you know? 'Cathedrals of Light'? The one about windows? It shaped my application essay to GSU, so I just wanted to say how much I appreciated it."

I grunt, abashed. "Thank you. That's very nice to hear."

He flushes, pink on pink, and retreats, leaving me alone with my thoughts. Not-so-nice ones. Try as I might, I cannot stop dwelling on Lance and Marcella. Their affair has polluted my brain, spreading out to taint every memory of my marriage. I run through the rosters of our acquaintances, professional peers, and Lance's friends, asking myself: "Her too? What about her? How many times? How many women?" Eventually, I'll have to incorporate this new injury into my arsenal of scars, but until I can bear hearing the elaborations he'll create to avoid responsibility for the betrayal, I will play possum to the truth.

However tired I am, I know I won't sleep well. Emilie's sad story is still fresh in mind, and Belle Rive feels haunted. Adelaide warned me to stay put but I'm antsy, constrained by these old walls bandaged up in gingham, paint, and wainscoting. The construction crews are long gone, along with Adelaide Randolph, Owen, and anyone else working on the property. I shudder, realizing just how alone I am here, how vulnerable. But outside my door the deepening twilight sweetens the cooling air, and thin vaporous veils drift overhead. Crickets play mourning songs, drawing bows across their violin strings with a melancholy air. A few lights blink and buzz along the road, but the rest of the plantation lies in darkness.

There is still enough light to navigate by, and I push through an oblique density of air, stepping over hillocks of dirt and rillets of water dribbling from a thick, black garden hose. The cane fields are gone, except for about half an acre planted to set the scene. Sagging uninhabited on its low rise, Belle Rive resembles a demented old granny, dolled up and lipsticked, rolled out to join a party in which she cannot participate. Strings and ground stakes mark off various parcels of earth. In the field behind the house, a stark, neglected patch of rusty-looking weeds juts up through a jumble of dusty glass reflecting flashes of moon and stars. Suddenly I recognize myself to be in a graveyard of sorts—here lies the ruined orchidarium, just as detailed in Emilie's letters—Isidore, ranting and smashing, terrorizing his own hopes and ambitions. Something crunches underfoot—a litter of discarded snakeskins and skeletons horribly heaped together as if collected by unseen hands.

Am I cold? Why do my limbs quiver so?

Must shake the clanking of chains, the songs and shouts, agonized screams rising from tormented mouths.

No, stop it. Imagining terrible things. Focus instead on the factual details, Belle Rive's looming bulk. Far fields whispering in the night, tittering trees, river lapping at the bank like a lion licking blood from a carcass. I'm drawn to the house, this feast of history laid out for my savoring. Run my fingers along the wooden veranda railings, feeling the layers of paint and subtle inconsistencies in the hand-hewn pillars. The wide double doors have been removed. Thick, milky plastic flaps in the gap—the fluttering lid in a sleeping eye. Myself a tiny Jonah lost inside the body of this enormous creature. Planks and timbers creak and shift as it breathes, absorbing the irritation of my intrusive presence in its gut.

Gentleman's parlor, ballroom, sewing room, or library perhaps. An indoor kitchen left over from some twentieth-century occupants with a gas stove and 1950s icebox. I can tell most of this by feel. A thin string of lights hangs in the main hall, and their wan yellow glow settles on various surfaces, deepening the shadows. Two stairs are missing.

Am I in Belle Rive, or a house of dreams? For the staircase seems to sway beneath my tread as I go upstairs and the house stirs from its slumber and widens its throat in a cavernous yawn.

An elusive, teasing whiff of perfume lures me down inky hallways, where I peer into empty bedrooms saturated in cool blue moonlight. One has a bay window set with panes of rippled glass, another opens through a closet into a second bedroom—Isidore and Emilie's marital suite? Another set of stairs, narrower, steeper, leads to the third floor. Is this Isidore's private room, this lonely hole tucked under the gables where cobwebs blanket the windowpanes and the cherry tobacco scent of heliotrope lingers in this dusty haven? It's warmer up here—must've been stifling in summer, but I imagine that this is where he came to hide from ranting Floriane or to escape M. Bilodeau's irritating demands, the sight of slaves toiling in the fields and Albert's back, flayed raw from a whipping. Where he did "unspeakable violence" to himself.

From the window, I can see the gray streak of river and distant, twinkling lamps. I feel as removed from my own life as I am from those lights. They are glimmers of activity and humanity blinking through a silent, lonely fog. I stand outside of myself, watching me watch me. The emotion I thought would come has not. I feel nothing, but feeling nothing is like being dead. Am I dead? Here in the dark, alone and forgotten, I have no body, no soul. I'm a creature carved from ice, and when the morning sun rises, I shall melt into puddles and evaporate.

Slide my fingernail into the wound, reopening it. Digging deeper, pushing through bands of muscles, veins slippery against the pad of my fingers. Two in. Three. Sweat beads on my skin. Cold waves of nausea break against my shores. I see myself look down at the blood falling to the floor. There—sensation. *Pain.* I am alive.

OWEN KNOCKS ON the cabin door and calls my name. Heat collects in pockets of skin and sheets, and I roll over, groaning and grappling for my phone. 7:00 a.m. Too fucking early.

Owen knocks again, his voice lost in the grating rumble of machinery as the Caterpillars grind into gear, engines revving. Finally, he goes away. Irked at being rushed, I rise and dress, careful to cover my wound with the large Band-Aids I brought and a long-sleeved cotton blouse. Owen is sitting on the tiny porch when I emerge twenty minutes later.

I'm a good actress, and play the part of visiting scholar well, exploring the grounds with Adelaide and two others from the Foundation, offering my opinion and answering questions with professional calm.

Later, the five of us drive in two cars to New Orleans and eat dinner at a lavish Brazilian churrascaria where a "wine angel" wearing a harness ascends a bar three stories high, pirouetting midair as she fetches wine from the top shelves.

We are all so polite and charming. Only Owen looks nervous and out of place, young and eager to please. His visible nerves strengthen my own. At one point, when he jumps into the conversation offering an ill-timed bon mot—and Tameka, the Foundation's interior designer, snickers—I catch his eye and wink. Maybe because he seems younger than his age or because I'm mourning the slow death of my own parental role, I feel motherly toward him. We are allies.

Tameka is very pretty and fashionable, with fabulous teeth and dark, glowing skin. I envy women like this, confident and genetically gifted, steadily working their way toward a picture-perfect life. She is everything I am not. I wonder if Lance would fancy her and quickly shake the thought away, pouring yet another glass of heady red wine.

"So, Lydia," she begins, pointedly watching my wine glass fill. "Any plans while you're here? Have you been to Bourbon Street yet?"

"Pfft!" Adelaide sniffs. "She'll learn more from staying at Belle Rive! Bourbon Street is for tourists, idiots, and drunks."

"Isn't that what New Orleans is famous for?" Kevin, a developer of indeterminate age and ethnic identity, cocks a bushy black eyebrow.

"Maybe to someone from Boston, like you. You believe we're all about witch doctors, vodou and *zonbis*, chicken foot charms and blood sacrifice! Too many fools tramping up the graveyard to pray to Mama Marie to cure their toothache or win the lotto." Adelaide grimaces, stabbing at a chunk of meat in front of her. "You come here to drink yourselves senseless on 99-cent hurricanes and spew vomit on historic buildings. French Quarter? Fool's Quarter, more like!"

Tameka laughs gleefully, flashing a flirty grin at Kevin. Owen has resigned himself to silent nonparticipation in this conversation, preferring to study the wine angel's midair acrobatics.

"Really? I thought it was all about prostitutes." Kevin amuses himself, oblivious to Adelaide's criticism. She is all about history, beauty, and presentation. Kevin only cares about the bottom line and whether or not Belle Rive's reconstruction will prove profitable. He's already pressured Adelaide to start booking weddings for the following summer.

"What about you, Lydia?" Tameka seems to have a particularly childish desire to annoy me. "Will you make a wish to Mama Marie?"

"I wouldn't know what to ask for." I sense that I am being made fun of, but also that I may be (again) paranoid.

"Oh, I don't know," Tameka trills. "Fame and fortune. True love." Again, she grins at Kevin, blinding us all with her fabulous smile. Those perfect teeth snip through a peeled carrot like she's biting the finger off a baby.

True love. Suddenly, my face grows hot and tears pool in my eyes. She knows. Even as I know that this is foolish, a part of me is watching from outside myself, seeing all the labels I've acquired flare in neon ink. Crazy. Victim. Lonely. Unloved. I've always found it interesting that there's a specific word for a man whose wife has cheated on him—cuckold—yet none for a woman whose husband has cheated on her, as if his infidelities were so trivial and their effects so harmless that it didn't even merit naming.

Adelaide "tsk tsks." "I doubt Mrs. Mueller is superstitious enough to believe urban legends like that one. How would she be able to sift through the remains of old buildings full of stories if she believed in ghosts?" She raises her hand, signaling a waiter.

An attractive man costumed as a gaucho sails over, brandishing masses of steaming, oily flesh impaled on skewers—barnyards full of carnage—red duck, fatty goose, chicken, six different cuts of beef, pork tenderloin, glistening bacon, and veal. The dining room is redolent with odors of burned blood. Singed hair, smoke, and dripping fat, popping in the flames. He wields an expert knife, shaving off thin slices of beef with quivering pink centers onto our plates.

A scream cuts the air and Owen gasps. The wine angel dangles fifteen feet above the tile floor, fumbling with the straps on her harness. It's over in a flash. She drops to the floor with a thud and a crunch that makes everyone wince. Bartenders and waiters throw down glasses and trays to run toward her. Diners rise from their seats, straining for a glimpse and dialing their phones, making simultaneous calls to 911.

Adelaide lays a bundle of cash on the table and gestures for us to leave. "Maybe it's a warning," she says. "Mama Marie doesn't like us talking about her, making promises she can't keep."

THAT NIGHT, MY sleep is tortured, grim. Is it the fallen wine angel, the talk of vodou curses at dinner, or the swelling heat that the night doesn't alleviate, leaving my clothes sticky and my wound itching? My dreams are chaotic, filled with shape-shifting monsters who chew on my hands with short, pointed teeth. I walk the dreadful halls of that house, trapped within its nightmarish labyrinth of empty rooms where wallpaper peels in moldy strips and the discarded belongings of former occupants clutter the floor. Unmade beds sag. Faded clothing litters the chairs, but a glass half-full of water sits on a nightstand, waiting to be drunk. In every space, I'm an intruder.

Drawn again to the room where the séance continues. The medium's droning commands echo through pipes, vents, and walls. "Come to us, Spirit! Show yourself!" But her voice is different now, a confident, whiskey voice. "Papa Legba, open the gates!" Three loud knocks vibrate the walls. "Old Man Legba, open the gates!" The cut I made on my arm falls open like a startled jaw, showing fleshy rolls of wet pink membrane. Slicing through my own meat, my fingernails catch on something and I dig it out, frantic. An emerald as large as a beetle. Blood pulses, spurts, fountains. There is no air to breathe. I inhale my own blood and choke on it.

Clawing my way out of that nightmare, I wake gasping and sweat-soaked. I have been summoned. I answered the call, and my spirit is no longer my own.

OWEN IS MY constant companion for the next three days. He trails me on my perambulations through the house, asking questions, taking notes. I like his company—quietly, but not intrusively, masculine. He's a good-hearted boy. Again, I feel the pang of Hackett's absence. We've texted a few times since I've been away, but he hasn't asked any probing questions.

I have to consider what will happen to us, to me, if Lance leaves me. Would Hackett choose to stay with his father? How would I manage on my own? I've always been afraid of living alone. The nuances of my various manias deepen and expand without the presence of others to check them. Although I grouse about being ignored, I am usually the one who removes myself. My insecurities are rooted in the paranoia and anxiety I have always struggled to keep at bay, and I must remind myself that I can be emotionally color-blind—seeing only stark patterns and not the variant shades of warmth that enliven my experiences. My family is my light in this world. My husband, my son—their love encircles me like a life ring. Without it, I'd surely drown in my own dark seas.

Electrical problems at Belle Rive stall our work for a day while the sparking old wiring is ripped out and replaced. The power will be off for hours, and the heat feels unbearable. This is Owen 's first visit to New Orleans, and he begs me to accompany him on a tour to explore the French Quarter and Garden District. Together, we drive into the city in his rental car, my eyes gobbling up every sight. Though I know that very little in this landscape appears as Isidore would have seen it, I feel that I'm gazing back through time to the days when the traffic on this country road consisted of horses and buggies. Before there were black power lines, dumpy little country gas stations, and pickup trucks gathered in the yards of weather-beaten clapboard houses. When the cane stood tall in the now empty fields, and canopies of giant oak hung lower to the ground.

With the others, we traipse through post-Katrina streets dilapidated or pristine, our tour guide spouting his patter in a jolly, booming voice. Scramble on and off the tour bus snapping photographs, posting and uploading every image for the benefit of friends back home. (Well, at least Owen does. I have none. I text a few photos to Hackett, who responds with "Cool!" and a thumbs-up emoji.) Owen and I are companionably quiet, our focus attuned to moldings, eaves, sloping gables, bowed verandas, and the various intricacies of wrought-iron balconies.

The bus slogs its way down long, dusty lanes. Spanish moss dangles from the tree limbs to trail against our windows. Feathery green manes of resurrection fern sprout from the oaks, and profusions of waxy pink blossoms adorn the sprawling magnolia trees.

I realize that I haven't eaten for a very long time. My head aches with a subtle pain both fuzzy and sharp. I am disoriented—gyral. The cloying humidity presses in and I'm relieved when we stagger from the coach into the shade of an overgrown turnaround beneath a street sign for Metairie Road. Everyone stretches, murmuring and shaking out their legs, making way for an old woman draped in layers who drags a battered shopping cart through the throng.

Owen offers me a snack bar from his pack, but as he holds it out to me, the woman thrusts her face before mine. It's wrinkled up into a ball like a scrunched-up paper sack; her slack lips gape and sputter. "Daughter, you home!" She grins wildly, showing puckered gums. "Why you been gone so long?" She kneads my arms with knobby fingers. "L'eau va toujours à la rivière, chou." Tapping her gray, cobwebby head, she winks a glaucous eye.

Thinking more quickly than I, Owen asks her, "Tell me, granny, what do you mean?"

"Water always run to the river." She chortles, snatching the snack bar from his hand and pushing past another knot of tourists.

Something crunches under my foot. I look down, my low heel impaling a crispy snakeskin. Owen steps on the tail and I shake it free, feeling queasy. Only when I turn around does the clear bright pane of my sanity shatter, for we stand before the strange, ever-shifting house I visit in my dreams. Gray paint peeling in strips, its dusty black shutters frame tall, lace-curtained windows. Double balustrade supported by blistering Ionic columns, a green painted door with a black metal knob. The air shimmers weirdly. My ears ache with the cicadas' swelling tympani and as if summoned, my gaze fastens upon a small, octagonal window on the third floor. I see the lace-garbed figure of Emilie's beautiful Mulatress, Petite Marie—the woman in my dreams of the séance—pull back the lace and peer down at me, her plush mouth curving into a grin from which drips a trail of crimson slime.

"Lydia, they're leaving without us." Owen shakes my arm and the vision evaporates. The rest of our group trails off down the sidewalk as the tour guide blathers on about the historic neighborhood. It's 85 degrees outside but I'm shivering.

"Come on," he says kindly, latching his arm through mine. "I heard there's a lunch waiting for us at one of the houses on the tour." Allowing myself to be led away, I turn back for another glance at that high octagonal window. No face appears.

Floating outside my body, I watch "Lydia" perform. She is careful, adept, and conscientious. She asks all the right questions, though her voice is sometimes stilted. She takes meticulous notes and photographs everything within sight. Adelaide seems to like her, and Owen watches her with the adoring gaze of a puppy dog. She is even polite to Tameka, though the girl's veiled barbs cause Lydia to absently reach for her wounded arm and run a finger along the pad of her bandages. I watch her smile and act her way through meetings and luncheons. It is a marvel that she keeps her secrets so well. I would think that her bad blood would seep between her cracks, turn her skin mauve and violet. I would think that poison would pool at her feet—but it does not.

Her job concluded, she packs up, bids goodbye to Tameka, Adelaide, and Belle Rive. Owen drives her into New Orleans. She wants to spend the afternoon wandering around the city, she says. Photographing the ornate French Quarter balconies, strolling along Dauphine and St. Anne Streets under the arch into Congo Square. She circles back, dragging her rolling suitcase behind her, sweat dribbling down her temples, between her breasts, and beneath her arms, making transparent patches on her long-sleeved shirt. She passes restaurants, shops, the Voodoo Spiritual Temple, and a leather bar. Her feet lead her down Basin Street to St. Louis Cemetery No. 1, and she pays for a tour. She slogs along between the tipsy crypts slouching into oblivion. Crumbling bricks, soft as wet chalk. Black-streaked marble tombs besmirched by centuries of weather. Angels with muddy faces and broken wings staring blindly at some yearned-for visitor.

A young man and woman break away from the group, giggling. Ahead, Lydia watches the woman laugh, calling to her lover. Her voice is an assault. Too joyous, feminine, and high-pitched for this most somber of scenes. Her boyfriend leaps out from a tomb behind her, moaning

"Brains! Braiiins!" She squeals as her knees buckle and she slaps him, falling into his arms, laughing.

They make her sick.

She tells herself it's the heat throbbing from a low sun hanging in a sky the color of flames. It is the casual death all around her. She wants her husband, but he is far away and she is alone. A stranger in this strange land.

If only Lance were here! She could focus on the texture of his sleeve, the pattern of hairs on his head. Distract herself with his words. Fold him around her, shield herself from this macabre onslaught with his strong body. But he loves another. The cord's been cut. Fluid drips and spreads.

She imagines the desiccated corpses stuffed in bags and crammed into the crypts that seem to tower over her, as if she's swallowed the red pill, nibbled a magic mushroom and shrunk to Thumbelina size. She can't see the sky overhead for her tunnel vision. Her suitcase is filled with iron weights, so she abandons it and begins to run. Cemetery maze. It's worse than treading over a burial ground because here the dead need simply sit up and throw back the lids and doors of their tombs to free themselves. Skeletons clambering out to enclose her in their bony bower. The spirits will crawl inside through her cut and take over her body. She panics. Trips over the rim of a crypt, stumbles through piles of offerings—bright flowers, coins, cigarettes, seven-day candles, trinkets, and colorful beads—and collides with a tall white headstone. Her shoulder smashes into the stone and rattles her teeth.

My head pounds. The world contracts and expands around me. I'm on my own. Lost my suitcase, somehow, I don't recall. Spiders scuttle over the ground. Rats skitter and slink just out of sight, stealing candy from gravesites and scurrying back to their filthy nests.

The fall jars me back to reality and frees my tears. They drip, fat and slimy, into the dust. I reach for the wall behind me, pushing myself up from the ground. Xs cover the crypt. Big and little scratches and scrawls made with knives, markers, pens, and paint. Wishes blanket Mama Marie's tomb in a snowfall of hope. What do I wish? I think of Tameka, teasing me. Adelaide, scorning the vodou tourists. My bright son, fumbling toward adulthood. My husband of almost two decades, peeling back Marcella's clothes, grunting and groaning, spilling himself inside her. All I want is someone to adore me forever and ever, to crave me as shipwrecked sailors pine for home and rescue, and men lost at sea crave rainwater. To thirst for my kiss as the vampire does virgin's blood and zombies lust for living flesh. To yearn for my touch as martyrs pray for death and reunification with God. Lust to make men brawl for the right to ask my name—Lydia. I will be the yawning, sucking vortex that none can escape. Narcotic enchantress, demon lover, succubus. I will be the addiction and the remedy.

No one is near to see me kneel in the dirt to muddy the knees of my linen pants, roll up my sleeve, tear a sticky bandage from my arm, poke my finger through crusting yellow pus and purple scabs. Searing pain floods my body with opiates, bliss and agony. Bright red finger paints *XXX* on the crypt door. Mama Marie hears me. I hope she will answer.

So DISORIENTING to travel. Feels like jumping in and out of dreams. New Orleans was a grubby, foggy nightmare from which I have awakened, alarmed by the unfamiliarity of my own surroundings. But the trip blew a bubble between Lance and me, and that space is filled with radio silence. We hug awkwardly. We cling desperately. I cannot bear the sight of him, just as I cannot drag my gaze from his. I am always searching for some sign of his monstrosity but find nothing more than an ordinary face, beloved and care-worn, a child's lovey with the satin rubbed off. We swim through anger as thick as pudding. Fractured but functioning, our lives lumber on as before.

WORK IS THE frame that contains the chaos. It is my only focus and my only escape until the day dwindles down and sleep comes, reluctantly, bringing disturbing dreams that daylight smears away, leaving no clear image. I plod through my papers, writing dull little descriptions of nineteenth-century building techniques, trying to make the addition of the new kitchen in 1849 exciting.

It is evening and the peace that twilight and moonrise usually bring evades me. Lance is out and my son is cloistered in his room, as usual. They have no purpose for me, I have become a ghost haunting my own house.

I pour another drink, add ice, strip down to my skivvies, and tuck myself into bed. The packet of Emilie's letters sits on my nightstand, a treasure trove of secrets. I've waited to read Isidore's journal, too caught up in my own internal agonies to focus on it, yet also antagonized by the thought of his words inside my head. To read it will be to deliberately expose myself to his pathology. His madness. (I've got plenty of my own, thank you very much.)

But even when sealed in a plastic box, Isidore's book emits a fusty perfume that is both repugnant and enthralling. Noting the fine-grained leather and flaking gold leaf, I open the box (releasing the genie) and take the journal in hand. Binding thread disintegrates and powders the bedspread. Again, the subtlest cherry tobacco hint of heliotrope evanesces from the rumpled leaves as I press my nose into its open seam to collect traces of century-old cologne. Inked in an increasingly cramped and splotchy hand, its later pages freckled by pale brown splotches of dried blood, the paper leaves a residue on my fingers. Without thinking, I place them in my mouth and suck it off.

Like me, Isidore has been abandoned in the labyrinth of his own capricious, untrustworthy mind. We are two of a kind, him and I. Serenaded by the autumn wind whistling through the chimneys and rafters, I fill my mouth with burning liquor, hold the old book open across my breast, and plunge into the shadows of a long-dead world.

The Private Diaries of
Isidore Saint-Ange
Belle Rive Plantation, Louisiana
1851–1854

Aboard the *Olympus*, Liverpool to New Orleans

FRANCE IS BEHIND me. The new continent awaits my embrace and I rush into her arms, eager for her affection. Emilie wrote that the whole of Louisiana Creole society awaits my addition to its ranks, and her enthusiasm and certainty of my favorable reception are dazzling. Emilie's father, Marcel Bilodeau, has written to assure me that my father watches from his perch in the arms of angels, and that he knows his cousin would be delighted to see the family strengthened in this way. My union to Emilie conjoins two branches of one bloodline, and assures that the Saint-Ange ancestral holdings in Boulogne will remain rightfully in possession of Bilodeau descendants, maintained by the profits of its cotton plantation.

I am aggrieved to face the prospect of setting aside my own interests to concentrate more fully on my role of plantation manager, but dear Emilie assures me that there will be time and a place for me to resume my philosophical studies of the natural world soon enough. She has already offered one of the empty slave cabins so that I might transform it into a workshop, but I refused the offer. My practice is confined to paper. She cannot quite conceive that one can be of scientific mind without the accoutrements of vials, beakers, and pipettes. No doubt she fears explosions of caustic chemicals and smoke wafting from beneath my study door. I cannot expect a rural girl, however bright and curious, to understand the masculine nature of metaphysic inquiry.

NEW ORLEANS IS IN SIGHT! Hustle and bustle animate its docks. So unlike Marseilles, yet there are skins of every color visible, from the darkest tobac to the ruddy, crustacean red of burned European flesh. A teeming sprawl of ships of every size and distinction jostle in the harbor while emitting bellows of smoke and steam. Clanging bells and voices compete with the bray of animals. A squalor of vermin scale the ship ropes, and squealing rats cling to and topple from pier posts and buoys. A slaver spills its foul litter of wretched souls, while another spits up white, canvas-wrapped bodies—trussed corpses that bring to mind the larvae of queen ants and bees. Crates, boxes, and barrels filled with every manner of comestible, from tropic pine-apples to Indian tea, line the pier and are shifted into carts on the backs of sweating servants and freed men. All told, it is a scene of both industry and chaos.

I shall soon disembark and begin my new, American life. Pray that this country, this land, will be kind to me.

The Dauphine Orleans, Dauphine St., New Orleans

I put in at a hotel in town to refresh myself before continuing on to the plantation. Heaven forbid that Emilie should first meet her fiancé when he is travel-worn, reeking of shipboard life and the grease of the unwashed hoards! *Ma mère* asserts that one never forgets that first glimpse of one's true love, and it would forever grieve me to have impressed the lasting image of a grubby foreigner in Emilie's mind.

I had intended to depart for Belle Rive yesterday, but calamitous events superseded my travel. It is only today, the smoke from the smoldering remains still darkening the sky, that I can even consider venturing out of doors.

I was taking an afternoon constitutional—for it was so good to extend my legs and get in a brisk stroll after such long confinement on the *Olympus*—and had elected to explore Conti Street, when the temper of the people took a violent change. Masses of American men, boys, and some women gathered and blocked the walkway, raising voices and fists in a hysteria of vengeance. Intent on bloodshed, they surged up Chartres as one body, carrying me along in their midst like a broken tree branch tossed on rushing floodwaters. However detached I was from these events, my horror was genuine. Never have I seen such a demonstration of aggression!

I have since learned that a hostile mob, spurred by news of the execution of a delegate of Americans in Cuba, attacked the offices of the local Spanish consulate and its newspaper. Its coat of arms and flag were torn down and demolished in a frenzy of hatred. To my great misfortune, two men descended upon me and beat me with their fists, sticks, and whatever weapons they could bring to hand. Only my repeated cries of alarm in French eventually extinguished their fury enough to convince them that despite my complection, I have no sympathies with Spain, nor do my veins carry Cuban or Spanish blood. I was knocked about quite a bit and lost my bearings, but managed to slip into a doorway and cling to a column to avoid being pulled along with the rapacious crowd. In time, I made my way back to the Dauphine, requested a bath and tea in my room, and retired behind a locked door.

A calming soak and a meal somewhat restored my vigor, but the City still ferments with a simmering rage. There are numerous wounds on my person where the flesh was bruised or split open, and blood now soils my good vest. Fisticuffs have left their mark upon my jaw, which means a further delay in reaching Emilie. I've dispatched a letter to Belle Rive, informing her that business concerns detain me for another three days but that my affection is with her, as surely as the sun does shine upon her face.

It's unclear what transpired yesterday, but reports from the concierge indicate that the riot continued past sundown, causing much havoc and damage to the homes and businesses of Spanish merchants. Even women and children were not spared the crowd's assault. This sudden descent into brutality fills me with grave concerns about the sanity of Louisiana's people, but human nature proves itself the same in every situation—a volatile combination of angel and demon, with neither one ever gaining much mastery for any purposeful length of time.

Presently I find myself feeling rather cloistered in this over-warm room. The river breeze—if one could so call such a humid exhalation of human, animal, and vegetal stink—seems to do nothing but soak into my clothing and make it weigh more heavily upon my skin. I pine for evening's release from this solar brutalism! In the meantime, I shall venture to the dining room to sample a selection of the avocado and citrus sherbets and praline iced creams advertised in the Dauphine's window. If I deem it safe, I'll venture forth once again to survey the mob's damage and perhaps make a few sketches upon my return. Who knows what this night shall bring?

EMILIE SENDS A letter inquiring of my delay and imploring me to allow her to join me at the Dauphine. She desires to bring her lady's maid and take a room on a separate floor so that we may at least dine together and tour the City, but in view of recent events and the general climate of unrest, I have advised her to remain at Belle Rive and assured her that my business, such as it is, will soon be concluded, then I shall spare no haste in making my way to her.

It was with a heavy heart that I dispatched that letter. It seemed to carry an additional weight of subterfuge, for I have not been honest with my betrothed about my doings in town. The horror of my introduction to this barely constrained wilderness was soon supplanted by admiration for the freedoms with which its various people commingle and the wildly astonishing array of languages, foods, nationalities, styles of dress, and mannerisms which assaulted me along Dauphine Street as I made my way toward the French Quarter. What I sought is unclear. Some gentle reminder of home, perhaps, some connexion to the motherland I may not see again in my lifetime, for none know what pleasures or violence await me in this teeming landscape.

As I neared a house of worship, the air swelled with song. Such a glorious music have I never heard before, for its tones were as deep and resonant as bassoons yet swollen with the sweetness of hymns sung by seraphs on high. This music was so unlike any other that has ever touched my ears, it lured me into the gloomy recesses from which it emanated. I followed the music into an oblong courtyard, tidy but congested with profusions of fragrant blossoms. A single door stood open, from which song poured forth.

Just as I paused, perforce to turn my feet and point them toward the street to continue my perambulations, a young woman appeared in the doorway. She had the loveliest face, with a glowing toffee skin and sparkling black eyes complementing plump, moist lips and shining black hair, plaited in mysterious patterns upon her head. Her beauty made my heart pound inside my chest, and I found that I could not move, much less speak, so captivated was I. Her dress was simple to the point of indecency, showing her delicate shoulders, as she wore no supporting garments and none of the frills and fancies currently so fashionable. She offered me a smile and beckoned. I went to her as if spellbound. The heat inside the small church was powerful, but the atmosphere was one of sublime joy. I slipped into a pew beside an elderly man, bent of back and tremorous with palsy, but as I rested my hands upon the rail, he pressed one of his own to mine in a gesture of brotherly welcome. The music, ah, I cannot do it justice! Suffice it to say that the conjoined notes of sorrow and jubilation have stirred something long dormant within me. I accepted the Host when the time came and allowed the priest to offer a blessing on my behalf.

That beauty who first enticed me positioned herself by my side as I departed at the conclusion of the service. She spoke to me with such a thick and confusing accent, it required the full efforts of my concentration to understand her. Her smile said enough. I allowed her to slip her arm through mine, a most daring gesture, and draw me from the churchyard. I followed her lead as we walked through the City's tumult. Thick and damp was the air, and so profuse were the aromas of gardenias, perfumes, human and animal wastes, and by-products of industry that I could scarce draw a breath. I tired quickly but pressed on, much encouraged by the urgings of the sweet princess on my arm.

We arrived at a place I now know as Congo Square. It is on Sundays, here, that slaves, servants, free persons of color, and immigrants of all stripe gather to celebrate their true religion. A sizable crowd had assembled amid an air of general excitement. Musical instruments were apparent—drums of every size, gourds and strings of shells, beaded rattles, and strange, carved horns I have never before seen. Dancers gathered while others cleared space for them. The woman on my arm pressed me tight to her side, and through the thinness of her gown, I felt her seductive flesh yield to me as a down mattress accommodates the weight of a sleeper. The dance began. A few of the performers were entirely unclothed. Others wore stylish costumes in the manner of American Indians—deerskin trousers and beaded chest plates, shells, bells, and dried pods, which made a merry jingle as the dancers moved. Swirling skirts of muslin, gauze, and brightly colored silks, female dancers dipped and swayed between the men, displaying ornately adorned petticoats and profusions of satin ribbon. The heat weighed upon me, perspiring heavily in my lightest summer suit. Velvet is no match for New Orleans weather, and due to the crowd's frivolity and casual attitude toward various states of undress, I was persuaded to remove my jacket and vest.

How I longed to capture the intensities of that ceremony! Such a soul-stirring profundity! Such an energetic expulsion of emotion and sound! If there were a way to forever preserve the music I have heard this weekend for my continued enjoyment, I should surrender the entirety of my estate to possess it. Voices lifted in praise and glory. Drums that echoed my fast-beating heart and its palpitations of fear, excitation, and arousal. A sensual feast of harmony and passion to rival or surpass the most stirring of arpeggios. I felt myself transformed, as if the music itself were a hammer to break open my cautious shell and expose the throbbing marrow of my soul. My princess never once let me go. She shared with me a tonic made of the milk of cocoanut, which, though warm and tinged with a not-unpleasant bitterness, I found refreshing.

As the sun descended, fires were lit and the dances continued well into evening. I could not help but surrender to the madness, swaying upon my feet and nodding my head in time to those ancient rhythms. Time seemed to melt away as if it had no consequence. At last, I became aware of pangs of hunger in my gut, and sensing my discomfort, the woman asked me (or rather, I inferred from her gestures) if I would like to dine. I acquiesced and again allowed myself to be drawn deeper into her enigmatic world.

We arrived at a private home in the French Quarter. A handsome woman I took to be the mother of my guide—for their resemblance was so strong as to be unnerving—greeted me warmly and invited me to freshen myself and join her in the parlor. We two shared a very pleasant conversation *en français*, until I remarked upon the daughter's unusual accent. I inquired if perhaps she had been raised elsewhere or received schooling in a foreign land, whereupon both *maman et fille* erupted with hearty laughter.

"My Marie is a skilled actress and she enjoys playing this little game with newcomers to our town. It's a harmless exercise. You are not offended, I hope?"

Mildly, yes, but one glimpse at the girl's mischievous expression soothed my irritation. I conceded that she was, indeed, a skilled performer.

"It would surprise you to learn what secrets people will offer when they perceive an inequality in social rank or intellectual ability. Marie is my little bird. She flits about collecting interesting stories to entertain her poor mother. I am often plagued by wakefulness and my nights are long and restless ones. It is a harmless occupation."

I agreed and resultingly, we passed a most agreeable evening over a simple supper, rum, and cards, glad as I was that I had not said anything of an intimate or confidential nature. My departure was a difficult one, for I feared never seeing her again and losing the light in those eyes, and so I begged her to see me once more before I left for my new life at Belle

Rive. She agreed, and tonight I lie here trembling in an agony of antici-pation until I can rest my gaze upon her once more.

MY THOUGHTS TURN continually to my old friend Gerald. *Le fol amour* I called him, for he was so consumed with passion for his ladylove that when she married another, he threw himself from the cliffs at Beachy Head. I never understood what drove him to take his life over a woman, for never having experienced a love as fierce as theirs, I could not com-prehend the recklessness of his actions. Now that I have met P'tite Marie (as she bade me call her to distinguish her from her mother), I do feel myself transformed into a rash man who would do anything to secure her favor. Indeed, I hardly slept last night for the fevered pitch of my excitement. My mind raced, my skin felt keenly alive with sensation as I imagined kissing her and making love to that exquisite creature. Then would come the crashingly cold wave of realization that such things could not be possible for me, as I am here only at the behest of the Bilo-deaus. Should I fail to marry Emilie, I will be left penniless in a strange land and cause great distress and embarrassment to our families.

I had finally worked myself into a position of staunch resolve and determined to hire a coach today to take me to Belle Rive, but then, mir-acle of miracles, the concierge came to my room to tell me that a visitor waited in the hotel lobby. I trembled with hope and excitement. Yes, it was P'tite Marie come to bid me farewell. She was even more radiant and lovely than the night before. Her hair unplaited was simply dressed. Long curls coiled over her shoulder, and she wore a gray silk gown trimmed in black lace. We took tea in the hotel dining room. My hand shook so that I spilled cream upon the tablecloth, fascinated and baffled by the intensity of my reaction to her.

I spoke of my longing to comprehend the mysteries of the natural world, its beautiful complexities and shocking contradictions.

P'tite Marie placed her delicate hand on mine, saying, "Because how else are we to understand the complex character of the human heart when we, too, are creatures of the natural world given to the same mys-terious fluxuations?"

"Exactly! And how are we to divine the biological origins of emo-tion from those engineered by the rhythm of the seasons, the influence of electrical impulses or magnetism?"

"Or the supernatural." She, the loveliest of women, gazed at me with the tender and shining eyes of a gentle forest doe, and my heart lurched within my ribs. "Remember, my handsome friend, there are elements and forces that we don't yet have the language to explain. Ancient, primitive energies of the cosmos that resist the rein of our control, like wild horses. How do they figure in your formula?"

It was indeed a most stirring discussion, unlike any I'd experienced, even among my schoolmates and professors. She was a Delphic oracle thrust from the depths of the sacred temple into the light of my adoring gaze.

We spoke with an ease I've never experienced with any man or woman, and in that short meeting I grew to understand the meaning of the term "soul mate." We lingered so long that the serving staff grew speculative and I sensed their eyes upon us. Sadly, I attested myself a man of honor and broke news of my upcoming nuptials to Mademoiselle Bilodeau. I proclaimed no hope of a future for us, and wept inwardly to watch that freshly ignited spark of hope in her lovely gaze grow dim. In silence, I walked with her through the Dauphine's lobby, where her maid sat waiting, and she offered her hand in farewell. I knew I should never again see her, and that I would forever regret my cowardice if I did not take advantage of the moment. Despite the presence of concierge, valets, and her own maid, I boldly flaunted social mores. Taking her chin in my hand, I expressed my devotion with a single kiss and felt the entirety of the world and its cares deliquesce and flow away.

I am reminded of Tennyson's words, "A man had given all other bliss, And all his worldly worth for this, To waste his whole heart in one kiss, Upon her perfect lips." Mightily do I struggle to put her out of my mind! I can only hope that Emilie will prove as attractive and exciting a companion. The lamp grows dim and my eyes burn with fatigue. *Bon soir.*

Belle Rive Plantation

The Bilodeau family does not count patience among its virtues. Yesterday, despite my letters, a coach was sent to fetch me to Belle Rive. The Dauphine's concierge rapped upon my door at quarter-eight to announce that my transport awaited (dashing the hopes that sprang so vividly to the fore). Despite my vexation—for forced, early risings do not improve my morning mood—I was glad for the coach, for it meant I must abandon the sloth that had overtaken me and put myself into the correct frame of mind. A transition from bachelor to betrothed was required. Admittedly, I had been tardy in donning my new role, for I was still shaking off the clinging veils of my introduction to New Orleans' hidden realms.

I was not brutish enough to insist on another night in New Orleans. Doing so would likely repel Emilie's good faith in me by proving myself of hardened heart. She desired my company and I would reward her by delivering my person at her command.

The coachman loaded up my luggage, and within the hour, we were off. I was sorry to leave behind the small gold cross my mother had given me, a family heirloom that had been worn by several generations of Saint-Anges. I searched everywhere in my room, but it was absent. The coach was dusty, with cracked, leather seats. Filth and manure caked its wheels, and the day's pressing heat drew every foetid odor from the gutters. We traveled River Road, following the Mississippi's west bank toward Belle Rive. It was a long and daunting journey. Sweltering heat much unrelieved by breezes, and acres of vegetation dying its natural death, the excitement and energy of the City center waning into a few houses, then fields and farms, swamplands, and the occasional glimpse of a far plantation. Limp of stalk and leaf, the cotton and tobacco fields sagged beneath the fierce sun. Slaves worked the rows, and for the first time, I felt the full horror of America's reliance on the industry of captive Africans. In France, we have our maids and servants, but these are discreet persons who labor quietly and receive pay. Never have I witnessed a grown man strike another upon his bare flesh, as I saw yesterday, one white man breaking a short whip upon the back of one enslaved. They stood by the edge of a dusty inroad while the others, perhaps the slave's family, stood nearby and watched, their manner one of lassitude and slack indifference. It shocked me at first, to think anyone so unmoved by the sight of such discord—the master beat his slave as a drunken farmer would whip a mule, with wild strokes and cursing. But were it me, I should not want to show my fear, lest it draw that wrath upon my own head.

Belle Rive was a surprise. Emilie had described it to me in her letters, but to see it for myself, its columns shining like glorious pillars of light, left me quite breathless. The style is Greek Revival, rebuilt after much of the original West Indies structure burned down in a fire some years ago, when Emilie was just a child. The house sits astride a gentle rise that slopes up from the river, its lengthy lane lined with young oaks. The land surrounding it is a shining emerald sea of indigo plants and snowy cotton bolls. Rolling up the road in our carriage, it was easy to imagine the tall, shading canopy that the oaks will provide in their maturity, and to envision my own happy *enfants* romping across the long grass, catching toads at the riverbank and dancing across the lawn on dusky summer nights.

How long she had waited for me I cannot imagine, but Emilie was there on the veranda, her skirts pressed and perfect, not a hair out of place, a smile upon her lips. The carriage stopped and the coachman opened my door. I descended, feeling like a god coming down from his mountain for the adoring looks she sent my way. She is effortlessly genuine and as sweet as a jar of honey. It is not her fault that I find her looks a touch common and her fashion outdated. She compensates for the snubness of her nose with a wide, rosy mouth and long, tapering fingers. She smelled of camellias, and when I took her soft hand in my own, I found her skin to be silken against my lips. Her touch is light as flower petals. Her manner is slow and deliberate. I should not think she walks across a room without carefully considering the placement and pacing of each step she takes. I had a moment of paralyzing worry, when I realized that this was to be my bride. That I should wake up next to that body, look upon that face every morning for the rest of my life. But I think I shall not mind the nose so much if my eyes are closed when we kiss.

Emilie's maman, Floriane, rushed from the house, scolds boiling on her tongue. Why had Emilie not waited inside? She should not stand on the porch like a housemaid! Emilie, whom I expected to buckle beneath her mother's corrections, merely brushed her aside. She is made of sterner stuff than it appears.

The women made much fuss over me. Monsieur Bilodeau and his son, Prosper, were away on a business venture, leaving the ladies to run the house in their absence. I must say, they man the place like army generals. Even temperate Emilie brooks no quarter from her staff. Unlike Mme. Bilodeau, Emilie's commands are softened with twin helpings of flattery and praise. Need one thank the house slave for making the doorknobs shine or the cook for preparing a sufficient meal? *Non.* But Emilie does, further testament to the kindliness of her nature.

My first night passed swiftly in the company of the Bilodeau *famille*. I have been given a guest room on the first floor, and after the wedding, Emilie and I will take a suite on the second floor. She could not resist showing it to me—a handsome bedchamber with adjoining dressing rooms. I commented on the luxuriousness of the four-poster bed and Emilie turned quite scarlet. I hope she will not prove a wife who has little taste for lovemaking. The penitence of a lifetime of silent, dutiful rutting fills me with dread.

Today, we toured the grounds and watched the slaves work. I witnessed no beatings such as the one I had seen earlier, and when I commented upon this to Emilie she remarked that she cannot bear the screams and so does not allow such punishments on her property. Mme. Bilodeau, however, shuns this sentiment. She is positively Old Testament in her discipline. It is she who determines which of her properties is to be sold, whether to allow them to marry, and how long children can remain with their families. She has stated that there is a lame eight-year-old boy she intends to sell at the slave market next month because "he eats more than he's worth." Her words rang in my head throughout our luncheon of fried oysters, lobster and potatoes in cream sauce, corn cakes, celery, pickles, cold ham, and calf's-foot jelly, and something called Tipsy Parson, a rather simple trifle of custard, almonds, and sponge cake lavished in brandy.

"It makes no sense to feed one that doesn't earn his way," spouted Mme. Bilodeau, heaping another quivering tower of cake onto her plate. I bit my tongue. Emilie seems all too aware of her mother's hypocrisy, for again, a scarlet flush inflamed her cheeks.

Later, when Mme. Bilodeau had retired, Emilie took the opportunity to knock upon my bedchamber door and offer apologies.

"I know that my sentiments are considered strange in the South," she said. "Abolition can scarce gain a foothold in such slippery soil."

She clung to my door, the color in her eyes rimmed with wide ribbons of white. She is small yet so certain of herself! Anxiety put a wrinkle in her nose, and I begged her to calm herself.

"My dear," said I, "we share those sentiments. We abhor slavery in France. Those in the French colonies succumb to economic pressure from the English and the Americans and cry 'tradition' to justify the outrage of keeping humans like animals."

"Traditions change." She smiled faintly. "Unlike people. Forgive her, won't you? She'll cling to anything that permits her to carry on as she likes. We shall be different, you and I."

Emilie met my gaze, her own strong and unblinking. Our brief correspondence has been inadequate. She is nothing quite as I imagined. Less—and yet so much more. Her skin has scarce the color of a sugar biscuit to match golden eyes which hold but a flickering shadow of depth. Her hair holds a curl well enough, but she could slip unnoticed into Society and none should ever suspect her heritage. I hope that Emilie's allure will be sufficient to eradicate from my mind the sterling vision and memory of that eloquent and mesmerizing woman, P'tite Marie, for it will require a hard scrubbing to wash away the impression she has left behind.

I SEEK TEMPORARY refuge in my study before the madness begins. Despite Emilie's sweetness and the welcome demonstrated by the Bilodeaus, I cannot help but tremble at what awaits me. My fate rests not upon the completion of the marriage ceremony, but the satisfactory fulfillment of my conjugal demands.

Speaking privately in his study, M. Bilodeau jested that should I perform badly, displease himself, his wife, or his daughter or fail to provide heirs, he should have no qualms about selling me off at slave auction. "An elegant Mulatto like you, French-speaking and gentlemanly, would fetch quite a price!" The knowledge that this jovial man conceals such menace in his soul leaves me uneasy. "But I am a free man!" I asserted. M. Bilodeau laughed heartily at my consternation but departed with a glower. We are both independent men, and while M. Bilodeau enjoys the freedoms of one traveling life's road "incognegro," African blood courses through our veins, however watered the Bilodeau strain—yet he is so far distanced from feelings of kinship with the slaves he owns that he may as well be a white man. Certainly, the line of his African affection is so lightly drawn as to be erased.

Emilie takes every conceivable opportunity to pull me aside and beg my confidence. Each intrusion begins and ends with an apology. Would I prefer quail or partridge? Which fish pleases me most? Have I enough water in the decanter in my room, and is the wine too sweet for me? Her endless queries are neither invigorating nor tiring, but I do hope that she shall soon learn my likes and preferences, so that each decision need not become a matter of such weighty consultation. When not hanging upon my arm like a climbing vine, she is occupied with her sewing and reading, thank God. I have little interest in the whole affair but for the wedding night and finding out what awaits me beneath those layers of petticoats.

THE WEEKS SINCE the wedding have been so occupied with travel, talk, and merriment that I have had not a moment to myself. At last, Emilie has departed for an afternoon tea with her Maman's friend, Madame La Foret, and Floriane's lady's maid, Lavinia, and I am glad to be alone. We have been fussed and fretted over at every turn, obliged as we were to bring Lavinia and Mainard on our Honey Moon. Mainard is a free man, and I have been sore tempted to inquire why he chooses to remain in employ of a slaveholder where so many of his brethren are treated worse than dogs while he is allowed but one afternoon off per month, and his allowance is not enough for him to purchase a new coat, much less one of the cream cakes on display in the patisserie window adjacent to our hotel. Emilie and I spoke at some length about the seemingly bleak futures of free men such as Mainard (whom they deem a body servant, not valet as I do), and are both aggrieved that there is little chance of his saving up enough to depart Belle Rive. For the moment, we are united in giving them fair treatment, as much as is possible.

Emilie's absence brings me welcome escape from public purview. As delightful as she has proven to be, I feel myself to be under constant scrutiny by everyone around us. I sense myself assessed by the family attending our wedding, by the slaves and servants over whom I am now master, by the members of society who control the gentlemen's clubs and houses of leisure, even the tobacconist when we stopped to purchase cheroots. All eyes linger upon me as if judging my fitness to be married, and I cannot help but twist like a bait worm beneath so many stares.

Emilie is amused to discover me somewhat bashful in crowds. She takes evident pleasure in speaking for the both of us. Marriage has transformed her! Gone is the blushing girl. In her place, a curiously attentive woman, quick to laugh and full of fire. I am beyond pleased.

Pleased as well that she has shown herself to be a receptive and loving mate, eager to accept my tutelage and pacing, but not devoid of admirable feminine traits. She possesses the most modest and demure of airs—she is a lady of the highest caliber—and yet did not disappoint me as I feared she might, being too proper and religious to embrace me with wifely vigor.

Tomorrow we venture to the public gardens in New Orleans so that I may make drawings of the humble specimens contained in the modest glass house there. (It takes my every effort to quash my optimism that I may catch a glimpse of P'tite Marie while there—even if from afar or fleetingly as she turns a corner, it will be enough to nourish my gaze, which is starved of her.) There is also a collection of Old and New World orchid species inhabiting the conservatory, as well as a superlative range of aroids, *heliconia*, *Palmaceae*, and ginger plants. It is my hope to persuade M. Bilodeau of the value in growing rare equatorials on the plantation, those which may be of botanical and medicinal value, on a small plot of land, east of the cane fields. There the light is open and fierce, and were I allowed to manage my own garden, I should be content knowing that my specimens would thrive beneath an undiluted sun, in air viscous with moisture. My needs are few and my pleasures small. I hope I shall be quite happy with Emilie, and she with me and meanwhile, smother any thought of P'tite Marie and the letter I promised to write but did not.

I AM A married man. Daily, I must remind myself of this fact. The peaceful existence which I anticipated has been disrupted by the reappearance of the one who so effortlessly captured my heart in New Orleans. Emilie had persuaded me to attend an Independence Day ceremony at the home of M. Bilodeau's acquaintance, the Englishman Mr. Badcocke. All was enjoyable and splendid until I spied a vision of loveliness in white lace—P'tite Marie.

Seeking her favor, Badcocke leered and groveled, singing his offensive tunes and making a nuisance of himself all the while. How my heart ached to see her so abused! But I remained silent, torn by yearning to seek her out but restrained by etiquette and the wish to avoid wounding Emilie.

P'tite Marie was not to be put off, however. She sought out my wife and struck up a conversation as if to deliberately needle me. She caught my eye and volumes passed between us in some unspoken communiqué before Emilie squealed at some new sight—a little dog wearing top hat and bowtie—and tugged on my arm to lead me away. I cast down my gaze, thus breaking the link between myself and P'tite Marie. When I looked again, she had vanished.

I pack my temptation into a small box and bind it tight with string. It must never be opened. It would release a love so profound, so savage, that none would recover from its wounds.

EMILIE AND I have entertained a steady parade of visitors and well-wishers since the wedding. Her parents' friends, mostly, or companions and classmates from her school days. My wife proves herself to be a charming and delightful companion in every way. She is quick-witted, curious, and thoughtful. My relief at the unfolding discovery of her person is great. The fears I harbored during the long journey from France—that she would be shrewish and simpleminded, falsely gay and shrill of voice, burdensome or overattentive, sticking to me like a tangle of furze, or that she be too repulsive to behold for any grave length of time—each of these notions is happily disabused.

But when not taking tea or being regaled with stories and advice about marital and business matters, I am dragged 'round Belle Rive to witness and learn every aspect of managing cotton, sugarcane, slaves, and merchant exchanges. There are account books to pore over, columns of figures to memorize, names and histories to learn, almanacs to consult, plantings and harvests to be logged, and a plethora of other discrete details requiring my rapt attention, memorization, and repetition. M. Bilodeau is exasperatingly fond of crying out "Écoutez et répétez!" after each of his pronouncements. I begin to feel quite the tropical macaw riding about on a pirate captain's shoulder, my only purpose to serve as his echo.

Emilie's older brother, Prosper, is a buffoon. Glib and full of bluster, spouting his insane and ridiculous ideas, swanning about Belle Rive in preposterous clothing—always with a flask in his hand—he is quick to laugh but just as quick to anger when events don't match his expectations. Absolutely his mother's son, Prosper takes a childish pleasure in goading and undercutting me whenever his father is away. Clearly M. Bilodeau sees qualities in me that his son lacks and makes no bones about his displeasure with Prosper's indulgent ways.

There is respite in the moonlit nights as I lie beside my bride, exploring the terrain of the body she is eager to offer into my hands. Marriage is so much more than I anticipated. So long has my head absorbed the melancholic musings of my elders, naturally I expected my wife to be like theirs, bitter about fulfilling her duty and offering as much pleasure as one would find rubbing up against an old, dry log. I had imagined that I would be confined to the occasional, reluctant acquiescence to my beastly desires and roll over after, sated but filled with repulsion for sullying the bed sheets, as if I had trampled a fragrant flower garden with my boots.

But she is tender and loving, eager to run her fingers along my skin and through my hair, and accept my kisses and advances. The shock of it increases my ardor, and she is content to oblige me as often as I place my hand on her belly or press kisses to her short neck. There is much affection between us, and we have become companionable friends. It is no fault of mine that the memory of P'tite Marie springs to mind during our lovemaking, intensifying my lustful sensations.

ALL CONTINUES TO progress at a rapid pace. M. Bilodeau appears very keen to ingratiate me with his business associates, local merchants, his overseer, Ramón the Spaniard, and those most vital to the functioning of this land. We spend much of the day circulating about the grounds, inspecting the plants for blight and signs of infestation. He hopes to educate me to know by touch whether a specific stalk or leaf is over- or under-watered, burned by sun, or ravaged by insects or fungi. I nod and give him every particle of my attention, but after hours in this clinging, damp heat, my mind is prone to wander and I sense my neck bend as my chin droops toward my chest. I make a most earnest effort to store all the information provided in the lockbox of my skull, but by the following morning, I find that it has evaporated.

My books and other materials from my home library arrived today, three crates dense with knowledge. Mme. Bilodeau has allowed me to keep a small bedroom as a private study. It's a rare pleasure to line up my beloved volumes on the shelves, and to know that I have my own safe refuge.

I've been invited to a *petite soirée* for members of M. Bilodeau's gentlemen's club in New Orleans. Entry into the club is not guaranteed me—first I must pass a series of social exams to prove my worth. M. Bilodeau assures me that these are the most rudimentary of tests, and that merely by virtue of being a man of the Continent, there will be nothing distasteful or inelegant to disturb me. I await the entertainment with a rather cynical eye. I have yet to find evidence of sophistication in this rustic world, yet everyone works to convince me that I'll be most pleasantly surprised by the depth of culture this side of the Atlantic.

I HAVE EARNED a new respect. Despite my ineptness in the sugarcane fields, my offerings of dinner table wit seem to have made sufficient impression upon M. Bilodeau's friends. Far from finding myself the object of speculation, I am embraced in their ranks as a man of taste. We had a lavish and hearty gentlemen's dinner (I listened more than spoke, for I had little to contribute to their topics of local business and gossip) and situated in the drawing room with cheroots, cigars, coffee, and brandy on hand, they commenced my hazing. Their "tests," at least the ones put to me yesterday, are most insipid and provincial. I was induced to pull the egg from a bound chicken brought in from the henhouse and drink its contents (most horrid) while the fellows chortled with glee. They allotted me plenty of whisky with which to wash it down before putting me to the next task. The fellows sought to prove me a *poisson d'avril*, yet the jape is mine. It was their intention to befoul my wine with horse's urine—but I smelled something amiss as I lifted a glass to my nose. Feigning a coughing fit, I claimed the need to withdraw to the privy to relieve myself. Frogs spotted the dewy grass and I easily trapped one beneath my coat. The jest was much improved upon secreting the little creature in the water pitcher. Again, they pushed the spoiled vintage upon me, and again, I feigned a cough, requesting water before wine. M. Arnot took pitcher in hand, turned perplexed eyes downward, and released a long, high squeal. M. Bilodeau nearly burst a gut with glee as the frog leapt straight at M. Arnot. Arnot fell backward, dashing a plaster bust of Socrates from its stand. The bust bounced just as would a head struck off by Madame la Guillotine and rolled safely away, but the pedestal toppled, crushing the innocent animal I had so recently plucked from its natural habitat.

M. Arnot grew squeamish and fled the parlor when his fellows dangled the deceased frog before his face, while M. Bilodeau heaved with sobs of laughter. My own hilarity was quickly tempered by the vision of Emilie's disapproving face and the knowledge that she would surely find me crude and filled with malicious intent should she learn of my ruse and its unhappy conclusion. Later, I requested M. Bilodeau keep my confidence and resist relaying the incident over the dinner table or any other such gathering. Though he finds the incident a source of amusement, I am certain the Bilodeau *femmes* would declare it a most disagreeable show of character. M. Bilodeau pronounced my concerns foolish. The members of his gentlemen's club are, he assures me, men of staunch moral fiber and much familiar with the delicate nature of ladies' constitutions—"You shall learn soon enough, Isidore, that honesty ill suits husbands and wives."

Is this to be what is expected of me? I little intend to burden Emilie with the intricacies of my private thoughts, but have no wish to openly deceive one who has shown herself to be calmly rational, docile of temperament, and expectant of a marriage woven of stronger threads than mere convenience and fiduciary obligation.

It seems there is precious little time for my own pursuits, as much as my company is demanded by M. Bilodeau for matters of grave importance. We spend a multitude of hours laboring over fiduciary minutiae, calculating to the penny the return on cotton harvests, totting up expenditures in the ledgers, and debating the merits of new equipment. Try as I might to make my contribution a participatory one, M. Bilodeau is content to both propose and answer his own questions. He needs little more than an attentive face toward whom to direct his speeches. I am like a fountain in which his verbosity continuously cycles its own stale effluvium.

Should I excuse myself with promises of a later audience, pleading exhaustion or answering the call of my own intellectual directives, M. Bilodeau will rise from his seat and attend my every step, following me to the door of his study and beyond, his tirade untiring. It is only upon occasion of a conversation with his wife that he withdraws and dismisses me. Often have I claimed urgency in my wish to speak to Mme. Bilodeau regarding some matrimonial trifle, to steal wind (hot!) from his sails. Only then may I creep up squeaking, telltale stairs to my sanctuary and my books. Left on my own, the hours are water draining swiftly away. I guzzle them in quantities but thirst for more.

M. Bilodeau and Prosper have been conferring about going to the slave auction I've seen advertised on the signs along the roadside, loud red planks with black and yellow lettering.

Yesterday, a slave processing sugarcane lost his arm to the grinder, thus spoiling the cane syrup and stalling production for half a day. M. Bilodeau cannot be divested of the notion that my interest in the natural world affords me surgical skill applicable to humans. As if to further prove my point, we visited the slave cabins to see the man and examine his wounds. My limited medical knowledge was tried and found sorely lacking. An unholy host of bluebottle flies (*Calliphora vomitoria*) had set to the man's stump. The stench of his overheated flesh, the raw meat of it maturating and rank with infection, was enough to draw the bile from my liver into my mouth. Writhing on a filthy cot and livid with fever, he is not long for this world. I shudder to witness suffering of a scale as I have only read about, on battlefields, where men like Fair Japheth are discarded to the elements to die of their wounds. Fair Japheth is prized for his endurance and M. Bilodeau is as loathe to lose him as he is eager to replenish his stock and redouble cane pressing.

They request my attendance at auction—nay, I say not "request," for that is too polite a term for the press-ganging they do upon me. My refusals are turned upside down and inside out. M. Bilodeau jokes that I am "sweet as bear meat" if I cannot withstand the auction square and will show myself unfit for Louisiana life. There is no overt threat but one most subtly implied—a withdrawal of his favor or worse, revocation of consent for my position. Master of Belle Rive was never my intended designation, but if I am to complete my work, I must take advantage of the best opportunity afforded me to do so.

When not socially obliged to coddle my in-laws, the evenings here pass with interminable bliss. Emilie's sweet company soothes me. Her tenderness more than compensates for the elder Bilodeaus' stridency, and it is some consolation for putting out the fire that P'tite Marie ignited in me.

FAIR JAPHETH DIED the day after we visited him, and M. Bilodeau gnashed teeth for his loss. "None stronger and none quicker with the machete!" He was unmoved by the wailing of a stout woman, who came running from the fields when she heard the news. Presumably his wife or kin, she set up a great cry, spurring several others to misery. M. Bilodeau ordered Fair Japheth buried immediately. Throughout the night, a terrifying expulsion of sound resounded from the slave quarters—pealing lamentations that filled the air and clouded it like a miasma.

Emilie was very drawn the following morning, with gray circles beneath her eyes. Floriane chided her for communing with slaves and sharing in a grief she had no right to. Still feeling somewhat the usurper in the household and unsure of the permanence of my position, I waited until Madame departed to take Emilie's hand and offer what little comfort I could. It is beyond my understanding that persons who share the same bloodline strive to possess others of their mien. Emilie is shamed by the complacency and conniving of her kin, that because of their skin color, they should hold the whip, rather than bend under it.

THE HORRORS OF the slave market surpassed my darkest imaginings. I am unsure which is worse—the Bilodeaus' casual acceptance of disenfranchisement or the knowledge that I have aligned myself with them and tar myself with the same guilty brush.

I have heard many tales of the cruelties with which the Americans treat the Negro, as if a man were no more than a dairy cow or hog for slaughter, but I did not anticipate the depth of suffering that saturated the market, the stench of agonized despair that emanated from those in chains. Many times, I gave thanks that my own mother had been spared such violations in France. A tangible element, it seemed to fill the air with its reek, run down those bared, black and brown bodies and soak into the ground like rivers of blood. Indeed, I could hardly keep my wits about me amidst the din of wretched sobs as babes were ripped from their mothers' breasts, and those same women paraded naked and cowering across the auction block. Men fared no better. Indeed, animals receive kinder care, for they are fattened with luxury and quickly killed, but the life of a slave is starvation, grueling labor, and a slow, brutal demise.

Returning to Belle Rive, M. Bilodeau called Floriane out to view Fair Japheth's replacement, a fierce-looking youth who towers above his master by a head. They call him Albert and his proud shoulders are already deeply scarred with the whip-marks of his insolence. Floriane praised her husband's eye, and was further delighted when he presented her with a gift, a small girl of nine or ten, to be her pet. Sullen Albert says little, but the child, who Floriane promptly rechristened Poupette, is yellow as a cheese, with rusty brown hair and a profusion of dark freckles across her cheeks. However, her English is good and she speaks French with precision.

Emilie's vexation at the arrival of two new slaves is evident. She has hopes of converting the plantation to one manned by freed, paid workers or allowing those who wish it to choose indentured servitude in place of captivity, which would grant them the good fortune of one day earning what is denied them. She has spoken to me about the maintenance expenses of the plantation and affirms that the family would spend less on wages than auctions. This noble plan is but a fairy-tale recited to the deaf. Confounded by their daughter's repugnance of the trade which feeds and clothes her (Prosper has no such reservations), the Bilodeaus do not, or will not, hear her.

EMILIE WATCHES ME always. Her gaze is one of gentle concern, and my guilt over my persistent fascination with P'tite Marie eats at me as ferociously as did the Guinea worm (*Dracunculiasis*) extracted from Albert's leg this week. (Unscrupulous owners sometimes attempt to sell those already infected with sprue, bloody flux, malignant fevers, or swamp sickness. The specter of *Dracunculiasis* infection haunts the slave market; it is painful to treat and renders its host weak and ineffectual.)

Albert developed a burning sore on his leg and soon a threadlike worm erupted from the wound. He works sullenly, as would anyone with a parasite writhing inside his skin and drawing sustenance from his intestines. The old housekeeper Clothilde visits each day, twisting the stick around which it curls, slowly drawing the worm from his flesh until it is completely expelled. I cannot but help feel my own pain echoed in this drama, for it is like P'tite Marie has wormed her way inside me, and I am the healer attempting to draw her out. I have convinced myself that if I do not speak of her, her memory will wither and die within me, but it is a seed cracking open inside me, struggling to sprout and bloom.

MY WIFE LIES abed in our chamber, and even from my study on the upper floors, I can hear the scratch of her quill against paper. Surely she uses tears for her ink, for they have not ceased their flow for six days. She lost the child conceived on our Honey Moon and has been painfully distraught since. Her body aches and all her womanly senses are in turmoil. She is blue-lipped from loss of blood and cold to the touch, but worse is the sight of the tears that dribble down her blanched cheeks. She came quite close to Death, I believe, and has been changed by her brush with the Netherworld.

Belle Rive is quiet as the tomb. Every servant and slave, and all the family, move about like shadow puppets. So great was their joy for the promise of this new birth that their sorrow is more than equal its measure. Mme. Bilodeau has donned mourning clothes and draped the mirrors with black crepe.

Clothilde has been worth her weight in gold, as they say here. She is the only one capable of assuaging Emilie's sadness. She tells many tales of Papa Legba and his vodou *loa*, assuring Emilie that the babe's spirit will be cared for in the afterlife, although the child is unbaptized. It seems that our Savior lacks the power of these heathen gods where life and death are concerned. Oddly, Emilie appears consoled by Clothilde's tales.

My once-rational wife has taken up the banner of Spiritualism, in as much as it concerns our lost child, who was but a blood clot, with no discernible features to trouble the eye. More concerning is her intrigue with séances. She received a letter from her correspondent and bosom friend, Geneviève Stockton, recounting a ritual she and her husband attended in New York. Mr. Stockton is some sort of lawyer, I believe, and as such has opportunity to hobnob with the local elite when conducting his business affairs. Emilie had an unnerving gleam in her eye when describing their experience to me. Her fervor for the Fox sisters and their reputed ability to contact the dead fills her with a terrible, grim hope. She has asked me to go into New Orleans to purchase a book by mesmerist Andrew Jackson Davis, who she claims is a foremost communicator of the Spirit realm through his trances, and to find any papers or magazines about the Fox sisters for her—about whom she becomes unnaturally excited—and even speaks of traveling to New York to meet Kate and Margaret and sit beside them during a séance. Though these mystical accounts reek to me of chicanery, I will not be the one to dissuade her from comfort in her time of distress.

Though we wake to ice flowers on our windowpanes, Prosper says it is unseasonably dry and cool this winter. He and M. Bilodeau spend many hours huddled over the almanacs assessing the coming weather and discussing last year's yields and profits. I find this work tedious and the cause of very heavy eyelids when I am asked to give my thoughts on the matter. M. Bilodeau ascribes to me a wealth of knowledge I do not have. He believes I enjoy superlative powers of prediction in relation to matters of planting. I assert that I am no farmer and my preoccupations give me no authority in this realm, but he is not dissuaded from his opinion.

It fills me with dread to know he gives my word such weight, for if this year's yields are poor, I am certain he will hold me to blame.

Belle Rive is aflame with speculation, gossip, and fiery proclamations about the evildoings of its slaves. There has been little peace since yesterday morn, when the overseer discovered Albert was not in his bed or cabin, nor to be found in the fields, barns, kitchens, or big house. Some supposed he was off fornicating in the cane, as a few are wont to do, but Sweet Liza stood fast in his defense, saying that Albert "never took no shine" to any of the slave women and always "keep hisself to hisself." The alarm bell rang thrice in quick succession, and M. Bilodeau, Prosper, and Floriane went running out to the fields in their nightclothes. The overseer, Ramón, was cussing up a storm, but when I joined the melee (taking time to dress myself first), I could see the fear gleaming in his wide eyes as he twisted his hat in his hands. He is responsible for the keep and guard of all field slaves and will be due punishment, loss of wages or his position, if the Bilodeaus accuse him of assisting in the escape. He made sure to point fingers in every possible direction away from himself. He clutched in his hand a leaflet printed up for free distribution that described the story of Henry Box Brown, a slave who had himself nailed up in a crate and shipped from Virginia to freedom in Philadelphia two years ago, and claimed it had been found in Albert's cabin.

M. Bilodeau went scarlet with rage. Never have I seen a man so puffed up and purple! Oh, the insult to his pride! Without doubt, he was fretting about the loss of face among the other plantation owners should they discover that one of his properties made such a fool of him with such a simple plot.

M. Bilodeau, Prosper, Ramón, and several others gathered to amass a plan. M. Bilodeau sent Mainard to fetch the slave catcher from LaPlace. The dogs were called out to sniff around the cabins and catch Albert's trail. Ramón and the slave driver, Mr. Plunkett, were dispatched on horseback to search along the river and roads. It was a dreadful commotion, made worse by the arrival of my wife, as scarlet of cheek as her *père*. Emilie launched herself at her father, bodily, with cries that he let Albert go and take the loss. I moved too slowly. I knew myself frozen in time as this sick, sordid world swirled about me, tossing me in its midst. The slavering dogs, the cracking whip and threats against the remaining slaves, who went about their tasks either quite meekly and downcast or with a lively resentment, the oppressive heat bearing down upon us all. I felt as if I stood outside of myself as Albert's cabin mate was dragged forward, lashed to the whipping post, and flogged without mercy. I smelled his blood in the air, thickly reeking and metallic, while Emilie's cries rang through my head. At last, I seemed to re-inhabit myself as if popping up from a lake bottom after complete submersion. I pulled her from that scene of terror into our private parlor, where she wept in my arms for her powerlessness and the terrible injustice of Albert's fate.

It seems that Albert is the first to attempt escape from Belle Rive. I have heard rumor that his forebears were royalty. If such a story is true, one easily imagines the great indignities accompanying their fall from such a lofty station. Such tales often circulated in France, recounting the travails of insubordinate African kings or princes sold off by their own people for refusing to accommodate marriages, tribal coups, or political rebellions.

The slave catcher has been about these parts with M. Bilodeau and Prosper trailing his wake, slapping up posters offering a $50 reward for Albert's apprehension or return—"Fugitive slave eloped from Belle Rive Plantation. Albert is a tall, handsome and well-formed Negro, very black. He speaks with a deep timbre, and cannot read or write. All reasonable expenses paid, compensated with the reward above. Additional $25 paid if proof delivered of Whites harboring fugitive slaves or assisting in transportation to any State in the Free North."

These posters have a crude drawing made by the slave catcher, which looks little enough like Albert to assure that none shall recognize him upon sight. This fact is of little consolation to Emilie, who continues in vain to plead with her father to cease pursuit. Her distress over Albert and the general atmosphere of heaviness and turmoil within Belle Rive leave her drained of the spirited joy to which I had grown accustomed. Clothilde has advised her to withhold her favor from me until after the return of her monthly cycle, and so our nights, so recently filled with pleasure and soft words, are quiet and early ones. We get much sleep and progress rapidly through the pile of books on the bureau.

Albert was apprehended in Hammond and held in jail there for two nights until the slave catcher could fetch him back. They arrived at Belle Rive in the late morning, and I watched from the veranda as M. Bilodeau paid out the reward and Plunkett dragged the shackled man to the whipping post. Emilie was away visiting a neighbor's new baby, and while that leaves me worried over her state of mind when she returns from holding an infant when she has so recently lost her own, I am grateful that she was not here to watch Albert's punishment. Prosper stood beside me, telling me that this dreadful spectacle was required to keep the others in their places, and keep the fear coursing through their veins in place of blood. And plenty of blood I saw, Plunkett wielding his calfskin whip, some four or five feet long, upon the man's raw, glistening flesh. Strips of raw, dripping skin stuck to the lash and flew through the air, spattering the ground and bystanders. My stomach was as hard and tight as a new melon and each crack and the resounding roars, like those of some demented lion (for I saw one once in France, a malnourished, violent creature who roared incessantly as if in great pain when taunted with beef haunches by his laughing trainer) seemed to burrow into my ears and transmute Albert's misery unto me.

Afterward, Plunkett summoned a kitchen girl to bring a cask of pork brine, which he splashed upon the open, hanging flesh to heighten Albert's pain. Prosper japed and clapped as if watching some grand entertainment, and my heart turned cold toward him. There we stood, two free men, removed from that spectacular torture by our fortunate origins as descendants of the Caucasoids. Albert was left bound, his legs strapped to blocks of wood and scarce able to turn his head to shake off the flies and mosquitoes settling on him.

My stomach heaved and I staggered to the bushes to empty my guts onto the grass until bitter bile stung my throat, then I fled, my eyes blurred with tears of horror and knowing myself trapped like the others in this diabolical maelstrom of wickedness.

Albert was released at sunset, and several others came to help him shuffle back to his meager abode. Unlike wounded Fair Japheth, Albert will not even receive the courtesy of a visit by a healer. I offer prayers very rarely, but this night I gave hearty thanks to whatever god dwells in the Heavens, that Emilie returned to Belle Rive after supper and missed the entire event.

M. Bilodeau brought me to New Orleans again to attend a card game at his gentlemen's club. M. Bilodeau insists that the company of wives is tedious to married men and the occasional escape is required to prevent us from being made too soft and womanly by their ceaseless chatter and trivial concerns. His opinion about the poor intelligence of his own wife is greatly exaggerated and inaccurate. Though Floriane is an obstreperous and shrill character, I have revised my initial assessment of her and concede that she is a very shrewd judge of character and tight with a penny. I think if the general keeping of books was left entirely to M. Bilodeau, Belle Rive would soon fall into ruin from his excessive expenditures on mechanical contrivances (while she spends toward the satisfaction of her own desires for dresses, hats, ribbons, jewelry, perfume, and the like). Floriane goes through the household accounts and those in M. Bilodeau's study with great regularity, revising when needed and loudly clucking her tongue. She is known to contact merchants to amend orders and keeps the kitchen cabinets locked to prevent theft or mismanagement of the stores. Of Emilie's character, he knows even less.

The club is in the French Quarter, and several games of draw poker and twenty-deck poke were already in progress when we arrived. We drank brandies in the parlor while awaiting an opening in a game, and M. Bilodeau passed me a stack of coins with which to place bets. Fortunately, I consider myself an astute player, having passed many a dreary English night deep in cards with my schoolfellows at Cambridge.

It was pleasurable to play with such jovial folk—M. Arnot made every attempt to part me from my cash to repay me for the water pitcher trick I had played upon him, but I rose from the table joyously undefeated when the dinner bell was rung.

Dinner was a grand affair, roast beef with onions, veal in whiskey sauce, crisp duck, grouse, sweet peas in beurre blanc, Queen fritters, ice cream and poached pears—worse than French cuisine but better than English. I spoke at length with my neighbor, a visiting Welshman who introduced himself as Cadwalader Eugene Crunn (he seemed to believe we had Cambridge acquaintances in common) and who shares my enthusiasm for the Natural Sciences. Mr. Crunn proved a delightful conversationalist, and it pleased me greatly to enumerate our mutual interest in the local flora. I spoke to him of my visit to the orchid conservatory, and he requests my company on a future expedition there to catalog some variations with which he is unfamiliar. What a delight to discover such a curious intellect amidst those garrulous buffoons!

Following the meal, we retired to the parlor for entertainment. With a belly full of food and brandy-warmed, and my pockets rich with not only the money M. Bilodeau had given me but the winnings from the poker table, my spirits were lighter than they had been in several weeks. I have not been able to shake off the grisly wickedness of Belle Rive, and my sleep has often been disrupted by the memory of Albert's screams when the overseer pickled his back. It was a welcome diversion when a veiled young lady came out to sing for us while Mr. Fetch played the pianoforte in accompaniment. Afterward, she lifted her veil, and I realized it was P'tite Marie, as lovely as when I first encountered her upon my arrival in New Orleans.

I had not seen P'tite Marie since my last brief glimpse of her in the autumn of last year, marching in a funeral procession in New Orleans. I had stood transfixed as she passed by, unaware of my longing. I worked to convince myself that it held no deeper profundity than mere coincidence. Had Emilie not been hanging on my arm, I'd have run after her and thrown myself into the procession of mourners simply to feel the heat of her gaze upon me.

No sooner do I manage to divest myself of longing then she materializes in my life, as if to remind me of her existence. Entrancing in her loveliness, with sparkling black eyes and gleaming, rosy lips, P'tite Marie acted as though we were strangers, for which I was grateful. She brought a lively joy to the gathering, casting her flirtatious glances at the others yet allowing that mesmerizing gaze to linger overlong upon me as she ran her pink tongue over the bright pearls of her teeth.

Sitting beside me, the Englishman Mr. Badcocke jabbed his elbow into mine. "I know all about her," he chortled. "Daughter of the vodou queen, some say a roller, she'll ride a man in the alley and pick his pockets clean, believe me. A toss with her'd be worth any black magic curse she'd scratch out in hen's blood. Pretty as a new copper penny, she is. Isidore, you'd better get your name on the list before all her slots are filled!" He leered at me, and a fierce rage boiled up inside me. I had to grind my jaws together to keep from making remarks that would raise uncomfortable questions.

Seated on Badcocke's left, M. Arnot grimaced. "I wouldn't risk it. You'll catch the pox or worse! That's a conjuring family, and they shouldn't be trifled with. Keep your pecker and your wallet in your pocket where they'll both be safe!"

Badcocke dismissed him. "I don't follow any of that nonsense. I'm a good Christian man, it's not in my make to fall for heathen hocus-pocus."

"All the same," M. Arnot warned, "keep your wits about you or you may end up in a grave with new copper pennies on your eyelids."

P'tite Marie excused herself to change costumes and as she left, I feigned a visit to the indoor privy. The whole episode was a ruse for us to spend a moment alone together so that I might taste those tempting lips which had continually commanded my attention. I found her alone in a small anteroom behind a changing screen, sequestered from view. The moonlit room was dark but for the oblong patterns of bluish light streaming in from the windows. Every moral fiber in me repelled her touch, and yet I craved it, would yield to her like Samson to Delilah, and let myself be stripped of power.

She smiled upon seeing me, and displayed a look of such intensity that I trembled. We ducked into the shadows and immediately, my hands found the opening of her gown, parting its folds of fabric to seek out their prize. She succumbed to me! I was inside her, an ocean of fragrant, silken flesh rising up to swallow me. She bit my ear, my neck, whispered my name and professed her undying love for me. It was heaven, so quickly were we transported beyond the ordinary concerns of the mortal world. Surely the heat of our passion would set the woodpile alight!

Voices intruded on our reverie and she wiggled away, gasping. I stood there for one dumb second, a mute and throbbing beast, my sodden organ spurting into my hand. I regained my senses (ears ringing, world spinning) just as M. Bilodeau appeared, illumined from behind by the lantern light in the tall windows. I could not see his face. Haloed by light, grizzled curls framed his head like question marks.

Quickly, I obscured myself behind the screen and flowing curtains while I tucked myself away. P'tite Marie patted my father-in-law on the shoulder and directed him to the privy before returning to the gathering without a backwards glance. I adjusted my clothing and followed her back inside.

P'tite Marie bounced upon the gentlemen's knees while I did my best to look away in vain agitation over the nearness of her and my desire to speak with her, touch her, and breathe in the scent of her once again. At last, she found her way to my side and greeted me briefly, politely, as though unaware of my turmoil. With much discretion, she slipped a small calling card into my hand and bid our gathering good night. I had no chance to examine it until I was alone—it is the address of a house in Metairie, La Maison d'Amour et La Magie, which I do not intend to visit.

I FEAR THAT M. Bilodeau has seen my heart, gifted to another at the expense of his daughter. I am a foolish man. He has pressed me with no end of questions since returning from the club in New Orleans. Questions burned in my father-in-law's gaze all night, but he could identify nothing wrong, so remained quiet. It was only in the close carriage, pressed up against me and exuding his sour odors of old brandy, that M. Bilodeau voiced his concerns. I dismissed them quickly, saying it would be easy to misconstrue a gesture in so little light. The shadows cast the expression he'd seen on my face, nothing more. I hear the words coming from my mouth and wonder who I have become.

Many a man has kept a mistress, and scandalous women in France and England have often been quite open in admitting their liaisons with famous men. Never having been moved by profound passion, I disdained both parties, thinking them bestial and without honor. Then, I did not understand the nature of passion and assumed myself far above such raw animal emotions, but now that love has claimed me (as a parasite claims its host), I am helpless to resist its demands or repel its impulses. That night remains enshrined in my memory, the feel of her limbs like a tangle of silken cords, the sound of her voice in my ear as I sink into her and become lost. Oh, how I am lost!

CRUNN CALLED OF a morning and said he'd hired a coach for the week. If I was free, would I join him on the expedition we'd spoken of? His appearance threw the house into *une grande panique*, for he is an exceedingly handsome fellow, very well turned out, who charms everyone he meets. Floriane and my own normally forthright Emilie went pink and fluttered about like mad butterflies, while Poupette sat shyly in the corner, gazing at him as if he were the statue of David. M. Bilodeau displayed his usual pompous bluster, strutting about like a proud cock with his chest puffed out and his chin high. Even Lavinia, who is ordinarily quite unflappable, glowed serenely in his presence. It was a relief to depart after coffee was served and the poor man plied with no cease of questions. I myself was doubly delighted by his request for my company, as it meant that not only was carriage provided and an afternoon of fine conversation with a like mind, but that I was also relived of another tedious day plunging through almanacs and account books.

Crunn has a sharp and engaging mind, and his knowledge of both what he knows and what he doesn't, is refreshing. He little fears showing his ignorance by asking questions, yet he is quick to share the knowledge he possesses and is eager to speak of matters unknown to me, such as the *Materia medica*, of whose philosophies he is an ardent follower. The conservatory was magnificent, and Mr. Crunn and I had the pleasure of speaking with the head gardener and being allowed to make several very fine drawings of a recently acquired rare specimen not yet on display, that delicately ruffled lady *Cattleya laelia grandis*.

Following, we had Ceylon tea and madeleines in the French Quarter and I was encouraged to share my own ordinary tale. He said, "Ahh" repeatedly and stroked his fine beard, as if my story were the most entrancing he'd ever heard. I told him that my family still owned the estate in Boulogne, but since my father's death and with my mother's minuscule income barely sufficient to pay the taxes, it had fallen into disrepair. There was little for me there, and because the Bilodeaus are cousins, my mother hoped that the marriage between myself and Emilie would inspire them to invest in the family holdings. Thus began a correspondence between matriarchs. When the betrothed discovered ourselves compatible, the Bilodeaus brought me to America.

It's astonishing to note that the entirety of my existence thus far could be so briefly summed up and all the complexities of my *affaires de coeur*, my triumphs and failures at school, my journeys and pursuits so tidily contained within a few simple sentences. It makes me feel my life greatly ordinary, and thus I have resolved to create some story for myself that shall enthrall upon its retelling.

He asked how I fared, a Mulatto among Creoles, Whites, freed men, and slaves, and inquired if I felt my treatment and reception in society to be affected by my color. Or was it worse, he joked, to be a Frenchman among Americans? I have thought about this often since my arrival, how I am an entity unto myself and somewhat an object of scorn, curiosity, and envy because of my complection, status, philosophical leanings, or education. The slaves are aware of my discomfort with issuing orders, of expressing impatience or cruelty toward women who resemble my own mother. The elder Bilodeaus and their society friends, however genuine their affection for me, treat me like a sideshow novelty—an attraction or object of amusement. I am an island unto myself, and until P'tite Marie washed up on my lonely shores, it was uninhabited and dispassionate. Crunn expressed much compassion for my station. The Welsh are similarly castigated in Britain, and Crunn sympathized with my sense of alienation and disenfranchisement, as did I his.

Crunn spoke much to me about his hopes to fund a venture in America, for he has a trust which needs investing and little idea what to put the money toward. He displayed great interest in my thoughts about orchid cultivation, and we spoke at length about the Crystal Palace and my desire to bring a portion of such elegance and beauty to Belle Rive. I was persuaded to confess my desire to one day build myself a conservatory to pursue orchid cultivation, and thus we arrived together at the notion that I build such a structure at Belle Rive. Not only would it be of educational value to others but a route to personal satisfaction for me. I left our meeting greatly encouraged and enlivened, feeling more cheerful than I have in many months.

I WOKE TO a day of longed-for solitude; Emilie, Prosper and the elder Bilodeaus had left at dawn to visit a neighboring farm to buy two foals. However, I soon discovered that my time was not my own. Sly old Clothilde brought my morning tea. Grinning widely, she announced "Lè chat pa la! The cat is away!" A perfect day, said Clothilde, for me to travel to the *loa* house to procure some "necessaries" from Mme. Laveau's daughter. The unusualness of her request was mitigated by her insistence that I fetch those items required for a native religious ceremony to ensure that my next babe is born alive and healthy. I would be a monster to refuse such a thing, and the urgency and secrecy of the mission were not lost upon me. Though the Bilodeaus grudgingly allow the old woman her religious indulgences, they are typically quick to suppress any overt practice that threatens their staunch Christian discipline.

I took a horse and rode alone to the House of Love and Magic, P'tite Marie's house in Metairie. Though there is a deep kinship and much affection between myself and P'tite Marie, I fear she is a bright star which will scorch my eyes and leave me blind if I do not break my stare. Like the sun, she casts a light over every surface and a heat which leaves one languid and thirsting.

A faint gray mist had draped itself about the house at the end of that long serpentine road, obscuring its features and lending it a mysterious aura, but it was a fine townhouse. Iron filigree balconies were strung between the slender fingers of fluted Ionic columns fronting the palest lavender façade. Young oaks dappled the walk and flowering jasmines scented the air. A large snake slithered out from the bushes and quickly moved toward the veranda as I approached. Before vanishing into the shadows beneath, it coiled around and lifted its head to fix me with a piercing stare as if daring me to enter. I shuddered with a sudden sense of trepidation, very glad that I was wearing high boots in case it struck out.

A handsome woman in a starched linen gown came to the door, and I did as Clothilde instructed, making the hand signal she said would introduce me as her agent. I was led into a parlor, well-furnished and comfortable, whose main feature was a large table and a very broad cabinet such as one would see at an apothecary's, crafted with many shelves and small drawers. She poured me a small tumbler of rum and we sat at the table as she asked my troubles.

I gave her Clothilde's list, and from this she discerned that it was a child we wanted. As I watched, she selected several herbs and stones and tucked them into a cloth bag. I paid for them and was dismissed. I confess, my loins had quickened at the expectation of once again glimpsing P'tite Marie and engaging her privately in conversation, for it would have been our first time alone since our furtive encounter at the gentlemen's club, but she did not show herself. For the sake of all concerned, it is best.

EMILIE CAME TO me in my study last night. She closed the door behind her and disrobed. There was little light but for the candle I read by, and after she pinched the wick, night suffused the small room. I could make out naught but the outline of her body. Starlight framed the glimmer of her long, unbound hair. Pressing silent lips upon me, she smelled of rum and herbs, her skin damply fragrant with strange odors and adorned with necklaces of strange design—feathers and metal coins hanging from a leather thong.

Excitement rose in me beneath the caresses of this new woman, my wife with powers multiplied. When we were satisfied, we left the study to go to bed, only to encounter Clothilde in the passageway, waiting with a candle and a gloating look upon her wrinkled face. I suddenly felt less a husband than a project or a pet, groomed and trained.

My lively wife's interest in the new Spiritualist movement has earned her the attentions of several prominent members of that community. She is keen to attend a lecture at the Société du Magnétisme de la Nouvelle-Orléans and is quite radiant at the prospect of being mesmerized by Joseph Barthet, for she has avidly read his tract *ABC des Communications Spirituelles* in her attempts to force a link to our deceased child. (I do not think of it as a child but a spark extinguished before it had the strength to catch, a wisp of smoke from stamped-out tinder.) She is adamant that Barthet's hypnotism and treatment with magnets will help to fortify her body and soul to bring forth a new, complete life. I persuaded her to remain at Belle Rive; I'm certain that Barthet is a charlatan intent only on parting her from her coin and filling her head with ridiculous notions. Emilie was irritated with me and we parted on unhappy terms. She does not perceive the social embarrassment I have diverted away from her. I would apologize but she is simply too provincial to understand the lack of integrity with which these sharpers operate.

The sky has been overlaid with noxious, heavy gray clouds that sting the eye and dim the sun. La Foret, the cotton plantation some three miles east, has burned for two days. M. Bilodeau sent over Prosper and several of Belle Rive's men the first day to help quench the blaze, but it spread very quickly from the kitchens to the cabins and devoured the barn, plough shed, and five acres of cotton. Their niece Loucille and six of La Foret's female slaves have been quartered at Belle Rive, one who has been badly burned along the arm. Clothilde tends to her with watered rags and poultices of aloes and plantains (*Plantago major*). I have noticed field hands harvesting this weed. When I next encountered Clothilde, I queried about this practice and she said that plantain gives the body strength to heal and when eaten, imparts those qualities to the consumer. Clothilde has a canny look about the eye and secret ways that everyone here is accustomed to, but her quiet, creeping steps and habit of appearing in rooms as if coalesced from the very air leave me rattled and dreading the appearance of that shrewdly wrinkled visage when one least expects it.

Emilie is rather absent of late, both in mind and body. She devotes many hours to reading the magazines and books sent by her friend Mrs. Stockton, each one about Spiritualism and the Spirit world, the summoning and appeasing of ghosts and life beyond Death. These are not tales of souls gone to God and dwelling in serene heavens, no, they are stories about the victims of Murder and Foul Play who seek justice for the evils done unto them, or recountings of conversations with departed loved ones who were unable to impart some final message before expiring. How it pertains to the lost child, I have yet to ascertain, and she speaks of it with some hesitation, as though I sit in judgment of her grief—I do not.

She requests yet more books of me, and I would not refuse her or the chance for a day away from the stink of char. All this talk of ghosts and spirits leaves me discomfited. To bed, I go.

THERE MAY BE salvation for the La Forets yet. Yesterday, a strong odor of ozone lingered in the atmosphere and the scent of impending rain filled my nose. The air was as heavy as mud, and so full of humidity that one could almost swim through it. We were all on toe tips, awaiting the breaking of the clouds and the downpour that could save the burning plantation. There is concern that the blaze will rampage unchecked across the fields and forest between La Foret and Belle Rive and destroy us, too. A thrashing rain was all we could hope for. As the clouds began to rumble and swell and thunder whip-cracked across the sky, excitement surged through each of us seated at the dining table, pushing ourselves through a rather dismal luncheon. A spontaneous cheer arose and even the serving girls smiled. Another fierce rumble made the walls tremble as a sudden darkness oppressed us and lightning split the heavens asunder. There were abrupt footsteps and noises from the pantry. Standing in her usual spot at Mme. Floriane's elbow, Poupette spoke as if to herself, but Mme. Floriane heard her and sat up, sharp as a poker. "What did you say, girl? What did you say?" In a moment, all was thrown into chaos. Mme. Floriane leapt to her feet in pursuit of Clothilde. Emilie asked Poupette to repeat her words, and Poupette's whey-colored skin appeared to curdle before our eyes as she spoke. "She gone to cut de storm in two. She wants La Foret to burn." *En suite*, we followed the shouts to the yard, arriving as Clothilde grabbed the ax from the woodpile, closed her eyes in prayer, and muttered some unholy incantation. She swung that ax into the ground with more force than a woman of her age should possess. Dirt clods flew and Mme. Floriane screamed for assistance, but it was done. Clothilde pushed off Prosper and Mainard, and pulled all that energy back into her shriveled old body, a blossom closing protective petals about itself.

Emilie has since told me that Clothilde despises the La Forets because M. Bilodeau's father sent Clothilde's grandson to them on the condition that he remain at La Foret plantation as a blacksmith's apprentice, but a visitor offered a good price for him, so they sold him off as an indentured servant and sent the boy away that same day. Clothilde did not discover their betrayal for two months, by which time he could not be traced. With the elder Bilodeau now dead, she has turned all her fury upon the La Forets. She welcomes any opportunity to assist in their ruination.

It rained all night, but such a light patter that it little damped the fire, and so La Foret still burns and Clothilde steals about Belle Rive with a look of satisfaction upon her ancient face. I asked my wife why the open practice of Clothilde's religion does not result in punishment as it does for the field hands, who are threatened with the lash if caught worshipping their own gods. Clothilde, said Emilie, is a blood relation. A cousin of M. Bilodeau's, she has always served the family, first as a nursemaid when he and his siblings were young, and then as housekeeper of Belle Rive when M. Bilodeau married Floriane. I confess, a shudder of revulsion quaked my bones. The convolution of ancestry and marital ties that divide servant from served in this family congeals my blood. If one is born on the wrong side of the fence in this country, there is no hope of ever climbing over it.

EMILIE IS AGLOW, certain that she will someday be successful in giving me a healthy son or daughter. While I harbor my own skepticism about its powers, Spiritualism and these vodou remedies have enlivened her body, mind, and soul. She has corresponded with several women who share her abhorrence of slavery and speaks to me of leaving Belle Rive to forge our own livelihood, freed from its blood-soaked fetters. These letters and conversations, the near-daily teas and salons to which she goes, fill her head with aspirations beyond our means. I admit, I am at a loss. She speaks with great and reckless optimism, knowing little of my occupational trials. What life can I provide to her? Am I the sort of man to drain his wife's income, that is, should the Bilodeaus consent to let her keep her portion if she cuts herself off from them? She is transformed by this new religion, while I fall further into doubt and dismay, for no spirits speak to me and no one seeks my company or conversation except Crunn, who becomes a bosom friend and confidante, my only one.

Mr. Crunn has written to me from Charlotte, North Carolina, where he has traveled to check on production from a gold mine he placed a stake on in 1847. He assures me that while production in Mecklenburg County has declined in recent years, his mine still generates several thousand troy ounces of pure gold per annum. He assures me that he will be in good straits to fund my glass house project and urges me to begin searching for all the necessary components. I am delighted at this prospect. It is more than I could have achieved with my own meager income. I have no hope that the Bilodeaus would ever be persuaded to invest in anything so frivolous and time-consuming. I have written to several manufacturers in England to request information about conservatory building kits and await their replies with a joyful heart.

Emilie seems to be returning to her former, fiery self. Clothilde has been most diligent in preparing hearty soups and teas to strengthen her blood, and indeed, color returns to the lips and cheeks that were so recently as pale and cold as Death. While the old servant's creeping ways continue to unnerve me, I cannot refute the healing claims she makes, for haven't I seen my wife change from a hollow creature wasted by grief to one again full of life? Emilie told me that Clothilde has taken a shine to Albert, perhaps because her own son is gone and she has no vector for her maternal urges. She treated his back soon after the pickling, and when I saw him recently in the yard, his bare skin glistened beneath a smooth web of scars, nicely healed. While she will not share the intimacies of their conversations, Emilie has confessed that the objects I purchased at the *loa* house formed the basis of a secret ceremony. Clothilde promises that we shall conceive soon, and be delivered of a healthy child.

I have had little time to write in my journal, so pressing are the demands upon my time. If not my wife begging me to read one of her Spiritualist books, then M. Bilodeau is constantly hammering at me for one thing or another. I find myself quite exhausted and pulled in twain. My only relief comes from poring over the catalogs which have quickly arrived, bearing many beautiful drawings of iron-framed conservatories in all manner of design or purpose—many with Gothic arches, leaded or stained glass and domed ceilings—lavish orangeries and pineries, and a fine selection of Wardian cases for shipping orchid bulbs and plants. There is an orchid show in Boston next spring, and Crunn has spoken of financing this trip and joining me to select specimens for Belle Rive's glass house, and it is my greatest hope to journey there with him.

M. Bilodeau wishes to venture into New Orleans on Saturday to attend a Quadroon ball at the home of Mr. Hollow, owner of the Greater Louisiana Shipping Co. and the riverboats *April Tides* and *Little Nineveh*. Why the event holds such a fascination for him, I cannot imagine. To my understanding, Mulatto, Quadroon, and Octoroon women are paraded about like show ponies for wealthy men to ogle and if they like, "purchase" a filly to keep in their own stable. The Bilodeaus are a prominent Creole family and as such, I would think he would find such an event distasteful. To my dismay, I continue to learn truths about Emilie's father which leave me sour-mouthed and untrusting of his true nature. To the eye and ear, on paper and in person, he might pass, but he is known in this parish as Creole because of his métis mother, and it is a mark he cannot wash away. He speaks pridefully of his white father, but inside, he simmers with a bitter resentment that he cannot keep up with the big boys in town, the wealthiest and whitest who run New Orleans as if all were racehorses beneath their broad bottoms.

I have refused attendance at the ball in all ways that are polite without drawing unwelcome attention to myself, but my heart sits in my throat at the thought of finding myself spectator to yet another type of slave auction. For didn't P'tite Marie once tell me that the practice of *plaçage* kept her in silks and satins and paid for the grand houses she and her mother dwelled in?

If her gods have any power, I entreat them to keep her at home come Saturday so that I should not have to gaze upon her face and be reminded of my sins.

Neither Christian nor heathen gods saw fit to intervene in my small drama. P'tite Marie was at the ball, boldly flaunting her décolletage for those pomaded, strutting cocks to crow over. I heard one man tell his companion, "She is not the most beautiful, nor the best dancer or most gracious conversationalist at the ball, but she is the liveliest and best for a tumble or two-penny suck." Livid with rage, I removed myself from their proximity to sit alone with my punch, stewing in the overheated, spicy broth of my rageful lust. P'tite Marie moved through the pressing bodies and swayed her hips as if ringing a Sunday supper bell, flashing all her large bright teeth when she laughed and offering everyone in proximity glimpses of her glistening, pink throat, wide open to suck up the air. She would not allow her eyes to rest on me, but I sensed her to be keenly aware of my presence.

Though M. Bilodeau spoke vilely of her character, he made a jackass of himself whenever she was near, pawing at the lace on her gown, leering at her swollen bosom. She played her part as if on stage at the Lyceum Strand. The show they enacted together served only to turn my stomach. I felt myself to have been played a great fool. How the two Maries must have cackled at my innocence! I shudder to realize myself so easily led astray.

M. Bilodeau became unhealthily fixated on P'tite Marie, despite all my efforts to divert his attention. She behaved as if we were nothing more than casual acquaintances (a falsehood, for could I not feel the air between us vibrating with unseen energies as the threads of our telepathic union wove together?), a favor I felt myself to be unwisely grateful for and which left me with a sense that it was a favor to be repaid. I managed the evening with some semblance of grace, and danced with the women though my presence there was a source of both wicked laughter and consternation from the gentlemen there—was I a monkey trained to dance for their amusement, or was I representative of some new, socially progressive threat, a colored Frenchman bidding at *plaçage*, flaunting my youth, position, and Continental connexions?

Once the dances were danced, the brandy, sherry, port, and champagne bottles emptied, the men could spirit their chosen playmate into one of many small rooms off the great hall. Curtains were drawn, giggles (and the hard bargaining) commenced. I kept myself removed from this sequence of events as I had no further wish to observe M. Bilodeau growing red-faced and crude or to endure the hostility of some of the other bidders. There was a lovely garden visible through the tall windows, and I eagerly took advantage of my opportunity to escape the perfumed heat of the ballroom for cool evening air and a river breeze.

There was little light but that which came from the moon to guide my perambulations as I admired the fragrant white buds of the *magnolia grandiflora*, some larger than my own palm. I soon became lost in my own musings, and did not realize myself watched until I heard the familiar laugh that had been pealing in my ears all evening.

"I had no idea that you were interested in buying a mistress, Isidore."

P'tite Marie materialized out of the darkness, bright teeth, shining eyes, glowing skin. Her pale-yellow gown seemed to draw the moonlight into its folds and radiate them around her in a vivid aureole. I resisted the urge to cover my eyes or turn away from the spectacle of her.

"I'm not here to buy or to lease."

My poor joke was as thin as workhouse gruel. Neither of us laughed. P'tite Marie flowed—yes, flowed, as a magnolia blossom sails downriver on a giddy current—toward me, her hands outstretched. She curled me into her butter-yellow glow, and the scent of her heliotrope perfume, and some lingering fragrance of earth and herbs, filled my nose.

"Just quenching your thirst, then?"

"I am here at the behest of my father-in-law. It's his desire, not mine, to enter into this society. He may encourage me to take a mistress here, but in my eyes, he is a sinful man and a poor father to urge my emulations of such gross conduct as this."

P'tite Marie drew her fingers along my collarbone, traced my ribs and counted the knobs in my spine. "Had your fill of me, Isidore? You haven't been back to visit. You promised my maman that we'd see you again. She's been waiting for your return. Or perhaps you were too ashamed to return to one to with whom you have been so dishonest."

I shucked out of her grasp and removed myself, but she clung and traced my every step. It would come down very badly should M. Bilodeau find us together in the dark garden—he covets her for himself.

"There was no future for us, however much I wanted it. Want it. Obviously, you understand that my days are no longer my own." I protested, but she advanced. "My wife...," I stammered. "You are a Siren calling me down to my death and I would gleefully drown myself to be with you, but"—I racked my brains, for no reason seemed adequate to refuse her or to reject this greatest of sensations when every cell in my body yearned for absolute union with this superlative creature—"I cannot." Spineless words!

"Give me just one taste of that sweet mouth, Isidore, and I'll leave you be."

"As charming as I find you, as much as I wish it, I cannot."

I moved away and tripped over a low stone bench, landing on my rump on the damp grass. P'tite Marie laughed and stepped over me, drowning me beneath her gown's silken waves. The moon was behind her, throwing her face into shadow.

P'tite Marie dropped to her knees, and I could feel the hot center of her grinding against me. Why did my traitorous body react? I knew I should not, but found my fingers grasping her thighs as she undid my flies and freed me. It was as if my mind, my rational senses, deserted me. I could think of naught but assuaging the ache in me, of being inside her. Starched crinolines scratched at my cheeks as she writhed atop me. She was hot and soaking wet, her quim milked all fluid from me and left me gasping. I swear I could see the magnolias on the low branches open and close like infants' mouths, clamoring for milk.

This was everything I had yearned for and desired. I felt myself expand in a thousand directions, every nerve alive and singing. My ears rang with the force of my climax, and P'tite Marie threw back her head and released the most horrifying, guttural groan as she convulsed over me. Pleasure coursed through my body and shame poured out alongside it. Her cry was the wail of a dying beast, and I feared the appearance of M. Bilodeau or worse yet, Mr. Hollow, come to see what wretched animal lay expiring in his garden. I pushed her from me and did up my trousers.

Mud in front and back, grass and soil matted into my hair, my jacket rumpled and damp—I could not go back into the house. I would be either chastised or laughed at and could abide neither option. P'tite Marie sprawled on the grass, her white-stockinged legs spread apart, flaunting her throbbing, dark flower. I could not tear my gaze from her face, the black, almond eyes that seemed to laugh at me as much as they praised me. The red slash of her mouth gloated at me, grinning with triumph.

"If M. Bilodeau asks, tell him I've taken ill," I said, and went to find the coachman to beg a horse or vehicle to remove me far from that temptress.

My good, Catholic wife would suffer a broken heart should she learn of my continued betrayal, which at the time of its first occurrence, was but a trifle upon my conscience, and now weighs like a millstone around my neck. I could console myself with protestations that I knew her not, knew not what awaited me and was ignorant of my blessings. Thinking upon it now (for it creeps up insidiously, no matter how hard I try to suppress its memory), my body becomes inflamed, just as my spirit bloats with misery. Emilie's good nature suspects nothing. She is always smiling, and the adoration in her gaze is sickening. How can I celebrate the child that will one day grow in her belly when I may have planted another in the belly of her rival?

MY DECEPTION DERANGES me. I push it from my mind with strong hands, but like vermin, it finds cracks through which to come slithering, creeping, or crawling back. Only letters from Crunn, detailing the promise of sale of his gold mine shares and the purchase of the glass house kit, distract me from toiling over the intimacies of my indiscretion. I have chosen a very fine model measuring twenty-five feet long, a near-perfect replica of the conservatory at Chiswick House Gardens, which I viewed once in 1847, and left an indelible impression on me that could only be eclipsed by the Crystal Palace, whose glorious paths I hope to travel again one day.

M. BILODEAU GOT quite drunk tonight and told me that he has submitted a bid to take P'tite Marie as his *placée*. Heart, stomach, loins, mind—all reel. He confesses his desires to me as though I, too, should take pleasure in them. He grows increasingly sordid in his descriptions, speaking to me like an equal (as if I would equal his loathing of his wife and the strictures of his life). I asked why he did not confide in Prosper, and he says I am a gentleman and French, therefore have a greater grasp of the world than his son, already thirty and still unmarried, who has spent his entire life on Belle Rive's acreage or thereabouts. He is planning to spend the weekend in New Orleans at a brothel, and if possible, he says, entice P'tite Marie to join him for dinner, if not more. He will tell Floriane and the others that he will be at the Dauphine (the damned Dauphine!) to entertain meetings with his solicitor. The dreariness of this task ensures that none of us will request to join him; I assume he'll have the company of one of his friends like the Englishman Mr. Badcocke, who shares M. Bilodeau's appetites.

I confine myself to my study and the planning of my garden in hopes of avoiding him as much as possible. Emilie and Floriane believe his tales, and I am left wondering if we are deceived so easily simply because we are gullible, or more worrisome, because we choose to be.

BADCOCKE WAS DISCOVERED dead on the bank of the Mississippi River three days ago. His jacket, vest, and other items were found at a nearby crossroads just beyond Metairie, and the *Daily Picayune* reports that his facial features were sunken and ghastly, as if he had suffered a long illness (though M. Bilodeau reports Mr. Badcocke had been in exceptional health when last they met) and was left, withered and aged, as if drained of blood and life force. His eyes bulged and his lips were shriveled and blackened. Poison is suspected, as there are no marks indicating violence upon the body.

I came upon M. Bilodeau still in his dressing gown, reading the newspaper at the breakfast table long after the family had departed and the dishes had been cleared away. He called to me and pointed to the article with trembling fingers. I noticed how long and brown his nails had grown, and for the first time smelled an odor of the sickroom about him. He told me that Badcocke should have watched himself more carefully. They had been to a soirée in the City, and Badcocke had caused grave offense to an important woman, who cursed him with a vodou spell. Naturally, Badcocke had mocked and ridiculed her, saying that no Negro witch had more power than Jesus Christ (for Badcocke is a proud Anglican), and that Englishmen, recounted M. Bilodeau, "hold the favor of our Lord and Savior!"

He told me that the whole room had gone silent save for Badcocke's laughter, and M. Bilodeau tried to ease nerves by buying another bottle of champagne, but the damage was done. The bartender, a huge Creole man, tossed Badcocke into the street and M. Bilodeau with him. They parted ways and exchanged no further words. My brain teemed with questions, the first being the identity of the woman Badcocke insulted, but M. Bilodeau declined to say. His hands trembled as he took cold tea, and I sense that he is very much afraid that the same fate may befall him.

Our conversation was cut short. Clothilde came in with a basin, tonic, and rags to attend to M. Bilodeau's rheumatic knees. She soaked each rag in tonic, a murky green, weedy-smelling liquid, and wrapped them around the old man's pale, knobby joints. Curious, I inquired as to the recipe of her tonic.

Clothilde answered that it was buckeye, which has a strong spirit. I pressed her further. Had she medical training? She replied that she was a healer, same as her mother before her. Born into healing, she said. As a child who came after twins she had been blessed with the power to hear the voice of her ancestors, and to cure sickness.

"Everything have a spirit," Clothilde told me. "Every plant, every creature that walk, swim, crawl, or fly. Good spirit like buckeye make a body better, but some are bad, cause illness, pain and suffering. If the spirit of one thing get into another, *il semé la pagaille*. Disaster! Two spirits cannot share the same house." She cast her sly gaze at me and made a motion as if wrapping a noose around her neck, crossed her eyes and poked out her tongue. (A distasteful pink slug, patterned with red and white patches.)

"Ask M. Bilodeau dead friend. He know."

At this, I found myself pushing away from the table and my chair clattered to the floor. Startled, M. Bilodeau dropped his teacup, which shattered upon the table. Only now, upon later reflection, I realize that Clothilde was the only one who was unmoved.

M. BILODEAU'S SULLEN mood has cast a pall over the household. I inquired after him and he looked at me very bitterly, his wiry gray eyebrows drawn together in a snarl. He said, "Sometimes we don't get what we deserve," and humped away, scowling. I can only assume it means P'tite Marie rejected his bid, a knowledge which fills me with immense, ridiculous joy.

I CANNOT FORCE P'tite Marie from my mind. Memories creep in like fog, clouding my clear view. The scent of magnolias stirs my blood, inciting my body to arousal as it did that evening at the Quadroon ball. Every moment I leave my thoughts unguarded, she appears, a longed-for yet unwelcome specter, begging my attention. Our last encounter remains for me as fresh and vivid as if I still wore her perfume on my skin.

QUAND ON PARLE du loup. The wolf has answered my silent howls. I have received an invitation to give a lecture about the collection and preservation of floral specimens to a gathering of amateur naturalists at the Garden Society. Naturally, my hands moved of their own accord, penning a reply and passing it to Mainard for posting, *tout suite*. Afterward, I suffered much guilt for the hope that leapt in my breast, and raging fire that I—in vain—attempt to smother. I am of two minds. One of which chides the folly of my hope that P'tite Marie shall be in attendance, the other which practically chains me to Belle Rive as if I were a wanton dog prone to straying.

Yet, as the angel on my shoulder urges me to remain with my wife, to toss away this adolescent fancy of mine, I realize that I have already conceded my powerlessness when confronted with my wish to again taste those lips like candied plums and to bury myself between those silken thighs once more.

And as I tell myself that I shall not go, I find my hands packing my specimen cases and preparing notes for this lecture, plotting to perfume my beard and don my finest waistcoat in the event P'tite Marie wishes to rest her eyes, or her slender fingers, upon me.

EMILIE DOES NOT wish me to leave tomorrow, fearing that I will be caught in the summer storm that hovers on the horizon. I placate my wife with promises to return bearing a copy of the new novel about which plantation society cannot cease discussing, *Uncle Tom's Cabin*.

I persuaded her that it was an honor to be recognized for my abilities, as there are no like-minded fellows in the environs of Belle Rive to appreciate them. Here, so far removed from the City's bustle and noise, I am left companionless and with no stimulation of the mind—save for Crunn's steadfast and encouraging correspondence—I fear I should grow enfeebled in my avocation. At this, she pressed me to attend, saying she knows I would become but a shell of the man she has come to love if denied opportunities to expand my knowledge. I kissed her warmly, knowing myself blessed to have secured such a tender wife, and departed, as two-faced as Janus.

RAPTURE HAS BUT one home on earth, and it is within the body of my adored. Had God not intended P'tite Marie to spend the small hours cosseted in my embrace, would he have constructed such a perfect farce for all His players? I'm grateful that Maman's Catholic inculcations never took root in me, for surely I'd dwell in fear of an eternity roasting in the fiery pit!

The sky was overcast when I departed July 7 after lunch, but the air was dry and my barometer indicated fair weather ahead, so I felt confident in leaving the wagon and taking a horse to make the journey alone. But as if intending to foil my plans, the Bilodeaus pressed upon me their desire that I deliver a set of dishes to La Foret. I could not refuse without good explanation or looking the fool, and so I grudgingly acquiesced. The Bilodeaus have purchased a second-hand Rockaway carriage and for reasons unknown to me, Emilie feels I will be safer as a passenger than a driver. Mainard must accompany me. How trustworthy he is, I am not certain. He has not impressed me as a gossip, but one can never know the heart of a domestic, be he servant or slave.

Once that errand was done, I stopped at the club to freshen myself and partake of a light supper and station a protesting, anxious Mainard at the club's servant rooms before continuing on to the house in the French Quarter, where welcoming lamps burned brightly, dispelling the evening's early shade. By then, the atmosphere was suffused with the scent of rain, and a chilly damp hung beneath the trees, pooling in pockets between the buildings. The sky broke open like an egg, delivering its weight upon the paving stones in grand, splashing draughts. Rain spilled down the windowpanes and hammered against the roofs, commencing a powerful din.

This was Madame Marie's home, but it was her daughter who opened the door to me. P'tite Marie wore a simple crimson frock; her unbound hair poured over her shoulders in glistening black coils. My heart throbbed at the welcome sight of her. I stumbled over the lintel and she grasped my arm, chuckling at my clumsiness. "My mother was called away; she has asked to postpone your lecture. Did you not receive her letter?"

I shook my head. Words would not form.

"Yet here you are," she said. "As if delivered by Erzulie herself!" How strange, she remarked, that the rainstorm had begun promptly with my arrival as if it had followed me from Belle Rive. We took tea in the parlor and drank glasses of rum punch made for guests who would never taste its sweetness. A shimmering excitation framed by grim suspicion traveled through my limbs. I could barely stay seated for the impious thoughts blossoming in my mind and dribbled out useless profundities to entertain my hostess.

The hour wore on and I often said that I should leave as soon as the rain stopped, but it lashed itself against the house with the vindictive fury of Plunkett's whip upon Albert's bared back. I should not be able to walk back to the hotel in such dire conditions. Circumstances indicated that I must wait for morning and drier roads. I said as much, the words leaping from my lips with a will of their own.

My eyes grew heavy from the rum. My mind clouded and my mannerisms turned languid. When that statuesque seductress took my hand and led me from the parlor, I climbed the dim stairway to follow those swaying hips, that delicate hand bearing the sputtering yellow lamp, aching for release from the heat that inflamed my loins. What followed was a night of unparalleled bliss in which I attained superlative heights of intimate pleasure and a deep sleep marred only by troublesome dreams of Emilie clothed in holy robes weeping red tears into a basin of blood, which she thrust upon me, pursuing me when I fled and spattering that awful liquid upon me.

Today, I woke up alone. My clothes had been pressed and hung. The house appeared uninhabited, for no one answered my calls. I returned to the club with a growing sensation of unease and suspicion, for not a quarter mile from Madame Marie's the dry streets were clouded by dust and the parched air carried not a lick of moisture. Certainly, I have witnessed localized storms, but the boundaries of the tempest that soaked the City last evening appeared to be part of a much larger disturbance for the density of its deluge. My confusion grew as I walked along River Road and saw straw-like yellow grasses and breathed the stagnant odor of the docks, unwashed by any cleansing rain. Mainard was in a tizzy, wild-eyed and haggard-looking as if he hadn't slept in days. He brushed off my apology for the delay and commenced to drive home with an exhausted air. (I write here in the carriage to preserve my thoughts before I return to Belle Rive and the mendacity of that place, which grows distasteful to me, tears them from my hold.) Mainard does not speak to me, but only regards me with a wary eye.

I BELIEVE LITTLE in Spirit realms, ghosts, or heathen gods, but if such powers exist, they trifle with me and take great pleasure in batting me about between their paws. Devour me now, I say! My cowardly soul has little use for this world as it is. I cannot account for my time, and my unquiet mind will not make sense of these events, nor find suitable explanation for what has happened.

Belle Rive was as I had left it. My discomfort grew to a vibratory pitch, the taut strings of my nerves plucked by unseen fingers, as the carriage drew up and I heard Poupette's high voice shouting for Mme. Bilodeau. The girl sat on the portico engaged in some domestic task and once she spied me, set up a great cry.

Mme. Bilodeau came to the front door with Emilie behind her, struggling to push past her mother before breaking free and running to me. She wept fresh tears, having feared some terrible fate had befallen me—highway robbery, crashing into a ditch or being snatched by the slave patrol.

I learned that the evening post, delayed by a swarm of hornets terrorizing the road, arrived shortly after my departure and with it, Madame Marie's letter canceling my engagement. The Bilodeaus had anticipated my return the next day and when I did not, began to fear the worst. I spoke of the delaying rain, which vexed them as there had been no hint of foul weather, and my claim to have spent the night at the Dauphine went unheard. Emilie asserts that I have been gone two nights, not one as I insist. The details are etched firmly in my memory as if on stone, and I cannot be convinced two nights passed when I know that I was gone for but one.

But again creeps that subtle sensation of alarm, a murkiness of thought and recall, for that night with P'tite Marie did seem to exist beyond the natural boundaries of time. If I allow my rational mind to dwell on it, I notice the holes in the fabric of my story. I wear my truth like a protective cloak, when in fact, it is as threadbare as old lace.

The whole debacle has framed me in an unflattering light. Emilie has spent the evening in silence. I took supper in my study, where I intend to remain until the household settles into sleep, and I may walk these halls without suspicion. Clothilde watches me always with that rapacious gleam in her eyes as she wanders the house warbling out this gruesome hymn in her mix of tongues:

Ezili Dantor matres kay la, Erzulie Dantor mistress of the house
Ke ou se nwa, your heart is black
Tet moin si ti neg konnen nom li, loa dance in my head
Prete'm dedin a, lend me the basin
Pou m vomi san mwen, I vomit blood

A LETTER FROM Crunn! He has sold his mine shares and requests the details of the glass house I've chosen. He will place the order and have the kit shipped directly to Belle Rive. M. Bilodeau has put Albert in my care. Though sharp-minded and strong, he is often glum and rarely speaks. Removal from mundane toil in the fields will perhaps bring some relief to his dour mien.

Emilie is kind as ever and appears to be in good health, though she sleeps much and subsists mainly on Clothilde's vile-smelling tonics, broths, and puddings. My lost day is no longer mentioned. I do not know what she thinks of me, and I do not ask. We put it to rest and leave it undisturbed, but sometimes I find her gaze resting upon me, the slightest furrow on her brow. When caught, she wipes the expression away as if polishing a dusty surface, and replaces it with a benign smile. The eyes drop and she turns her head, her thoughts unspoken.

MY MIND WILL not rest. I've decided to journey to Metairie to speak to P'tite Marie about my lost night. I cannot explain how much these unsettling events have distressed me on the heels of that strange storm.

I contemplated engaging another errand for Clothilde, but should that old witch mention it to my wife, she may rightfully deny all knowledge of the incident and claim it a ruse. (I should like to have Albert drive me, but the Bilodeaus keep him—quite literally—under lock and key after his escape attempt.) I sent a letter to P'tite Marie and asked her to meet me in the garden adjacent the Orchid Society's offices. Fearing Emilie would intercept a reply, I asked her not to respond to my letter. I shall just have to trust that she comes to me.

How GLAD I am that I've accustomed myself to carrying this little journal everywhere with me, for it gives me the opportunity to capture my thoughts before they are lost and is a true friend in those times when I have none to confide to.

It was never my intention (at least that I would admit to myself) to make love again to that glorious girl. I've made every effort to push from my mind any memory of those infinitely sweet kisses served up by a velvety mouth, those bewitching smiles or the clever nuances of a conversation so deft and intelligent it challenges me as well as any man's! But the closer I drew, the more my heart began to pound with eager anticipation and my blood heat with desire.

Mainard left me at the offices just after the appointed time, and it was all I could do to dismiss him with any measure of calm. Was she there? I forced myself to enter the building and converse, however briefly, with the curator before excusing myself for a tour of the gardens. The sun hung from the sky, a glowing golden pendant that suffused the grounds with gentle pulsations of heat. Garden heliotrope (*Heliotropium arbo-*

rescens) were in bloom and their scent evanesced from the profuse purple blooms in dizzying waves. It is a scent I shall forevermore associate with this wondrously terrifying day.

She arrived like a freshening spring rain, bringing with her the hopes of a fertile and abundant summer. There is no greater pleasure in my life than her company, and though I fully inhabit each moment I spend with her, those minutes are accompanied by an abiding sorrow that we shall have to part and I'll know not when or if I shall see her again.

My love was an inquisitive little bird flitting from one topic to another, teasing out my thoughts with skill and gently inquiring about my wife. I admit I was relieved to have a sympathetic ear to hear my concerns about Emilie's growing fascination with Spiritualism. She told me that the ancestral gods of her religion, the *loa*, sometimes have loud voices and demand to be heard, so it is with Christian saints and souls. Too often they speak and we refuse to listen. We could not see the air we breathed, she said, or grasp it in our palms, but it was within and without us, a sustaining and vital force. So it is with the spirits. Like air, they can appear as destructive winds or caressing breezes. It was not rational, she said, to deny their power or presence. To do so was an affront, and I would arouse their anger if I did not heed their commands. Again, my reasonableness was found lacking.

That sparkling conversation thrilled me in new ways, for she is knowledgeable about many topics dear to my heart and can discourse as easily on the natural sciences as the philosophies of Kant, Rousseau, and Kierkegaard. Her humor is an ever-present grace, and throughout our walk, I found myself stirred to new depths of emotion. As dear as Emilie is to me, there are many subjects which languish between us for her lack of interest (or, in the case of her new religion and those associated with it, my own). Her affections seem clumsy and naïve in comparison to the ardor that P'tite Marie arouses, and my wife's comparatively childish caresses generate the most insipid of animal responses in me.

Alongside this keen passion of the mind, an attendant passion of the flesh was stoked. I could conceive of no greater pleasure in life than to hold P'tite Marie in my arms, taste her lips, run my hands along those succulent limbs, fill my hands and mouth with her tantalizing flesh. I begged to kiss her once more. Though some remote part of myself urged restraint and caution, I heeded it not. I was aflame! I cared not for the dangers in our being caught or what those damned Bilodeaus and their society should think of me. (I include the following details because it allows me to luxuriate in the retelling, to experience anew every thrilling tremor and flush of excitement with each reading.)

Together we tumbled into a grove inside the sweltering greenhouse, where taut stalks of tropical plants and their giant leaves acted as curtains to shield us from curious eyes. We fell upon one another in euphoric agitation; I could not get my flies undone quickly enough. Biting her lips, I pressed my bruising mouth to hers to quiet her noises. My climax was immediate and overpowering, but my zeal never waned and we tussled like fighting spiders—legs and arms locked and gripping. She rode me in waves that ebbed and crested, drawing me closer to the pinnacle of a second release but denying it me. I thought I should burst. Sensation pumped through me, blinding and deafening me to all cares or concerns. My angel removed herself to catch my seed in her mouth, sucking as if drawing out my very soul and I was lost, absolutely lost in her. She tapped the vein of my physical and spiritual essence, gorging herself to the point where pain overtook my pleasure and I could not push her away. It was like being smothered in the intoxicating, hypnotic embrace of a vampire. My desire to surrender absolutely was equally matched by my need to reclaim my sanity. The green garden spun around me. A nefarious sense of doom closed in. My heart shattered and I knew myself forever marked and claimed.

She vanished in the moment I closed my eyes to catch my breath. I stumbled from the garden to the waiting coach as if in the throes of fever. Mainard assumed me overcome by the sun and I encouraged this, retreating into silence.

The Bilodeaus, no doubt, begin to think me delicate, but I don't care. An incomplete man, I have blundered through all the moments of my life before she made me whole.

I HAVE STAGGERED through the days in a delirium, preoccupied with my fantasies of her. I inhabit dual realities—days filled with tedious details and obligations, lantern-lit nights spent gazing at the river and the stars, reliving the delicious torments of the garden tryst, pacing the boundaries of my study as if it were a prison cell. The very air is suffused with new gravity and each whispered breath runs over my skin, rousing new awareness.

More than once, I have taken myself in hand, stirring myself to ecstasy while reveling in the fragrance of heliotrope perfume daubed onto my handkerchief. My lust is equal only to my shame.

EMILIE IS ALL-CONSUMED by her Spiritualist studies and has become convinced that she can practice like the famous mediums and communicate directly with the departed. I do everything within my power to convince her that it would be wise not to exert her sensibilities at this delicate time. She says she will put these ideas aside and does, although I see they do not rest lightly within her, but fester like a boiling wound.

ALBERT AND I have cleared a plot for the glass house. Crunn writes again to encourage me to remain patient as there are legalities involved in the sale of his mine shares that must be settled before the transaction is final. The delay is an additional frustration when I have already waited so long to begin this project, but he assures me that all is well, and indeed, he may earn more than previously thought upon a second evaluation of the mine by assayers.

Belle Rive will hold a summer ball for the neighboring plantations. Emilie says it is a way to gain favor among the wealthier, white planters and that her parents intend to use the occasion to bolster their social standing. I find their motivations frivolous (as are they), but Emilie says it is good fun. She and Floriane are deep in planning, making crepe paper banners and chattering away amiably. It is good to see Emilie put aside her annoyances and enjoy pleasant conversation with her mother, for once.

Clothilde and the kitchen staff have been busy baking, and two hogs have been slaughtered for pit cooking. Being the strongest, Albert is always assigned the most arduous of physical tasks and now digs the pits (I can see him from my study window, dwarfed by distance and gleaming from exertion). The squeal of the hogs as their throats were cut nearly sickened me, but I held my ground, observing alongside M. Bilodeau and Prosper even as the creatures' bellies were slit and their shining, plump entrails pulled out by the handfuls to make sausages and chitterlings. Clothilde caught the blood in buckets for puddings, grinning and smacking her lips as the hot crimson flow splashed over her fingers. I fled, I admit that I did, my stomach clenched tight in revulsion, Clothilde's macabre song ringing in my head, "Lend me the basin, I vomit blood." The Bilodeau men laughed at me, but I do not care. Let them think me overly sensitive upon this grisly occasion. Isn't it enough that I have uncomplainingly withstood the brutalities that daily inhabit this place? I thought myself removed from it all here in my study, but the climate overwhelms me and the open window admits the rank odor of burning hair as the hog hides are cleaned.

It is in these moments that I feel myself most like an accessory in this household. A trivial decoration with no practical use. The temptation to flee to P'tite Marie is overpowering. I have not seen or written to her since our assignation in the garden and work mightily to keep her from my thoughts, but she is omnipresent, a lush and seductive ghost forever haunting me.

A GHOST WHO haunts me, unrelentingly! My guts lie in tight coils after this most arduous of days. Why does the universe insist on flaunting my marital failings by introducing P'tite Marie into every social event we attend? Just when I have at last convinced myself that there shall be no more contact, that I must never see her again and have made peace with that fact, she appears. Ubiquitous and unerring in her unacknowledged pursuits.

We attended a celebration at Oak Alley Plantation along with some thirty guests. Our hostess, Mme. Roman, is famed for the extravagance she flaunts at these summer balls and the circle of social elites and artists who top the guest list. In attendance were our neighbors and kin, several merchants with whom M. Bilodeau does business (or desires to), a riverboat captain, a few fellows from the club and their wives, and as entertaining novelties, a traveling Chinese aerialist and his protégé, and a female Tarot reader. The place had the air of a Russian traveling circus, foreign and slightly ominous. My noble-hearted wife and I circulated among the noisy crowd, smiling and greeting the revelers, answering their benign, pointless questions while I grew evermore agitated. The glaring sun pressed us toward the foetid ground like some punishing hand from the heavens. The cane flapped and rustled as if yearning to uproot itself and walk into the cooling river. Bluebottles swarmed in thick black clouds through the pit smoke, and the sounds of laughter and merriment pulsed in my ears like some cacophonous tune.

Our hostess pushed us toward her prized guest, the French novelist Alexandre Dumas, who arrived accompanied by an arrestingly bedecked woman wearing an enormous hat and veil that completely obscured her face. My heart convulsed with turmoil and every hair on my body stood on end when I recognized the wearer. A dagger of cold fear stabbed into my belly. It melted there like an icicle, pouring its sick dread into me. How profoundly I ached to lift that lace and reveal my beloved's precious face, but I knew I could not. What agony to feign disinterest, to appear aloof and train my hands to my sides when they longed only to caress her! She, too, played the game with grotesque ease, wringing the pain from an aching soul starved for her touch as if it mattered not to her that my mind was in turmoil and my body all aquiver with a desperate desire. Thus did I master my turbulent emotions and don a mask of polite indifference to distract from the chaos swirling within me.

M. Dumas introduced Mlle. Laveau, and as I accepted her gloved hand with my own trembling one, she lifted her veil and kissed me thrice, twice on one cheek, once upon the other. I faltered a moment, saying I had turned my ankle upon the lawn's uneven ground. M. Dumas caught me in his eagle-eyed stare and a twitch played at the side of his mouth. P'tite Marie cast a sly look at me and dropped her veil.

Relief came as a voice beckoned to the crowd, announcing that the aerialists would begin a show of contortions. M. Dumas shooed the women away and Emilie bubbled quite excitedly, clutching the arm of the woman in white to lead her toward the performers.

M. Dumas took my elbow, leaning in conspiratorially. "Forgive me, Isidore, I did not know she was an intimate of yours."

"No one does. It is a shame I try to forget, but she has beguiled me. I cannot rid myself of the thought of her."

He seemed to take particular delight in my discomfort, adding, "I know American attitudes are much less advanced than ours. I shall keep your secret, *mon frère.*"

I strove mightily to maintain my façade, but my pulse beat with such exertion that I feared others could hear it. I begged the gods to intervene and remove her entirely or to bring us together in some remote corner where I might steal a kiss from the lips as luscious as the icing that she licked from them as she hovered by the desserts table, cake in hand. Strong emotion is unfamiliar to me, and it took all my self-control to puppet myself through the celebrations, every moment achingly aware of her closeness.

Relieved to be free of the women, I enjoyed the novelist's charming stories (what a luxury to converse in my native tongue with a compatriot) and remained at his side while his companion kept company with my wife. M. Dumas was curious about how a gentleman like myself keeps himself occupied amid the grim conditions of a plantation, and so I commenced to tell him about my orchidarium, but all too soon, the aerialist took his bow and the performance ended.

Arm in arm, my wife and my mistress returned to me, Emilie gushing about P'tite Marie, "We have been having the most fascinating conversation about the Spirit world and the practice of vodou!"

The sight of them together held me in thrall. It was the cruelest jest. To be so close and unable to kiss her, to watch her gift her smiles so freely and know myself the only one whom she saw (but pretended not to see) was torture. I drank too much rum punch and my head spun. I could no longer observe that parody of life. Is this what they deem "love"? This demented suffering and agonizing, bodily pain? My heedless obsession wrested control of my senses and I lurched from that euphoric jubilee, staggering blindly away through the sweltering rickyards. To where I knew not, merely that her presence was the sweetest torment and I must escape it.

Grouped on their coarse porches, the slaves of Oak Alley enjoyed a reprieve and ate vinegared pork, greens, yams, and hoecakes. With blank faces, they watched me falter through their humble truck patches, trampling runner beans and okra. I fled to the riverbank and secreted myself aboard the Romans' keelboat anchored there, sobbing and laughing at the mess I'd made of my life.

The notion gripped me that I must categorize these feelings and learn if they were reciprocated or whether I merely wandered through a fantasy of my own creation. Unholy Lorelei that she is, P'tite Marie hearkened my silent calls. What succor, what corporal relief and pleasure filled my skin's envelope as I observed the soft patter of approaching footfalls, and smelled the perfume which announced her like a retinue of trumpet-blowing heralds!

Wordlessly we fell together, lips and bodies seeking total union. A fire raged within me and we tumbled into the empty cabin and fell upon the floor. She lifted her skirts and gave me what I desired and I thrust into her, pinning her long arms over her head as she moaned and writhed beneath me. "I love you," I murmured, "more than breath or life!

More than the sun or stars! You possess me, body and soul. I am yours, only yours, evermore."

She shuddered and heaved beneath me, biting my arm to stifle her cries as droplets sprang from her eyes and poured down her face. Her tender voice was broken as she spoke the words that bound us: "Yes, beloved, you are mine and I am yours. We are twain, cleaved souls sharing one mind, one heart. Ours is a love that will never be sundered, forsaken, or forgotten. *Cher* Isidore!" and we kissed again with hot, wet mouths while the distant band began to play, and stirring notes filled the stifling air.

We forced ourselves to disembark and returned separately to the picnic, moving through its charade. I saw the scene for what it was: a stage filled with marionettes twitching on invisible strings, a tableau of wooden mannequins. P'tite Marie and I circulated among the false figures, marveling at the love that enlivens us while others feel nothing at all.

GRAND NEWS! ANOTHER letter from Crunn arrived this morning. He has secured a buyer for his shares and writes that he will receive his payment within the week. I have completed the order for my glass house and composed a letter to the Orchid Society for the purchase of bulbs, which I will post upon receipt of Crunn's bank draft. Albert levels the plot for the glass house and digs the post holes after his day's work in the field is complete. As I do not want to deprive Albert of the few solitary hours allotted him each day, I have elected to join him in this task. Sunset finds us stripped to the waist, rakes and hoes in hand, breaking up the great mats of native grasses in this unused square of land. Albert's size dwarfs my own frame, and his back is striped with glistening ridges of mauve flesh where the pickling scarred the skin. I try not to stare, but on our first day, he met my gaze with his own inscrutable one. I attempted to convey some piteous apology for his sorry station, but he rebuffed me and turned away, his black eyes revealing no thought or emotion, for he is accustomed to thinking of himself as an object in the Bilodeaus' eyes and likely views me the same, someone from whom he must obscure his true emotion. We work till exhausted and I call a cease to our labors, then we cast our tools aside and allow relief to settle into our bones.

Emilie comes out and sits in a chair and reads till the light is gone, or sometimes she brings us lemonade or mint water with shortbread or slices of cake left over from dinner. I'm not sure what Albert thinks of her generosity. He merely thanks her and eats or drinks in silence before departing for his cabin. But we three sit on the blanket that Emilie spreads out and the night swells around us, warm and velvety, and I am content in some small way to be relieved, if temporarily, from my libidinous afflictions.

Tonight while undressing, I dropped my cuff link on the floor. When I bent to retrieve it, I discovered a jar of yellow liquid under the bed. This is one superstition I know, as there is a French variant. It's a binding spell. Emilie must be storing her first morning's urine in it to keep me from straying. This knowledge fills me with a disquieting mortification, for I have experienced true passion in the arms of my mistress, while for my wife, I am her first, only, and should I outlive her, her last lover. Whatever affection we have for each other is a product of duty as much as genuine emotion, whereas what I have felt (and continue to suffer) for P'tite Marie is a yearning so profound that it eclipses any other thought or sensation, an ardor which pervades my waking and sleeping hours and all the twilight moments between. Ours is the desire beyond all reason which drives a reasonable man to commit deeds once unthinkable.

SURELY I AM cursed. Madame Marie has asked Emilie and me to attend a séance in New Orleans. I humor my wife, for nothing convinces me that the departed remain on Earth in some ghostly guise to aid or harm us as these Spiritualists believe. By nature, a soul is an incorporeal thing. It is like the heat from a comforting fire contained within a house or hearth. Lacking bricks and walls to enclose it, heat dissipates, as the soul does when the body dies. It cannot remain intact in any form and surely does not linger among the living, taking an interest in situations and people it can no longer affect. Does the wind care for what we do? No. It blows without regard to our wishes; likewise the sun shines oblivious to our petty human dramas and the rains fall according to their whims, not when summoned by prayers, pleas, or magical dances.

This journey is merely an opportunity for me to put the shadow of my deception behind me and to strengthen the affection between me and my wife. I must not scan the streets for a glimpse of that bewitching temptress and stamp out any hopeful spark of a chance encounter. To entertain these thoughts would preoccupy mind and body so completely as to leave little room for any other sentiment.

SUMMER IS A grueling, bleak season in Louisiana. Belle Rive is focused solely on wringing as much profit from its lands as possible. The days grow long and excessively hot, sometimes oppressed by a layer of gauzy gray clouds which seem to retain all atmospheric heat and moisture. My sweat does not dry in this airless world but settles into the fabric of my clothing, dampening my hats and curling my hair. I am not pleased. England's balmy seasons and France's luxurious summers seem a remote fantasy, long ago dreamed.

Crunn again writes of a delay in selling his shares of the mine. It is a cruel blow. I have fixated upon the idea of my orchidarium with singular fascination and intent with the purpose of distracting myself from unruly thoughts. The only reprieve from this misery is Emilie, who has regained some of her luster and appetite. As she becomes more deeply enthralled by her new religion, the opinions she has kept relatively private now begin to find expression in her voice. She buckles under the yoke and seeks to throw off her parents' restraints upon her.

Spiritualism, she tells me, is concerned with liberation of mind and body, not solely the spirit. A woman should be free to speak her mind without fear of censure, ridicule, or defamation. She should be free to engage in intellectual pursuits with as much vigor as a man, and her involvement in the subjects which interest her should be respected as if she were a man—a free, white man of good standing. Why, she asks, should she be consigned to the traditional role of helpmeet when she aspires to something much greater?

"Truly, my darling," she said to me, "would you rather see me hide my light under a bushel and keep this world in darkness than be free to shine with all the power that is my birthright as a holy child of God?"

Those rosy cheeks and gleaming eyes affirm me that she possesses a high measure of self-belief, and I count myself fortunate to be married to one so charmingly fearless. Of late, she has spent nearly all her free time with her nose in a book or newspaper, reading about spiritual communication and the recountings of various mediums and their witnesses. She grows increasingly agitated about slavery and speaks wistfully of a free life away from the evils of Belle Rive. Could we not, she pleads, move North and join her dear friend Mrs. Stockton in New York? Emilie has an inheritance bequeathed to her by her great-aunt and insists we use this money to leave Louisiana.

However much I agree with her and would like to leave Belle Rive, thus freeing ourselves from the odious grasp of this place, to do so would put me far from P'tite Marie. I cannot bear the thought of doing so, very likely never meeting her again—no matter that I know it best—and so I contrive reasons to remain.

Tomorrow, we take part in the Société de Magnétisme et Hypnotisme event at Mme. Laveau's house in the French Quarter, where time once deserted me as I lay enraptured in the arms of my mistress. I hunger for my beloved's presence as much as I dread her appearance there. (What a shameful lampoon to play the doting husband in front of her! It is an insult to all involved.)

I have realized it is much better to avoid P'tite Marie altogether, for there is no future for us and every moment I spend in her presence or entertaining thoughts of her only fortifies my compulsion. I feel that if I am away from her long enough, my fascination will sputter and die. That one day I'll be able to look upon her with as little emotion as a stranger, but that day feels very distant indeed. I may well be old and gray before she slips from my mind entirely, for I am often reminded of her in the simplest things, a sunset or perfect blossom I would share, and my work on the orchidarium. None of which belong to her but are mine alone or mine to share with Emilie. Sometimes I feel that I function with only one arm, one eye, for my beloved possesses the others.

We spent two days in New Orleans to attend the séance at Mme. Laveau's. I was pleased to see M. Dumas in attendance, along with four other men and women. P'tite Marie served as her mother's assistant, and neither one mentioned our long-ago dinner—acting as if I were merely another curiosity seeker and adherent of the new faith. P'tite Marie seated herself between myself and Emilie, much to my wife's delight and my consternation. Her bare hand fit into mine perfectly, smooth and warm, and I fought the urge to kiss it. The lamps dimmed, the incense burned, and Mme. Laveau summoned the spirits, calling for Papa Legba to open the gate. A tremor of anticipation ran through me as the ritual began. Dual currents of desire and repulsion traveled along my network of nerves. How I longed to be alone with her and yet how mightily I resisted the attraction!

Two of the women there, sisters, sought contact with their deceased father. Mme. Laveau called him and the sisters asked their questions, murmuring and softly weeping as Mme. Laveau answered for him. Next, M. Dumas queried about a departed friend, a soldier killed in action some years ago, and received word from beyond that his fellow was well and at peace.

Mme. Laveau asked the room if any others had questions. From the corner of my eye, I saw Emilie squeeze P'tite Marie's hand and ask for a message from the child she lost or about any other troubles plaguing Belle Rive. There was a lengthy silence. Emilie's hopeful expression turned worried and grew dull as no response was forthcoming. No spirits answered her call. Suddenly, Mme. Laveau hissed, "Spirit! I sense your presence! I smell your perfume and feel the agonies of your soul in the air around us! Come forth and speak to us."

The candles in the center of the table smoked violently and their flames danced as if in a strong breeze, but the windows were tightly closed, their curtains drawn. A shudder ran through each of us. I heard Emilie's voice as if calling from another room. P'tite Marie gasped and her hand went limp in mine. I smelled the sharp odor of spilled blood, musty and thick. Terror gripped my heart. The candles extinguished themselves and the sisters shrieked and moaned.

The decaying fumes of antique parchment and burnt meat filled my nose, and the unmistakable odor of a woman's sexual organ. Something the texture and temperature of a monstrous eel that has lain at the bottom of a frozen lake swam into me, overtaking me with its viscous evil and stealing my air. I choked on it as if on a rank clot of jellied blood but could not expel it from me.

Emilie cried out in horror as the table leapt and juddered beneath our clasped hands, its four legs thumping violently against the floor. I watched in helpless horror as my adored fainted, barred from doing anything more than observing with mild concern as my heart raced with agonies of anxiety. It took all my strength to restrain myself from clasping her in my arms and kissing her back to life in front of my wife. I lingered as long as was polite, rent in two with my desire to invest body and soul in caring for P'tite Marie and my fervent need to flee before I gave myself away.

My hands will not cease their trembling. Look how shaky my writing! I feel myself to be in all ways bedeviled and my firmly held beliefs, those which I have always trusted to steady me through life's storms and to serve as the Gibraltar to which I cling during moral and spiritual crises, have deserted me. All is thrown into chaos.

IN THE COACH Emilie asked repeatedly if I "had seen her" hovering above the table, a vicious mirage with tragedy-twisted features and blood-soaked hands. I had not, but Emilie insisted that some violent specter had stared directly at me and flung itself into my open mouth just before I began to gasp and choke.

"It looked like you inhaled a swarm of bees, Isidore. I was terribly frightened, but I knew that spirits have no wish to harm us and so I could bear it." Only later, when settled in our hotel bed, did Emilie point out that she had asked her question in vain, for unlike the others, she received no reply.

AT LAST MY turmoil settles enough for me to begin to analyse the events of the 7th. I've suffered two days of intermittent spells where I am beset by cold fears, fevers, and distressing dreams while asleep and awake, in which I find myself approaching some ominous house with a vague resemblance to my beloved's but whose dimensions are grossly magnified and twisted into monstrous shapes. Whatever Spirit latched onto me at that séance will not release me. There are three components to my internal disturbance:

First, my intellectual processes are disrupted by the evidence and appearance of something which defies logic, thus confounding all my suppositions about the physical nature of the universe.

Second, I now question my philosophy professors and the metaphysical instruction I received in Catechism and from Maman, and wrestle mightily with existential questions about the afterlife. Is it a place of peaceful respite? If Spirits remain on Earth after death, what is their nature? How can a being exist without a body? Is there life everlasting, truth to the message we are spoon-fed from cradle to grave?

And third, if such dimensions exist, then it would follow that all other things are possible—angelic and demonic realms, limbo and purgatory, even black magic and witchcraft. If Emilie's Spirits are real, as has been shown to me, then mustn't Clothilde and P'tite Marie's vodou *loa* have as much validity?

These contemplations plague me with their endless harangues. I have always considered myself a reasonable man, even of temper and disposition, a humble drone in service of Philosophy's great questions, yet also a man who is firmly entrenched in Reason. I have never experienced any existential crises about my place in this Universe of ours, but now…

I must make a staunch effort to repel the tendrils of fear that snake through the dark hours of my imaginings. I am greatly disturbed. It as if someone has opened a door in the floor of my house to show me the flaming fields of devils who lurk below our familiar and beloved Earth, waiting to devour our Souls.

At last, a letter from Crunn! The assayers have valued his shares at a significantly greater price and Crunn says that he has met a Mr. Quincey, the English glazier who helped build London's famed Crystal Palace. He desires to engage the man to make the frames and plates for our venture. I am beyond myself with delight. However, the cost increases significantly, to sixteen thousand dollars from eight. Crunn assures me that we will earn back our investment within a few short years as my orchidarium will rival the botanical gardens and conservatories in Washington D.C., Philadelphia, Boston, and New York.

The legal delays in selling the mine shares for the higher price mean that Crunn will not have my bank draft for another month or so, and he asks if I would consider paying the glazier myself to secure his hire and Crunn will reimburse me as soon as his transaction is final. He included the necessary information for a wire transfer should I find a way to make it possible.

Sixteen thousand is far beyond my own wealth. I consider asking M. Bilodeau for a loan, but I have felt a distinct coldness from him of late—perhaps he resents my refusals to accompany him to his club for more sordid shenanigans—and a bank would require significant collateral, which I cannot provide, having little in my own name. I sent a response telling Crunn that I am working to obtain the funds—we cannot let the glazier get away—and will write again soon.

I have written to P'tite Marie to request a spell to help me get money to hire the glazier. Perhaps I wrote because at last I had an excuse to contact her even though I felt a fraud in doing so. Often have I ridiculed the heathen vodou religion, cast aspersions on Emilie's belief in spirits, and denigrated the superstitious practices of this Catholic family, but my experiences at the séance begin to worm into my mind, hollowing out my own rationale to make room for those dark mysteries. M. Bilodeau has great faith in Clothilde's ability to ease his pains, just as Emilie believes that mediums can speak to the dead and Floriane is convinced that the Eucharist is the transubstantiated body and blood of Christ. What beliefs have I? Faith in the power of reason, science, and nature? Before Leeuwenhoek first spied bacteria under a microscope, we had no knowledge of that invisible world. How can I continue to cling to my rigorous notions when events contrive to dispel them?

P'TITE MARIE HAS responded to my request for aid. I received a package today with a red flannel gris-gris bag which I am to carry on my person at all times and reveal to no one lest they draw the luck from it. The instructions say to bathe with goat-milk water, then stand at a crossroad beneath a waxing or full moon, anoint the ground with salt and rum, and chant *Oshun besta ke lo bu* three times while I cut a lock of my hair and add it to the bag. When I return, I am to empty the contents of a wax envelope into a glass of red wine or brandy and drink it. I write them here because I will burn her letter, as she asks, along with the packet of dry herbs I cannot identify, despite scouring my books for their names. This should bring me my heart's desire and I will soon procure the funds to begin the glass house project with Crunn. Tonight, the moon is nearly full. I will not hesitate to follow my adored's instructions, no matter how lunatic I seem.

I WAITED UNTIL midnight last night to sneak from my bed and traverse the half-mile from Belle Rive to the nearest crossroad. A wispy river fog snaked over the ground with the insidious deliberation of some creeping apparition. Still I carry the lingering fear that I should again feel the slimy, cold intrusion of that lake eel, or find my throat clogged with insects. I shivered as I turned in a circle, sprinkling salt and rum on the damp, clinging dirt. The incantation felt like froth in my mouth as I choked it out, my face aflame with embarrassment. My only consolation was my solitude, but as I walked back I spied a lantern flickering beneath distant trees. The light soon winked out, leaving me with the discomfiting sense of having been watched.

At breakfast, Clothilde said she'd sent my boots to be cleaned as they were covered with mud, provoking curious looks from Emilie, who had herself removed my clean boots before we crawled into bed. That stupid old woman! Was she the source of the light I saw? Had she followed me?

It does nothing but convince me that I must be very cautious about my personal activities and correspondence, for she is not to be trusted with secret keeping.

MY WIFE GROWS plump and rosy, and we lie together at night, our hands on her belly, feeling the child within stir. I must smile and nod and play the role of doting husband, allowing her these indulgences because it turns up the flame in her eyes and gives her comfort.

THE SPELL WORKED! I would dance a jig if there were not always so many eyes about this place. I don't know what results P'tite Marie's spell intended, but a solution presents itself. Two days ago, M. Bilodeau called me into his private study and changed our fortunes. Since my arrival last year, he affirms that he has come to trust me as a reasonable, practical man with his daughter's well-being ever present in my thoughts (at this, I was careful to maintain a straight face) and my signature would transfer the holding of Emilie's inheritance (some twenty thousand dollars) to me. He made me promise that I would not give credence to her ridiculous pleas to leave Belle Rive. M. Bilodeau would see her die and be buried here where she belongs, rather than leave Prosper alone to manage the plantation after his father's death.

Today he received a letter from his solicitor confirming the change. I will draw against the inheritance to hire the glazier and purchase the kit, with the intention of replacing the money as soon as Crunn sends payment. I dispatched a letter to him immediately informing him that I would wire the money to him by week's end.

EMILIE IS TERRIBLY distraught today and rages against her parents and this place. She found Poupette sobbing in the stable in a torn and bloodied gown with fresh gashes on her legs, presumably from a belt buckle. Upon examination, Emilie discovered that the girl had been intimately assaulted. She took it upon herself to summon every male person at Belle Rive and line them up in front of the whipping post, then M. Bilodeau and Floriane came from the house, M. Bilodeau limping quite badly from rheumatism and shouting that she must stop her ranting. He was infuriated that she had called cease to the field work and caused delay during such a busy time. At Floriane's urging, Clothilde took Poupette inside while Floriane tried to soothe the anger between father and daughter, but Emilie was not to be silenced. Her face turned scarlet and ugly as she moved along the row of men, searching their clothing for tell-tale stains, their faces for guilt or some obscenely loitering pleasure.

Mr. Plunkett sported raw scratches on his dirty face. Blood seeped through the scraggle of his black beard and his collar was torn. Plunkett's admission that he had had sex with the girl at her request tripled Emilie's fury. Emilie raged and wept, while the slaves looked on with a dull horror and Plunkett exulted in his crime, a lurid grin upon his lips.

She begged her father to tie the driver to the post and give him the whipping he deserved. M. Bilodeau slumped against the veranda railing and said he was sorry that Poupette was hurt, but she was no better than a beast, and he would likely punish a man more for doing the same to one of his goats. He shouted that vile verse that all slavers hold up as truth, Peter 2:18, "Slaves, be subject to your masters with all reverence, not only to those who are good and equitable but also to those who are perverse," before limping back into the house.

Floriane slapped the man, and announced that he would lose a month's pay if he touched her "baby doll" ever again. Prosper and I watched glumly. For once he had no opinion, and I was frozen by the frenzied wailings of my wife as she clutched her round belly and fell to the dirt, howling in grief.

Together Floriane and I helped Emilie inside and laid her to bed, and Prosper rode off to fetch M. Fournier. He gave her a sleeping draught and confined her to bed for the duration of her sickness. Any exertion may bring the fetus to bear before its time, and we are to treat her with utmost care.

PLUNKETT HAS DISAPPEARED from Belle Rive. Emilie and Floriane are pleased that he has run off, but M. Bilodeau says Plunkett is a dutiful man and loyal worker who would not abandon his post just because of a misunderstanding. Prosper and Ramón are searching the grounds. I assume the man is lying drunk somewhere and worry little for the fate of one such as he.

PROSPER AND RAMÓN sent word throughout the nearby parishes asking for news of the slave driver Plunkett, but received no reply. Emilie has requested Poupette serve her, alongside Clothilde. Floriane was displeased to give up her toy but has allowed the girl to become Emilie's companion as long as she is bedridden. Together they make the baby's layette, and Poupette improves her limited reading so that she can entertain Emilie by reading the newspaper and ladies' journals.

These theatrics serve as a welcome distraction from my own racing mind and its efforts to put the séance behind me. I haven't slept very well for the memory of that cold eel slithering into my body like some lethal vapor. There is no news from Crunn. Awaiting a change of fate, I languish in this fulsome heat. Work songs echo from the cane fields and thus do I accept the slaves' instruction to keep my hand on that plow and hold on, hold on.

MAINARD INFORMED M. Bilodeau he observed Albert prowl the night carrying a small bundle of something which he dumped forthwith into the fish pond. Albert was summoned before his master but refused to speak, even when threatened with gibbeting. M. Bilodeau, Prosper, Mainard, and I went to the pond and watched Mainard root through the muddy shallows in the spot where he'd seen Albert. Prosper joined in, eager for something to do, and shortly pulled several bones from the mud. I identified them as broken rib bones and the knobby end of a human femur.

Next, they searched Albert's cabin, tearing up the floor and hearth, where they found a belt buckle, identified as Plunkett's by Ramón, and several burned and crumbled bones. Again, I confirmed that they were human. I wished to God that they were animal bones, but the gritty, sticky ashes were too much like crematory remains to be mistaken for anything else.

Albert is chained to a post in the yard awaiting the sheriff's arrival. Dismay weighs heavy upon me, for Albert's punishment will most likely be execution, no matter that he was defending Poupette, whom he adores like a sister.

NEVER HAVE I ever passed a more dreadful fortnight than here at Belle Rive. Every person—slave, master, or mistress—is tainted by the murder of Mr. Plunkett. Tensions run very high and each of us rests uneasily in our beds. We have ascertained that Albert likely ambushed Plunkett sometime at night, killed him, and chopped the body into several pieces to fit it into the fireplace. None of the other slaves has admitted to hearing or seeing anything, even under the threat of whipping.

Poupette wept for several days after Albert was arrested, until Floriane grew despondent and banished her to Emilie's full-time care. My sweet wife is the only one around whom Poupette is somewhat cheerful. Emilie is teaching her lace-making and crochet patterns. She even shares her lunches with the girl. I wonder if Poupette knows that this time with Emilie may be the best she will experience here or elsewhere in this cruel country.

The excitement wears on M. Bilodeau. His rheumatism flares, and his face is gray with pain. His usual ribald humor is absent. Even though I do not always like the man, it is preferable to see him lively, fiery-tempered, and vivacious than the grizzled ghost who has taken his place. In his stead, Prosper has eagerly taken over some of his father's duties, but he manages people poorly—working them too hard or too little. He is careless with equipment. He pulls slaves from the tasks they do well and assigns them some other to learn. Floriane spends much time fretting over her husband, and so I am left to serve as intermediary, arguing with Prosper, fielding M. Bilodeau's many questions, and handling Ramón's complaints.

Prosper sent word to Belle Rive's neighbors and business acquaintances looking for a "strong, good-natured, and agreeable" slave to buy. We have placed an ad looking for a new driver, but few are eager to apply since our last ended up burnt to bits. We feel the lack of Albert's strength. His crime, and Plunkett's, have cast indelible shadows on each of us here.

M. Bilodeau's physician, M. Fournier, came today to examine Poupette and informs us that despite her small size and sweet, simple nature, she is likely a woman of thirteen or fourteen. Emilie had urged Clothilde to brew herbal abortifacients for the girl and was certain to make sure that she drank them, but only time will tell us if Plunkett has sired a child in her.

Upon examining Emilie, Fournier recommended that she remain in bed until labor commences. With the recent stresses and her loss, he fears that she will give birth too early. She grumbled about his prescription, but she is willing to do anything to ensure we have a healthy babe.

ALBERT IS JAILED and awaiting trial. I am greatly saddened to think of that large, peaceful man locked up in a tiny, stifling cell where the futile stench of decay pervades every corner and death is imminent. I am powerless to help him.

Crunn writes that he has secured the glazier and they are drawing up plans. Once completed, they will mail me a copy and place the order for Rolled Glass plates made at a factory in Albany, New York. The iron trusses will be completed and shipped separately, and then the glazier, Mr. Quincey, will accompany the glass plates to Belle Rive to help me assemble them. Crunn adds that he will also ship a selection of bulbs that he intends to buy at the winter Flower Show. One bad thing is balanced by a good thing, and I am left even-keeled.

YESTERDAY I ACCOMPANIED Prosper to the town of Convent, some twenty miles east, to assess a new purchase—Albert's replacement. This fellow is older than Albert, but also very large. He appears to be fashioned entirely from tree trunks, so solid and thick are his limbs. Coffee, as he is called, seems more placid or at least more stoic than Albert, and after excessive poking and prodding from Prosper (to which Coffee mutely surrendered), I intervened. He speaks no French and cannot read or write, but his master assures us there have never been any problems with him. He seemed genial if reserved and somewhat downcast. I suspected him so beaten down by his life in bonds that it no longer mattered where he lived or what fate befell him. Upon further questioning about his history, I learned that Coffee's wife had died in childbirth. The infant was stillborn and very small. The remaining two children were sold off shortly after. His palpable misery had been an aggrievance to his mistress, along with complaints that it took too long for him to eat his meals. (An examination of his oral cavity reveals several rotten teeth, which the smithy will likely pull.)

We bought Coffee for the sum of $600, and he was given a moment (at my urging) to gather his few meager possessions. He settled himself in our cart, clutching a cloth bag and a stack of neatly folded clothing. Prosper babbled like an idiot the whole drive home, congratulating himself on his financial acumen and elaborating on his plans for Belle Rive. I sweltered in the humidity, covering my nose against the smell of labored horses, unwashed bodies, and the alcohol on Prosper's breath. Relief came only once or twice, when breezes gifted us the fresh scent of sweet grasses. Coffee stared at his feet or at the Mississippi's greenish water and I wondered what he was thinking. How would I feel if some stranger came to Belle Rive and purchased me?

All manner of strange thoughts filled my head during that long drive. Every longing, question, fear, hope, and impulse forced open the sealed doors I had sequestered them behind and burst forth to crowd my mind. My constant battle against my desire and longing for P'tite Marie, my guilt, my fleeting fantasies about returning to France to farm the broken-down Saint Ange estate, squelched worries and uneasiness about the glass house project, my discomfort with plantation life, my station here and the alienness of the South. I felt myself beset by imps who plucked and prodded me just as Prosper had done to Coffee. Of late, I find unwelcome thoughts manifesting in my brain. A stranger's words overtaking my own. Impulses that must be crushed and discarded. I try not to be troubled but dismiss these as impressions left on a weak mind after troubling events.

A LETTER FROM Crunn arrived containing the plans for my orchidarium. It is breathtaking. I had not dared to imagine that it would be so glorious! He received the funds and set Mr. Quincey to work immediately. He says I should be proud of my countryman, Henri Giffard, and encloses a newspaper illustration of Giffard's steam-powered dirigible about which he is very enthusiastic. Delivery of my glass plates and iron framing should occur within two months' time.

DAMNED CLOTHILDE! THAT snooping old woman will be the death of me the way she creeps about this place with her eyes upon me, watching, waiting. I had a bath three days ago, in our chamber. Emilie had made one of her rare excursions to the first story and I was alone. Sometimes she grows so tired of confinement she gets up and wanders about until Floriane catches her and returns her to bed like a naughty child. After the water was carried away and the tub removed, I could not locate my gris-gris bag. I searched everywhere I had been in the past day and did not discover it. I suffered superstitious worries that my plan would somehow go awry, the entire project falter and collapse if I did not find it. This worry ate at me throughout supper. I feared its discovery, perhaps to be thrown away or worse, someone else wearing it and destroying its magic.

It is the only tangible link I have to my beloved and is therefore infinitely precious.

My wife and I were abed in our nightclothes when Poupette came in, bringing a posset for Emilie. That foolish child had my bag in her hand and told me that Clothilde had found it and asked it returned to me. Knowing, without doubt, that Emilie would inquire about it, which she did.

"Give it to me!" We said it simultaneously, but favoring her mistress, the girl placed the bag in Emilie's hand. She frowned, undoing the leather thong and displacing the tiny metal talisman of a two-headed human body. I quivered as she emptied the pouch's contents into her hand, scattering ashes and broken herbs onto her round belly, and I finally saw what I had been carrying with such protection and care all this time. A small, jointed bone, terminating in a claw. A knot of black hairs tied around a nail. The small gold cross belonging to my mother I'd lost at Congo Square. A shard of purple crystal and a dull silver stone that Emilie turned over and over in her fingers. Poupette stood by the bed, observing. Clothilde must have instructed her to bring back news of my reaction.

"Isidore, can this be yours?" Emilie inquired.

I denied it half-heartedly, lest I initiate a Shakespearean tragedy by protesting too much. Playing my part, I feigned mild interest in her find. "I know this one," she said, fingering the purple gem. But the rest? Eager for distraction and a chance to show off her knowledge, Poupette detailed the contents, curdling my blood.

The Venus stone, an amethyst, for love and psychic power. The joint snapped from a skeletal paw would be a black cat bone. The cross? A personal item sacred to its owner. Magnetic lodestone, to draw your desires to you. "The nail and hair?" I asked, swallowing the wobble in my voice. Rocking on her heels with excitement, Poupette said it was a "twine"—the twisted hair of two people—knotted around a Saint Elena nail to join hearts and souls together. Poupette added, "Red bag for love. If someone made it themselves, it draw the one they want to them. If made for another, the stone draw the wearer to the maker!"

"Why, Isidore," cried Emilie. "Your face! Are you ill?"

I claimed the smell of that foul heathen token was an affront to my sensibilities.

P'tite Marie had tricked me, conjured me like some ordinary, uneducated fool. My love was not my own. I had believed that I dabbled in the dark arts to secure means to build my orchidarium. Instead, I conjured myself into an unhealthy *idée fixe* whose insoluble bonds betoken permanent ensnarement.

"Take it away and burn it!" I cried, unable to smother the fire that raged within me, snatching the stones from my startled wife's hands and flinging them at the door. In the second that I held it, the lodestone had grown hot in my palm, and I rubbed at the red mark it left. Quaking, Poupette crawled the room, collecting the items before scurrying off to Clothilde. I denied Emilie's attempts at conversation, cutting down each query as if it were a stalk of cane beneath my gleaming machete. I closed my eyes to the fire simmering within me. I have slept poorly, that night and every night since, for that is the night I entered the perfidious habitation that stalks my dreams and encountered the vampiric wraith therein.

P'TITE MARIE THINKS she has a claim on me. She calls up the spirits of her country religion to smite me. She begs her dark gods to turn my head and stir lust in me, to curdle my loyalty to Emilie and render it foul and unfit. If any should ask, I claim ignorance.

But no matter how I resist her lure, no matter the heat of my anger and the shame of my gullible betrayal, still, I yearn for her touch, and long to see and speak to her, to kiss her lips, to lose myself in her embraces. Am I ensorcelled? Cursed? Enslaved by magic?

Strangely, I have been consumed with nocturnal visions of a diabolical house looming at the terminus of a long road that snakes beneath tall, crooked oaks, whose dusty moss drapes nearly to ground, brushing my face, clinging horridly to my clothes as I pass. In this dream, I walk through an oppressive twilight toward the house, trepidation assailing me, irresistibly drawn forward while knowing I should not enter where nightmares with scrabbling claws await my imperiled soul. She visits me there, a shadowy beauty creeping through the halls of an enormous house—always the same house—her black hair flowing as if moving on underwater currents. My desire is its own force, a longing so powerful that it stirs my sleeping flesh to response.

I wake drowsy and spent, as if from hours of lovemaking, to drag myself through another day, haunted by memories of my dreams, her touch, a pleasure so intense it is akin to agony. My own moans disturb my rest and yank me from slumber. I am vaguely aware of pushing myself into the soft heat of a feminine body whose firm, round belly at last asserts that it is not P'tite Marie's alluring specter I embrace but Emilie's sturdy, earthly form.

Despite the turmoil of my emotions at P'tite Marie's deception, a small part of me inflames with joy. She so desired me that she endeavored to bind me to her by commanding the powers of her gods to make me hers. She wants me with an intensity that matches my own. This knowledge is a scintillant star forever guiding us toward one another.

LABOR BEGINS! I am here in my study, listening to the muted voices of the women in our chamber. The house is abuzz with anticipation and we men have been shooed away like pesky flies to await the presentation of our newest family member.

It is a welcome diversion from my own thoughts. I thought writing would help to settle my brain, but I can scarce concentrate, and resign myself to pacing until I am summoned.

THERE WERE MOMENTS today when I thought my entire life lost in a gush of blood. Emilie came through the birth with ease and strength. *L'enfant* came quickly on a surge of water and greeted the world with a lusty cry. How my chest swelled with pride at the sight of him!

All had been well until then. Clothilde was by her side, and for once, I was glad of the old woman's presence. The babe was cleaned, swaddled, and set to breast. I thought the whole process ended, but Clothilde waited with a grim expression. She and Floriane conferred and only hastily explained their concerns when I pressed for an answer. The afterbirth had not come. It must be expelled or infection quickly sets in. Clothilde palpated Emilie's abdomen and dispersed a tincture to her while Floriane took the baby. Poupette held Emilie's hand, murmuring encouragements as Emilie at last began to cry out and writhe, her body clenched and spasming upon the bed.

I have seen sheep and pigs give birth in my youth, kids and piglets sliding effortlessly from their mute mothers, but human women do not endure their pains with the same stoic grace. Emilie turned quite gray and wept from pain as Clothilde manipulated her belly with cruel hands. The blood came and a glistening, crimson organ rode its tide, as thick and wide as a man's liver. But the flow did not stop. It soaked the pads and dripped onto the floor. Emilie's eyes met mine, a gaze of such naked fear and desperation I thought my own heart should shatter under the weight of my helplessness.

At last, however, the treatments worked. My wife is saved. My child lives and I utter thanks to the powers beyond that they survive.

WE HAVE A son—Théodore Marcel Bilodeau Saint-Ange. He is a perfect specimen with a firm grip and full head of dark hair. They sleep now, but I cannot. I don't want the intrusion of my wretched imaginings to spoil this perfect day and so I remain awake, sitting in this chair by the fire where I can watch my wife and child in peaceful, blessed repose. Truly I am a man transformed.

I AM TWENTY-EIGHT today. Emilie served a sponge cake she baked herself, and we ate it together on the veranda while Poupette served tea. Théodore lay in his bassinet, entranced by the colored ribbons and feathers Poupette tied to its handle, and Emilie, kind Emilie! bade her sit with us and eat. She was happy to do so. Emilie speaks again of moving North and does so in front of Poupette. She believes that I share her enthusiasm to leave this place, but I cannot conceive of removing myself from the poignant, indelicate torture of my affair, nor exclude any possibility that I may see my beloved again, however keen my agonies.

Floriane has charged me with visiting St. Augustine's in New Orleans to arrange the christening and make an offering to the church. Increasingly, I am a soul divided. The gleaming light and promise of my new family is overcast by the impertinence of my salacious dreams. I have concluded that there is a supernatural agency at work within me. Why else would this stubborn affliction persist despite all attempts to vanquish it? I consider asking the priest to remove P'tite Marie's spell from me, but chastise myself for even giving it credence. If I do not believe in her magic, surely it can have no power over me. I did not believe in spirits and yet I saw one at the séance and see it again in my dreams. Belief, I find, exists independently of any physical evidence to prove or disprove anything. I had thought that whatever is, *is*, and whatever is not, *is not*, but now I must revise my opinion. What *is not*, is simply *unseen* or *unknown*.

EMILIE TELLS ME that Plunkett's attack has borne fruit. Poupette will bear a child. She is oddly excited about the arrival of her own baby, and greatly enjoys all the preparations for it. Again my wife presses me to take her from this place. The Stocktons await our decision and no doubt grow impatient with Emilie's persistence and my resistance. Daily, she offers her pleas and plans, which now include Poupette. Why not replace Lavinia and take the girl with us? She would be our paid domestic, and her child would have the chance to grow up in the free North. Since she has proven herself woman enough to entice a man and birth a child, Floriane has abandoned her pet to Emilie's care.

I cannot tell Emilie that her funds have gone to buy my glass house, for she would not approve the hasty secrecy of the expenditure. Though the money is legally mine, for I am her husband, I want our endeavors to have a sense of cooperation. In that I have failed. Once Crunn returns the money to me, I will tell Emilie to write to the Stocktons and procure freedom papers for Poupette and her child. (A date has been set for poor Albert's trial. I wish it were in my power to aid him as well.) I'll build my glass house and perhaps can train Mainard to manage it. The Bilodeaus will benefit greatly from its presence and the added income it will bring from visitors.

Though I write these plans on paper, I already know myself for a fool and a liar.

TOMORROW, MAINARD WILL drive me to New Orleans in the Rockaway carriage to speak to the priest at St. Augustine's. The whole day long, I have plotted to place myself where I might engineer a chance encounter with P'tite Marie—on the street, at the church or a café. Wishing that my longing would metamorphose into a physical force to compel her to me, as surely as a beckoning hand or a rope that I might pull. My desire for her is a desiccated kernel rooted in an open, leaking wound, disrupting my sleep and disquieting my mind. Whenever I allow my thoughts to linger too long upon her, I am suffused with an inescapable voracity. I hunger for her. Thirst for her. Can scarce direct my thoughts into any other channel, for they build, coalesce, and overflow their boundaries, pooling again in that same, worn groove. I know that I should keep to my task, but I am compelled, as if by magnetic forces, to seek her out.

DARK CLOUDS HAVE cluttered the sky all day and the warm air is malodorous with the stench of blood, faeces, and death from the butchery where they slaughter hogs and cattle for the week's market. St. Augustine's is the church where free Negroes, Creoles, and Mulattoes worship. As such, one must traverse unsavory areas where the City's worst industries reside—tanneries stinking of urine, paint factories, smelteries and foundries, all of them belching fumes, smoke, and sparks into the polluted air.

The Bilodeaus worship here because Clothilde is allowed to attend Mass. Although she is hardly treated better than a slave at Belle Rive, she is still *à la mère de famille*. The priest is a free man of color, even-tempered yet fiery in the pulpit, and much admired for his passionate embrace of the sacraments. Our meeting was brief. Théodore will be baptized on All Saints' Day. Floriane wants it to happen as quickly as possible. His soul is not safe until then, and she says that the souls of innocent children are sweets to entice the Devil from his hiding place in Hell. I do not object to this display of their faith for once, knowing now that the Spirit Realm so closely overlays our own, and there are powers both Dark and Light at war in this world. Worse, I fear the influence of vodou upon my child—that my mistress may take offense to this new life that demands my attention and seek to reclaim that attention through means fair or foul. (I do not know why these suspicions have taken hold of me in recent weeks. I fear myself the recipient of some Spiritual Contagion that seeps into my skin and organs, poisoning my dreams, infecting my rational Self and filtering all my perceptions through a diseased veil of superstition and paranoia.)

I told Mainard that he may have the weekend to visit his family in a nearby parish. He carries his freed man's pass upon his person at all hours and so I little fear he will encounter any trouble for driving alone. His delight was fierce. I believe it is the only time I have seen the man smile. Once he departed, I sent a brief letter to Emilie, telling her that I will remain in the City until Monday to purchase items for Théodore and manage my own business affairs. A glorious sense of expansion set upon me. My fetters fell away. Immediately, I dispatched a note telling P'tite Marie that I am in residence here. Although she has vilely deceived me with her vodou trickery, I begin to find the sin forgivable. Her actions were driven by yearning and an all-consuming desire to hold on to what was once so dear to us both. Now, I sit in my room anticipating her arrival, every part of me humming with a strange, glorious energy knowing that she will stand before me, close enough to touch and to kiss. How desperately I await her touch upon my skin!

WORDS DO NOT adequately describe the depths of the ocean of pleasure in which I swim. Never have I been so passionately transported! She speaks to me in my own language, and I am understood. It is as though I am a solo traveler in a foreign world and have finally encountered my kindred. She makes me whole. She remakes my fragmented body as Isis once did for her beloved Osiris. She pours honeyed wine for me to sip, feeds me sugared beignets from her rosy lips, and clings to me. She opens beneath and above me and showers me in the fragrant dews of her magnificent body. It is as if I do not inhabit my own familiar self, but that of a god, diaphanous and eternal. I scarce mind her rituals when she anoints and burns her candles or sets out offerings to her *loa*. We speak of great things and those trivial and silly, and she laughs low in her throat with the satisfied rumble of a purring lioness. My anger is a childish and faint-remembered thing. Let me be bewitched then! Let the *loa* braid our souls together, for there is no greater bliss than what I have found in her arms.

Emilie and Belle Rive leave faint impressions upon my memory. My wife has become as unreal to me as a character in a novel. I have striven to love her heart and soul but discover it an impossible task when my heart and soul belong to another. The only intrusion in this idyll is the threat of its destruction. She has gone to pay her visits and will return soon, bringing with her awareness of time's passing and the inescapable necessity of my re-entry into mundane, waking life.

THE CART OF treasures that I brought home from the City was at best a distraction. A hand-carved French cradle decorated with gold fleur-de-lis, tiny leather boots, bolts of printed cotton and rose-colored silk for Emilie's dressmaking, crates of orchid bulbs, two new books by the Spiritualists, a box of chocolate truffles, lily-of-the-valley soaps, and musk perfume for Floriane—I dispensed these trinkets like Father Christmas, but Emilie was not dissuaded from her persistent questioning about my dealings while in New Orleans. Who had I seen? Did I have an assignation? Why had I sent Mainard away? My anger, seldom seen and rarely felt before I landed at Belle Rive, exploded like some prehistoric monster roaring to the surface of a placid lake.

I accused her of spying upon me and called her a bitter and jealous harpy. A pathetic country girl of dull wit and senses, for she had not the mental capacity to engage in the deft mental gymnastics with which I excel in games of words. Jabbing my pointer finger into her birdlike little breastbone, I taunted that should she be foolish enough to engage me in such a battle, her defeat would be swift and crushing. She stood slack-jawed and quivering as if recovering from a physical attack.

The ferocity of it surprised me, even as words flew like arrows launched from the bow of my mouth. Who is this man who slings cruel words about with so little care? What is the source of that sudden red rage? I am remade, but wrongly so, less a god than a flawed and ordinary mortal. Remorse and bitter confusion fill me. The taste of my bilious complaints leaves my mouth sour, as if I have vomited up true bits of myself and recklessly splattered them upon the soil.

FALSE PATTEROLLERS TRAVERSE the county stealing from plantations. M. Bilodeau warns that these men are not associated with the law and have no claim to call themselves a legal militia. Ramón says that the slaves speak of these men as wards escaped from a lunatic asylum in Mississippi or possibly members of a chain gang who fled a prison farm. Our neighbors have reported the theft of lay hens, piglets, smokehouse meats, clothing from washing lines, and vegetables from kitchen gardens. Guns, knives, and axes are stolen, and a horse or mule when possible. They tell the slaves they are patterollers and must be obeyed, while they rob and plunder anything not nailed down and sometimes abuse the women and girls. We have set up an armed watch and sleep little, marching the perimeter with our lanterns all night. I am glad for the diversion from the exhaustion of my nightly wanderings through that lonely dream house.

Albert was found guilty of murdering Plunkett. He is to be hanged to death Sunday next. Emilie was very distraught at this news, and redoubles her efforts to secure the patronage of any influential Abolitionist to raise a hue and cry. She speaks rashly of hiring men to break him out of jail and smuggle him across state borders to freedom, and appeals to the Pennsylvania Society of Friends and a tiny congregation of Reformed Presbyterians in Georgia to apply Christian charity by petitioning for a stay of execution.

She grows agitated and ill-humored, and I am certain this aggravation has a poor effect on her health and will doubtless sour her milk (for she insists on feeding our son herself, and disabuses Floriane's notions that a wet nurse would be better for all). She calls me a coward because I adhere to the rule of law, however distasteful. She insists that I risk my own neck to break Albert out of jail and assist his escape in clear defiance of the Fugitive Slave Act, never minding that the penalty for anyone abetting a slave's escape may be imprisonment or death. I managed to appease her with a promise to visit Albert in jail and offer whatever succor he might take from my company.

EMILIE AGAIN PRESSES for a move to the North. She doesn't wish her son to grow up on a plantation, to be served by slaves and grow indolent of mind and morality. She hammers at me persistently, and I am always left to evade her designs by means of distraction, outright deception, or by physically removing myself from her presence. How I laugh at her, for she doesn't know what I know, that her money is already spent.

Crunn has not responded to my letters, and I am fearful that something has happened to derail our project. I sleep poorly most nights, and when dreams come, discover myself wandering through that enormous house of shifting rooms, peeling wallpaper, cavernous coal pits, rotten wood that gives under my touch, and dastardly staircases that tumble and slide. I lurk in lightless rooms, searching madly, fruitlessly, for something I cannot find and little recall the details of that object which so possesses my faculties.

THE JAIL WAS a grim and despondent place. Albert's once fierce countenance holds true, however, and he flames with an inner light fueled entirely by wrath against the injustices done to him. Unlike the two other men contained therein (the mournful, gray specter of a man whose crimes I cannot imagine, and the wide-eyed, crouching stance of another whom I assume to be an escaped slave), Albert remains defiant. He will not be cowed, despite the punishments or deprivations heaped upon him. He took little comfort in my presence, and refused the comestibles and blanket I brought.

Hostile and filthy, he approached the iron bars. "I want nuttin' from you. I be jus' fine when death come fo' me. De lord bring me to his kingdom an' his light warm me fo'ever."

He closed his face to me and turned his scarred back upon me, retreating to the shadowy corner of the hot, dank cell to await his fate. My offerings were quickly appropriated by Albert's cell mates, but he did not stir. Although darkness has already claimed him, sun will shine upon his skin once more.

I hold no such beliefs in sun gods or heavenly realms and wonder at my fate when I pass into the grave. I fear that all will be silent as stone, an engulfing black emptiness that guzzles me down and keeps me forever in its belly.

THERE IS LITTLE scandalous entertainment among the plantation communities, so a crime and the ensuing legal wrangling stir up a hornet's nest of fear, anger, speculation, and interest. One and all within a forty-mile radius will turn up to watch the public hanging of the man who so recently spent twilight evenings sipping lemonade with Emilie and myself. Albert was never talkative, but good and pleasant company, who was sanctioned with the most irrevocable of sentences for daring to protect the innocence of a girl he cared for.

I sickened at Prosper's insistence that I attend and begged off, citing a need to complete work here. I would have fled to my rooms, but M. Bilodeau held firm that the three of us would represent Belle Rive at the hanging, and let others know that we did not take Plunkett's death lightly (though even M. Bilodeau has confessed that he found the man sour-tempered and disagreeable on most occasions). We are, it seems, setting an example, and depart shortly to watch a stolen prince swing from the end of a rope.

IF HIS BELIEFS held true, Albert is gone to Heaven. I pray it is so, for no man should suffer so gruesome and violent a passing as I witnessed, nor endure the cheering of a crowd at the creak of the gallows wood or the crack of a breaking neck. I couldn't bear to watch him swing. I pushed through the rowdy, excited throng to seek a moment of peace in which to compose myself. As if knowing I needed her, P'tite Marie found me taking refuge by the troughs where the horses watered.

She wore her gloves and the hat with a lace veil as if to hide her identity (or her color) from the bloodthirsty mob. Her touch was so tender! My skin ached in her fingers' wake, as if seeking to rise up and join with hers. As if we might become one through divine osmosis and fuse into a single supernatural being.

But her kindness quickly turned to an icy fury. Why had I allowed Albert to languish in jail and suffer the noose when I could have sweetened the guards and freed him? Secreted him in the hold of a steamboat and shipped him North? Why had I not sought her help? She kept the confidences of governors, mayors, landowners, and ship captains alike. When coupled with her mother's, her influence could be a tool of reckoning or grace. "All are in my debt, beloved," she said. "Even you. Especially you."

Despite the warm day, chills ran over my arms, and she vanished so quickly I wondered if she had ever been there at all.

Thus, heavy of heart am I, having failed Albert, Emilie, and P'tite Marie. My purpose at Belle Rive, and indeed in this life, diminishes in accordance with the increase of my apathy and cowardice.

WHAT DOES SHE play at? My love writes to Emilie and invites us to a gathering at the Société de Magnétisme et Hypnotisme to hear a speaker tell of séances in New York, and to report on the spread of the Spiritualist movement into the South. Emilie is naturally eager to attend. My dread accumulates in equal proportion to my eagerness to see her, to court her laughter at my silly dreams and hear her prove their merit. To attend would be to court torture. Emilie balked at my insistence to decline the invitation. She chafes under her constraints but remains a bridled mare; she will go where she is led.

THE ROGUE PATTEROLLERS came to Belle Rive last night. What might have become a gruesome conflict was repelled by a surprising guardian. Coffee has taken to training the gander as a watchdog, and indeed, at nearly forty pounds and two yards from wing tip to tip, that bird is better than any dog we have! Prosper, Ramón, and Mainard were on watch outdoors while I kept watch in the main house—Prosper guarding kitchen buildings and garden, Ramón on horseback, and Mainard on foot, keeping his eye trained upon the fields and slave quarters.

A commotion broke out near the stable, a cacophony of shouting and squawking, spooked horses braying like asses and kicking their stalls. Someone rang the warning bell and I raced out toward the sound, carrying my lantern high. Prosper and Ramón rode up, and we three arrived to catch sight of Mainard and Coffee shouting and waving garden tools at something which the gander had cornered behind the barn. Disturbed by the ruckus, the pigs added their own alarmed squeals to the noise, tramping through the mud and dirt and buffeting the rails of their pen.

Prosper and I closed in, Prosper pointing his pistol into the gloom where the gander danced and jabbed with sharp thrusts of its beak. I raised my lantern. A man cringed there, his shabby clothes shredded by that furious goose, his face crumpled and bleeding. He gripped a writhing piglet in his arms, holding firm against the sow who rammed the rails separating them.

Only Coffee could calm the gander with soothing words and entice it away from the man while Prosper snatched the piglet and threw it back to its mother. Together we subdued the interloper and bound him with rope, locking him in the tool shed, where Ramón kept guard till morning and the sheriff's arrival. Prosper was so pleased, he told Coffee, "By rights that piglet's yours now. You earned her. You can raise it to sell and keep the proceeds." Coffee was delighted, and I resolved to draw up some contract of ownership to ensure Prosper kept his word. Slaves are property and as such, cannot own property. The document would have no value except as to remind Prosper of his gratitude.

In the morning, we found evidence of theft and footprints from our captive's accomplices running off into the fields. We beat the cane and searched the grounds but found no trace of the others. When the sheriff arrived at noon, he hauled out our thief and we got a good look at him in the daylight. He was a scrawny bleeder, gap-toothed and dirty, pockmarked from illness and full of complaints about the injuries sustained from the gander's attack. Coffee grinned to see the scabs his guardian had created. We'd caught one of the false paterollers and the elder Bilodeaus were so pleased, they saved a portion of supper to send out to Coffee. (The leftovers and scrapings of their plates, along with a pitcher of milk and last Sunday's tea cake.)

Emilie blushes with excitement at this unusual display of my masculine virility, and I admit to being pleased that she sees in me a man worthy of her love.

THÉODORE'S DEAR SOUL is saved from limbo. Mine, however, feels in jeopardy. When did I begin believing in the powers of spirits, the call of the supernatural world? It is as if this place has cast a dark spell upon me—the violence and superstition we steep in leave me saturated with anxieties not my own. I had hoped myself recovered, for I slept well and easily for several nights after the excitement of the patteroller's capture. I convinced myself that those disturbing dreams had ended, but during the mass at St. Augustine's, as the candle flames guttered and smoked, and passing clouds cast shadows overhead to dim the light of the stained-glass windows, I shuddered with a terrible sense of foreboding, for my son is blessed and innocent, while I have no such expectation of redemption or the undoing of my sin. There is no water that can wash me clean, no prayer or blessing that will restore the scales to my eyes or polish my tarnished soul.

EMILIE AND MRS. Stockton continue to plot for our move to New York City. Mr. Stockton has significant dealings with several European companies and has offered me a position in his firm as a translator and cultural ambassador. It is clearly a favor orchestrated by wheedling wives. What of my orchidarium? The land has already been cleared, the plans under way. It is perhaps the only time I have shown anger toward Emilie. How could she think me satisfied to work in dour, dark buildings all day, completely removed from the natural world? To accept a position of such low rank simply to satisfy her desire to be near her friend and pursue her absurd fascination with Spiritualism? I have explained that in England, I served the professor in numerous capacities and we did not confine ourselves to dusty libraries, but rather traveled to attend stimulating lectures and dined with learned men, and much of our conversation occurred on our perambulations in Kew Gardens. I admit myself grown agitated and quarrelsome, sensed a keen and brutal irritation stirring within me and seeking a victim, as if I were a venomous serpent desperate to discharge the load of poison in my fangs.

She turned her back on me and went to sleep with tears in her eyes. I lay awake for several hours, only to sleep fitfully when it finally came, and suffer dreams of P'tite Marie floating at my bedside, lifting her white skirts to straddle me, pressing fiery kisses to my mouth and wringing the hot seed from me.

IT IS WELL and good that I do not believe in destiny or an all-powerful being who manipulates human lives for its own diabolical amusement. If I did, I would surely think myself its favorite plaything, written into a cruel picaresque and made to suffer continued humiliations and indignities. Yesterday my crates arrived, sixteen of them loaded high on a wagon driven by one of M. Bilodeau's sorry "country crackers" and two broken-down nags. Disappointing my visions of a gentleman's meeting, Crunn had said Quincey was too busy working on a project in Washington to accompany my delivery, but that he would attempt a visit at some future date.

I commandeered a crew to help unpack the cart while a drunken Prosper stood around sucking his pipe and offering useless commentary. The Bilodeaus have had little interest in my project—they find my hobbies frivolous and effeminate—yet this did not divert from their intrusion and vexing questions about the pieces, the projects, my ambitions, and the importance of my mission.

We stacked the crates up in the area I've chosen, and with Coffee's help I pried open the first one. Upon first glance, I felt myself somehow deceived, for the iron struts appeared flimsy and much smaller than anticipated. Several of the crates held the shattered remains of glass plates. Once completed, I suspect I'll scarcely have room to stand inside of it, much less grow the majestic palms I envisioned.

I could not display the wild emotion surging through me, and forced myself to smile and nod as if in deep appreciation for my investment while Prosper poked through the pieces and offered his lamentably stupid observations. I shall never reveal my disappointment to anyone. Surely there has been a misunderstanding which Crunn will remedy. I was grateful when the evening finally cooled and I was left alone to assemble the puzzle pieces of all my trod-upon phantasies.

THIS FESTIVE CHRISTMAS season brings heavy rains which keep us all indoors for a day of merry diversion. We are all able to cast aside our work in favor of rest and jollity. Floriane oversees the distribution of the slaves' new clothing (they get coarse linsey-woolsey, while Floriane's gowns are made of satin, silk, velvet, and polished linen. I had suggested to Emilie that they give their surplus dressmaking fabrics to the slave families to create their own items, but she says Floriane keeps every scrap and cutting for herself), while Emilie dispenses individual gifts she has purchased or made, such as needles and thread, pewter dishware, small Bibles, rags for quilting, soap, candles, and bags of sweets for the children. Clothilde oversees the serving of Christmas dinner to us in the dining room and the slaves on the long veranda.

Emilie gave me a new pocket watch, engraved with a quote from Keats, her favorite poet. She appreciated the emerald necklace I gave her but felt it much too grand for daily wear. I cannot imagine P'tite Marie saying the same, for I chose it for her and took a duplicate for my wife, not wishing to acknowledge her as lesser, even to myself. Emilie is as showy as a common garden daisy, while my beloved is the exotic, violet *Iris germanica*.

Dear Théodore was passed around like a sack of precious gold. Everyone wanted to get their hands on him and hold onto him. We have no other babies at Belle Rive (yet) and he is a source of wonder to the older children. Poupette carries him everywhere on her skinny hip next to her enormous belly. It looks as if she is smuggling a melon under her dress. The children love to squeeze Théodore's hands, marvel at his tiny fingers, and chuck him beneath his fat chin. Such a good-natured boy, he squeals and burbles with constant delight. He is the handsomest child, and softens the hardest heart with his charming manner. I wonder if my own father felt this way about me. I remember little of him. He was always away in my youth, marching in the ranks of King Louis-Philippe, and when I was at school I saw him briefly but once or twice a year. Did he take pleasure in my presence? Was I the light beaming in his eye or merely his progeny, disappointing in my lack of militaristic fire, a boy who would rather read than ride into battle? Whatever Théodore's inclinations, I shall support them.

Thus Christmas concludes, my wife and child sleeping peacefully downstairs. Myself in my study, full-bellied and brandy-warmed. The day's diversions have sufficiently numbed me to my predicament. It is a pleasant state I should like to inhabit for as long as possible.

PROSPER HAS BEEN fevered and ill-tempered ever since that stray cur attacked him and took its pound of flesh. M. Fournier came again to examine him and prescribed doses of calomel to expunge the infection from his system. Prosper has been heard barking up effluvial all afternoon, and his loud complaints distress everyone in the house. Clothilde is brewing up a foul-smelling poultice and Emilie insists on keeping Théodore confined to the bedroom or parlor to avoid exposing him to disease and Prosper's unseemly anger.

The rain ceases and I resume a muddied assembly of the glass house. I tolerate Coffee's chatter because it keeps me from my own worries. I persevere despite all signs that I have been swindled by Crunn's glazier. I wrote yesterday to advise Crunn to have no further dealings with that man, for he is of unsound and duplicitous character.

A MISSIVE FROM P'tite Marie. Her letters arrive via some acquaintance at the Garden Society who scrawls an illegible name upon the envelope, and their arrival makes my heart lurch. I must pretend that it is routine, dull correspondence from some musty old botanist concerning orchid bulbs, when in fact, I must hide the trembling of my hands until I can read them in private.

She is with child. My heart swells, breaks, bursts. This cannot be, no matter how every part of me is alight with joy. Men have endured much worse than this. I consign her letter to the flames and with it, my happiness.

M. FOURNIER BLED Prosper today, for the man grows worse almost by the hour. The bite upon his arm shines an angry, vicious red, as if freshly inflicted. He thrashes about in his bed in a state of indecorous, priapic agitation. The ladies have been barred from nursing him because his uncontrollable, frequent erections and emissions would prove too deeply shocking to their feminine sensibilities. Indeed, I find it distasteful and resist assisting M. Fournier, but Prosper is lost in the throes of such violent fevers that it takes several hands to restrain him enough to bleed.

The bleeding does calm him, but does not drain the infection or its advances. He refuses all liquids, choking and gagging when water is forced down his throat, reeling in horror at the very smell of it! I have never seen the like. Prosper's anguished howls echo through Belle Rive's halls and out across the fields, making the slaves cringe and whisper frightening tales of the *lougawou*.

After this latest session, M. Fournier gathered the family together in the salon to proffer his diagnosis of hydrophobia. It is completely fatal. Prosper shall not recover from this illness but instead, he will die gruesomely, frothing and spitting, raving like a lunatic while his body withers from lack of hydration. It is an ugly demise. Floriane wept mightily, wringing her hands and wailing for the loss of her only son. Emilie's tears splashed onto Théodore's head, a second, terrible baptism. M. Bilodeau visibly shriveled before my very eyes, a leafy stalk withered by Helios' glare. He said nothing, merely drew himself together and shuffled off, the weight of his years bearing down upon him.

M. Fournier advises heavy sedation until the end comes. We can do nothing more than ease Prosper's suffering while the disease takes its toll.

PROSPER DIED IN the night, gibbering and spasming, despite the heavy doses of laudanum we dripped between his bubbling lips. Livid and furious, he tore at his clothing, crying out for release and begging God to spare him his agonies. Théodore slept with Poupette in her room as dutiful Emilie spent the final night by her brother's side, dabbing his fevered brow with cool water. Mainard and I tied his wrists and ankles to the bedpost, for he had often lashed out, nearly striking Emilie across the face and chewing on his limbs in his fury.

Finally, bloodied and lathered with sweat and saliva, Prosper uttered a long, tortured moan and succumbed to the Reaper. Now he lies in bed, frozen in an agonized rictus, fingers clenched, mouth drawn into a fixed scream. Horror overtakes me! It is a quicklime pit, a foetid swamp that sucks me down into its dark and seething throat to chew the skin from my skeleton.

The slaves wear charms against the *lougawou*, and these jangling clutches of bones and bells sound to me like a restless, unholy spirit dragging its chains across the floorboards. I cannot sleep, for this place feels haunted by pain, illness, death, and wandering, vengeful spirits.

PROSPER'S PASSING HAS had a sobering effect on me, yet I am also stirred to deeper analysis of my life and with it, discover myself aroused to great emotion. My nights remain labored and restless. I dream of an angular woman, not familiar to me, tallish and thin with long, curling dark hair who pursues me up and down stairs among the endless corridors of that monstrous house. I dream of her riding a slavering, red-eyed creature, half-man, half-wolf, and I run, for I know they would drink my blood, make pâté of my liver and gnaw the marrow from my bones. But sometimes, in these dreams, I find myself slowing, wishing to be found, captured, and devoured, for I know that it will be sublime to feel those lips and teeth upon my flesh.

I wake throbbing in all of my limbs, my blood hot and rushing. For I desire this consumption, nay, *eradication*, as much as I dread it.

Emilie takes comfort in her Spiritualist readings. She is convinced Prosper has gone to Summerland, and that she can speak to him again as easily as calling him to come in from the fields. These beliefs persist despite repudiation. Coffee digs a grave beneath the biggest oak tree. Despite Clothilde's urgings to bury Prosper in hallowed ground to anchor his restless ghost, Floriane will not consign him to burial in St. Augustine's graveyard, as it is too far away. She has become unreasonable in her grief. Clothilde mutters about Prosper's *iwin* taking to the skies at night, flying about the countryside looking for new victims. She has tied a glass evil eye amulet to Théodore's gown and decorated our room with various charms to protect him at night, for his chaste soul is especially holy and much desired by the untethered dead.

My heart and spirit shudder with tremors today, for I have been made the fool! The *Daily Picayune* was delivered this afternoon and M. Bilodeau sat reading it on the veranda while taking his tea. I was crossing from the house to the yard, on my way to the glass house to continue its daunting and frustrating construction when he hailed me, glad only, I think, to have an audience, for he has been lonely without his only son. I was disinterested but forced myself to show empathy for a grieving man and pulled up a chair beside him. He read aloud snippets of society gossip, news of criminal activities, and a review of Mary H. Eastman's new novel, *Aunt Phillis's Cabin*, praising slavery, while expounding upon his opinions about Franklin Pierce's recent sweep of November's presidential elections. M. Bilodeau cannot conceive that his way of life may be imperiled or ever change, so certain is he that Belle Rive will endure the ages.

I listened with but one ear until he commented upon the capture and arrest of a notorious flimflam man in Boston, one Cadwalader Crunn, alias Eugene Crumb alias Wallace Quincey. A sickening vertigo rose within me and the world swam around me in dizzying eddies that threatened to drown me. I felt the blood drain from my face as M. Bilodeau read the article, cackling at the reports of the dupes Crunn had swindled. The man perpetrated his mine share investment scheme up and down the Eastern Seaboard and throughout the Southern states, defrauding nearly forty investors of $260,000.

So many questions raced through my brain I found myself unable to speak and abruptly departed, M. Bilodeau shouting insensibly at my back as I fled. I ran to the partially constructed orchidarium and suddenly saw it for what it was—a crude and shoddy imitation of glory crafted from cheap, brittle glass and soft iron already rusting from the river's exhalations. I puked up my lunch and left it steaming on the ground, fury swelling and choking me. Something manic overtook me. Possessed by a demon's dark urges, I dumped a lantern's flaming oil over the wooden scaffolding. Flames spread and I snatched up a broken iron bar and set to, smashing every pane to smithereens. Shards flew and the ringing peal of breaking glass brought Coffee and the others running. (Even now, the cuts on my hands split open and draw gruesome trails upon the leaves of this book!) Coffee pleaded with me to cease my destruction and Ramón wrestled the bar from my grasp, suffering many bruises for his efforts. They thought me mad, but I could not cease until I had razed my aspirations to the ground. Someone has thrown dirt over my murdered orchidarium to extinguish the flames. The smell of smoke lingers in my hair and clothing.

Emilie's money is lost. I can never tell her. How will I manage to earn it back? I cannot. She will despise me if she discovers it and our charade of domestic tranquility. This home which—for all its strangeness and miseries—is my only haven in the world, will be closed to me, leaving me to stumble through desolation, an outcast from Eden.

THE BILODEAUS LOOK upon me with suspicion, and Coffee regards me with wary dismay. He must have liked the reprieve of working on the orchidarium in Albert's place, for it freed him from the fields and the threat of the lash. Emilie continues to press me for information about the glass house. I am resolutely close-mouthed. I have naught to say, for what excuse could I give that would explain my actions, save some temporary madness? I cannot speak the truth, so let them all think me lunatic. What does it matter now?

SINCE THAT DISASTROUS day, my mind wanders ceaselessly, unmoored by dreadful worries and anxieties. There is no peace nor rest for me. I slip into unconsciousness as if tumbling from a steep cliff into a morbid abyss. Emilie tells me that I often cry out in my sleep and I wake exhausted, as the climb up from that slumberous void saps both mental and physical strength. I feel battered and bled dry as if I have performed hard labor throughout all the hours of the night. I am reminded, oddly, of the Brothers Grimm tale of the "Worn Out Dancing Shoes" and the princesses who cavort all night at a secret ball. I cannot conceive of the source of my fatigue and dismiss it as the result of the emotional strains of having an infant and the intense effort required to puppet myself through the motions of my life while my head, heart, limbs, and organs lie miles away in the possession of my beloved. My son brings me much pleasure, however, and is my sole source of joy.

AGAIN, LAST NIGHT I found myself in that enormous house whose dangerous walls bowed around me, threatening collapse. This time I climbed over broken boards to wander through serpentine corridors and cramped passages smudged with rusty brown blotches and black smears of soot. The carpets felt damp underfoot and spongy. There was little light, but I could see well enough, as if illumined by some mystic agency, and a woman's sobs reverberated throughout. I found a small, crooked door and opened it upon a moonless night. Wind soughed through the naked tree limbs and made them rattle. I stumbled upon a cemetery encircled by an iron fence, pushed open the squealing gate, and followed the worn path to a grandiose, white marble tombstone. Shiny beads, flowers, and tiny bottles of rum lay strewn about the ground. The crying came louder, and I saw her there, preternaturally glowing as if lit from within. Sorrow weighed down the features of her handsome, angular face. She wore clothes of strange design—trousers with dirty knees, like a working man—and as I watched, she dug into a gruesome sore upon her arm. The skin gaped open and shone black inside. With her blood, she drew an X thrice upon the white tombstone, and the ground complained and shook beneath us and the heavens shuddered above. Within the strange logic of dreams, I understood that Papa Legba had opened the gates and I had passed into his realm. Turning to run back, I saw the path occluded by a bewildering crowd of headstones so closely pushed together that even a breeze could not pass through. The tombstone split open with a great crack and P'tite Marie emerged, her arms raised, turning her palms to me so that I might witness the markings there: a blood-red X and other strange symbols. She spoke with a voice foreign and booming, a voice to instill terror within me and cause my bowels to clench and my lungs to cease drawing breath.

P'tite Marie took the skin of the sobbing woman, put it on as if it were a cloak, and moved toward me, chanting, "I desired to do thy good will, O my God: yea, thy Law is within mine heart." And she spoke with two voices, saying, "I waited patiently for my Lord and he inclined unto me, and heard my cry. He brought me up out of a horrible pit, out of the miry clay, and set my feet upon a rock, and established my goings. He hath put a new song in my mouth and many shall hear it, and fear me. Let those who seek after my soul to destroy it be ashamed and confounded together; let them be driven backward and put to shame that wish me evil."

The sobbing woman's face glimmered through my beloved's like a mirage, and her eyes gleamed black and malevolent.

P'tite Marie intoned, "You shall not forsake or forget me. Your soul is mine to make and keep, to trample and split, to consume as the blood that is my offering to you." The strange woman opened her mouth—*Prete'm dedin a, pou m vomi san mwen*—and out poured jets of steaming blood which flooded the chaotic ground and swirled up around me like sea waves. Beseeching, I staggered to my adored and watched her hands penetrate my skin, and felt her cold and bony fingers close around my beating heart to squeeze it dry.

I woke screaming and made Théodore cry for he was so startled. The sheets were wet beneath me and my nightclothes soaked with sweat. I could little calm myself. Hours later, the horrible thrill of it consumes me still and causes my hands to quaver as I write this. I did not want to put it down on paper, as if doing so would lend the nightmare extra power, but I cannot dissuade myself of the notion that some dreadful fate stalks me. I have been cursed and shall be consumed entire, whether by lust or terror.

CLOTHILDE FOUND ME poring over the Bible in the library, repeating the words that P'tite Marie had uttered in my dream. She crept up behind me, and her voice so alarmed me that I dropped the heavy book on my foot. "Psalm 40," she said, "is what you seek. Be careful, Monsieur! St. Expedite a trickster and love to serve any master who call on him. He give with one hand and take with the other. I see from those wisps 'round your head that you already under the conjure man's cloud. No gris-gris goin' help you now."

DAYLIGHT IS THE charwoman who scrubs away night's filthy stains. All is well when the sun shines, and I am invigorated and whole, yet as dusk dims the sky and shadows crawl across Belle Rive's façade, my mood darkens with an oppressive, unrelenting trepidation.

Emilie presses me to reveal the subject which troubles my sleep, but I cannot bear to give voice to my most miserable and private of experiences: the unbearable shame of Crunn's swindle and the knowledge that my beloved carries my child. For at its core, there exists a dreadful pleasure, and as much as I abhor those visitations, my animal nature will rouse and waken, seeking only the satiation of its appetites. I hunger for the apparition of this woman, be she a visionary aspect of a vodou spirit or some unholy succubus summoned by my spurned lover to antagonize me into madness. Her face is ever-changing and liquid, a fog in which burn two crimson eyes and gapes the cavern of her insatiable mouth.

P'TITE MARIE ASKS when I will visit her. Her tender words are balm upon my troubled soul. I long for her with a hunger rivaled only by the famished. How I long to escape this nightmarish place! Sometimes I think I should run away, steal aboard a steamer and lose myself in some new city, Philadelphia perhaps, or join the westward movement and become a frontiersman like Daniel Boone, some desolate place where the wilds are fierce and beg taming. I could ride horses across the Great Plains' vast prairies like a cowboy, or travel the Oregon Trail, get a land patent and settle in the Territories. I could disappear, that is. The orchidarium is no more.

Emilie would be better off without me mucking up her life. She'd be free to pursue her own desires and join the Stocktons in New York. She would soon forget me and find a husband who craves her, soul and body, as I do P'tite Marie.

But if I choose those things, my son will forget me, grow to manhood with no sense or memory of me. Strangers will raise him. I will lose my toehold in his heart and consign myself to invisibility. It is too great a loss, and so I remain, a poor fool in love with the one he cannot have, loving the one with whom he remains and devoid of love for himself.

EMILIE WISHES FOR another child. Théodore is such a bonny babe, she yearns to double her delight with a second. Her touch does not repulse me, but it is a wan and pallid match to my beloved's burning caresses.

Even the frightful ghoul in my dreams arouses me more than my own dear wife, who has become like a sister to me. I care for Emilie dearly and have no wish to injure her, but I grow limp in her hands! The reproach in her eyes, the fumbling neediness of her grappling fingers snuffs any feeble flame of desire I may have had.

I flee to my study and spend too many nights there, tossing on the narrow divan, hankering for the grim and chilly halls of that dream house and She who haunts them.

I have come to believe that She is the supernatural manifestation of my beloved, for Emilie has spoken about the Spiritualist belief in Astral Projection, and the soul's ability to depart the body to travel celestial realms at night. My experiences in Les Etats Unis have steadily eroded my faith in science's meticulous order. One can effortlessly adhere to the cold logic of chemistry, philosophy, and mathematics when spirits, magic, and monsters remain elusive to tangible experience. I had no cause to believe in the supernatural when it was unreal to me, but slowly, slowly, its insidious illness creeps over me, infecting my organs. Brain, heart, liver, lungs, spleen—all bite the lure and ingest the toxin. It warps my reason, renders me irrational and hot-tempered, ridiculous and frightened. It wakes the beast in me, and the beast demands feeding.

POUPETTE HAS DELIVERED a boy. He looks like one of ours, pale as a toasted biscuit with eyes like amber drops and curling brown hair. Nature proves a cruel mistress to my wife, who suffered a lengthy, difficult birth, when this girl-child's labor should commence and terminate within a single afternoon. She was up and walking about afterward. She would have gone to the yard to wash her sheets had Emilie not made her get back into bed with the infant.

The baby has roused Floriane's diminished interest in her former pet, and the Bilodeau matriarch has announced that the boy will be called Prosper. Poupette might have named him Henri or Didier or something of her own choosing, but she cannot counter her mistress's wishes. She doesn't like it, but the choice may prove auspicious, for the Bilodeaus may be less inclined to sell a slave named after their own dead son.

M. BILODEAU CONTINUES to force me into Prosper's empty shoes, however poor a fit. I am practically chained to the man! We spend many a tedious hour observing the seeding of a second cane field and I am called upon to evaluate every aspect of his agricultural enterprise. I have wasted much breath attempting to explain the differences between my horticultural knowledge of European florals and herbs with what little I know of American crops, pestilence, and growing seasons. He has managed very well for himself thus far, but insists that I deliver an expert opinion on every aspect of his farming ventures. It is maddening. My temper frays. He becomes more obdurate and absent-minded every month. Prosper's death sucked whatever youth he still possessed right out of him, leaving behind an obstinate, addled old man.

But as we made our usual pass around the fields this morning, M. Bilodeau grew strangely pensive. His words chilled me, and I repeat them here, for I do not understand how one so devoted to the satisfaction of his own libido can be so moralistic.

"I never shoulda taken you to the club, Isidore. I misread you. Thought you a true gentleman of the Continent, but you're just a no 'count pica-yune with no knowledge of life outside the schoolroom. I paid your family's debts and let your colored mother stay on her precious estate because I wanted it for myself. But this god-damned rheumatismus wears me out, and now I'll never get to France! I'll likely kick over soon, a backwater planter, respected by none."

He had never spoken so frankly before, and it alarmed me. I spoke to defend myself but he cut me off, flinging his cane up from the dirt and smacking my chest with it. "You can drink the wine, but don't get drunk on it! Only fools fall in love with their mistresses. Cut your heart in pieces, but give the biggest one to your wife. You can't afford to be this stupid." Anger strengthened his limbs. He jabbed his cane into my toes as if to break them. "Your trifling ways are going to ruin our good name. I forbid this, you hear me? Forbid it! See her again and I'll see you strapped to the whipping post. God has no pity for craven, yellow fools, and I don't either." He snatched my hand and crumpled his gnarled, spotted fingers around it before he limped away, his cane gouging deep dents in the wet soil.

I stood in shock, the hot sun thrashing my bare head. Sweat ran into my eyes and stung them. I opened my hand to find a purloined letter from P'tite Marie that said how much she missed me and longed for me, that our child would be a beauty and to fly to her as quick as a bird. "Remember," she wrote, "we are forged from one metal, twain souls, never to be forsaken or forgotten." I shall not forsake. I do not forget.

I WONDER IF M. Bilodeau has spoken to Emilie. She watches me even more intently now, and I feel her fiery stare upon me even in the cold bowels of night. I can do nothing but sever this flower at its root before it bears fruit. As much as the thought of never seeing, touching, or making love to P'tite Marie again leaves me weak and weeping, I must end it. Accept my place in this world, set aside my own longings and ambitions, and become the respectable man all expect me to be.

Numbed to all sensation and emotion, I move through my days a squirming blind worm rooting through excrement, conscious only of satisfying its most essential needs. The soil encasing my pathetic, limb-less soul smothers and entraps me, but I welcome it! Welcome the suffo-cating darkness of this dreary realm. I have no appetite. My heart races inside my chest. My hands shake. Only brandy and claret calm them, and I am diligently working my way through the family wine stores. If my father-in-law doesn't want me spending time with my mistress, he shall have to acclimate himself to my taking up with this new love.

I SIT ALONE in my study, certain that M. Bilodeau can hear the thoughts flitting through my hollow brain like moths bumping beneath a lamp-shade. I recognize that I do an injustice and cause grave harm to those I love. It would be better if I were not even here. "Yes," replies a voice, as strong and clear as day. "Better if you were not here. The gate swings open for you. Legba waits for you. Legba waits."

I write to her. "I cannot do this. I should serve my wife my heart on a plate and beg her forgiveness, but I am the hooked worm, the pinned insect, and I cannot move to change our fates. Do not write to me. Do not call on me ever again. My love for you is dead."

I am the cruel and ruthless executioner. I swing the ax, I cut the storm in two.

SHE HAS NOT yet replied to my letter. Every inch of me aches with long-ing, knowing I have caused her great pain that I'm unable to soothe. Forcibly, I stay my hand from writing, arrest my steps in their march toward Metairie. I cannot feed this beast in me. With a cold eye and cal-lous heart, I watch it wither and weaken, anticipating my release upon its expiration. I shall kill whatever weakness in me would give in to her, for I am a man enslaved by none, not magic nor the pull of seductive succubi. If only the nights were not so long, and lonesome! The sun burns away her ghost, but when I wake in the small hours, she leaps to the fore of my consciousness and remains ever-present in my mind until morning comes and reason stamps out my desire.

M. Bilodeau reads his letters to us in the evening and through them, we learn of the City's troubles in the wake of a spreading disease. M. Bilodeau's friend, M. Jacobs, blames the German and Irish immigrants who stream into the ports in such great numbers they overflow the City. He says they cluster their families into squalid hovels, crowd the rooming houses with their filthy bodies and numerous children, and spread contagion and pestilence. Fleas, lice, and bedbugs infest the boarding and wash houses. Some sailors on the *Camboden Castle* were reported ill with black vomit, and New Orleans has taken to burning tar in the streets to purify the air of the scourge that sickens so many. We are glad to be isolated here, miles from the turmoil.

M. Bilodeau and Floriane have been in mourning dress since Sunday. Fever has sickened several of their acquaintances and they received word three days ago that M. Arnot and his wife lost two children to the illness. Floriane's cousin in St. Charles parish has sent word that her daughter and two-year-old child are gravely ill, along with several of their slaves, one who died from it. If I could explain my reasons for doing so, I, too, would wear black, hang crepe and adorn my study door with a mourning wreath to lament the death of love.

More letters from New Orleans. Yellow Jack runs rampant through the City, and corpses heap up in the public graves faster than the diggers can bury them. This somber news only increases the morbid air at Belle Rive. The sweltering heat is unbearable, and no breezes blow to freshen the stink of overworked human bodies, the putrid marshes and pig pens reeking of excrement. The slaves labor in the burning sun, singing dreary hymns. Aside from this, the long days are nearly silent but for the constant slice of machetes through cane and the swishing of leaves as the stalks fall. The cook complains of mosquitoes in the kitchen, and I have urged her to keep the rain barrels, cooking pots, and kettles covered, for the insects are drawn to still water. The mood here matches my own, and my dour mien is not out of place.

Devious enchantress! A locket with P'tite Marie's portrait inside arrived this morning, nestled in a box of paper-wrapped orchid bulbs (does she not know of the rusting glass house lying in ruins?). My heart convulsed with sudden agony at the sight of that face I have so long striven to forget. Misery surged afresh on a swelling tide of sorrow. How long does it take for love to die?

P'tite Marie complains of her wounded sensitivity and her lusting soul. She threatens to reveal all to Emilie if I do not do so myself. In one page, she wheedles and threatens, line by line softening or hardening my resolve, for I yearn for her as does the imprisoned man release from torment. She uses my own words against me and promises the satisfaction of my every carnal desire—her heart on a platter served with sauce for my delectation. I weaken. My God, how I weaken! Her angelic words are prayers to her heathen *loa*, Christian saints, the fates and tides, any power that will compel or move me closer to her side.

My body flares with want as my conscience (such as it is) dashes itself upon the rocks like a splintering ship in stormy seas. I read her letters a multitude of times, committing each word to memory before I burn them in the grate as if consigning the body of our romance to the pyre.

I have no strength against her. To spy that lovely face would be to surrender once more to her spell. I desire her touch, her scent. Crave her the way fiends crave crime and sin. Covet as did Eve the apple the serpent bade her eat, but silence is my name and attribute. Like the Great Chinese Wall, I stand unyielding against her onslaught.

I have always allowed myself to be tempted and to give in to P'tite Marie's pleas, my emotions, or the stirrings of my loins, but I cannot have peace until this sickness is purged from flesh and spirit. The only conceivable resolution is complete and total abandonment. I must quarantine myself from her, lest she contaminate me again. But I shall do her the kindness of rebuffing her advances in person, for it is only right to make amends for the sorrow I have caused.

Today I took a horse and rode before daybreak for Metairie. Emilie stirred as I dressed. I told her sleep was impossible in this heat, that I would work in my study today and should not be disturbed. Furtive, I abandoned Belle Rive and set out alone over the dim and empty roads.

There was little of the usual morning traffic and commerce, and as I neared town the stench of death assailed me. The pestilence is everywhere. Issuing from the docks, the low taverns, pig-yards and ditches along the roadside, wafted a cloying, unmistakable fetor. Smoke clouded the air, while beetles and ants streamed over the ground in army trails, feeding on the dead and returning to their nests, bits of cadaver flesh in their pincers. People dragged themselves through their work, each one scowling, mournful, fear contorting their faces, each one wondering, "Am I next? Is tomorrow the day I sicken and die, turn yellow and melt away into pools of my own rancid, black shit?"

Without delay, I ventured to the lair of my tormentor. I am shocked by its apparent decay. When I first visited the house, I recall it being slightly shabby but possessing a dowager's faded beauty. That is not the case. The house is a harbinger of the grave! Tattered fringes of lace hang from the open windows like graying shrouds. Yellow trumpets grow to obscene heights and their pitchers stagnate with malodorous luring liquid that jostles with the rank marsh mud for olfactory supremacy. Sulphur-yellow witch hazel blossoms shower the high, weedy lawn, and the old oaks clutch at the house with gnarled black limbs, draping their loathsome shapes across its bowing portico. Worst was the discovery of a discarded snakeskin some four or five feet long lying across the road as if to bar my passage. A second viper's transparent specter dangled from the tree limbs overhead, some gruesome decoration for the Devil's fête.

Dread filled me as I rode upon it, braving languorous clouds of mosquitoes which gorged on my blood like peasants at a king's banquet. There was no sound to be heard from what had been a place of bawdy merriment. Only the croakers and buzzing bluebottles gave voice to their misery. Such was the heaviness of the atmosphere, a malevolent, suffocating heat and air so burdened with moisture, that I began to panic, for it seemed that I could not fill my lungs but only inhale more of the noxious damp. Perspiration soaked my clothes, so much so that I had to remove my jacket and vest, and knock upon the door wearing my sodden linens like some washerwoman just done hauling up laundry.

Gone was the attentive maid from before. A *jeune fille* answered the door in her stead, a rusty-colored thing with lank braids pinned to her bulbous head. She stared at me with her wide, colorless eyes (for she was blind as a mole), asked, "L'amour ou le magie?" and impatiently gestured me inside.

Both love and magic have sourced my present troubles, but I would choose *le magie* to break the spell cast upon me by P'tite Marie and her terrifying dream doppelganger. I should like to sever the chains of that dreadful attachment with my bare hands and render them rusted and useless! I hesitated but a moment before answering that I had come to see her mistress.

The girl led me into a parlor decorated with buckling, dark green wallpaper frescoed over in a vile print of primordial black leaves. The heaviness of design in the room, its black velvet drapes, heavy candelabras set with tall candles slouching in the heat, and corpulent, overstuffed settees, made me feel quite suffocated. Worse were the many lewd portraits of naked women twisted into vulgar positions. Bulging breasts and callipygian excess adorned the walls, leaving no feminine secret to the imagination.

The blind girl left me there, sweating and clutching my coat. She did not offer me a tumbler of rye or a glass of water. It was then that my eye caught the subtler decorations of that dreadful parlor. Human and animal skulls sat upon a mantel decorated with dried herbs, feathers, bones, and an assortment of small, stoppered jars filled with murky liquid and gelatinous scraps of flesh. Nearby, on a small table, a large deck of well-thumbed Tarot cards lay spread upon the lace cloth beside a wine cup, pewter bowl, and gleaming knife, its cunning blade the length of my thumb.

Just as I began to fear that I would be left alone in P'tite Marie's house of sin, she emerged from a second, smaller side door. How can one properly give credence to notions of fidelity when resolve crumbles so quickly upon sight of a sorceress such as she? I had been firm in my resolution, adamant of position and refusing all physical appetites when I arrived at her door, but the sight of her again undid me. I am a bundled knot whose enchanted laces unwind with demonic ease at the witch's behest.

Inwardly, I quaked and sobbed, but outwardly, I was as unfeeling as a pillar of ice. I told her, "This affair destroys my peaceful mind and marriage, spoils my sleep, tortures my body with its unquenchable lusts, and spreads ruination to all within its sphere of influence." I commanded her to rein in her nocturnal doppelganger and insisted I would engage her no further—she must cease her letters and find another.

She wept, lamenting the fate of our child. The sight of my beloved in pain was a mortal wound upon my soul. If only I could take that knife upon her table, cut us from the present scene and paste us into another more pastoral and removed from all the obstacles which daunt us! I spoke rashly and promised to take her back to France with me (anything to dry those tears!), for at that moment I had no greater desire than to leave my life behind and begin a new one with her.

Although my reason is set against her, my body fails to obey its commands. She clung to me, so softly warm and wonderfully fragrant. My hands rose of their own accord to enfold her in my arms. I watched my fingers cup her cheek and my thumb press against the fullness of her lips. As if frozen in horror, I was dimly aware of myself grappling beneath her skirts, blood pumping fiercely within me as if to make my heart burst. How she cleaved to me! And how I pursued my goal with a madman's ferocity, convinced that no other remedy could ease the pain nor settle the mind.

We exchanged not a word! It was only from some vague sense of danger and self-preservation that I was able to notice how quickly the time had slipped away and I found myself half-clothed and dripping before managing to button my trousers and slither from her grasp. She moved so quickly, I had no warning as she slipped up behind me and sliced a lock of my hair with that little blade. She smiled as she flaunted her trophy. "You belong to me," she said. "Key and lock, brain and body. There is no existence for us without the other, you see, for I dwell within you and you"—she patted her belly—"dwell within me. There is no knife or magic that can sever the ties that bind us. Your wishes are useless against me." Grinning wildly, she reached beneath her skirts, maneuvered her fingers and removed my viscid ejections from her cunt. She spread her fingers to show me the milky web strung between them and I grew nauseous as she anointed a red candle with our fluids. My face burning with shame and pleasure's dying fire, I fled that house. P'tite Marie's laughter echoed from parlor to portico, bouncing between the oppressive oaks and ringing down that dark and endless road behind me.

Now I take refuge in my study, too ashamed to face Emilie, whose eyes search mine for confirmation of her fears as she hammers me with persistent, unyielding questions. Bedeviled and bewitched, I am enslaved by women at home, away, and even in the solitude of my dreams.

WHY I THOUGHT myself protected against scandal and the violent emotions of woman, I cannot parse. For as I turn in my pit, digging afresh at those cascading cliffs which threaten to entrap me, as I begin to clear a path from misery for myself, so does the dirt take on its own life and rain down upon me with vengeance. Most of my life has progressed with relative ease; mine was not a world of strife and disagreement. My few *affaires de coeur* began and terminated with sensible words and sentiments. Never have I been demented by passion, made unreasonable or spoken promises which I did not intend to keep. One—one!—brief instance of folly and all is destroyed.

No longer am I entranced by the memory of strange music and the summonings of beautiful young girls in Congo Square! On the contrary, such things are distasteful to me. That woman has taken what was once a pleasant dream, a satisfactory memory, and crushed it into something hateful and hideous. All manner of anxious thoughts tumble in my brain. With the rising sun, this day has taken on a very ominous portent.

WHAT FRESH HORROR is this? Sending that wretched blind child to knock upon Belle Rive's door. I tremble at my good fortune, for Emilie and Floriane were occupied in the bedroom taking measurements for new drapes, and M. Bilodeau was napping during the day's worst heat. Lavinia found me in the parlor reading, thank goodness, and I came straight away. Imagine my agonized tumult of giddy hope and acrid revulsion upon spying that child whose clouded lenses tracked me unerringly from parlor to foyer. That insipid woman, Lavinia, hovered uselessly until I dismissed her with unnecessary harshness.

That rusty, hideous girl pulled a crude poppet from her apron bib, and I saw that it had my hair stitched to its head and P'tite Marie's emerald necklace wrapped tight 'round its neck. How my spirit quailed as the awful child drove a thick needle into its head, her white eyes probing the air as if to latch onto my expression and rip it from my face!

"You have offended the mistress of *loa*," intoned the girl. "Erzulie Ge-Rouge does not suffer the likes of one such as you, weak, deceitful man." Again, she drove needles into the doll, stabbing hands and feet. Scarce could I breathe, for though I assured myself that her magic had no effect when hurled against the bulwark of my reason, sympathetic pains blazed in response.

"Forever bound to my mistress's will, you shall suffer the injuries you have inflicted on others. Because you speak untruths, your words will always ring false. Because your words are lies, Erzulie Ge-Rouge claims your voice, the voice of your children, your children's children and theirs. You are cursed to suffer tenfold the miseries you have caused." With that final utterance, she stabbed one last needle into the poppet's heart. Fluid as inky and viscid as blackstrap oozed forth, coloring her fingers red and dripping to the floor planks. Disgust reared in me. I feared attacking that odious creature, so intently did I long to dash her brains against a rock or gouge out her pointless stare. I pushed the door closed, but not before she blew a handful of chalky soil at me.

Frantic, I brushed it from me, then ran to change my garments and wash my skin, for I remembered that most appalling of vodou tales—that curses are sealed with grave dust and the ashes of the dead.

MY DETERIORATING HEALTH is of grave concern to Emilie, but I am assured it is simply a temporary maladjustment and will be soon relieved. M. Fournier has been attending me at Emilie's behest. He is certain that poor sleep persisting over several weeks has left me in a state of nervous exhaustion, the cause of my hallucinations and tremors. He prescribed *élixir parégorique* (*tinctura opii camphorate*) to temper my aching head and the feverish heat of my agitation. He advised Emilie to close the windows at night to repel those river vapors that leave the bed curtains and counterpane damp with dew and no doubt contribute to my unhealthy state.

LAVINIA, COOK, AND Floriane have taken sick. Poupette is diligently washing every article of clothing, bedding, or toy belonging to the boys, and Emilie wipes down all the furniture with carbolic acid solution to sanitize it. Even so, Théodore has become agitated and cries frequently. He refuses food and milk but he will swallow barley water from a glass dropper if I give it to him. Clothilde mutters her heathen incantations and secretes vodou charms in the baby's crib, which I destroy immediately.

At sunset, we heard the far-off eruption of cannon fire, discharged to disrupt the ozone in the air and scatter the miasma that hovers over the City. M. Bilodeau's contact warned him of this plan by City politicians, but we could not believe such desperate measures would truly be taken. Adding to the greasy smudge of cannon fire on the flaming horizon is the obnoxious stink of burning tar, which leaps and cracks in pits in the yards of the genteel and poor alike. The hazy air takes on a choking effect and even at this distance, our eyes water.

M. Bilodeau agonizes over his sugarcane in this torpid heat. He must earn a full profit from the new fields we planted or his income from cotton will not be enough to cover our expenses for the year. Several slaves complain of illness but M. Bilodeau allows no reprieve from the fields. I, myself, have felt slightly unwell but ignore my symptoms. There is too much to do to sicken, and I am grateful for any distraction that diverts my thoughts from ruminating upon my sorrows.

M. Bilodeau summoned M. Fournier to deliver relief to all here who languish. Floriane complains of pain in the legs, back, and head, costiveness, and unrelenting thirst. The doctor suspects Belle Rive has been stricken by yellow fever of which he has seen a great deal of late. He asks if anyone, slave or free man, has had any contact with immigrants or sailors, and took the males aside to inquire if any had had sexual congress with women in the City. All could earnestly say no but for myself, who lied with uncharacteristic ease.

Floriane was prescribed bloodletting and a croton oil emetic to purge her sluggish bowels, which Emilie confided were full of a foul, pultaceous matter. Lavinia and Cook languish in their shared room, and because so many are ill and we are short-handed in the house, I accompanied M. Fournier to assist with their treatment. Cook's complection had gone quite yellow and her eyes were the color of thick urine. Both women bled from the gums and evidenced petechiae on the neck, face, and exposed flesh. Lavinia hemorrhaged blood from her nose when coughing. M. Fournier drained several ounces of blood from each woman and dosed each with cathartic tincture and laudanum for sleep.

I know myself snagged in some terrifying eddy, helpless to dam this flood of pestilence threatening to sweep away all that is known to me. I cannot stop thinking about P'tite Marie and her child, wondering if she is ill and how I will cope with the pain of heartbreak should she fall victim to the Great Fever. I fight with myself, arguing in various mental voices the advantages of recommencing communication with her and the absurd danger of doing so.

THÉODORE CEASES CRYING and only whimpers. His skin turns gold, his diaper fills with bloody stool, and my wife wails aloud, praying to all and sundry to spare our boy's young life. While my wife does not speak of death, fear of it sucks the color from her cheeks and permeates our atmosphere like a ghastly mist.

I have had some reprieve from those odious dreams about the house and the woman who haunts its halls, but now I find the visions returning whenever I close my eyes. I leave this house of decay and decline only to find myself imprisoned in another, stalked by that voracious specter and perversely aroused by the chase.

Some primitive part of me wonders if my beloved has died and it is she who seeks me through those lightless and sinister rooms, yet I duck and run, cowering in the corners as I flee her approach, my body quaking with erotic thrill and terror. When at last I succumb to her frigid embrace, monstrous gropings, and asphyxiating kisses, it is a welcome surrender. It is walking into death again and again, being pulled out from my skin and shaken free of my obligations. Now when I close my eyes, immediately I find myself walking that eerie path or climbing those derelict stairs, hungering and erect, telegraphing my submission to a floating phantasm.

A GHASTLY LONG night! Cook went first at 11:00 p.m., spewing up black vomit the texture of ground coffee beans until she lost consciousness and died. Next Lavinia, hemorrhaging from nose and mouth, became delirious and raved so loudly that Mainard was called to restrain her. She extruded a copious quantity of offensive black faeces and soiled the bed so much it shall have to be discarded. Died of the black vomit at 4:35 a.m.

It's now noon and none have slept. We have had a devil of a time removing the bloated bodies, which have quickly putrefied in this heat. Those slaves who are not ill are charged with digging graves as M. Bilodeau expects several more deaths.

Floriane is still abed and slightly yellow, but shows no sign of black vomit or hemorrhage. Emilie prays that her mother will make a full recovery and asks Clothilde to wash Floriane's body with blessed herbs and apply poultices of hot mustard to help drive out the evils that poison her. Her willingness to believe in these native rituals strikes me as both wonderfully trusting and absurdly naïve, symptomatic of the seductive allure of this alien land.

Ramón has just come in to tell us that three slave children are stricken along with their mother and one of the older men. Emilie prepares more carbolic wash to mop out the slave cabins, but I feel our puny efforts will be wasted.

M. Bilodeau hears Thibodeauxville is nearly deserted, all the shops closed and the streets empty with everyone either sick or hiding in their homes. There is public outcry to increase sanitation measures and roust out the poor from their hovels. Quarantined ships clog the harbor, their sailors crying out for release from their pain and disease, while the fit ones sometimes leap into the water, hoping to swim to land and vanish into the City's throngs. The harbormasters hire brutes to beat back any sodden sailor attempting to scamper up the riverbanks or ladders on the quays. We are all sick with dismay and agonizing worry, lurching about Belle Rive with glazed, ringed eyes and hopelessness draining the blood from our cheeks.

Emilie cries out with a dreadful pitch. I must go to her.

WE COULD NOT wake him. I rushed in to the bedchamber and my son was there, tucked up beside my hysterical wife, his small body as vividly jaundiced as a dandelion, fingers and toes already blackening. She had fallen asleep with Théodore breathing and woken to his still corpse, his delicate mouth open as if to suckle and his tiny fist clamped tight around a lock of her hair, frozen in this grim imitation of Life.

We drown in the horror of it.

Clothilde came soon and, weeping, took the baby to be washed and dressed for Christian burial. I cannot remember what I did or said to my wife, whose countenance bore such a grimace of pain I could not bear to witness it. My words dropped heavy to the ground, spoiled, malnourishing fruit with no power to strengthen or sustain.

Our love, our beautiful boy, is gone. A voice in my head whispers ceaseless invective, rousing me to fault, naming me a foul and selfish creature, and I perceive myself to be a murderer. Whether by my own actions or some invisible agent that has taken my hands in its own and used them to wring the life from my precious son, this blame is a fever that rages within me as bright and hot as hellfire.

WE PLACED THÉODORE in the ground today. I drift about this place, senseless and numb as a ghost, for I cannot feel a thing.

EMILIE WEEPS EVEN as she works, and we have all grown used to watching her minister to the ill, and assisting Clothilde and the girl Zulimé in the kitchens with tears cascading from her eyes. She appears perfectly rational and shockingly normal, but for the water streaming over her cheeks, dripping from her jaw and leaving a wet, pattering trail on the floors in her wake.

I do not cry. My heart is formed of lead, heavy and immobile. I am shocked that it still beats. Nor can I eat, for my throat closes and refuses all food from broth to bread. Claret sustains me now. Perversely, I feel that if I drink enough, I shall be cleansed of sin, for at St. Augustine's, claret is the blood of Christ, Emilie's beloved Lord and Savior, and served to bring souls unto restitution—or rum, for that is what Clothilde offers her vodou *loa*. Though I shun my Catholic education, I remember my verses well—Proverbs 31:7: "Let him drink, and forget his poverty, and remember his misery no more." Though my lips and teeth purple with my indulgence and I lie with Dionysus as eagerly as a ruined maiden, wine maketh my heart glad, and I shall be filled with the Spirit.

YELLOW JACK CLAIMED two more slaves, but no others grow ill. As if to flaunt the tragedy of our survival when our own dear boy is lost, Poupette's boy is in robust good health, untouched by disease. Would that I could trade his life for Théodore's! None dares speak of the hope we feel that this plague has stolen its last victim.

I am meant to work with M. Bilodeau and Ramón to rouse the slaves to hard work. We are in deficit and the aging cane begins to wither in the fields, as if it shares Belle Rive's affliction, but too often I take my claret and walk to the riverbank to sit and watch those solemn brown waters flowing away from me, ferrying my grief on their tides. Too often I sleep on the ground to wake drowsy and sun-burnt and stumble back to Belle Rive to lock myself in my study with another bottle.

Despite remonstrations that I drain the cellars and forsake my wife, the river is my only solace. The light illuminates my dreams, rendering them fleeting and pure with none of the murk of that god-damned house and its sinister inhabitant. No, I dream of happier days and dance with my child in my arms, his sparkling eyes alive with laughter as if he had never died.

I CANNOT PARSE what is happening to me. My melancholia intensifies day by day, when I thought it should by now ease. Sleep does not come easy, if it comes at all. I dream of serpents weaving through satiny hills of flesh. I dream of iniquitous magic and see evidence of its machinations everywhere, for surely I am cursed to suffer so! Emilie grows dour and quiet, but still she marches through the hours, a stern sergeant intent on her duties. Sometimes she smiles. Once or twice she has reached for me in the night, seeking comfort from this discomfited body of mine, wanting love when I have none to give, for all has been drained from my ravaged soul.

I AM RESTLESS. Too nervous to settle into any of my appointed tasks, too fretful to mind M. Bilodeau's ceaseless lecturing, and mightily forgetful of my wife's requests. I sit here below the oak, between the graves of my brother-in-law and my darling boy. I must keep guard at night, for the witch patrols my dreams looking for an entrance into this world. She taunts me with her hot mouth, her grasping cunt, she would drain the seed from me to breed her own devilish child and dig my boy from the earth to serve her. I have learned a thing or two about vodou here, and I know how these demons deceive the good and kind and living. But none can take him while I watch, and the sun repels those dreams, and so I reverse the natural order of my days and claim the night as my own.

PLEASURE TRUMPS MY shame. Too often, I choose the poor comfort of the hard divan in my study instead of the chamber I share with my wife. At first, I sought Emilie's company in hopes that her kindly presence would repel my Night Visitor, but now I flee from my wife's sight under pretense of protecting her. In truth, it is because I welcome those ghostly touches upon my sleeping skin. As much as I despise them and disgust myself, so am I compelled into intimacy with ethereal hands that draw pleasure from my bones as if draining the pith from them.

Elsewhere in the house, Poupette sings her nightly lullaby to young Prosper and Clothilde swings her keys as she checks the locks on the French, front, and kitchen doors. I imagine that Emilie is busy with her lacework again. I should go to bed and be with my wife, but too great is the temptation to linger here in anticipation of my Visitor.

I DRINK PAREGORIC to drown out the grisly realization that my beloved, that deceitful villainess, has again manipulated me by sending her malicious agent of vodou to dispatch with my child, thus freeing me to be with her. That little blind rat spewed death into this house, I know it.

A TRAVELING PREACHER came to Belle Rive today, a free Negro man of some repute named Obadele Logue who has received permission to orate to the slaves. Always pleased to Christianize his flock, M. Bilodeau consented to a revival tomorrow night in the fallow field beyond the canebrake. Emilie tells me she will ask Reverend Logue to bless our dear Théodore's grave and say prayers for young Prosper, who has remained miraculously vigorous. She entreats me to hear Reverend Logue's oratory and let his ministrations soothe my troubled soul, but I can't imagine any sermon adequate to staunch my bleeding heart.

REVEREND LOGUE RETURNED just after dinner and Emilie served tea on the veranda. He is extremely loquacious and a man of such fine character that M. Bilodeau limped out and joined us, drinking in the visitor's talk of neighboring plantations, the Fever's insidious spread, and the efforts of the politicians to contain it. Logue consulted with Emilie about which verses and hymns might be appropriate for a revival at Belle Rive. That was the first time I had seen Emilie smile and regain a portion of herself in many days. I could not jeopardize her happiness.

I hadn't much interest in their discussion till Logue spoke of a house in Metairie untouched by illness. He described it thusly: a grandiose but shabby home with lacy porticos decamped at the end of a long swamp road and distinguished by an unusual number of large snakeskins hanging from the trees. A young blind girl lived there in the company of her mistress, a fetching woman, who despite her choice of profession as a flesh-peddler and the excess of supernatural items in the parlor, struck him as delicate, kind-hearted, and devout. This Creole woman and her associates avoid the Jack through some miraculous means; none there have taken sick. Some speak of this as proof in the powers of vodou or witchcraft, but she assured Reverend Logue that she was a God-fearing Catholic. Despite an absence of protective measures such as employed in the City, her house remains pure. As the source of this wicked disease, she blamed the excesses of blasphemers, and entreated Reverend Logue to bless her home so that the Lord might take pity on those lost fools who sought comfort there.

At his mention of the blind girl, my heart throbbed with a sickly will. I could scarce remain seated and it took all my strength to conceal my agitation. I had no doubt he spoke of my love, that silken-skinned purveyor of fascination and pleasure. She sent him to spy on me! How I yearned to wring his memories from his brain, so that I too might once again see her and hear her melodious tones. It felt as though a thousand *Solenopsis*, those biting red ants endemic to the soil here, crawled beneath my skin, injecting venom with their cruel mandibles and pricking me with their sharp abdomens. I grew restless, overheated, yearning vainly for a bottle of claret, but Emilie had issued strict instruction I was not to drink. I promised myself a glass of wine as soon as she dismissed me. With an uncanny sense of awareness, I turned and met M. Bilodeau's darkly intent gaze—a warning look filled with threatening intention. I forced myself to settle, though I yearned to leap up and run over the fields and far from him.

M. Bilodeau rang the dinner bell early, and the slaves could be seen rushing from the fields to their cabins to eat and wash for the revival. Despite the plague and the loss of so many, there was a palpable excitement among everyone, and M. Bilodeau entreated Reverend Logue to ask Ramón for anything he might need for his sermon. The good man requested only a tin washtub, so that that his words might gather within and rebound with additional fervor. It's unclear whether M. Bilodeau's endorsement of the revival is due to a genuine belief in its succoring powers or if he does it solely to please Emilie and Floriane, but it is a welcome diversion when so many here are ailing.

Now one and all have gathered for prayer, and the cadence of voices joins the usual night sounds of the lapping river and insect song. Emilie is out in the fields tonight, chanting with the slaves for salvation and respite from the insidious plotting evils of Yellow Jack as if this contagion were a He, and not an It, an entity without conscience, pity, or remorse. I have half a bottle of claret, but it little eases my suffering.

I HAVE JUST woken and pulled myself up from the floor of my study after the vilest of dreams, which left my trousers stained and my organ most uncomfortably swollen. The Night Visitor pervades my dreams. Weeping bloody tears in flowing silky layers like translucent ruby bridal veils.

There is chanting in the fields, a hammering of noise, men and women slapping their hands together, rhythmic pulsations of hammers on metal. Spirituals or Catholic hymns? Like none I've ever heard. Where is Emilie? This claret is warm but settles my head. How long can such religious reveries endure? I must interrupt, tell them to quiet and stop their superstitious conjuring. They will wake the wrong spirits.

DAWN BREAKS. I have not slept for I am afraid of the terrible things I saw in the fields. Shapes twisting up from the fire in some deranged ecstasy of possession. Dancing with such vibration it rattled my teeth, Logue raising a long, fat viper above his head, ululating and thrashing it about like a whip. A shadow against the raging red fire behind him and air thick with smoke. He called my name and entreated me to come closer, but that terrible reptile leered and licked at me.

My own dear wife moaning and weeping, circumventing the leaping fire and shedding her clothing, her skin. No! I confuse myself. But if not Emilie, then who? That spirit from my dreams? Has she found a gate for entry into this world? Papa Legba's still swings open. I cannot entertain such ridiculous notions, but she comes to steal my son and dig him from the ground. I must protect him.

EMILIE SAYS NOTHING of last night's furor. When pressed, she denies any such dancing. Says I have confused good Christian prayers for invocations and lamplight for bonfire. She lies to me to hide her wickedness from me, and sheds *des larmes de crocodile*, saying that grief has turned my soul dark and clouded my mind.

M. BILODEAU GROWS agitated with me and I do try—how mightily I try!—to be as Before. Surely they all sense something amiss in me, and as hard as I work to hide my confusion, they work harder to discover the source of my decline. The *parégorique* leaves my thoughts muddled. Sometimes I spy Théodore standing beneath the big oak, his skin as yellow as fresh pollen, his tiny fingers frozen into blackened claws, his sweet mouth a rictus of agony. I wipe my eyes, shake my head. Such things cannot be, and yet I see them! Prosper claws his way out of the dirt, foaming at the mouth, wild-eyed and groaning. I sense that no locks or walls will repel him, so intent he is on finding me and sinking his teeth into my flesh so that I should become a ravening animal like him and die thusly, writhing and senseless. I suspect he knows about Crunn and the loss of Emilie's trust, and seeks revenge on me.

Fear pours its bitter taste into my throat. I see the ghost in daylight! She lingers over the grave of my darling Théodore as though charming him up from below the soil and I shout at him to refuse her call! Cover your ears, boy!

Now I am too fearful to sit beneath the tree, filled with these abhorrent fantasies that my own sweet son will lay corpse hands on me. Emilie cannot know that her brother and Théodore stalk Belle Rive's grounds, revenants lusting for vengeance. When M. Fournier comes again, I shall tell him that his remedies do not work, for still she plagues and haunts me, and I want little more than to surrender to the inferno and let it consume me.

THE EFFICACY OF the *parégorique* diminishes as my mania grows. I have increased my dosage to 260 drops per dose, sometimes 300 if the first has no effect. My appetite remains dull, and for that I am grateful. Clothilde puts ashes of the dead in my food to sway me to her bidding, and so I will not eat what she prepares for me. Even when my wife swears that her hands alone prepared my meal, I know Clothilde has deceived Emilie and exchanged flour, sugar, and such for these ashes. Emilie plies me with every delicacy in attempts to coax me to eat, but I want nothing. I take my medicine in a glass of claret and that is enough to sustain me.

M. FOURNIER RETURNED in the guise of taking tea, but his true aim was to leach me of my lifeblood yet again, for did he not come prepared bearing his loathsome bloodletting kit? Of course, only wine and *parégorique* flow in me these days, a fact proven when M. Fournier applied the lancet and out gushed a fount of the finest garnet vintage, filling his cup. I should be surprised that he did not put the cup to his lips and gulp, so fine and frothy was my offering. He insists on keeping the bedroom windows closed, and Emilie and I lie together in our sweat-damped sheets, fighting for breath in that muggy, unbearable room. But the efforts of Clothilde and M. Fournier are unmatched by my beloved. Although the dreams have waned of late—due in part to the efficacy of my treatment—they cannot be murdered or deterred, and She comes to me again, ever more determined.

I dream of the house of love and magic, a looming hulk of lacework and shadows glorious in its menace and ruin. Therein throbs the pulsing heart of my desire, the Night Visitor, the Weeping Woman. She whose mouth is serenity and bliss—the manifestation of my beloved, shedding tears for the loss of me and the death of our love. Weak and helpless, I drift up the stairs through those rotting halls to a room papered in dark green foliage, like P'tite Marie's parlor. The blind girl guides me to a bed draped in winding sheets stained by the grave, and wields lancets that slit my skin. The vaporous essence of my Self—all that I am, have been, cease to be—issues forth, and She appears. Coalescing from the shadows, her black curls soaked and streaming, to inhale my soul, strip the clothes from me and wipe her sharp tongue the length of my aching flesh until pleasure bursts forth and she may sate herself on my hot seed.

It has come into my mind lately to kill Clothilde. That sneaking, spying old biddy fills Emilie's head with absurd superstitions that make my wife tremble in my presence. Clothilde convinces Emilie that I am possessed! I heard them in the laundry yesterday whispering about me, but every word was clear, for my hearing grows ever more acute, such that I can hear the worms writhing in the ground and the sound of maggots chewing on dead flesh.

"Isidore be kept by a witch, *ti boubout*. She's got to keep him in her power or the Devil come and take her soul in exchange. Find where she keep her gris-gris and consecrate it with holy water to free him!"

Sweet Emilie dismissed Clothilde's accusations, but I watched the panic scurry beneath her skin and twist her mouth. No doubt I will find her in the bedroom or my study, searching through the cabinets and upending the drawers in guise of housekeeping. But she'll find nothing. Everything that P'tite Marie has ever given me is buried half a mile away in the weeds beside the crossroads that divert my path from Belle Rive to Metairie.

My unquenchable desire for that spectral manifestation of carnal sin is a hardy weed. I have plucked it, poisoned it, and dug down into the very soil of my being to sever its roots, but still it grows. I have deprived it of all nourishment, blinded and parched it—it shall not receive the light of her eyes or the delicate rain of her touch. I have murdered my lust with a hundred instruments of torture, and still it grows. Erzulie

Ge-Rouge comes to me at night; she claims me body and soul. It shames me to admit that I have wept for her, wandered the halls of that nightmare house calling out to her, yearning for her touch.

Only morphine numbs my agonies. Only bloodletting strengthens my resolve to resist her by leaving me too enfeebled to act, for surely I would weaken a hundred times over and write to my beloved. Had I the strength to rise from this bed I would mount my horse and ride to her, beg forgiveness and fall prostrate at her feet like a beaten dog. Instead, I take up the lancet to drain the melancholic humors from this impoverished vessel.

I saw Her last night, a vague and spectral shape wandering the cane fields, climbing among the shattered ribs of my ruined glass house. Torment flared within me, understanding that my own sweet boy had likewise been seduced by the witch's spell and kept prisoner in her house. P'tite Marie? The Weeping Woman? Why does she claim my dead child for her own? I pushed myself through cloying lightless rooms as if wading through muddy swamp water, following the sobs of a crying child. I call his name but he does not answer except to weep and wail. Futile are my efforts and I seek him in vain through every vile and insidious room of my beloved's strange and twisted house.

Emilie spoke true. The spirits *can* cross over. I have seen evidence of this with my own eyes, but still I turn my mind to that mystick realm longing to discover incontrovertible evidence that she is, or is *not*, real. None believe me when I assert my theorem and all remain adamant that a rest cure is required. Rest will not settle my spirit nor ease my sick, vile desire. Yet a change of surroundings, a cooler clime, sea air and freshets of mineral water, drawn daily from healing springs, should afford me respite, however brief. I have agreed to go, per Emilie's less than gently worded request and to appease M. and Mme. Bilodeau. My illness is a vain agitation to Floriane. She fears the shutting of society's doors should anyone in her elevated circles learn that her son-in-law may be a madman. As a pig to market, they pack me off. Emilie does not travel with me; I am Mainard's charge, as powerless over my fate as an infant. Oh, they wept! How they moaned and blubbered, but I am not deceived. One and all are glad to be rid of me. Doubtless it was Clothilde, filling my wife's head with her vodou lies, poisoning the Bilodeaus against me. Mainard is meant to dispense my drops whenever he sees fit, but I have taken my own precautions and carry a bottle of Dover's Powder to ease the stress of travel and to sleep, for I must know if She travels with me or is somehow tied to Belle Rive.

January 16, 1854

Dearest wife,

Assure yourself that I am safe and protected. These demons shall not best me though their terrible faces leer from the stone cliffs with abysmal black sockets and howling mouths melting, sliding out from the bleak rock. They watch me but I pass by unmolested for I shall not be cowed! Every town that we pass through, the inhabitants whisper about me and their gossip burrows into my ears and tunnels through my brain box dribbling trails of toxick slime everywhere. But I outsmarted them! I protect myself by wearing upon my head this sturdy canvas sack I did adorn with scientific symbols to repel their chatter so their thoughts do not seep into my eyes and imprint my lenses with their vicious words.

Though the travel is arduous and suspicious Mainard spies on me with malevolent purpose, I endure his attacks and go to Castile with every hope of healing the rift in my soul, curing myself of that dreadful affliction of nightmares and those derangements that steal my authority. Please tell Théodore I protect him from afar. I nailed a charm to the oak tree overlooking his grave so that the witch cannot steal him from his bed, for she summons him from death to torment us with memories of the past and our own dear boy.

Sleep in peace, dear wife, and know that my poor health and wandering fancies shall trouble you no further.

Isidore

CHRIST-LIKE, I am resurrected. After my months away, I return to Belle Rive clutching the thin string of my sanity, dragging it behind me as young Prosper pulls the wheeled horse in his wake. We are too alike, that child and me. Weak and infantile. (See how the pen trembles against the paper!) In thrall to our impulses and fully at the mercy of every other adult in Belle Rive. Even Clothilde treats me like a child, speaking to me slowly but ever, ever with that wicked, cagey look I recall so well. I hear her speaking through the wall…no! I promised Dr. Greene that I would not entertain these thoughts but let them rush away from me as does the frothing tide. No matter how much Castile water I drink (for I guzzle it now, cloudy and stinking of eggs, as if to wash the sickness from my mind), it cannot cleanse me of past sins or sorrows.

It is good to be home with my dear wife and to rest in my very own, dear study once more. The Sanitarium deprived me of writing utensils, for Dr. Greene feared my musings an enticement to madness. I could not even read my books there, but instead hunched submerged in steaming springs crying out for relief as I trembled and puked up guts and brains, retching until my corded intestines streamed from my nostrils and I had to snort them back in. The gardens were good and green, however, peaceful, and after a few weeks I began to feel the stirrings of my discarded fascination with botany, even serving as consultant on the nurturance of Dr. Greene's rose bushes. Most refreshingly, my sleep was untroubled but for my fears that I should see the Weeping Woman again and allow her to feed on my soul's wretchedness as she has always done.

There was a Spiritualist there, a glib young man with a nervous condition that caused him to shout out profanities at the most inopportune moments, for which he apologized profusely. He had attended several séances and lectures in New England and it was he who provided the utmost comfort to me in my manic throes. I confessed that I feared Théodore's revenant, and he held great conviction that my boy's innocent soul dwelled in Summerland among verdant restful pastures and the souls of helpful friends. Fear, he said, was only a manifestation of the mind's clumsy attempts to understand those greatest of universal mysteries such as the afterlife and spirit communication. To which he told me that the Weeping Woman sought me for a purpose. Why did I not speak to her in these dreams or ask why she wept? I had no answer, but now that I am home among familiar things, his query drifts back to me.

WHY DO THESE visions harangue me? I was in the yard performing the daily stretches taught at Castile when a leering brute of a cottonmouth slithered out from beneath the woodpile. It made for me with evil intent, and I fled. P'tite Marie's familiar pursued me to the orchidarium ruins, where I fell back onto some shattered glass, cutting myself. I knew the snake drawn by the scent of blood and huddled terrified, for it said it would slither around me and pierce me with its fangs. I called for aid but only the cicadas replied, singing their aimless song. Hideous monster! Poison clung to its teeth as it curled over my ankle. I knew myself lost. The wound would fester and blacken—a rotten limb grown gangrenous. Fournier would chop it off. Already I felt the agony of the severing stroke, the crunch of bones, and I screamed aloud. A woman walked from the far riverbank, a haze of pale linen and flowing black hair. I stretched out my hand to gain her attention. Her face was hidden. The world wavered before my eyes. My ears rang. I became conscious of her figure floating beside me, watched her pass a hand over the serpent and felt it recoil and vanish into the seething Hell from whence it came.

She took my bloodied hand in hers—its skin as cool and dry as paper—and pressed rose petal lips to my pulsing wound. Bliss shuddered through my form. Involuntary ecstasies wracked my body and I knew myself, once again, claimed. Tossed in the storms of my pleasure, I closed my eyes. When they opened, I was alone, my hand thrust into the air as I convulsed in the dirt. Some field hands passed by and I begged them to find my rescuer, but none had seen her, and they threw many glum looks my way when questioned.

I keep the wound open. Even now, it dribbles into the pewter dish. It is my offering to Her. Would that I could stab a wick into those gelid bowls of cruor and burn them as sacramental candles, summoning her to me!

Yet as I write this, a portion of my mind writhes in discomfort, doubting the veracity of my experience in the field and rejecting the appearance of that visitor. With one eye, I watch the gore clot on my palm and fear the loss of my good sense, while the other sees a crimson rose in bloom, a flower to proffer that haunting figure. I hear myself speak to P'tite Marie, conversing with her in the crumbling sanctuary of my mind while yet knowing that she rejects me and turns her heathen gods against me.

MAINARD STOLE MY protective hat because he coveted it for himself, thinking that it would work in reverse and he would be able to hear my thoughts but I cannot find it and he refuses me when I ask it back.

I CANNOT FORGET the silken caress of those rose petal lips on my raw and open flesh, nor absolve myself of longing, for I crave the touch of that woman, P'tite Marie's agent, a projection of her wounded spirit come to bedevil me. Our passion still lives, and mere spirits are not immune to its power.

Fournier returns, promising a cure for my diseased thinking. Now I know it not false or wicked—I have incurred a second sense just as Emilie's mediums who speak to the dead, for cannot I see beyond this waking realm into the world of dreams? See my boy languishing in that dream house of horrors, knowing my paltry attempts to rescue him fail? For I mount the steps which stretch out and draw ever longer, an endless shifting cascade beneath my tread. P'tite Marie disinterred my son and carries him close to her, a lure to draw me in as if I were a fish so easily caught. She shall do anything in her vast and wicked powers to pull me close and capture me—but I am canny like her, wary as the wild tiger, and I shall not be deceived. Though she speaks against me and sends her familiar to torment me, I will not bend! From the study window I see a figure lurking by the canebrake, white orbs glimmering in its vacuous, lurid face. Hear I the ceaseless susurration of the serpent and the wind, hissing about the evils that dwell within me, taunting me to leave the safety of this room and venture forth. All around, I drove nails into the doorframe to snare the malevolent souls that try to enter. Here I am safe from vodou spells and none can harm me but in dreams, and so I do not sleep.

THAT SHAM DOCTOR gives me chloral hydrate and Emilie watches to be certain I swallow my doses. But I know it meant to poison the Weeping Woman so that she appears to me no longer. If they murder her, the house will close its doors to me and my boy will be locked inside that prison, for sometimes the Weeping Woman is my adored and my heart breaks anew to know how I have ruined her affection, tramped over our love as if it were an insect to be quashed, and yet her face changes and her clinging touch overpowers me and sets the eels writhing within.

I pretend to sleep and proclaim myself a vessel of boundless health but when they go, take the lancet to my thigh and drain the tainted blood. Fournier's poison spills out of me in vile blue streams to take the form of thwarted shades and moaning ghouls. It soaks into the floor and traps them there beneath the boards but I hear them howling indictments against me.

POUPETTE OPENED MY window and let her in. Now I cannot escape her. She follows me from room to room, evanescing through the walls and doors—smoke trickling through a keyhole, water beads on the glass— her gaze, always watching through its hundred lenses, like the multifaceted eyes of a housefly. There is no place I go and remain unseen by her. She rides me at night and milks the vital fluid from me, and though I thrash and resist her, though I wear four pairs of pants to bed, she finds a way in.

That blind girl cursed me and stole my voice. It is why no one trusts my assertion that the Weeping Woman stuffed bees in my throat to choke me so that I cannot breathe. To suffocate me into death and her realm, to bring me through the gates. Emilie does not believe in the Weeping Woman, even when Ge-Rouge hovers over her as we speak and follows her from room to room, crying her bloody tears. Pins me beneath the weight of voluminous skirts like rising tidal waves, drowning, drowning me. She will not release me until I proclaim my eternal devotion, let her suck the very spirit from my body.

The image of my old classmate Aurelius Jacobs haunts me—that lurid face with its gushing third eye, exposed brain blinking at us wetly— operating theater alive with murmuring waves of unsuppressed sound knocking between our heads, leaking from our mouths and pooling around our twitching feet. Jacobs full of himself, flaunting that Cyclops eye and boasting of renewed vigor and health, oh yes, I remember he would not inherit till his mania was subdued and so he gave himself up to the knife and we teased him that he sold his soul for a £1000 a year. I saw it done with a trepan saw, Jacobs's eyes closed against the flow dribbling over his brow, hush of the theater amplifying the gurgling "pop" when they at long last extracted that ivory plug of bone. Jacobs got his inheritance. Said that his thoughts had clotted up like spoiled cream in his head, gone rank and green and until the surgeons scooped it out, he could not think. Likewise does the whirring of the hornets and whispering of ghouls dement my thinking and suffocate my internal voice so shall I endure the drill and gush to secure my own future.

How I TREMBLE and wail! All these many months I have convinced myself that my senses were cast into turmoil because passion had addled my wits, or because Belle Rive's shocking cruelties had so disturbed my sensibilities that I grew prone to internal mental disruptions and lunacy of a most severe form. I cast myself into the role of a delicate soul tossed amongst brutal storms of reason, made feeble-minded by the insensibilities of this atmosphere. Are dreams and fancies the working of an overheated imagination pushed past its healthy boundaries into realms of chaos and doubt? And so have I striven to retain this fallacy that the ecstasies experienced in the ghastly rooms of that lurid, terrible house were false, wickedness rising like smoke from the fires of my sinful lusts. Punishments and retributions. How eager was I to sacrifice my good sense (flesh) to turn among the silken arms of a ghost and thrust myself into its hot, wet, gaping jagged mouth—unholy angel! I can feel her licking the filling from me as the uncouth suck the crème from an éclair and all my powers drain away as down the whirlpool.

Yesterday I heard Clothilde speaking to my wife though they were in the parlor two floors below my study, their words rang up amplified as if through a horn, quoting her Christian miseries, for her saints close their ears to all prayer and *loa* gods dance uncomprehending in their foreign heavens guzzling the rum and spending the coin those jackanapes heap in forest piles.

IT's NOT MADNESS this plan, no, it makes perfect, eloquent sense, for how else should I rid myself of this cloying stench of rot and confusion? I can smell it, you know, alluring! festering! stink of the brown pus under a wet scab—keep asking Emilie to clean the window ledges where it gathers but she does such a poor job swiping dirty rags over it all she does is spread it and makes the stench accumulate everywhere it touches. The Weeping Woman shows me the sugar devil hanging in the curing house and I know that this shall be the instrument of my liberation. I give Poupette a gold dollar to fetch me the auger and so she comes with the precious corkscrew in her little fist. They tell one and all not to mind me, for my words are trickery and lies, the workings of a sickly man but she is a good girl and very simple to my mind and so proves easy to deceive.

But she trembles when taking my money as if afraid I will bite her hand.

"What you gone do with it Monsieur?"

"Important work," I say. "It's not for your young eyes to see and if you tell anyone that I have this tool I shall take it to them and snatch them from your head." I laugh but the child doesn't see the jest and she snatches up the coin and runs.

I ready myself for the Operation and to secure my own thousand pounds. I lie back and turn the crank and free the spirit locked inside the mental compartment and How I Shall Rejoice at the auger's bite and know myself soon Freed.

WELL, THAT DID not proceed as planned. I forgot that my door has no locks on the inside thus being removed by M. Bilodeau who would close me in to hamper my wanderings. I could not stuff the screams back into my gullet but they spilled and erupted as did fountains of blood from a severed artery. How they poured from the door! a torrent of bodies with gawping mouths stretched into long Os and my own gullible Emilie with the tears simmering and the corpse-pale complection of the white gentry her father so strives to emulate dashing to rip the sugar devil from my hands. Oh the cries and lamentations and ducky old Fournier again summoned with his vile bag of tricks. Now I find myself bandaged and tied, a lamed horse tethered in his corral while the barn goes up in cinders 'round me and though I batter the walls and yank the planks from their moorings, I cannot escape this room—once my refuge, now my prison.

Fournier stitches up my forehead porthole, closing that cracked window as if to stem its draft but the flies are here bzzbzzing, they creep and dig their skittering pointed legs into the seams and deposit eggs in my throbbing flesh. They want to gobble the luring rot inside my mental compartment but this is not the way for it will be unclean and leave me scarred and blind. Only way is to crack the window, pry apart the frames and let spill the ghost. I shall dig in with my own hands to wrest her from her moorings inside my mind. I will capture and devour her. I will fly to Metairie and string her up like Chinese lanterns so that one and all will see the Truth and know me for an honest man. Once again, some supernatural agency comes to my aid in dreams and wakefulness to illuminate the remedy for my suffering. I see clearly as if illumined the line of metal bits hooked on the wall—saws, axes, augers, picks. One tool will do the trickety trick, a center bit to carve out a perfect little hole through which the cerebral pulsations may alleviate their torment of confinement. Every sanguine drop that spills I catch into my jar, a holy vessel of crimson martyr's tears, and I shall make a doll of Her and drench it for my semen smells of heliotrope and my blood of orchids. Lo shall I set the ghosts upon her and transmit the agonies of my longing/

repulsion to her. A mirror I will be, my third eye burning in the dawn light—a beacon, a fount—shining its kinetic beams throughout all the realms of heaven and hell. No longer will she have claim or hold on me. When the sun has long set and all are abed, I will break the panes and climb down to the woodshed. Take the center bit and press through flesh and bone, open the window, open the portal, set free the ghosts.

The slaves shuffle through the fields and their voices rise to float on the stifling air, a sonorous trembling wave of sorrow. They sing this hymn when one of them sickens or dies, their voices forming a cradle of sound to bear away the departed soul, and again their wails knell across the fluttering cane—

Graveyard, oh graveyard. I walk in de moonlight, I walk in de star-light; I lay dis body down. I know de graveyard, I walk troo de graveyard, To lay dis body down. I lay in de grave an' stretch out my arms; I lay dis body down, I go to de judgment in de evenin' of de day. When I lay dis body down and my soul an' your soul will meet a'gin de day I lay dis body down.

Lydia and Lance Mueller
Philadelphia
Present Day

HORRIFIED, I WIPE the tears from my face and close my slack jaw. I lie staring at the ceiling as the sun crosses from the eastern to western windows without me moving from my station in bed, because I can't release the image of Isidore drilling a hole in his own head, of fucking his mistress in the conservatory garden, this genteel couple—him in his velvet and linen, her yards of fine fabric and lace—rutting among the blooming perfumed flowers beneath the blazing sun. That this is how I once felt about Lance and he about me. Aroused and hot-blooded, my body craves its own release. Tented over my face to block the light, Isidore's journal shares my heaving breath, filling my head with long-dead exhalations and the scent of decay.

I am undone, and oddly so, by the story of Isidore's thwarted grand passion and his mental decline—a delicate flower who wilted and spoiled in the wrong environment. A timorous dove pinched in the claws of a voracious eagle, he was no match for P'tite Marie's wily ways, her masterful manipulation of his emotions. Or were her feelings genuine? Was theirs the clashing explosion of soul mates, earthly forms shattering from the heat of combustion, naked souls merging into a blinding supernova?

Was vodou responsible for his possession and madness, the ghosts drifting amidst the turmoil of his Gothic nightmares? Maybe he truly believed that Petite Marie's curse manifested the murderous *loa* spirit, Erzulie Red-Eyes—righter of wrongs—to avenge his spurned mistress by draining him of his vital fluids and secreting his dead child in her house of horrors to lure him in. Plausible, perhaps, that he circulated lost in a labyrinth not of his making, running in terror from the pernicious jizz drinker who stalked him night after night, heard disembodied voices vilely hissing and whispering, instructing him to take the awl, that spinning sugar devil, to his skull and cut windows into the walls of his tormented brain. I, too, hear the voices, and cannot discern real from fake, internal from external. I, too, suffer my own haunting and the steady, oppressive presence of a ghoulish wraith who follows me from room to room, crimson-eyed and lusting. And maybe I should take the awl into hand and cut the demons out.

Raw and weeping, I know there's but one killer for the pain of these preternatural sorrows transmitted across the centuries to broadcast themselves inside my brain. Isidore's blade, his pewter bowl. Lifting myself from the tangled sheets, I make for my toy box. As I take it into the bathroom, I glimpse myself in the mirror: angular and wild-haired, long dark curls drifting about my head like Medusa's curse. Manic-eyed, scarred and terrifying in my long, white gown.

NINE O'CLOCK on a Saturday night finds me driving along South Street, looking for a parking spot close to the Blue Iguana, a trendy dance club that serves fifteen-dollar cocktails to newly minted lawyers and political strivers. It's early and the pickings will be slim, but I prefer to skim my cream early, before the boys get drunk and aggressive. The music throbs, bass filling up the empty dance floor. Hackett doesn't realize that the reason I confiscated his E was not to punish him, but to take it myself. The little pink pills reside in my glove compartment. I ration them for emergency situations, like tonight.

I care for nothing. No one. Lance has dealt my self-esteem a fatal blow from which I will not recover. Does it matter if I seek a petty revenge? Lance won't crumble from the discovery of my treachery; he'll say that he deserves it. That it's my right to serve him a helping of the same bitter victuals he fed me. He will play the martyr. The good saint bending beneath whip and flail, he will proclaim my punishment his due. It will be he who earns the pity, not me. And so, I proclaim myself entitled and seek out vengeance with predatory surety.

Three vodka tonics later, I've snared a little mousie. Thin, dark-haired man in a red T-shirt and khakis. I don't need to know anything about him. Not his name, his age, or his occupation. The way he dances, fluid and unselfconscious, with a sense of self-aware humor, tells me that he'll meet my needs for tonight. Chronic laryngitis serves me well on this occasion. A few gestures and my hoarse explanation eliminate the need for introductions. When I suggest we leave the bar, he complies with a smile, shepherding me from the dance floor with a protective hand on the small of my back. We walk in silence to his car, drive to his flat with nary a word exchanged, and fall into bed, heaving and moaning. My body opens under his like a voracious, carnivorous plant, swallowing, grasping. This is the moment I live for—the sucking surrender, the inner pull and resulting explosion, my brain full of spangles and electricity. Why does it never feel this way with anyone but a nameless stranger with little regard for the transmogrification of my sensual self? This man smells like lemons and leather. When he comes, he grips the back of my neck so hard it hurts, and I know there will be bruises beneath the skin come morning. This makes me smile.

He offers to drive me back to my car but I decline. We're close enough that I can walk and I need the night air to settle my head, cool my body's heat. The bright moon will wash away my sins, and the darkness cloak my subtle shame. He kisses me and locks the door behind me, turning me out onto the streets without a care. I find my car, and take myself and my wet crotch home.

I VISITED THE house again last night. This was the fifth dream in as many weeks, and now, through my midnight perambulations, I'm beginning to get a feel for the place. The layout doesn't change, but there are new rooms linked by tall corridors so broad as to be rooms themselves. Its design defies logic. Touring its floors, wending among the docents, visitors, interlopers, ghosts, and groups of schoolchildren on excursion, I am just one more body occupying space in the vastness of its heaving history.

A SECOND VIOLATION and another terse, tight-lipped call from St. Agatha's secretary informing me that Hackett is in the headmaster's office and will not be released to anyone but me or my husband.

"It's imperative that you come immediately to retrieve him, Mrs. Mueller. The disruption to the school day has already been enormous and there's been talk of calling the police. We'd like to keep this matter private. Naturally St. Agatha's has a reputation to consider, but there are other students at risk here, too. In light of your husband's contribution to this institution and your family's support, we're extending you this courtesy …"

The voice goes on and on, a chastising mother wagging her finger in my face.

My god, what has he done?

I drive like the devil, racing through cold gray streets to the U-shaped drive where St. Agatha's looms like a Victorian madhouse. Stringy clouds tatter a foreboding sky and the school flag snaps in a brisk wind. Softness and golden autumn light, all gone. Crows dot the yellowing lawn. Déjà vu—the same nun waits to open the doors, but this time we go upstairs to the headmaster's office, not down to detention. Hackett sits in a small armchair in luxuriantly morose repose. The man in charge of his keep, that vile old priest, stands beside my son, a tower of glower. He casts a spiteful glare my way. Isn't it decidedly un-Christian to so savor an "I told you so"? But he's Catholic and according to him, my loins are a fertile seedbed for evildoing.

Brushing past him, I follow the nun into the inner office. She leaves me standing before a massive oak desk and the creaking leather wing chair occupied by Father Talbot. Talbot doesn't wear robes or a clerical collar, but a small gold cross hangs around his neck over a blue Oxford shirt and a tie striped with the school colors.

"Mrs. Mueller. Thank you for coming down so quickly. You can't imagine how distressing it is for me to have to share this news with you." Talbot has the buttery remnants of an Irish accent. He's a theologian from Galway, and it was all over the news sites when he took over for the retiring headmaster two years ago. Talbot is decidedly progressive, openly feminist, and in full support of women's rights and gay rights, but remains stoically mum on hot-button issues like abortion. I was relieved when he joined the school and pitied his morning tussles with picketing parents and politicians.

"Sit down, please. You're hovering there like one of the Sisters!" He laughs at his own joke and I force a smile.

"Hackett's been struggling a bit lately," I begin, clearing my throat. "But he really is a good boy. I hope you know that."

"Indeed I do. A very bright boy, your son. But sometimes it's the clever ones who get themselves into the worst trouble because they can't fathom that they'll be caught, or worse, punished."

I know the feeling.

"We've had a time of it getting the whole story sorted, but your boy's been up to some very naughty things. Apparently, he's conceived a very clever racket. Writing other students' papers in exchange for drugs, which he then sells on school property. One might admire his creativity, but the papers he'd claimed to write are plagiarized. Granted, anyone can buy a term paper online these days and pass it off as his own, but your son has lofty ambitions. He guarantees each paper he sells to earn an A. He's copying published theses and dissertations, award-winning scholarly papers, and passing them off as his own. The levels of deception are really quite grand. St. Agatha's prides itself on honor and honesty, but teenagers are still children, and children do idiotic things. We do check, periodically." Talbot pauses for breath and I realize I've been holding mine.

"We've no choice but to expel him. As a courtesy to your family for your ah, delicate personal history, we will not press charges."

Delicate personal history. There are few worse feelings than sensing that others know your intimate secrets. I feel as though I've swallowed steel wool. My throat tightens. "What happens now? What about his record?"

"Ah," he murmurs, his pale blue eyes locked on mine. "That's the subject of another discussion. I'm meeting with the district superintendent next week, and I'll bring it up then and see what our options are. Hackett's career at St. Agatha's is permanently concluded, but we'll keep mum about the charges should you immediately enroll him in a public high school. He's a very intelligent boy. Some of history's great minds were troublemakers in their youth." Talbot pauses, his gaze intensifying as if probing the secrets of my warped mind. "Believe me, I've dealt with worse. All hope for him is not lost. Perhaps if he had someone to talk to, a professional, it would provide some relief from whatever he's been feeling lately."

I nod stiffly. "Yes, I understand. Thank you." I have the urge to either break into hysterical tears or stand and hurl my chair through the window behind Father Talbot's head. One inner voice laments the loss of my boy as he wanders further down his delinquent path, while a second, more urgent and nasty than the first, insists that my presence on this earth is a terrible poison that sickens all who draw breath in my vicinity, and that all would be better off without me.

I'VE NEVER SEEN Lance so angry or so defeated. His accusing eyes follow me everywhere, though he tries to hide his antipathy and commiserate with me as a husband and parent should. But it's still there; blame gleams fiercely inside that gaze. Sometimes I catch this pathetic, lost look sliding across his face. He wonders who we are, Hackett and I, what kind of people could do such damage to his orderly, pleasant life.

Hackett stays in his room. He has no computer, no phone, tablet, or TV. Maybe he's actually reading. After winter break, he'll start at the neighborhood high school six blocks from us and graduate from the very institution we strived so hard to avoid.

I exist in a state of constant pressure, some space-training chamber where outside sound and sensation are muted, amplifying the internal noise of racing mind, thumping heart, blood rushing noisily through my veins and arteries like high-speed traffic.

Isidore's gorgeous antique scarificator makes twelve precise cuts, all lined up in a tidy row. The blood drops out and the noise mutes.

THE MAN I fucked last weekend found me on Facebook. I don't know how. I don't remember telling him my name, but maybe I did. He wants to see me again. His request has floated around the edges of my consciousness like a gnat. I flick it away but still it circles, whining and distracting. Should I respond?

It's easy enough to text a time, date, and meeting place to the phone number he provided. Hackett's never around, and Lance—will Lance even realize that I've left the house? If he's fed and liquored up, if I make a show of playing the good wife and slip out the door, he won't argue with my absence.

Paul is already seated at the bar when I arrive. He rises and kisses my cheek as if we're old friends and I sense the other patrons watching us with disapproval. It's as if they know. They smell my treachery, my hunger.

"Lydia, hey. Thanks for meeting me." Paul's slightly less attractive than I remember. Maybe it's the neon bar sign's unforgiving blue glow or my clear head that hardens the line of his lumberjack jaw and narrows already-squinty eyes. He smiles and hands me a menu. "How's your throat?"

"Better, thanks." I'm still a bit scratchy but at least I can speak. "We had a good time the other night. I'm a little surprised that you wanted to see me, though. Is everything okay?" Here we go. The admission of a communicable disease. The plea for forgiveness. The pledge of love. It feels as though I'm the guy and he's about to drop a baby-bomb on me. Thank god I don't have to worry about getting pregnant. I had my tubes tied in the hospital immediately after Hackett's C-section birth. Sort of a "while you're in there" thing.

Paul licks his lips, a gesture I despise for it always makes me think of the smell of spit. "This is kind of an unusual proposal, but you strike me as an unusual woman." He pauses, waiting for his compliment, or whatever it is, to sink in and lubricate our social gears. When I don't reply, he starts over. "So, you seem like someone who's not shy about getting her needs met and I—"

An ill-timed server bounces over to our table and brings me my order of iced coffee, black. I watch her walk away, ponytail swinging, before I turn my attention to Paul.

"I get it," I say, tilting my head and gazing at him from beneath my lashes. It's an automatic tic, soon followed by my hand on his knee or leaning over the table to afford him a better view of my breasts. "You're interested in an arrangement. Something casual. Am I right?"

Startled, Paul nods and breaks into a grin. I decide that he's cute enough after all.

"String-free," I say. "Just for shits and giggles, right? No drama, no jealousy, no promises." I sound like a woman who knows what she wants and I am, it's just that I never ask for it in such blunt terms. Today, however, my veins are filled with cold fire. My bloody escapades have drained the sentiment and fear from me. I am transformed in a thousand small and invisible ways.

"Are you clean?" I ask. "No diseases or creepy-crawlies that want to hitch a ride in my undies and come home with me?"

Paul shakes his head. "I got tested for everything when I gave blood last week, actually. I'm like an Irish spring." He grins. "Clean as a whistle."

"Ditto. Well then." Here comes the table-lean, and sure enough, Paul's eyes drop to my breasts. I take a deep swallow of coffee, liking the sharp bitterness that drains down my throat. "Are you free this afternoon?"

He checks his cell phone. "I have two hours. What do you think?"

"I think we can do a lot in two hours." I stand and offer him my hand. "Let's go."

I'm HOME COOKING dinner, standing at the stove stirring a pot of putta-nesca while Paul's cum dribbles down my thighs. I'm not wearing any-thing beneath my skirt—too sore for that, but sore in a swollen, good way that I want to relish for a while longer. Maybe I'm foolish to take his word for his HIV and STI status, but at least I've regained the pulse of awakened flesh between my legs. Lance is home from work at an early hour and in a rare good mood. He will attempt to Make Amends. Rebuild the shaky bridge he's burned down. He wants me to know that It's Not My Fault. That I'm Still Beautiful. Desirable. He will sate himself with my body and I will allow it, because I need the closeness. Because I am lonely and love him. Because sometimes the only way to move past something is to pretend that it never happened.

He kisses the back of my neck and slides a possessive hand around my waist. "Mmm," he murmurs in my ear. "Going commando? What's that about?"

Shrugging, I allow him to turn off the burner and slide my skirt up over my hips. He unzips and nudges inside me, groaning. "You're so wet."

I swear I can smell Lance's semen, that familiar fungal, slightly sweet odor that used to make my head swim. Lance grips my forearm and squeezes. Twelve punctures on my arm crackle, burst and ooze. Red serum wells beneath his fingers, soaking the cotton sleeve of my blouse. It's not him but the sight of the blood that tips me over the edge and leaves me gasping with pleasure.

He shudders and collapses against my back. Instinctively, I grab a dishtowel and wrap it around my arm to hide the blood. After a moment, Lance pulls out and says, "I'm going to change. See you in a minute."

I nod, offer a tight smile, and peel back the towel. My sleeve is clean and dry. No bloodstains. My breath quickens. Didn't I see it earlier? It's there in my memory, the tiny explosions of fluid beneath my scabs, the flowering bouquet of poppies between Lance's fingers. I roll up my sleeve and run a finger along the small, healing purple marks. Jesus. I'm seeing things again. Hearing and feeling things that aren't real.

Shaking, I finish making the pasta and begin on the salad, unsur-prised when the knife slips and gashes my thumb. Concentrate. Trying not to cry but the tears are there, a child's astonishment, seeping up from inside some deeply buried place. I gulp a glass of wine and call to Lance. Dinner is relatively pleasant, at least until Lance finishes the bottle of wine and pours himself a scotch. It isn't often anymore that I get to enjoy the company of the man I first married, charming, glib, and startlingly intelligent. He rises to depart the table and leaves his dirty dishes behind. The reconciliation effort has ended. Flimsy scaffolding crumples. The fragile bridge collapses. I try to speak but nothing but a cracked whisper escapes my swollen vocal cords. Lance makes a dismissive noise and retreats to his study, as evanescent as a guilt-shrouded ghost.

BLOOD STIRRING, I shift inside my skin thinking of Paul. I've ignored his messages for days, but at last I text him back and head upstairs to slip into a silky red dress, relishing the feel of the fabric upon my bare skin. Whereas many women long for a full, heavy bosom, I've always been more than satisfied with my smallish breasts, firm enough—even after bearing a child—to confidently go braless. I strap my ankles into high-heeled boots, run my fingers through my ringlets and leave my life behind.

Paul's already wasted when I meet him at the club. His pupils are glossy and wide. His lips are pink and wet, his kisses hot and sour. I sling back a few shots of tequila and move with wild abandon, my dress skimming my flesh, flashing my thighs when I grab my skirts and shimmy like a can-can dancer. A girl with messy green hair sidles up and rubs herself against me, ass, thighs, and tits sheened with sweat and spilling out of her tight black dress. Her eyes are the same color as her hair, and she drunkenly flutters lashes heavy with layers of mascara. Paul whoops and runs his hands over our bodies, pushing us closer, squeezing whatever flesh he can grab hold of. The girl smells. Her scent cascades under my nose as she moves, undulating currents of musky armpits and some expensive perfume that doesn't suit her natural chemistry.

She whispers into my ear, her words distorted by the music's throbbing bass. I allow myself to be led by the hand to the ladies' room, where she and I curl into a stall. She offers me a candy-colored tablet of molly and a lurid grin. I accept—why not? My life is my own. I am not needed in a home emotionally vacated by both husband and son. The girl places the tablet on my tongue and strokes my hair, wrapping a ringlet around her finger. The pill catches in my throat, as sharp as glass shards. She kisses me, her voluptuous mouth deep and slick. I part my legs for her, give her access to my most intimate self. I will do anything, anyone, to make myself feel better. Lips traveling over my skin, she kisses my scars, nibbling at the scabs as her fingers pry me open. It is dirty and rough and violent. It is silken clouds and happy psychedelic haze, and I let her break me open like an egg to guzzle up my liquid insides. Panting and glassy-eyed, we return to the dance floor hand in hand, where Paul greets us with open arms.

THE HOLIDAYS DRIFT past like wraiths. We eat Thanksgiving and Christmas dinner in restaurants. Hackett is content with cash, and Lance and I do not exchange gifts.

Paul and I meet whenever time allows. There's not much talk. Just animal grappling and grunting. It does the trick. Soothes the ache in me for a while, fills up the hollows. For even if my blank spaces are filled with smoke and vapors, there is, at least, something there.

THE DREAMS ARE horrifying but addictively so. They haunt my head. The smell of camphor in my nose, the taste of old dust filling my mouth when I wake, like vapors of dreamtime wine drunk in the land of Nod. The balance shifts. From a state where that which is unreal and irrational can be pinpointed and examined, to one in which the absurd is logical. I feel myself sliding along the plank, skidding from one extreme to another and then *I am there, pushing through that dank, clinging grove, pushing aside curtains of Spanish moss. Breathing air thick and hot as the noxious green steam from a witch's kettle. Entering that house, purple and pulsating, black and stagnant with decay, a devouring entity eating away the space between its walls. Black night lit with tarry black stars defying all physical laws, smell of grave dust and heliotrope. I come alive then, peeling back my skin, unrolling that fine, fawn suede from my redbones and gristle. Growing new joints and tendons, I am slinky, sleek. I slide through the tall rasping cane with serpentine ease. My hunger's in my mouth, oh but I can taste the salt of him coiled up and waiting, the stinking, delicious, putrescent cadaverine of his essence as I take the sagging stairs and search the house for him. I can smell the blood throbbing in his veins. But even better is the smell of his tense arousal, its fluid sluicing fierce and fine through that one fat pipeline and rising to greet me.*

He calls to me. His voice is a guide wire tugging me closer. Through the double doors, their mauve paint flaking in strips upon the unraveled rug, I enter, I enter, I enter, I am infinite. I am everywhere. Creep upon the bed with my clinging claws, the fingers so bony and barely there, my hair stands on end. Isidore, writhing in dreams. King of glossy golden skin, his panting, tipped-open mouth like a trampled rose.

Open your eyes. See me.

THE HOUSE, THE house! That cursed landlocked shipwreck. Pasted like a flyer onto my sleeping mind's eye, I cannot unsee it or spend a peaceful nocturne without wandering its spiraling, ruined halls. A seducer of the night stealing into sleeping women's rooms, I discover myself prowling and furtive, sure that I can't be seen because I have no skin or limbs or breath in me. I'm just a figure in a dream who preys upon the energies emanating from these night-capped bodies in their beds, windows locked against the dangerous, intrusive night. I am only a river mist, a creeping cat who pounces onto their chests and suctions the air from their deflating lungs, stealing oxygen from blood, cord, placenta, fetus. A vengeful spirit glimmering in their murky cheval glass, hovering a foot above the floor and trailing sanguine tears in my wake.

WORK SEEMS TO not be going as well as I imagine. Adelaide calls me to complain. I've missed my deadline. Her words disintegrate into a spiky trail of letters, float right out my other ear and leak from my nose. She wants her boxes back. I will not relinquish the journals, letters, or scarificator. They belong to me now. As I hang up the phone, my laptop screen stutters and freezes. Twenty-eight open tabs showing the same scratched, monotone image of a single structure, the house with the octagonal window I saw in Metairie: "Reputed brothel, The House of Love and Magic. New Orleans, LA. Circa 1854."

I WANT TO quiet this noise in my head. Like bees but ghost bees, their sound more vibration than noise. Ease the pressure. Because the blood, the cutting, doesn't do it for me anymore. The scarificator has tasted the flesh of my every limb. The bowls have been filled and filled again and yet I cannot drain this sickness from myself. This dark mood that has descended into the pits and crevices of my very personhood, as Isidore said. Like him, I fear the crumbling of my reason, the subtle disintegration of the fibers that bind my reality.

SOMETIMES PAUL REFERS to something I don't remember. He says I come to his house in strange outfits, long white dresses with voluminous skirts.

That I wear a manic stare and red opera gloves to hide all the scars on my arms and fuck him until he is spent and dehydrated, begging off another go because he's exhausted. One night, I clench my scabby thighs around his waist as pleasure floods me, momentarily blotting out the world. Opening my eyes, I look down at the lover lying naked and flushed on his back beneath me, his face pinched with agitation.

"Do you love me?" he asks. Sweaty, warm palms grip and release my hips, squeezing flesh in nervous handfuls.

"I don't but I wish I did. Are you sorry you asked?"

He shakes his head, but I know him for a liar.

LANCE CORNERS ME, barging into the bathroom while I cower in the bathtub with my tall glass of scotch. Tepid, milky water sloshes over the rim and splashes his suede shoes.

"What the fuck is this?" he shouts, waving a credit card statement.

There are things I do to make myself feel good. I thought a new look might make me into someone else, someone better. More loveable. More normal. But I don't say this aloud.

"Three thousand dollars at a costume shop? When did you get this card? What the hell are you buying all this crap for?"

It's too much. His voice amplifies in my brain until feedback squeals drown out his words. Then I'm standing. Water drips down my hide. Lance's eyes morph into shocked Os. He hasn't seen me naked since I locked up my honey-box and tossed away his key. Opening my mouth to aim my scream at him, I launch a volley of deadly arrows that pierce his lungs and silence him.

DR. OLIBEROS JIGGLES her foot as she listens to Lance describe my behavior for the past few weeks. This movement is the only sign that she is alive—her gaze is unblinking. She's as steady as a statue except for that foot, tap-tapping against the leather leg of her chair. She's a stripe of beige, skin the same color as her nondescript, boring clothes. Her eyes are the same color as her skin. Hair so short she could pass for a nine-year-old boy. But little boys don't favor shiny carmine pumps with gold-studded heels. I can't take my eyes off those shoes. They feel like a bad omen. Red shoes dancing their way into a cemetery plot. Even if I chop off her feet, just like in the fairy tale, those red shoes will go on tap-tapping.

Lance's voice runs through my head, hamster on a wheel. I know he's Concerned. Desperate to patch me up, maybe so that he'll feel less guilty when he finally leaves me. In intimate detail, he describes the marks upon my body. The night terrors. My belief that I am being summoned into that hideous house. That I no longer need to eat because "she says the house feeds her." Lance glancing my way, his eyes settling upon the sharp knobs of my wrists, the new bones that push themselves up beneath my skin. That I forget simple things. Get up from the table to pour myself another drink when I already have two sitting before me. Forget that I must drain the bathtub or seem surprised that Lance and Hackett are angry and fed up with me.

"Tell me about the dreams, Lydia," says Dr. Oliberos. "Lydia. Lydia? Do you hear me, Lydia?"

"Yes, I hear you." My voice is low, scratchy. She offers me a glass of water. It is like swallowing nails. Maybe I'm rabid and this is hydrophobia.

"Tell me about the dreams you've been experiencing."

"The house," I mumble. "It feels like it's watching me. Listening. That all the dark rooms, all the secret passageways and shape-shifting walls can hear me and want to stop up my mouth." I know it can hear me talking about it, that it will summon me back there tonight just to correct me. Punish me.

"What do you feel happens to you in these dreams?"

"They're not dreams," I say. "It's real. I used to wake up hungry. I've always wanted breakfast right away in the mornings. But not anymore. I wake feeling full. Satiated. Sometimes there is a strange taste in my mouth, like bloody meat. Sort of raw and metallic."

Tap-tapping. "Go on."

"I meet a man there. He wears a velvet vest and jacket. He has long, wavy black hair and sad eyes that turn down at the corners. Sometimes when I visit, I try to ignore him, to go explore other rooms, but he calls to me. His body calls to me. We make love."

Lance shakes his head and lets out a huff of air.

"You make love to this man? Is that all that happens?" Dr. Oliberos asks.

"There is more to it than that. He gives himself to me, utterly. He desires me, absolutely. He is the beach and I am the sea. He is the fisherman and I am the catch. He reels me in from a great distance away. Even when he fights me …"

Dr. Oliberos's eyelids flicker minutely. "Continue."

"When he resists. When he screams and tears at his hair and clothes, when he tries to dig the eyes from his head so he doesn't have to see me, he is crying out to me. Begging me to release him. He thrusts and turns upon the bed. He bursts into white flame and only I can quench that fire. I put my mouth on him. I pull him into me. He spurts endlessly and I drink from him. I take his life force and I am satisfied. But when I wake I feel heartsick and evil."

"And how do you manage those feelings?" Oliberos asks.

"Just look at her arms!" Lance interrupts, pretending to gouge my flesh with a knife.

Automatically, my arms cross over my chest and I hug myself tight.

"Lance, let Lydia answer. Right now, we're only here to listen."

He makes a strangled, gurgling noise. It is, I think, like the sound the man in my dreams makes thrashing beneath me when I'm fastened like a lamprey on his swollen penis.

"I step outside of them." I'm not liking this "sharing of secrets" malarkey. What I do to myself is nobody's business but my own, but I promised Lance. It's either this or the hospital, and so I spill my guts. Nearly all of them anyway. I skip the part about Paul. He's not mine to share.

The good doctor says, "Lydia, from what Lance has told me, you have a history of mental illness and self-injury but you've been stable for quite a while. Typically, in cases like yours, there's a traumatic event that precedes a breakdown. Has anything particularly upsetting or painful happened to you lately?"

"Lance loves me," I say. "He didn't do it on purpose."

Dr. Oliberos fastens her gaze on my husband, uncomfortably probing him for family secrets. "Lance?" But the idiot just shrugs.

"Liar, liar, pants on fire," I whisper in a voice like the drone of bees.

She schedules another session and sends us away with prescriptions for Risperidone and Pentobarbital. I think Lance would like to origami-fold me up into a tiny square and mail me off to Timbuktu in an envelope with no return address.

THE DRUGS DO not arrest the insidious seepage of dreams into my waking mind, and so I quit taking them. I'm certain that my blood (fresh, red, wet) exerts some mystical influence upon Isidore's artifacts, somehow summons me through supernatural dimensions to an otherworldly plane where past and present cohabitate. I decide that the best way to avoid visiting the Nightmare House is to hide the alluring scarificator so that it no longer beckons. Get rid of the journal, page by page. It tastes like the ghosts of garden heliotrope. I can taste the salt of Isidore's skin that coats the pages and the grime from his labored, sweating hands. The paper dissolves on my inky tongue like a stale Communion wafer. I'm supposed to stay home but when Lance has to leave, I am free to roam. Free to fuck. Paul is terrified of me but also in love. He's my panting little puppy, a cum-slave spurting into my voracious guzzling vortex, and I intend to wring him dry.

I FEED THIS fire. Daily, I wrestle my thoughts from its hold, rip the trailing ribbons of my sick obsession from its greedy, devouring flames, but this fire is unquenchable, its appetite unsustainable. It cannot be contained. I fold myself into my nightmare and seek him out, the words filling my mouth. *Mad, unholy man of my dreams. How I hunger! I thirst for you. Bleed for you. Your body is the sacrament I take on my tongue. The tongue I would bite off and feed to you.*

CERTIFIED MAIL DELIVERY from Adelaide Randolph. Lance picks it up at the post office after becoming annoyed with the number of pink slips stuck to our door frame.

"Open it," he says. Voice dry, hard, tight.

But I won't. I can tell by looking that it's bad, a lethal message, a vodou curse sent by that witch to destroy me. He's shaking the letter in my face, making its despicable magic fly off into the room.

"Stop!" My hands fly out, flailing.

"Goddammit, Lydia. Open your fucking mail." He swats my arm with Adelaide's envelope. Fear shudders through my bones. I can't let it touch me again.

"You do it." I moan, hiding my face as he tears into it, releasing spell-spores into the air.

His eyes scan the letter. He looks at me and sighs. "Read it."

I peer at it, trying to make sense of the sentences dancing around on the page. My voice is raspy as I read, "'Every good tree brings forth good fruit but a corrupt tree brings forth evil fruit.' That's not nice at all. Who would send such a thing to me?"

Lance frowns and rereads the letter aloud. "Please return all archival materials to the Belle Rive Restoration Foundation using the express mail account information below." He waggles the page. "Look at it again. What does it say?"

I recite, "And a man will choose any wickedness, but the wickedness of a woman. Sin began with a woman and thanks to her we all must die."

"Jesus Christ." Lance collapses on a chair.

"It doesn't say anything about Jesus Christ."

He laughs weakly, wiping away the solitary tear leaking from his right eye. After a moment he gets up, and soon I hear the low drone of a one-sided phone conversation.

The letter sits on the counter, face up. The words stop dancing and order themselves into neat rows. "Please return all archival materials to the Belle Rive Restoration Foundation."

I make it to the sink just in time to pour out the watery pink puke spilling from my mouth.

HACKETT IS MISSING or absent or a teenage runaway. Terrified of his mother's raging insanity, which perplexes me. I always held it together, was always a good mother. Until I wasn't.

"Where is my son?" I ask. Lance gawks at me.

"Seriously? You were freaking him out. It's not healthy. We mutually agreed that he should live in a more secure environment until things improved."

Yes, maybe I should have noticed my boy's absence, but he likes to party and hang out with his friends in Callowhill. What child wouldn't choose the company of friends in lieu of his spiritually bankrupt mother, his cheating asshole of a father? I resolve to forget this annoying conversation.

"No one feels sorry for someone who makes such poor choices. This is the work of your hand, Lydia."

"Me? More like the work of your uncontrollable lust, you dick. You're the one who broke us. You and Marcella."

254

Lance's face hardens. "When things settle down and I no longer have to babysit you, he'll come back."

This is one catastrophe after another. The skin of my face crackles into an agonized rictus. I hear juicy chunks of it peel away and plop into my lap, but when I look, there's nothing there. Maybe I remember Hackett peering warily at me from my bedroom door. His hesitant embrace, the concern distorting his features when he tells me he loves me, his childish plea to "Get better, momma. Please." How long ago was that? A day? A week? I can't recall.

"Is he?" I murmur. "Where?"

"Staying with Marcella for the time being. Her townhouse has a spare room."

Ezili Dantor, mistress of my house. "My heart is black!" I wail. "Mwen kriye dlo nan je san!" *I cry tears of blood.*

Isidore's scarificator works its magic on my skin. Inner thighs dotted with thick scabs I peel off and pinch to spur fluid to the surface of the reopened wounds. But I leave my tools out. I've grown sloppy, careless. Forget to clean the blades, my skin. Make myself sick. Fever, infection. Yellow-white rings of pus bubble on my skin. And I keep picking, squeezing, digging. Scraping the edges with plastic knives to dig out the infection, making the holes wider and deeper with every turn.

Lance drives me to the ER when I faint at home, smacking my head on the edge of the toilet. He tells me later that the admitting doctor looked nauseous when he came out to describe the damage I'd done. The chewed-up paper they'd excavated from my stomach which clogged the tubes and dripped ink onto my gown. They say the psych ward has a bed waiting for me.

Dr. Oliberos comes to my rescue. She gives me Haldol injections and prescribes Naltrexone. She tells Lance that cutting releases the body's natural opiates and if the drugs sap my pleasure in it, I'll stop. She talks the ER doctor into keeping me for observation and releasing me into her and my husband's care. If not for her intervention—spurred on by what? Lance? pity? medical curiosity?—I'd be in lockdown. (I learn this two days later, when the IV antibiotics have kicked in and I'm finally awake.)

There will be scars. But I don't care. In the hospital, I do not dream.

PAUL WANTS TO see me. He will not shut up. He will not leave me alone. He's infatuated or addicted or obsessed. Says I have turned him inside out like a coat. I have lost my job, my son, my husband. My sanity. My skin stretched taut over wire-hanger bones, I am scars and scabs and sail down the streets toward him, a sleek ship, a racing shell, sharp prow parting the night air.

When we are together he says I am so beautiful and terrifying he cannot exist without me. I am a terrorist. I terrorize him with lust and sin, dump out all the trinkets in his turned-out coat pockets and pick through his life's minutiae. But we are better together when we don't speak. We inhabit simple pleasures. I spread myself over the cold sheets while he rolls a blunt and sprinkles it with white powder from a baggie. He winks and licks the paper, sealing it shut before flicking his lighter and firing it up. Wordlessly, he passes it to me—ever the gentleman. I suck in the smoke, coughing at its unusual bitterness. Paul takes a toke and passes it back. I don't care how it tastes, I'm just waiting for those waves of ambient pleasure to roll over me and mute the Dark Mood's static inside my brain, so I pull the smoke inside me again and again.

Paul welcomes Dark Mood into our trysts as if it were a playmate, another lover to convert our folie à deux into a ménage à trois. Our sex is raw and silent. Barebacked and sticky. We are naked, but there is something more than being unclothed in our communion, there's a level of exposure that makes my bones hum. The sort of intimacy you can only experience with someone who doesn't know you very well, who hasn't seen you birth a child, suffer through the flu, or trip over a curb and skin your knee. I retain my mystery and float inside its cloud, ethereal as the icy spirits we drink in great swallows straight from the bottle. He licks the drops that dribble down my chin and splash onto my collarbones. He kisses my scars, pushing his thumb into tiny craters on my flesh.

"Look at that," I say. "Your thumb's growing out of my arm. Do you see it?" My heart races; everything grows faint and flickery about the edges. My arm stretches into a long thin twig from which Paul sprouts, a vine growing straight from the woody pith of my skeletal frame. He's all the way across the room. The room is a hollow tunnel, but he can still touch me with fingers like sharp and shiny bird claws. He is a growth grafted onto me, and we inhabit the same euphoric realm. Our hair sprouts magnolia blossoms—infantile mouths clamoring for milk— and our skins tremble together, like leaves in a spring breeze. Then he is the tree and I am the slithering rainbow serpent Aida-Wedo, a bridge between heaven and earth, infinite and omnipotent. I am the Source and the Light, the Great Mother.

"Show yourself, Spirit!" cries a voice from dreamland. "Spirit, speak your name!"

But I'm not a source of Light. I am a spitting, spinning creature, Erzulie Ge-Rouge crying tears of blood. I am the manifestation of P'tite Marie and Emilie and Lydia, scorned, wasted, tossed aside. I am bitter and vengeful—unloved, childless—and restitution will be paid.

LANCE

My wife is covered in blood. The shock of it arrests me for many long minutes. Time freezes around us. Ice settles into my heart.

I will not remember dialing 911.

Listening to the recording of my call during her competency hearing, I will be shocked by the grave, toneless voice that purports to be mine and is completely foreign to me. Nor will I recall prying her fingers, one by one, from the knife she still clutches and carrying it carefully to the kitchen sink, as if I mean to soap up the blade after carving our holiday turkey.

Something cakes her hair into sticky coils—more blood. She is rufous with death. I drape a blanket around thin shoulders as taut as high wires and sit beside her on the staircase as we wait for the police, the ambulance, and her removal from my life. I would kiss her; I would murmur into her ear reassurances that everything will be all right, but she won't hear me.

Why did you do it, is the obvious question. What else are you capable of is next, the one that will ruin my sleep and tunnel through my days, leaving holes behind in all my memories. Hackett was right to leave us behind—spoiled, selfish boy.

Sirens wail and blip. Heavy fists bang upon our front door. They will take her from me, at last. She has orchestrated the grand finale of her mad symphony, and now I begin my requiem.

Lydia turns toward me with the slow precision of a wind-up doll, sucking a stranger's blood from lips that I have kissed a thousand times. Black and lightless, her eyes are not her own. She motions me closer, her whisper needling into my ears: "Give me any plague, but the plague of the heart, and any wickedness, but the wickedness of a woman." For the first time, I am afraid of her.

AMPHETAMINE-INDUCED PSYCHOTIC disorder with delusions. That's the official diagnosis. Tests showed high levels of PCP mixed into the cocktail of pharmaceuticals in her blood. It explains nothing; my wife was not taking amphetamines when her visions began. She was not psychotic when she spoke to me about the man in her dreams or the house she inhabited there. She was perfectly lucid—frighteningly so—until the moment that I found her sitting on our front step with a bloody knife in her hand.

I can't explain what happened to her, that fey tragic creature whom I loved fiercely and unrelentingly upon first glance. She believes herself transformed, possessed. *Hell hath no fury.*

As sick as she's been, she's remained present inside herself. I could always see her, find her, somewhere inside that beautiful shell. Until suddenly, I couldn't.

LYDIA

WALLS HERE THE same sickly, dusky color as bloodstains on an old sheet. Smells the same, too— pukey, rotted sugar-fish smell of paralytics and castaway needles. Light too sharp and yellow, light too brightly blue and flickering. Endless noise of orderlies, clanging bars and bedpans, locks clicking back and forth, in and out, grinding keys and hinges. TV blaring, a body moaning in the room next door, but none of it real. No windows with glimpse of soothing sky. No sunlight streak-painting its heat on my skin. Lights on. Lights off. Silence. Heart beating inside my ears. Soul slithering inside my skin, looking for an exit hole. Soul slinking into dreams, my body a house abandoned—a ruin.

And it comes back. Not Soul, for that is gone and I am empty, but Memory.

"She's the youngest patient we've ever placed in solitary." Tinge of pride in that voice. I start to shake. Can't get warm even while I'm sweating. Tears of blood leak from my skin, run down and drop onto the shiny floor. Cutting is the way. Cutting is what put me here, sawing my flesh with a plastic blade, digging in with pencil points. They'd taken everything away, tied my hands. But alone, I found a way. For my teeth were sharp as vipers' fangs, and the taste of my blood was sweet. O beauties! O breath of my breath! Glistening drops like rare rubies balanced on a thread, filling, spilling over. Crimson delight. And the ease of it, the sorrow draining away.

Now I remember. I was here before. Blue and cold. Fingers and toes like icicles. The Snow Queen of Solitary. The shock. Electrical odors of burning hair and skin. Ozone stink and black eyes meeting mine in the mirror. My saintly, ancient grandparents intoning, "The Lord gives and the Lord takes away. He forgives all transgressions, and the fires of hell burn not for thee, child."

Memory burned from my brain because "It's better that she forgets. Gets a new lease on life." Who was I? What had I done to be taken away, treated that way? They made me a monster, or culled the monster in me. They leashed me. Kept me small. Made me docile. How could I have forgotten?

VERY LATE ONE night Lance calls me, drunk and sobbing, begging forgiveness. His words will ring, sing, within me for eternity. "I'm an imbecile! The intensity of my feelings for you has always frightened me. I behaved in the worst possible manner. I shat where I ate and closed my doors to you. I always feared your disintegration, the loss of you. Always! And I tried to keep a wall between us, to love you from afar so that it would hurt less when I finally lost you. I wouldn't even admit to myself that's what I did because the admission of my guilt, my deliberate blindness, was abhorrent to me. Lydia, you are the exception to every rule. I have loved you since I first laid eyes upon you and felt God stirring in my soul. It frightened me. As much as I craved you, I wanted to run from you. And as much as I desired you, I wanted to crush that desire within myself."

I have dragged myself up from a deep, drug-induced sleep and crawl over the minefield of my husband's words, trying not to get blown up. The room around me is stuffy and filled with ambient light from the nurses' station. I recall a few lines from a poem and I offer them to Lance. "The very tones in which we spake had something strange, I could but mark; The leaves of memory seemed to make a mournful rustling in the dark."

"Until they made themselves a part, of fancies floating through the brain, the long-lost ventures of the heart, that send no answers back again." He sighs deeply. "Longfellow's 'Fire of Drift-wood.' You remembered."

We share a minute of silence as I push back the strange images that bob up from my buried conscious—myself, much younger, in a hospital room much the same as this one, waiting for my mother to call and to come and get me. The call, the visit that never came.

Lance speaks. "Lydia, you don't understand how difficult it is to be married to someone like you—always frozen in wait for the other shoe to fall. You are a killing weight, a stone sewn into this wolf's belly. But, beloved woman, know that whatever becomes of us, my heart will beat for you until the coroner cuts it from my body."

RED SHOES DANCING over the cold linoleum, Dr. Oliberos arrives one morning for a consultation.

"How are you feeling now, Lydia?"

"Can I go home now? I want to go home." My fingers rise of their own volition to skitter and fret over the strings of my peony-pink scars. Remembering. Thirsting. I don't like this empathy, the way my own frail sanity begins to seethe and recoil from my efforts to comb its unraveling strands into order.

Dr. Oliberos watches impassively. Taking notes, I'm sure, in her mind. "Not yet, but soon. When you're better."

THE INJECTIONS SPREAD a blanket over my mania, smothering it, beating it out like a fire. At last I can receive visitors. Lance comes with the lawyer he's hired to tell me that Paul survived my attack and refuses to press charges.

"Count yourself fucking lucky, lady," the lawyer remarks. I might like to give him a taste of the knife next, but the impulse that drove me to attempt murder (was it?) has dissipated, leaving behind nothing but an ugly stain.

My beautiful bittersweet boy arrives one afternoon, bringing me a tablet loaded with word game apps, a pair of headphones, and a music mix he's compiled filled with songs from Bauhaus, The Clash, Joy Division, Skinny Puppy, Einstürzende Neubauten, SPK, and even Nurse with Wound. As much as he's grumbled about my affinity for punk and industrial, it's the music he grew up with, the music I've always played while I worked, and he knows those songs as well as I do. It's a genuinely thoughtful gift.

"You look well," I say. Marcella the traitor has done a good job of caring for him.

He smiles wanly. "You too," he says, though I can't imagine that I do with these gray shadows beneath my eyes, dressed in camouflage patterns of yellow and green bruises.

"Death warmed over, as they say."

"At least you're warm." At last, a real grin. He hasn't entirely forsaken me.

THIS IS WHO I am. How can I reconcile myself with that fact? Am I meant to revel in my uniquely warped reality, or am I to coddle it like some weak and atrophied limb? On the one hand, my reality seems perfectly normal to me; it's what I've always known. It's as familiar and comforting as a dark and dirty burrow when I've fled the light, the slithering snakes on the prowl, the ominous black clouds swirling overhead. Yet I know there exists an entirely other, outer world which I, from the sanctuary of my underground hovel, cannot envision or understand, even when I am forced to exist in it.

I mean, it's *my* brain. My head, my thoughts, my jig-jaggedy, see-sawing emotions or flatlining affectless drift. It's what I know, and even in its unreliable state, I must trust it to be Truth. But now there is another Truth, a chemical language written in pharmaceuticals, and I must reconcile myself with the knowledge that my world was false. A faulty product of genetic construction, and I cannot trust my own disordered thoughts or my seismic emotions because they are inherently flawed.

However much I yearn to be someone else or to behave/feel/think differently, this is all I have and I must make do with it. This antiquated jalopy, this shit-bucket of butterflies. And crazy or sane, I am always me—a restless, distorted soul.

LANCE VISITS AGAIN, bringing flowers this time—a bountiful bundle of magenta cabbage roses to brighten the tiny, cheerless room. Shocking. He stopped buying me flowers years ago after I shredded his bouquet of lilacs and tossed them into the dinner salad.

"Don't worry, they're not from me," he announces wryly.

"Will you buzz the nurses' station and ask for a plate, knife, and fork?" I say, poker-faced.

My husband blanches, an "oh no, here we go again" look scrolling across his face.

"I'm kidding!"

He frowns. "Oh, ha ha." But then the clouds break and a smile creeps out. "You haven't made a joke for a long time."

"I'm rusty. Maybe that was in poor taste."

"I don't mind," he says, propping the flowers in my plastic water pitcher. "These are from your little admirer, Owen. Believe me, if he wasn't such a fan of yours we'd be in much worse shape over that whole Belle Rive fiasco." Lance pulls a chair up to the bedside, resting his hands beside mine on the cotton blanket. "He told Adelaide that the scarificator was damaged in shipping and reimbursed the Foundation with the insurance money. They weren't technically aware that you had the letters and journals, so you're safe there. They did, unfortunately, send a notice of intent to sue if you don't pay back the funds they advanced you, including expenses for your trip to New Orleans."

I groan. "This hurts my head."

Lance shrugs. "The lawyer's responding. At worst, we'll have to give them a few thousand dollars. Anyway, Owen wants to visit you. I thought it would be okay but I said I'd ask you first."

For a panicked moment, just one, bees vibrate in my throat. Choking stingers, claws, and brittle cellophane wings flutter against my palate. Then they're gone.

"Yes, I would like that."

Scruffier but still pink-cheeked, Owen comes the following week and I get to wear street clothes. We skip niceties.

"Why are you here?" I say, skewering him with a look. His attention feels odd but unobtrusive.

"I meant it when I said I really admired your work. I was sorry to hear that the Belle Rive restoration was a wash. Well, they hired someone else, anyway. Your son contacted me. He said you'd mentioned me—as a colleague, of course," he adds hastily. "I think he believes we're friends."

Hackett, my darling one. Hope still lives behind that cynical façade.

"Like I said, he emailed me. Said that this assignment was making you sick again and asked if I knew why it would affect you so much." He pauses, baby face piqued with concern. "So I did some research, starting with Isidore's institutional records. I shared his story with my boyfriend, Lucas; he's earning a master's in abnormal psych at Brown. It's his opinion that Isidore suffered from adult-onset schizophrenia. He was what, twenty-seven, twenty-eight when he first mentioned the voices? The visions? And that comment that Emilie made about Isidore's eyes particularly struck me. Lucas showed me some new research proving that schizophrenics have detectable abnormalities in their visual patterning, which may in future be used as markers in neuropsychological assessments. Again, all signs point to severe mental illness. Fournier treated him with morphine, paregoric, and chloral hydrate, all of which are narcotics—opium was the primary ingredient. And all of which can cause or exacerbate visual and auditory hallucinations, paranoia, insomnia, and cognitive dysfunction. Plus he was regularly bled to the point of anemia and emaciation. They thought they were helping him but their treatment just made him worse."

The meds slow my speech. When I speak, it feels like I'm holding a giant slug captive in my mouth. "What's my excuse?"

"PCP, I hear." His eyes sparkle with mischief.

Touché.

Owen continues. "Isidore was institutionalized for the rest of his life. He spent two years locked up in Jackson before Emilie could transfer him to a reformation asylum in New York. He died in 1869 after a third attempt at self-trepanning."

"He never really had a chance, did he?"

"He was probably genetically predisposed to mental illness. It's unlikely that he would've remained well. Lucas suspects that the move to America and plantation life, especially the traumatic events of witnessing Albert's whipping and hanging, Prosper's death from rabies, and the yellow fever deaths caused PTSD, culminating in a psychological break. All of the religion and vodou would have fed into his paranoia. Plus, he seemed to exist in a permanent state of culture shock and never adjusted to his new life."

"There's no further record of him? No letters or journals?"

Owen shakes his head. "The only reference to his state of mind or what he thought about while at the asylum is a note in a medical file that Emilie kept with her papers. I found them all archived in a university's historical documents library. A doctor remarked to her that Isidore had drawn three large *X*s on the wall of every room where he was housed. Those same marks were also discovered carved into his chest postmortem."

XXX. A pray, a plea to Mama Marie, just as I had made. What wish did my dead diarist want fulfilled?

Owen continues. "Part of their story does have a happy ending. Emilie went on to become a doctor. She graduated from the Boston Female Medical College in 1860. Geneviève Stockton's daughter Fanchon also attended college and was renowned in her time for her mathematical theories. She became a professor of astronomy later in life, working in conjunction with her artist sister, Sylvie, to produce some of the most beautifully illustrated science books of the era."

A chill travels over my skin. "My mother used to read to me from a yellowed book of fairy tales with eerie pen and ink drawings by Sylvie St. Cyr. I keep it on the bookshelf in my office."

"That's her." Owen lifts his eyebrows, adding, "So, here's where it gets juicy. There's no definitive proof, but anecdotal documents of the time confirm that in 1854 P'tite Marie gave birth to a child, who spent the first few years of its life in the brothel with its mother. The child vanished when it was about three years old and was presumed dead. Some said it was washed away in a flood on the property, others reported that it was snatched up by the *lougawou* or buried alive. Mention of the child ends shortly after its disappearance."

"Lougawou?" My tongue is clumsy with the unfamiliar word.

"*Loup garou.* Werewolf."

I nod. "The shape-shifter."

"But then there's this." Owen unfolds a color copy of a yellowed newspaper entry from the *New Orleans Parish Liberation Reader*, a newspaper for the newly freed colored community, and pushes it across the table for me to read.

On June 12, 1857, a light-skinned Negro female, aged three to four years, was found wandering the road at night and covered in fresh dirt. She had soil embedded beneath her fingernails and ground into her hair. She wore a white, lace burial gown. She does not know where she is from and cannot name her mother. The girl gives only her Christian name, Celestine. A further search the following day revealed a small hole, two feet deep, 15 yards from Providence Road, with no other evidence of trauma or disruption to the area. Foul play is suspected. The child is given to the Indigent Colored Orphan Asylum, and any who know of this child or her circumstances may lay claim to her therein.

"That was my mother's name," I interrupt. "Celestine. Queen of the heavens, daughter of the stars." But she is long dead, her ashes sprinkled in constellations across the Allegheny Mountains.

Owen chews his lip and continues, "Record of P'tite Marie's daughter only exists because she was an anomaly. Celestine left the orphanage at age nine when a woman named Paris took custody of her. At age fifteen, she was working as a seamstress and was hired by a traveling troupe of actors. It's suggested that she joined them to sew costumes, set pieces, and tents. At any rate, she traveled with them up the East Coast to Philadelphia—this was after the Declaration of Emancipation, and so she was free, you know. At nineteen, Celestine sang on stage at the Union Theater in San Francisco billed as 'Velvet Orchid, the Voodoo Queen's Daughter.' She toured music halls and saloons under the management of a man called Bottleneck Jim for several years until marrying a white businessman who saw her perform and became entranced. Records from the 1880 census list Celestine Lavelle, her husband, William Dillard, and a young daughter, Isidora, living in Boston."

"Now look," Owen sets aside the clipping and spreads out a worksheet.

A family tree.

I take it with shaking hands, fighting against the clouds that swarm the rim of my consciousness—a tempest impending. Where is my ax? *Gone to cut de storm in two.*

> Marie Célestin Paris, b. 1827, Louisiana (Petite Marie)
> Celestine Marie Lavelle (Dillard, Brown), b. 1854, New Orleans, Louisiana
> Issie Dillard Brown, b. 1896, Charlottesville, Virginia
> Dora May Dillard (Peyroux, Roup), b. 1923, Annapolis, Maryland
> Celestine Merry Roup, b. 1948, Philadelphia, Pennsylvania
> Lydia Lovell Roup (Mueller), b. 1974, Wilmington, Delaware

Owen clears his throat. "Um, obviously because of the date and place of birth, and the name, we can safely infer that Celestine is the daughter of Isidore Saint-Ange. I suppose if you'd had a daughter, you would have carried on the family naming tradition. Issie, Dora, May, Merry—they're all derivations of Marie and Isidore's names. Lavelle and Lovell are variants of Laveau, and P'tite Marie's mother Marie Laveau sometimes used her married surname, Paris." He drags his finger down the trunk of my family tree. "You see, if you follow the maternal line of descendants, you come to…you, the great-great-great-great-grand-daughter of Isidore and P'tite Marie."

The world stills completely and goes silent as if someone has turned the volume all the way down until the only audible sound is the speakers' electronic whine. And I know that although Legba's gate is closed to me, the house still sprawls, looming ominous over the moss-curtained path like a slavering predator hunched to pounce and devour its prey. Awaiting my inevitable return.

At last I speak. "Did Adelaide know this? Is that why she hired me?"

Owen shrugs. "It was a lot of work to figure this all out, so I doubt she had any idea. If my research is accurate, you're a descendent of the most famous vodou priestess in history. Maybe there's magic in your blood."

The curse, the bloodlines. Emptying myself into those pewter bowls in faint imitation of my long-dead ancestor—a vessel of retribution pouring his torment into pitchers to slake his lover's endless thirst. How long had she lain in wait to find one whose borders between fact and fiction, dream and waking, were porous enough to allow her to cross? P'tite Marie the broken-hearted, sorrow spilling out through the crimson eyes of Erzulie Dantor weeping bloody tears. Mama Marie answering her daughter's call. And this fresh-faced youth before me, who looks as innocent as a cherub, has invited himself into the viper's nest.

"So I got hit with a genetic double whammy. Madness and super-natural power."

Owen shrugs. "That's one theory."

"And the others?" I ask.

"Shared psychosis. Suggestibility. Empathic possession. Does it matter now?"

Only because I don't think it's over. But maybe I'm just bat-shit crazy.

Then it's my turn to shrug. I keep turning the same small details over and over in my mind but never find any solution. There is no easy way to rationalize my experience.

"Everything can't be so easily explained away, though," I say. "Both Emilie and Isidore described seeing me in their dreams. I was the spirit who haunted the graveyard, the house. They described my clothing, my hair. How is that possible?"

"Coincidence?" Owen examines me with a probing gaze, and it's clear he's trying to discern where reality intersects with fantasy, and on which side of the line I stand. "Lucas says recurring thoughts affect our perceptions. We look for patterns and ascribe meaning to random events or groupings of events rather than evaluating them individually. It's called a self-reinforcing cognitive bias."

I frown. Owen's echoing my own dismissive tendency to negate the possibility of supernatural intervention. Maybe I just like the complex and alluring idea of magic and spirit possession more than I like the simple fact of mental illness. A nurse knocks briskly on the door and leans her head in. "Lydia, it's time for your session. Dr. Oliberos is waiting for you."

I nod and tell Owen, "I have to go get my head shrunk now."

We rise simultaneously and move toward the door.

"Thank you, Owen," I say, watching him flush with pride. "Send me your paper. I'd be glad to have something interesting to read in here."

Beaming, he moves to shake my hand but changes his mind and clasps me in an awkward but tender little embrace. My friend, Owen. We wave goodbye to each other and I follow him down the hall to my session, amused by his jaunty walk. But then he calls out to me, arresting my steps.

"Hey, weird coincidence about May 13. I almost forgot to mention it. You and Isidore were committed on the same date."

And that old black magic, that Cimmerian shade, blooms inside my head and spills down my spine to nestle in my belly, as cozy as a hibernating asp in its subterranean lair. As if to remind me, "I'm still here." I consider Isidore, awl in hand, driving the sugar devil into his bloodied skull and wonder what it will take to wake me from this unending nightmare.

LANCE VISITS ON a sunny Sunday afternoon, overheated from helping Hackett ferry his stuff from Marcella's house to ours. We play checkers and Scrabble at the table in my room, joking about our long-standing competition to outdo one another with the most obscure, arcane words. We do not speak of Paul or Marcella. Isidore. The dreams. The soft web of memory weaves itself around us, snaring the good and bad among its strands. The pinkening day softens and lengthens. I lie down and stretch out my arms, and he climbs into bed beside me, nestling into my body as if made for it. We are at home in each other.

Is this what love is, storm and stagnation? An eternal ocean in ebb and flow, the shore and the sea moving away from and toward one another in ceaseless motion? For now, my waters soak the sands and lick the stern rocks, and the dry beach drinks me in. We drift in and out of sleep until the windows fill with night and shine their blank, black gaze upon us. I do not dream.

Author's Note

The flesh of this novel is the muse's creation, but its bones are as real as you or I. What I aimed for was to imbue the dead with life (for there is certainly something Frankensteinian in humanizing fictional characters), and it was crucial for me to understand as much as possible about their daily lives. I read a number of books and consulted more than two hundred sources, including scholarly journals, academic papers, historical archives, newspapers, museum collections, and more. The rabbit hole was deep, dark, and long. It tunneled through the cruelest and bleakest chapters of American history, unearthing fresh horrors along the way. I took comfort where I could, drawing inspiration from the efforts of abolitionists and private citizens to end slavery, the Spiritualist movement, which provided the first public speaking platform for women, and the pioneers of asylum reform.

Belle Rive is loosely modeled on the Laura Plantation, a Creole-owned plantation in Vacherie, Louisiana. (*Creole* is a term of confusion and the topic of some debate itself. The characters in this novel are Louisiana Creole—American-born people of European, typically French, and Afro-Caribbean descent). Mixed-race people have long been stereotyped as tormented by their own racial schisms and supposed "confusion" about ethnic identity, but that schism runs much deeper, exposing fundamental flaws in our cultural psychology. It's been a treat for me, as the child of a Black father and white mother, to write about the nuances of the mixed experience through a historical lens.

The rabbit hole also yielded treats and treasures. I'm the sort of casual armchair historian who takes a particular delight in reading Victorian menus and lists of nineteenth-century slang or old-fashioned names (there really were people named Coffee and Prosper, for example), drooling over pictures of antique medical equipment, and discovering the unique culinary history of some of our most common foodstuffs— pineapples, avocados, marshmallows. This novel gave me the delicious opportunity to swan dive into the trivia of the past.

The House of Erzulie was a personal exploration as much as a literary one. Research is an excellent distraction. To create its grimly gorgeous fabric, I wove my own darkness among the threads of its Gothic conventions and motifs. Much of it was written during a very tumultuous year and its aftermath. Herein are the warp and weft of heartbreak, reclamation, sacrifice, and faint glimmers of hope. For me, this novel embodies catharsis and transformation—welcome or unwelcome—and the journeys we take that lead us away from, or bring us back to, ourselves.

Suffice it to say, while I've taken liberties with the truth, nearly every situation and many of the characters in *The House of Erzulie* are supported by historical fact. Here are a few:

Although Isidore is swept up by an angry mob of rioters in April 1851, the event this refers to (**Anti-Spanish Riots**) actually took place in August 1851. Responding to the execution of fifty American soldiers who, led by Narciso López, had attempted to annex Cuba to the United States, New Orleanians destroyed the Spanish consulate on Bourbon Street and several Spanish-owned businesses.

Linden trees share a rich lore across many cultures, but figure in Southern Gothic literature as spooky or haunted. In her dissertation *Scented Visions: The Victorian Olfactory Imagination*, art historian Christina Bradstreet comments on the semen-like smell of linden trees. Semen itself contains the aptly named putrescine and cadaverine—toxic and foul-smelling diamines—which are by-products of putrefying animal tissue. Nothing could be more appropriate to signify the sexual obsession and decay that haunt my characters.

A **succubus** is an entity or demon in attractive, female form that preys on sleeping men and steals their vitality through sexual intercourse. Hence, the pernicious drinker of jizz.

As a curative, **bloodletting** has been around since the time of the ancient Egyptians. A desire for improved precision, speed, reliability, and functionality inspired the invention of adjustable, automated scarificators during the eighteenth century. Dispensing with lancets and leeches, a physician could employ a scarificator's spring-loaded blades to more easily open a vein or inject substances into the skin. A typical bloodletting kit would contain a scarificator, glass cups to draw blood to the skin (cupping), and manual or spring-loaded lancets.

May 1853 signaled the arrival of a deadly recurrence of **yellow fever**, a mosquito-borne virus that thrived in swampy New Orleans. Attempts to purify the air included shooting off cannons and burning open barrels of tar, whose fumes further sickened city residents. Strange weather patterns intensified suffering. A heat wave speeded the decomposition of dead bodies, and coffins awaiting burial burst open. Arriving ships were quarantined; desperate sailors would jump overboard into the bay only to sometimes be beaten back by panicked citizens. Immigrants and impoverished slum-dwellers were frequently targeted as the source of disease and suffered not only social ostracism but high rates of death. Nearly eight thousand people died in New Orleans in 1853 due to yellow fever. Lafayette Cemetery Project records show that between 1817 and 1905, the disease killed more than forty-one thousand people.

Emilie's outrage over her father's refusal to free his slaves is based on records that show plantation owners spent more on the purchase and keeping of slaves than they would have by shifting to a system of paying wages or freeing them and hiring them as day laborers.

The gruesome story of Poupette's rape and the death of the slave driver Plunkett is based upon the case of **Celia Newsom**. Celia was the frequent target of her master's sexual assaults. When Celia's pleas for help were repeatedly ignored, she beat her rapist over the head until dead and burned his body in her fireplace. Once the remains were discovered, the pregnant woman was jailed, where she delivered a stillborn child. Following her conviction (by an all-white, male jury) for first-degree murder, Celia was hanged in 1855.

With the help of abolitionists and a free Black man, **Henry "Box" Brown** did indeed escape slavery by mailing himself in a wooden shipping crate from Virginia to Philadelphia in 1849. He lived the remainder of his life a free man.

The **Fox sisters** were the first documented mediums to launch the Spiritualist movement. The girls became famous for channeling ghosts during séances, whose presence was made known through a series of knocking sounds. The Fox sisters were quite well-known until their hoax was discovered (apparently, the girls could loudly crack their toe joints) and they were discredited. Many of the people and Spiritualist publications mentioned are real. Spirit communication, séances, magnetism, and hypnotism (mesmerism) were the basis of a cultural phenomenon that originated in America and spread to Europe during the mid- and late nineteenth century.

The fascinating case of first lady **Mary Todd Lincoln** served as a partial template for both Isidore and Lydia's deterioration (although the details of Lincoln's decline are hazy and the subject of speculation). Her mental illness was reportedly treated with opiates and chloral hydrate (the predecessor to barbiturates), which only exacerbated her symptoms and intensified her visual and auditory hallucinations and her strange beliefs and behaviors. Opiates were standard-issue treatments in the nineteenth century. They were prescribed but also available over the counter in a variety of patent medicines touted to cure every conceivable ache, pain, or illness. The primary ingredients were narcotics and alcohol (laudanum, for example), combined with a variety of substances such as hashish or herbs like belladonna, which can be toxic.

Before Fannie Farmer standardized measurements in her 1896 *Boston Cooking-School Cookbook*, a tea spoon would have meant the smaller spoon used to stir tea, and a table spoon the larger one set at table for eating. Most silverware sets today still include **tea and table spoons**.

Ganders have actually served as watchdogs. If you've ever spent time around geese, you know how vicious they can be. Now imagine an angry, thirty-pound bird coming after you, hissing, pecking, and flapping. You'd probably run, too.

Spooky castles, manors, and houses are hallmarks of the Gothic genre. For years, I've had a recurring dream about a house that has evolved from a creepy monstrosity with a haunted coal cellar and collapsible walls to a renovated marvel complete with a swanky rooftop bar and live jazz. There are always people in that house—a few are malignant and ghostly, but most are friendly or harmless, like the docent who gives historical tours to visiting schoolchildren. These dreams seemed to summon me into them, to hold a power over me, and they lingered throughout my waking hours. It's where I first climbed the swaying stairs and saw the scene of Emilie attending a séance. Dreams are their own marvels. Fantastical or mundane, they serve as portals into other lives, worlds, and points in time. It seems plausible, then, that we might somehow walk through those doors and discover ourselves merely a character in someone else's dream. Sleep tight!

For Further Reading

Anne E. Beidler, *The Addiction of Mary Todd Lincoln*

Born in Slavery: Slave Narratives from the Federal Writers' Project, 1936 to 1938, Library of Congress

Ann Braude, *Radical Spirits: Spiritualism and Women's Rights in Nineteenth-Century America*

Bret E. Carroll, *Spiritualism in Antebellum America*

Hannah Crafts, *The Bondwoman's Narrative*

Thomas De Quincey, *Confessions of an English Opium-Eater*

Jason Emerson, *The Madness of Mary Lincoln*

Harriet Jacobs, *Incidents in the Life of a Slave Girl*

Monica Murphy and Bill Wasik, *Rabid: A Cultural History of the World's Most Diabolical Virus*

Albert J. Raboteau, *Slave Religion: The "Invisible Institution" in the Antebellum South*

Andrea Rock, *The Mind at Night: The New Science of How and Why We Dream*

Lori Schiller and Amanda Bennett, *The Quiet Room: A Journey Out of the Torment of Madness*

Daniel Paul Schreiber, *Memoirs of My Nervous Illness*

Marilee Strong, *A Bright Red Scream: Self-Mutilation and the Language of Pain*

About the Author

Kirsten Imani Kasai is a writer, editor, and educator who has published poetry and fiction in a range of literary styles, including the speculative fiction novels *Ice Song* and *Tattoo* (both from Random House). *The House of Erzulie* is her third novel. She's the publisher of *Body Parts Magazine: The Journal of Horror & Erotica* and owner of the Magic Word Editing Co., which helps writers of all stripes achieve their goals. Kirsten holds an MFA in creative writing from Antioch University Los Angeles and is certified in the teaching of creative writing. She lives with her partner and children in California, where she quietly advocates for introvert rights from the privacy of her home. Find her at KirstenImaniKasai.com.

Also from Shade Mountain Press

NOVELS

Vanessa Garcia, *White Light*

A young Cuban-American artist distills her grief, rage, and love onto the canvas. Praised by Nobel laureate Wole Soyinka for its "lyrical pace and texture." One of NPR's Best Books of 2015. "A lush, vibrant portrayal, told in rich, smart prose" —*Kirkus* (starred review)

Yi Shun Lai, *Not a Self-Help Book: The Misadventures of Marty Wu*

Marty Wu, compulsive reader of advice manuals, ricochets between a stressful job in New York and the warmth of extended family in Taiwan. Semi-Finalist, 2017 Thurber Prize for American Humor.

Lynn Kanter, *Her Own Vietnam*

Decades after serving as a U.S. Army nurse in Vietnam, a woman confronts buried wartime memories and unresolved family issues. Silver Award, Indiefab Book of the Year. "Well written, compassionate, and perceptively told"—*Foreword Reviews*

SHORT STORIES

Robin Parks, *Egg Heaven: Stories*

Lyrical tales of diner waitresses and their customers, living the un-glamorous life in Southern California. Hailed by *Kenyon Review* as a "welcome addition" to working-class fiction. "A stunningly gifted writer"—*PANK Magazine*

The Female Complaint: Tales of Unruly Women, edited by Rosalie Morales Kearns

Short story anthology featuring nonconformists, troublemakers, and other indomitable women. Finalist, Indiefab Book of the Year. "Spellbinding… A vital addition to contemporary literature"—*Kirkus*

POETRY

Mary A. Hood, *All the Spectral Fractures*

New and collected poems by the microbiologist/naturalist/poet.

All books are available at our website,
www. ShadeMountainPress.com,
as well as bookstores and online retailers.